Expresso
Bongo

Expresso Bongo

A WOLF MANKOWITZ READER

THOMAS YOSELOFF, PUBLISHER

New York   London   Toronto

Library of Congress Catalogue Card Number: 61-13929

A. S. Barnes and Company, Inc.
11 East 36th Street
New York 16, New York

Thomas Yoseloff Ltd.
123 New Bond Street
London W.1, England

Printed in the United States of America

CONTENTS

Expresso Bongo

A KID FOR TWO FARTHINGS

IT WAS THANKS TO MR. KANDINSKY THAT JOE KNEW A UNICORN WHEN
he saw one.

He also knew that the Elephant and Castle was the Infanta of
Castile, a Spanish princess. He knew that Moses was an Egyptian
priest, that the Chinese invented fireworks, that Trotsky was the
best revolutionary, and that pregnant was going to have a baby.
Joe was six, and thanks to Mr. Kandinsky, he was educated, although
he didn't go to school, for he had to look after his mother till they
came to Africa.

His father said to Joe when he was still five, "Look after mother
till you come," and Joe said he would. Then he went down to talk
to Mr. Kandinsky in the basement. No teacher knew what Mr.
Kandinsky knew, about the Elephant and Castle, that is, and the
unicorn. Soon after, Joe's father went to Africa, with two suitcases
and a Madeira hat for the hot weather.

Joe lived upstairs at number 111 Fashion Street. There was a bedroom and a kitchen, and the kitchen had a fireplace and a gas stove,
but no sink. The tap was at the top of the first flight of stairs, and
Mr. Kandinsky used it, too. The lavatory was in the yard at the back
and smelled of Keatings Powder. Mr. Kandinsky lived in a room
on the ground floor, and had a workshop in the basement. The workshop had a window below ground level, and there was an iron grille
over the pavement for the light to come through. In the little area
outside the window were bits of newspaper and an old hat and a
sauce bottle, and Joe wondered how they got through the iron bars,

9

because it was a top hat and the bottle was the tomato sauce kind with a wide bottom.

"We ought to look, Mr. Kandinsky," Joe said one day, "because maybe there are some pound notes or even sixpences mixed up with it all."

"Joe," replied Mr. Kandinsky, "who has pound notes or even sixpences to lose in Fashion Street?"

So the window was never open, except in the summer it was lowered a few inches at the top, and a lot of dust came into the workshop.

Mr. Kandinsky was a trousers-maker. In the workshop he had a sewing machine, and a bench with the surface all shining from where he and Shmule pressed the trousers. In the fireplace were two big gas rings with two big goose irons beside them. When the cloth was soaked in a pail and spread over the trousers, and the hot goose iron pressed on top, a great cloud of steam arose. Mr. Kandinsky always said it was bad for your health and the worst thing in the tailoring, even bringing on the consumption. On the wall were three hooks with large brown paper and cardboard patterns hanging on them. On the mantel were two boxes with flat pieces of white tailors' chalks in them, and hundreds of cloth patterns in books, and dozens of reels of cotton.

Mr. Kandinsky had two pictures. Over his bench was a big print of a lady with her head bowed sitting on top of a large gray-green ball. Her eyes were bandaged and she was holding a broken harp. Joe thought the lady was a street musician who had been in a car accident; she was crying because her harp was broken and she couldn't live by singing any more. Mr. Kandinsky looked at the picture for a while and said, "You know, Joe, maybe you're right. But what about the ball she is sitting on?"

Joe thought it over while Mr. Kandinsky hand-stitched a pair of fine worsted trousers, but in the end he had to give up. Then Mr. Kandinsky told him:

"This ball is the world and this lady is Hope who is always with the world. She is blindfold because if she could see what happens she would lose hope and then where would she be? What this broken harp means, I don't know."

"Maybe it's a bit of another painting," Joe said.

"Maybe it is," said Mr. Kandinsky, "who knows?"

"Who knows?" repeated Joe, because he liked the way Mr. Kandinsky said things. "Who knows?" he said again, putting his head to one side, opening his hands and trying to lift his eyebrows.

The other picture was a brown photograph of an old man with a long beard and side curls, and bushy eyebrows, and a great curved nose with curved nostrils. This was Mr. Kandinsky's father. "A pious man, Joe," Mr. Kandinsky said, "very respected in the village, the finest coat-maker in the whole country."

"Not a trousers-maker?" asked Joe.

"Certainly not," said Mr. Kandinsky, "he was a great man and he would never lower himself to be a trousers-maker."

"Why aren't you a coat-maker, Mr. Kandinsky?" asked Joe.

Mr. Kandinsky, who could answer all questions, replied, "Because my wise father put me to trousers-making, thinking that Kandinsky and Son would be able to make complete suits. And you know what that means, Joe? It means bespoke tailoring—no more jobbing for other people. You can be an artist, not just a workman, somebody can send you sackcloth you will make it up into a pair of trousers. But it was not to be. It was a dream, Joe. Never mind. Life is all dreams—dreams and work. That's all it is."

After this talk, Joe nodded at the photograph of Reb Zadek Kandinsky when he came into the workshop. The stern eyes looked past him into the future, a lost future of Kandinsky and Son, be-spoke tailors. The curved nostrils turned disdainfully away from Mr. Kandinsky, the Fashion Street trousers-maker, well-known in the trade, but not in the same class as his father, a master tailor, who died cross-legged on his bench, stitching the reveres of the first coat he made in London. "May he find his place in peace," Mr. Kandinsky said, "that last coat was beautiful I tell you, Joe, beautiful."

"I think your trousers are lovely, Mr. Kandinsky," Joe said, to cheer Mr. Kandinsky up.

"Thank you, Joe," he answered, "I will make you a pair of blue serge trousers." And he did, a real pair of trousers, with turn-ups, and a cash pocket. Everything, even proper flies.

The whole house was Mr. Kandinsky's, not his, but he paid the whole rent and Joe's mother gave him ten shillings every week. He was an old friend and the arrangement was made before Joe's father went away. Mr. Kandinsky could spare the room. "I am the only Kandinsky extant—which means the last Kandinsky," he told Joe. Joe thought how it must make you old to be the last one extant. He looked at Mr. Kandinsky. He was very old but his face wasn't worn out. In fact he had much more face than Joe, and Joe wasn't extant at all, having both his mother and father as well as Mr. Kandinsky. Joe kept a pet in the backyard, a day-old chick, which sometimes lived for two or three weeks. After Mr. Kandinsky told him he had no people he called his pets Kandinsky in memory of that family.

At Friday night supper, Mr. Kandinsky and Joe's mother talked about Africa and Joe's father and what he was doing there and how soon Joe and his mother would go out to him.

"You know, Rebecca," Mr. Kandinsky said, "your fried fish is not just fish—it is manna from heaven."

"You are always paying me compliments, Mr. Kandinsky," Joe's mother said.

"And why not, Rebecca?" said Mr. Kandinsky, "you are the prettiest girl in the whole East End."

"Girl," said Joe's mother, and laughed, blushing so that she did indeed look quite pretty.

"Isn't she pretty, Joe?" asked Mr. Kandinsky.

"I think you are very pretty and nice," Joe said to his mother, although she had stopped smiling, and her face looked sad and not so pretty.

"For how long?" she said, "how long is anyone pretty? Mr.

Kandinsky cleared his throat which meant he was going to say something important. Joe looked at him, waiting.

"You are pretty as long as someone loves you, Rebecca," he said, "and so many people love you that believe me you are very pretty. Look at me. I am ugly, and old, but even I am pretty when someone loves me."

"I love you, Mr. Kandinsky," Joe said. "One morning you will look quite pretty." Mr. Kandinsky put his hand on Joe's head.

"Thank you, Joe," he said, "I feel a little bit prettier already. To celebrate I will have one more piece of this wonderful fish which the miracle of your mother's cooking has made as sweet as honey." Mr. Kandinsky, Joe thought, never got tired of fried fish.

"So what does he say in his letter this week?" Mr. Kandinsky would ask. "How is the Kaffir business?"

Joe's mother read parts of the letter out aloud, with Mr. Kandinsky stopping her every so often by raising his hand and asking a question. Then they would discuss the matter for a few minutes before she went on reading. Sometimes they were very long letters, full of business details, five gross of steward's jackets, twenty gross denim trousers, add ten per cent for carriage costs, a hundred pound company, five pounds paid up, salesman's commission on a hundred ex-army bell tents, and so on.

These letters were full of excitement, with little stories of Kaffirs drinking their white beer and singing, or Kaffir boys met late at night marching down the street beating a drum, and Joe's father walking in the road, otherwise they would beat him up. The long excited letters and money in them. As Rebecca opened them, the corner of a five-pound note, and once a ten-pound note, and always a few pounds, would be seen. Unusual, exciting notes they were, not ordinary but African money. But other letters were very short. There was no message in them for Joe or Mr. Kandinsky at all, and for Rebecca just a few words. These were the bad letters, and if Joe asked too many questions after they arrived, his mother's face would look at him as if she couldn't see, and if he went on asking questions, it would suddenly begin to tremble and then she would cry, hugging him and making his face wet with her tears.

In the mornings Joe's mother went to the Whitechapel Road where she worked in a millinery shop. She trimmed hats with bunches of artificial fruit and flowers, and Mr. Kandinsky said she was the best and most artistic hat-trimmer in the millinery trade. Because she didn't come home until the late afternoon, Joe ate with Mr. Kandinsky and Shmule at twelve o'clock, downstairs, in the workshop. Mr. Kandinsky never allowed Joe's mother to leave something cooked for them.

"I am an old cook myself," he told Joe, "although your mother is the best cook in the world, Joe, I am not saying anything against her cooking."

Mr. Kandinsky cooked on one of the gas rings in the workshop. On one of them a big goose iron was always heating, and on the other a large cooking pot with two handles bubbled quietly all morning long. Into the pot Mr. Kandinsky threw pieces of beef or a small breast of lamb, with plenty of onions and pepper and salt, and some large potatoes. Or a large marrow bone cooked with carrots, or mutton cooked with haricot beans. At quarter to twelve Joe went up the street to the baker on the corner to buy three onion rolls. Then they all sat down with big enamel plates full of steaming stew, eating and talking. Joe liked Mr. Kandinsky's cooking very much. "The best cooks are men, Joe," said Mr. Kandinsky. "Some men cooks get thousands of pounds from the Kings of Europe for cooking dinners no better than this."

Mr. Kandinsky talked a lot, but Shmule was often quiet. Shmule was short and broad, and very strong. He had bright red hair which curled into small flames, although after a haircut it was more like a piece of astrakhan. His skin was pale and his eyes gray, and every Saturday he spent the whole day at the gymnasium developing himself. Developing yourself was the only thing Shmule wanted to talk about, which was the reason why he said very little, because Joe was too young to develop himself much, and Mr. Kandinsky was already too old. Occasionally Mr. Kandinsky would bring Shmule into the conversation by saying, "You got a new muscle to show us?"

Shmule at once took off his jacket. He rolled up his shirt sleeves and clenched his fists and bent his elbows till large knots appeared everywhere. Sometimes he took his shirt off as well. He put his arms over his head, and enormous bands of muscle stood up on his back and chest. Joe clapped and Mr. Kandinsky called Shmule "Maccabeus," which means "The Hammer," and was the name in which Shmule wrestled. But once or twice Shmule tried a new muscle and though it came up a little distance it fell down straight away. Then he blushed from his forehead to his neck, and went into a corner to practice.

Shmule was going to be a wrestling champion, which meant he had to beat Louis Dalmatian, the Stepney Thrasher, Turk Robert, Bully Bason, and the dreaded Python Macklin. He didn't have to beat them all at once but even one at a time was enough, especially the dreaded Python Macklin, who had broken limbs with his powerful scissors grip. Shmule showed them the scissors. He took a chair and fought with it on the floor, twining his legs round it and pressing hard, explaining all the while, until one of the chair legs cracked and Mr. Kandinsky shouted, "The furniture he breaks up!"

"A chair I can mend," said Shmule puffing and blowing, "but supposing it was my leg?"

So between Shmule and Mr. Kandinsky, Joe learned a great deal about the world. Though he was a bit young, Shmule taught him the position of defense and how to give an uppercut. But it was Mr. Kandinsky who told Joe all about unicorns.

It was the afternoon that Joe's chick Kandinsky was found dead on its back, legs in the air, a ball of cotton wool and two matchsticks. Joe was worried because he did everything the day-old chick man in Club Row told him to do, and yet the chick died. Mr. Kandinsky suggested that perhaps it could happen that Joe wasn't a natural-born chicken-raiser. Chickens just weren't his speciality. Maybe he should try a dog or a lizard, or a couple of fish. This made Joe think why not write to his father for a big animal, because naturally small animals only have small lives and naturally they lose them more easily.

Mr. Kandinsky had been studying Africa in some detail since Joe's father went there, but the parts in the book about the gold mines and the diamond mines were not as interesting as the chapter called the Fauna of Central Africa. He was, consequently, in an excellent position to advise Joe on the habits of larger animals.

They discussed the lion with some hope, because many cubs have been trained into good pets, but lions only eat meat, and where would they get enough to feed it? You couldn't fool a lion with vegetable stew; even Mr. Kandinsky's cooking would only make it angry and then there would be trouble. The giraffe was nice, but with such a long neck, you couldn't get it in the house. A zebra is only a horse with stripes and horses you can see any day in the street.

"Maybe," Joe suggested, "maybe my father could send a unicorn."

"A unicorn is a public house," Shmule said, looking up from a small book he was reading, *The Principles of Judo*.

"Don't show your ignorance on the subject, Shmule," Mr. Kandinsky said. Then he told Joe about unicorns.

"Every animal when it was made by the Almighty was given one extra-special present," said Mr. Kandinsky. "The squirrel was given a wonderful tail to hold on with so he wouldn't fall from the trees; the horse was given strong fine legs so he could run fast; the lion great jaws; the elephant a trunk so he could take a shower whenever he felt like it, because an elephant is so large, how else could he keep clean? But the unicorn got the most special present of all. He was given a magic horn which could cure anything anyone was ever sick from. It could grant anybody's wish—straight off. And this horn consequently was worth £10,000 cash on sight, anywhere in the world. Don't ask me why the unicorn got this present. Someone had to get it, so why not him? Anyhow, he got it and no one else. But because of this very gift unicorns became so scarce you won't even find one in the zoo, so it is in life.

"At one time unicorns were common as cart horses, wherever you went in the streets you would see half a dozen. In those days no one was poor. You needed something so all right, you just reached out your hand and there it was, a glass of lemon tea, a new hat. Then, when people became poor, all the unicorns had their horns stolen and sold. You can imagine what that did to them. Could a lion live without his jaws, could a squirrel swing from the trees without his tail, could an elephant go on without a shower-bath, could I eat if I stopped making trousers? Of course not, so how could a unicorn live without his horn?"

"Ah, Joe, they died in their thousands the lovely unicorns. They gathered together in dusty yards and at the bottom of those streets which lead nowhere. They nuzzled one another for comfort, and closed their eyes so as not to be reminded of what they had lost. Their fine white coats became spotted, their beautiful sleek muscles slipped away into twisted sinew. They pined, they shrank, they faded, they died, and their death was sad for they had been eaten up by poverty, swallowed in the darkness of a pit with no bottom, so that no one ever saw them again."

Mr. Kandinsky sighed as he bent to throw his cold goose iron on to the gas ring. He looked at Joe with big eyes and sighed. "This was the pity of it, my Joe," he said. "The unicorns passed away, but poverty was still in the world, poverty and sickness. Strong men have wasted away, beautiful girls have grown ugly, children have been lost before they could yet walk, the unicorns are all gone and yet poverty is still here. Don't ask me why. What do I know?" He sighed again, then put his hand on Joe's shoulder, pressing so as to feel the small fine bone. "Never mind," he said, "sometimes in spite of everything, a child grows well, a man goes from strength to strength, a woman's face does not fade. In the same way some unicorns must have lived. They were the clever ones. They saw how things were going and didn't waste time blaming men or cursing life, or threatening God, or any other foolishness. Instead they came forward and said to the rest, 'Listen, friends. If we don't do something soon there will be no unicorns left in the world.'

" 'Be quiet,' some of them shouted, 'can't you see we are too unhappy to do anything.'

" 'Don't be blasphemous," others cried, 'it's the will of God.'

" 'Don't interrupt us when we are crying,' others said, 'it is the only thing left for us to enjoy.'

"But some gathered together to escape, some with hope in their hearts, some with doubt, a few with the spirit which does not care either for hope or doubt. These said, 'Living means waste, but let who wants to live, live.'

"One old unicorn who had been told about Africa when he was a baby had never forgotten. He told them, and to Africa they went that very night. In Africa they are today, although their terrible experiences made them careful about being seen by men, so that nowadays you don't see them so often. But they are even bigger now, and stronger even, and so fierce they fight at the drop of a hat. Without doubt, Joe," said Mr. Kandinsky, "without doubt, Shmule, you wrestler," he said, "there is absolutely no reason why there shouldn't be unicorns in Africa."

"What do I know?" asked Shmule.

"Could you get a unicorn into the house?" Joe asked.

"A small unicorn," Mr. Kandinsky said, "certainly. There is no reason why a small unicorn couldn't be got into the house. Would you like another spoonful, Joe?" He stirred the carrots in the saucepan on his gas ring so that a great cloud arose.

TWO

After Kandinsky the day-old chick died, Joe went to the animal market, because if you wanted a unicorn, the best place in the world to look for it was Club Row.

Joe had his own way of walking through the market. It made it much larger if you started in the middle where the herring women fished salted herrings out of barrels with red hands, dipped them in water and cleaned and sliced them thinly with long thin knives. From there you walked up to Alf, the singing-bird man, then cut round the back, coming through to the other end where the dogs were. But if there was something you wanted to buy it was much better to start at one end by the singing birds and walk through, looking carefully at every stall.

Alf, the singing-bird man, came to Mr. Kandinsky for repairs so he knew Joe and always spoke to him, even if he was busy selling someone a canary. Alf was against day-old chicks as pets. He pulled his light brown overall coat down, pushed his cap back from his eyes and told Joe when he bought Kandinsky, "You ain't doing that chick no favor, Joe, taking him away without his mother, alone, he doesn't know how to give a peep-peep yet, putting him a box with a drop of water and a handful of straw. That rotten day-old chick man should be put in a box himself, the louse, selling chicks to anyone with a sixpence. A chick like this needs his mum or a special hot-box; he don't just grow up any old how any old where, he must have special care, he shouldn't catch cold." Alf turned to a fat lady with a big gray fur round her neck. "That canary, lady," he said, "is such a singer I should like to see better."

"He don't appear to be singing much just now," the lady said, taking a handful of potato crisps from a bag and crunching them. "Tweet-tweet," she said to the canary, spitting a few little bits of potato crisp at him, "tweet-tweet."

"Here, Oscar," Alf said, because all his birds were sold with their right names on small red certificates. He whistled softly to the bird. Oscar turned his bead eyes towards Alf, listened for a moment, and then began to sing.

"Lovely," the fat lady said, finishing the crisps and brushing her fur, "how much for the bird?"

"That Oscar," Alf said afterwards, "I had him nearly a year." And he started to whistle softly to a dark gold canary.

Near Alf's stall there was a jellied eel stand with a big enamel bowl of gray jellied eels, small bowls for portions, a large pile of lumps of bread, and three bottles of vinegar. There were also orange and black winkles in little tubs, and large pink whelks. People stood around shaking vinegar onto their eels and scooping them up with bread. A little thin man in a white muffler served them and sometimes dropped a large piece of eel on the ground. Behind the stand a very fat man with a striped apron and an Anthony Eden hat waved a ladle in his hand and shouted, "Best eels, fresh jellied, buy 'em and try 'em, eels." Over the stand a red white and blue banner flapped. "The Eel King," it said. The King himself never served.

Opposite the Eel King was a red barrow with dark green watermelons, and a white enamel table top with halves and slices of melon and a large knife. Joe pretended he couldn't make up his mind whether to buy some jellied eels or a slice of melon. He watched people eating eels and shaking vinegar on them, and then looked back at the large wide slices of red melon with glossy black seeds bursting from them.

In the end he bought a twopenny slice of melon and pretended it was jellied eels, scooping the red flesh with his teeth and saying "Blast" and "Bloody" when the seeds dropped to the pavement. Some of the seeds he saved so that when they were dry he could crack them between his teeth and get the thin nuts inside.

While he scraped the thick skin of the melon, Joe watched the Indian fortune teller who wore a turban and sold green, yellow and red perfume in small bottles. Whenever a woman bought a bottle of perfume the Indian looked at her strangely. "A little moment, dear lady," he said, "a little moment while I look into the bowl." He looked darkly into a large glass bowl which turned purple or orange, and sliding his hand beneath brought out a small envelope with a fortune in it; the pavement all round his stall was covered with torn envelopes. Once when the market finished, Joe kicked his way through empty boxes and newspapers past the Indian's stall. He saw him counting sixpences into piles, and putting them into small blue bags, but the bowl looked like an ordinary bowl for goldfish. An Indian girl who wore a long blue silk robe was packing the bottles into boxes on a barrow. When the Indian pushed the barrow away, the girl walked behind him; they went to the bottom of the street and turned away into the darkness under the railway arches, back to India.

The Sunday came when Joe had saved enough of the sixpences Mr. Kandinsky gave him every week for helping in the workshop, to buy a unicorn, should one appear. Mr. Kandinsky was always busy on Sunday mornings, and he hardly noticed Joe leave. He was arguing with a customer who wanted a zip fastener on his trousers, something to which Mr. Kandinsky could not agree.

Joe ran quickly through the crowd to the singing-bird end of the market. Alf was talking to a budgerigar and a tall thin man with a sad face. The bird wasn't replying, but every so often the thin man said, "It's no good, Alf—it's no good," till at last Alf put the cage down. Then the bird suddenly said, "Hello" and Joe said hello back. The thin man looked sadder still and left, and Alf said, "Talks better English than I do—hello, Joe, what are you after? No more chicks remember."

"Do you know where I can find a unicorn, Alf?" Joe asked.

"Try down by the dogs, Joe," Alf suggested. "Hello," the bird said again.

"Hello," Joe replied and started towards the other end of the market.

On the way Mrs. Quinn, the hen woman, called him over.

"Joe," she said, "tell your mother I'll bring the eggs over meself tomorrow." She was holding a fat hen which squawked as an old woman pinched it and complained. "If you don't like the bird, for the love of St. Patrick leave it," shouted Mrs. Quinn in Yiddish. "So tell your mother now," she said to Joe.

"Do you know where I can buy a unicorn, Mrs. Quinn?" Joe asked.

"What do you want with heathen animals?" she answered. "Get yourself a nice day-old chick."

"That day-old chick man, the louse," Joe said, "he should be put in a box."

"Will you leave the bird alone now?" screamed Mrs. Quinn at the old woman who was still pinching its bottom.

"There's no harm," Joe thought, "in at least having a look at the chicks."

At the stall, hundreds of them were running about in a large glass enclosure with a paraffin lamp in the middle of it, all squeaking like mice. When someone bought them they were put into cardboard boxes with air holes, and the squeaking became fainter. It was a pity they had such small lives.

"Another one already, cock?" asked the chick man.

"Not today, thank you," said Joe, "I'm not a born chick-raiser."

"You got to know the trick of it, cock."

"I'm going to buy a unicorn this time," Joe said.

"You do that," the man said, "you do." He bundled two dozen chicks into a box and tied it up with string.

Just about the middle of the market, near the herring women, was the fritter stall which also sold hokey-pokey ices and sarsaparilla fancy drinks. The smell rushed up so thick from the great vat of frying oil that if you stood nearby for a while you had a whole meal of fritters. The hokey-pokey man called out, "Get your hokey-pokey, penny a lump, the more you eat the more you jump," but Joe hurried on. He passed the cat-lady with her basket of kittens mewing, and the long line of hutches where the rabbits were always eating. He waited for the bearded sandwich-board man to shout at him, "The wages of sin is death, repent lest ye perish," because he was studying to spit when he spoke, "Sthin—death" Joe spluttered as he hurried on.

The dog sellers mostly stood in the gutter or against the billhoardings holding a puppy in each hand and one in each pocket. They didn't say anything unless you patted a pup. Then they told you he was a pedigree Irish retrieving elkhound, his mother was a good house dog. A few of them had cages with bigger dogs in them, and one or two men just stood around with four or five dogs on leads, trying to make them stop walking round in circles and jumping at people. There were dogs with short legs and long tails, and dogs with short tails but long ears. They were all dogs all right, all yelping and barking, just dogs.

Joe walked right to the end of the dog end of the market, hurrying past the man who bit off exactly at the joint dogs' tails that needed lopping, to the very last man standing by the arches under the railway. The four sixpences and four pennies in his pocket clinked and three men tried to sell him pedigreed pups, but the last man stood by the dark opening of the arches without speaking. He held a large white rabbit under one arm, and in the other hand a piece of tattered string, and at the end of the string, a small unicorn.

While Joe looked at the unicorn, a little man with three pullovers on came up and took the white rabbit. He held it up by its ears, and it kicked its feet at him. Then he handed it back saying, "Flemish?"

"Dutch," the last man said.

"Thought it was Flemish," the little man mumbled as he turned away.

"Dutch," the man said again.

"Funny thing," the little man mumbled, pulling his pullovers down, "funny thing."

People pushed past with bags of fruit and dogs and birds in cages but none of them spoke to the man. Then a tall boy came up and stared at the white rabbit for a while.

"How much?" he asked.

"Twelve and sixpence," the last man said. "It's Dutch."

"Half a bar," the boy replied.

"Done," said the last man and handed over the rabbit. The tall boy left, talking into the rabbit's ear. The last man pulled at the string on the unicorn as Joe came up to pat its head. The unicorn licked Joe's hand.

"He's a bit twisted," the man said to Joe, "but he'll grow straight in time."

"He is a bit twisted," Joe replied looking at the unicorn's hind legs, "and one leg is shorter than the other at the back."

"He's a runt all right," the man said. "Still."

"How much is he?" Joe asked.

"Only five shillings," the man said.

"Give you two shillings," Joe said.

"Come orf it," the man said.

"He's a bit twisted," Joe said.

"What if he is a bit twisted," the man replied, "he'll grow."

"Give you two and fourpence," Joe said.

"Kids," the man said, "Kids." He turned into the arches, the unicorn limping beside him, and Joe behind them both.

Under the arches the air smelled of smoke and horses, and footsteps and voices echoed through the smell. In the corners old men with long beards and old women with feathers stuck in their hats, all wrapped up in rags, sat on sacks talking to themselves. As Joe passed, an old man took a long draught from a bottle, and coughed. At the other end of the arches the last man began to hurry, and the unicorn tripped and skipped after him.

When Joe caught up with him the man stopped and the unicorn sat down.

"You still 'ere?" the man asked. "Kids."

"What will you do with him?" Joe said.

"Have him for dinner," the man said.

"Oh," Joe gasped.

"With a few onions," the man said.

"How much is he?" Joe asked.

"How many more times?" the man said. "Five shillings. He cost me that to raise."

"If you come back with me to Mr. Kandinsky at Fashion Street," Joe said, "he'll give you five shillings."

"All that way?"

"And I'll give you two and fourpence as well," Joe added.

"Give me the two and fourpence then," the man said and Joe counted the coins into his hand.

"I don't mind leading him," Joe said, "if you're a bit tired."

Back at the workshop Mr. Kandinsky was fixing the zip fastener into the trousers because, after all, the customer is always right, even when he's wrong. He was talking to the baker from the corner. "You know," he was saying, as Joe came in leading the unicorn, "the black bread agrees with me better, only I get the heartburn something terrible."

"I'm telling you," the baker said, "it's the black bread. I'm a baker, shouldn't I know?"

"Hello, Joe," Mr. Kandinsky said, "what you got there?"

"Cripple, ain't it?" said the baker.

"It'll grow," the man said.

"Can you lend me five shillings to pay for this unicorn, Mr. Kandinsky?" Joe said.

"For a unicorn," said Mr. Kandinsky, reaching for the box he kept his change in, "five shillings is *tukke* cheap."

Later, Mr. Kandinsky made a careful examination.

"Clearly," he said, "this unicorn is without doubt a unicorn, Joe; unmistakably it is a genuine unicorn, Shmule. It has only one small horn budding on its head."

"Let's see," said Shmule. Then after he looked and felt the horn bud he said, "Granted only one horn."

"Second and still important," continued Mr. Kandinsky, "Joe went to the market to buy a unicorn. That is so, Joe?"

Joe nodded.

"Consequently," Mr. Kandinsky continued excitedly, "it follows that he wouldn't buy something that wasn't a unicorn. In which case, he bought a unicorn, which is what this is."

"There's a lot in what you say," replied Shmule, "although it looks like a baby goat, a little bit crippled that's all, not like a horse which is after all, a unicorn except for the horn."

"And this has a horn, yes or no?" asked Mr. Kandinsky.

"Definitely," replied Shmule, "it has an undeveloped horn."

"One horn only?" asked Mr. Kandinsky.

"One horn," agreed Shmule.

"So," concluded Mr. Kandinsky, "it's not a unicorn?"

"What do I know?" said Shmule shrugging his shoulders. The shrug reminded him of his shoulder muscles, so he went on flexing and unflexing them for a while.

Then Mr. Kandinsky sent Joe to the greengrocery to buy a cabbage and some carrots. "And a couple of heads of lettuce as well," he added. "What he don't eat, we can put in the stew."

While Joe was gone, Mr. Kandinsky examined the unicorn again, while Shmule practiced a half-Nelson on himself.

As he ran his hand over the unicorn, Mr. Kandinsky sang:
One kid, one kid, which my father bought for two farthings.
Shmule looked around. "That's what I say," he said. "A kid."

"What harm will it do, Shmule," asked Mr. Kandinsky, "if we make it a unicorn? Oy," he added, "he really is crippled." Sadly beating his fist on the bench Mr. Kandinsky sang:

> *Then came the Holy One, blessed be He,*
> *The angel of death to destroy utterly*
> *That struck down the butcher*
> *That slew the ox*
> *That drank the water*
> *That quenched the fire*
> *That burnt the stick*
> *That beat the dog*
> *That bit the cat*
> *That ate the kid.*

Shmule's low voice joined Mr. Kandinsky's cracked one in the chorus. Together they finished the song.

> *One kid, one kid, which my father bought for two farthings.*

THREE

All the excitement about the unicorn was one thing, but Shmule had his own troubles. Second, there was the dreaded Python Macklin, but first there was Sonia.

Sonia was the daughter of Hoffman the butcher, and maybe plenty of meat was the reason why she was the strongest girl between Bow Church and the Aldgate Pump. She was four inches taller than Shmule, and she had only three muscles less than him, and those muscles anyway it didn't suit a girl to have. She could lift Shmule as easily as he could lift Joe, and though she had squinty eyes and a bad temper, she had a very good figure. One day, Mrs. Levenson, the corsetière, who did a bit of match-making on the side, got him over to Hoffman's for Friday night supper, and in no time Shmule found himself engaged to Hoffman's daughter Sonia. That was his number one trouble, for although a promise is all very well in its way, what is the use of being engaged if you haven't got a ring to prove it? And Sonia hadn't a ring.

That ring. Sonia didn't forget it for a minute. In the evenings or at weekends when they practiced weight-lifting together and catch-as-catch-can, she never forgot. Shmule might say, "I pulled a muscle"—that's all. Just "I pulled a muscle."

"You got a muscle?" Sonia would ask, insinuating.

"Don't worry about me," Shmule would tell her, "I got enough muscles."

"I forget," Sonia would answer, lifting up the heavy bar, "it's diamonds you are a bit short of just now." Always on for a ring.

Do Sonia justice, the other girls in the blouse factory where she worked wouldn't let her forget. Every day one or other of them tried to needle her about the ring. "Funny thing," Dora the blonde —blonde!—said, "funny thing a fellow proposes but no ring. You sure, Sonia, he said *marry?*" And even worse. Sometimes girls ran up and down showing off the rings their fellows had given them, and then Sonia felt so small. But she couldn't tell Shmule all that. The only thing to do was keep at him, because, give credit, a girl engaged is after all entitled to a ring. Say what you like, right is right.

Because of that ring Shmule went in for the wrestling. Before that, he took three pound seventeen he saved in a slate club the baker ran, and bought a gold ring with a little tiny diamond in it. Shmule went into fourteen shops until he found a ring for that money, because everyone knows nothing but diamonds is right for engagements. But he could have saved himself the trouble. He went round to Sonia that night, pleased as punch, and when they were sitting in the front room just as Sonia was about to start nagging him, he jumped up, ran round the room, and shouted, "Say no more—

you got yourself a ring." He gave her the ring and held his face forward for a kiss.

Who can satisfy women? A fine kiss that Sonia gave him. With the back of her hand she gave him a slap on the cheek and burst out crying.

"Two years I've waited you should make me respectable with a ring, and what do you give me in the end? A little tiny bit of rubbish, I wouldn't be seen dead in it. Why did I ever say yes to you? Why am I such a fool? Why did I let you take me to Epping Forest that time?" Because that was something else she never let Shmule forget, although there had been no trouble.

To cut a long story short, Shmule explained to Mr. Kandinsky, Sonia couldn't wear that ring because such a small diamond after such a long time would make her look ridiculous. The other girls might say, insinuating, "For such a small ring you must wait two years?" And that was why, answering Mr. Kandinsky's question, "Why be a wrestler?" Shmule took up wrestling. Wrestling he could win enough money to buy Sonia a large ring, and then perhaps, she would stop nagging him.

"Why don't you just marry the girl straightaway, and save yourself trouble?" Mr. Kandinsky asked. "Surely this is a practical solution?"

"You think I haven't tried?" said Shmule. "She won't let me come near her until she gets that ring."

"Why don't you marry someone who's got a ring already?" asked Joe.

"What can you know about these things?" asked Shmule.

"My mother hasn't got a diamond ring," Joe said.

"Do me a favor," Shmule replied, dismissing the whole matter. "I got enough worries. This dreaded Python Macklin I got to fight soon is no joke."

But although Shmule had worries of his own, he helped Joe to build a house for the unicorn. They got four orange boxes and a hammer and some nails, and while Shmule knocked them together he told Joe what he would do if he didn't have to develop his mus-

cles to fight the dreaded Python Macklin. Because wrestling kills
you for perfect efficiency, Shmule said. Take Fred Hercules, for instance, no use as a wrestler at all, but still the best developed man in
the world. And if you could win a title like Mr. World, or Mr. Universe, or just plain Mr. Europe, you were made. That's what Shmule
might have been if he didn't ruin himself becoming a good wrestler.
Mr. Universe. That was something to be. Mr. World. You could
sign adverts; I grew my muscles on Brymaweet, signed Shmule. I
always use a Rolls-Royce car, signed Shmule. It was a gold mine, and
he had to give it up. "Turn all that in, my future, Hollywood even,
because plenty of Mr. Worlds have finished up big stars, just because
Hoffman's daughter Sonia must have a bigger ring than any other
machinist in Gay-day Blouses." And Shmule gave one of the orange
boxes such a bang with the hammer the side caved in and they had
to repair it before going on.

After the house was finished, while Shmule filled up a few cracks
in it with canvas, Joe went back into the workshop.

"So, how is the unicorn's house coming along, Joe?" asked Mr.
Kandinsky, peering through the steam from pressing, and wrinkling his nose, because after all these years he still didn't like the
smell.

"Shmule is worried about that Sonia," answered Joe. "She wants
him to turn in his future, and not have a Rolls-Royce car."

"Women," said Mr. Kandinsky. "But we can't do without 'em."

"You do," said Joe.

"I'm old," replied Mr. Kandinsky. "I have had my share of
trouble."

"Did you want to be Mr. World, Mr. Kandinsky?" asked Joe.

"Mr. Kandinsky is already enough for Mr. Kandinsky," said Mr.
Kandinsky, pressing hard with his iron and making a great cloud
of steam. "The only thing I could do with, because all this bending
over ironing gives me a creak in my back, is a Superheat Patent
Steam Presser." Mr. Kandinsky leaned back from the bench. "You
know, Joe, with this patent steam presser all you got to do is open
it—so. You put in your trousers—so. Close it—so. Press a handle.

Pouf. Up comes the steam. Open. There is your trousers pressed. No smell, no consumption. Not like this, hot up the irons, press a bit, they get cold, wet the cloth, press a bit more, hot up the iron again, breaking your back, your heart, day after day."

Whenever he thought of it, Mr. Kandinsky ran on about the Superheat Steam Presser. Once he took Joe to see one working at a factory in Commercial Road. They watched a boy open and close it while another boy put the trousers in and took them out, and Mr. Kandinsky looked sad when they left.

"If a man has to be a trousers-maker," he said, "it's a pity he shouldn't have a Superheat Steam Presser." On the way home he took Joe into a restaurant and they had sweet lemon tea and biscuits.

Usually when Mr. Kandinsky mentioned how he would like a patent presser, Joe spent some time suggesting ways for them to save up for one. But now all he said was, "Maybe my father will send you one from Africa for your birthday," because his mind was too busy thinking about the unicorn.

Until the unicorn's own house was finished, he lived in the workshop under a shelf, in a nest made up from odd pieces of material. Joe fed him morning and evening, leaving a bowl of water and milk for him to drink should he feel so inclined. Joe talked to the unicorn between meals so that he shouldn't feel lonely, but though he would make quite a good breakfast, he didn't care much about anything. He just looked at Joe with sad eyes and slowly folded another lettuce leaf into his mouth with a long pink tongue.

"I think," Joe told Mr. Kandinsky, "that this unicorn is missing his mother and father, but what can you do?"

"What can you do?" agreed Mr. Kandinsky.

"But where are they?" asked Joe.

"In Africa, no doubt," said Mr. Kandinsky.

"But how did the baby get here?" asked Joe.

"Who can say? Maybe he was left here when the unicorns left."

"But by now he should be grown up," Joe said after a while. Mr. Kandinsky put down his iron.

"There, Joe," he said, "you have a problem. That unicorn should be grown up."

"But he's not," Joe said, "he's no bigger than a dog, not a big dog, either."

Mr. Kandinsky thought for a while.

"He is not grown up," he said at last, "and you know why? Because unicorns can't grow up on their own. They have to be told how by grown-up unicorns. Same as you have to be told by me, otherwise how will you grow up? Same thing with unicorns, which are, after all, only human."

He took up his iron again, turned the flat of it towards his face, and spat lightly on it. There was no fizz. "These blankety irons," he said. "What I need is a Superheat Patent Presser."

That evening when Joe's mother came home from work, she asked first and foremost how the unicorn was. Joe said the house was nearly finished, but the unicorn didn't seem to care, and he told her what Mr. Kandinsky said about why the unicorn happened to be there at all.

"Mr. Kandinsky knows," Joe's mother said, "because he reads so many library books. I've got a surprise for you, Joe." She brought out a bar of *halva,* a sweet made from honey and nuts wrapped in thick silver paper.

After his supper, Joe ate a piece of *halva.* He broke it into very small bits, arranged them on the table, and ate them one at a time. He was thinking and he thought better this way.

When Joe was in bed his mother kissed him and said good night, and was about to leave when he sat up.

"You know," Joe said, "Mr. Kandinsky wants a Superheat Patent Presser, and Shmule wants to be Mr. World, and Sonia, that's Shmule's girl, wants the biggest ring in Gay-day Blouses, and that unicorn wants its mother and father."

"And what do you want?" Joe's mother asked.

"I'm thinking what," Joe said. "What do you want?"

"Whatever you want," Joe's mother answered. Then she said

good night again; the whole thing all over again; a cuddle with kisses, a cuddle without kisses, one big kiss, and a few little kisses as she had done since he was young.

FOUR

They called the unicorn Africana, because Mr. Kandinsky said that was the name for everything to do with Africa. Straightaway the unicorn began to look a little better. Everybody needs a name, otherwise how can they know who they are? You couldn't call a unicorn Charlie or Hymie, or Kandinsky even, so they called him Africana.

Every morning when he had finished his breakfast, Joe took Africana for a walk up Fashion Street, then across the road and back again past the shirt factory. Africana wore a tartan lead and collar which had belonged to the baker's dog Nicolai, named after the Tsar of Russia, both of whom were dead. The shirt factory was dead, too. It was set back a little from the road, and the whole of the front was covered with torn posters. The big door of the factory was painted a sort of purple which flaked off all the time, and had initials carved on it by the boys in the street. Above the height to which the boys could reach was still part of a large colored poster which showed a magician in a top hat taking a blue rabbit, two blue pigeons and a large bunch of blue flowers out of another top hat. The roof of the shirt factory had small roofs on it and Mr. Kandinsky called it the Kremlin. Beside the door there was a faded board which still said, "Wanted: Machinists," but no one ever went into the factory and the door had a large iron padlock chained on to it.

The two corners where the pavement curved round to meet the far walls of the factory were sheltered from the wind. In one or other of them there often sat one or other of the old men and women who wandered about the East End wrapped up in rags and carrying sacks, with feathers in their hats and crusts of bread sticking out of their pockets. They only talked to themselves, mumbling all the time, sometimes having arguments alone, and once in a while shouting out so that crumbs of bread flew from their toothless mouths. They were wanderers, wandering through the small back streets, poking into dustbins and hiding empty bottles and rags in their sacks, begging stale loaves from the baker shops, and sleeping under the arches or in the sheltered corners of the shirt factory. No one knew them, or where they came from, or where they went. They had always been there. They were very old.

On Africana's morning walks Joe introduced him to the neighbors. Their first call was the baker, who gave them a coconut biscuit each and remarked on how Africana was growing.

"Do you really think he's growing?" Joe asked, because it seemed to him that Africana was no bigger than before.

"Growing?" said the baker, "I should say so. And he's walking better into the bargain. Fashion Street agrees with him. You want another biscuit?"

"No thank you," Joe replied. But Africana said nothing. He didn't even finish his biscuit.

Whenever it wasn't raining, even in the winter, Mrs. Abramowitz, who had a small fancy button shop, used to sit by the open door on a bentwood chair watching people pass. Joe knew that Mrs. Abramowitz meant no harm, but he wished she wouldn't pinch his cheek like a hen's bottom, because it made him feel as if he was going to be cooked, and also it hurt. Whenever she called out, "So, my Joe, how is your Mummy?" so that Joe would have to stop and talk to her, he tried to keep his cheeks out of her way. But it was difficult to talk to people without turning your cheeks towards them, and Mrs. Abramowitz was very cunning. While he was busy and off his guard telling her something, a bony hand suddenly jumped up and two bony fingers caught one of his cheeks. "What a boychick!" Mrs. Abramowitz said, licking her lips as if she was tasting him. She smelled of wintergreen ointment and camphor balls, and wore a cardigan with fancy buttons on it.

Another cheek-pincher was the man with the twisted mouth who had the confectionery and tobacconist. He wore a black Homburg

hat all the year round, and tried to cover his twisted mouth by growing a bushy moustache which although his hair was gray, came
out red. But you could still see it was twisted. Everyone got their
sweets and tobacco from him, but he was not well-liked, being as he
was a fence and an informer, a friend to the police. No one trusted
him because he got the street a bad name, although he was very pious
and quoted Gems at you when you went to buy a bar of milk chocolate or some Polish fruit bon-bons. His favorite Gem was "Go to the
ant, thou sluggard, consider her ways and be wise," which he said
all the time to his daughter, who also had a twisted mouth, although
she couldn't grow a moustache so well to hide it. To Joe he would
say, "There is a time for all things; please don't bring the animal
into the shop." Then when he took the money, "Two and a half to
make you laugh." Joe never laughed because suddenly, if you got
too near, the fingers crawling over the polished counter quick as
spiders, jumped up and bit your cheek, harder than Mrs. Abramowitz. But it was the only shop which sold Polish bon-bons, Mr.
Kandinsky's favorite, so what could you do?

The only one in Fashion Street Joe discussed Africana frankly
with was Mavis from the greengrocery. Mavis had a money box in
her shop for Our Dumb Friends, although she agreed with Joe that
animals talked to one another. She was always helpful with hints
and suggestions so Joe let her into the secret that Africana was a unicorn. He let her feel the one horn bud which was still very small,
and asked her if it was rubbed with wintergreen would it grow
faster. Mavis didn't think it would, but she showed Joe how to brush
Africana's coat, and always saved the best leftover greens for him
and didn't charge. She said she was sorry she couldn't do anything
about the limp, except ask Her Holy Mother to help. Mr. Kandinsky
thought it was nice of Mavis and Her Holy Mother to go to the trouble, and besides, it might do some good. The unicorn did get a bit
better at walking, so thanks were due to Mavis and Her Holy
Mother, although Shmule helped as well.

Shmule studied Africana carefully. One day he said to Joe, "Remediable exercise is the thing for that limp. Oliver at the gym told me. Works wonders." And he massaged Africana every night for a week with a little white oil. But even with Mavis and Shmule both working, you couldn't honestly say that Africana was growing much.

"Why should you worry if he grows or not, Joe?" asked Mr. Kandinsky. "Take everything for what it is, don't try to improve it, Joe. A chicken is a chicken. A man is a man. A little unicorn is a little unicorn. It's enough." Mr. Kandinsky thought Joe expected too much sometimes.

Joe didn't answer. He could see Mr. Kandinsky wasn't in the mood to talk about things. He and Shmule were finishing off a big order. They had to work overtime to make it pay, and there was hardly enough time to eat. So naturally something had to be sacrificed, and of course, it was talking, especially as Shmule had his fight coming off soon, and never talked much in a period of intensive training, not even to Sonia. Joe was very lucky then to have Africana's company. When the weather was dry they played in the yard together, Joe in a muffler and overcoat and Africana in a woolen coat Mavis knitted him.

Joe's favorite game was called Africa. In it he and Africana explored a jungle looking for a lost city. Africana was very big and strong with an enormous solid ivory horn with silver bells on it. Joe was tall and very brown and carried a rifle and two pistols. He rode Africana through the jungle where they fought a lion, two tigers, rogue elephant, a dreaded python two hundred feet long, and a cannibal king who looked like one of the wanderers. They beat them all. Joe wrestled the cannibal king and caught him in the dreaded scissors grip, so that his back cracked like the chair Shmule broke that time. The cannibal king was stuffed full of bits of stale bread and rags which fell out because he had wanted to steal Africana's horn and sell it. Africana defeated the elephant, and speared one of the tigers, and Joe shot the rest. Then they stopped under a big tree for a picnic dinner, and Africana had some greens while Joe brought his meat and potatoes into the yard to eat. After dinner they went on through the jungle. It was a long trek but down by the lavatory they suddenly came upon the lost city.

In the distance it looked like the shirt factory, with hundreds of cupolas all made of gold shining in the sun. In the city, which smelled of Keatings Powder, everything shone with big diamonds. Joe put one in his pocket to take back for Shmule to give his girl Sonia. The city was empty, although everything was neat and tidy as if his mother had just cleaned through. In one of the treasure vaults they found a large brand-new Superheat Patent Steam Presser which Joe put on one side for Mr. Kandinsky.

Joe and Africana walked down a long road paved with silver cobbles. All the way along were stalls with singing birds and hens and hokey-pokey ice cream and fritters and jellied eels and Polish bonbons, and you could take whatever you wanted. At the end of the road there was a huge palace like the Roxy Cinema in Whitechapel Road, shining with colored lights.

As they walked up to the palace there was suddenly a great thunder of hoofs, and hundreds and hundreds of unicorns came galloping towards them. At the head of them there was an enormous unicorn, his great golden horn studded with diamonds, and beside him a milkwhite lady unicorn with a very kind face. Africana shouted out to them, and they ran up to him and licked him all over, because they were his father and mother. On Africana's father's back— and this was the best of all—rode Joe's own father, who lifted Joe up onto his knee.

Then Joe and his father and Africana and his mother and father packed the diamond for Shmule and the Superheat Patent Steam Presser for Mr. Kandinsky, and went back through Africa with all the unicorns following them back, back, all the way back to Fashion Street. That was how Joe brought the unicorns back from Africa where they were lost for all those years.

The afternoon Mr. Kandinsky and Shmule went to deliver the rush job, it was raining, and Joe and Africana played the game called Africa in the workshop.

Joe was wrestling with a chair which was the cannibal king. He was having a hard time because the cannibal king was becoming a better wrestler all the time because of all the practice. Joe was twisting round into a better position to put the old scissors on him, when he saw a very old torn pair of boots stuffed with rags standing near his head. He looked up. It was one of the wanderers.

The wanderer had an old cloth cap with tickets in it, a big red nose, and a dirty beard all over his face. He held a sack in his hand, and a bottle stuck out of a pocket in one of his two overcoats. His little pink misty eyes peered all around the workshop. He asked Joe, "Is the old guvner in?" although he could see that he wasn't.

Joe knew at once who it was. He watched him carefully, clenching his fists, but when he walked over to Africana he nearly screamed. It was the cannibal king all right. Joe had no rifle and no pistols and couldn't wrestle and it was real. He stared up from the floor as the cannibal king came closer and closer to Africana.

Then, thank God, Joe heard clattering on the steps and Shmule's voice say he was wet through. He jumped to his feet and ran out of the room. "Quick, quick," he shouted, the tears running down his face, "quick, quick, quick." They rushed into the room while Joe, biting his lip, followed behind.

The wanderer looked up, squinting his misty eyes at them. "Ow are ye, guvner?" he said. "Got any old bits of clorth terday?"

Mr. Kandinsky sighed.

"You frightened the boy," he said. "Shmule, give him some of the bits and pieces. It's all right, Joe," he said, "nothing to worry for, Joe."

Joe didn't answer. He watched the wanderer fill up his sack. All the time he looked secretly at Africana, with a look like Mrs. Abramowitz when she was giving a pinch.

When the wanderer went, Joe saw him stop on the steps. Before turning out into the driving rain he pulled the bottle from his pocket and took a long drink from it. Afterwards, Joe went slowly up the stairs and looked out into the street. The cannibal king was stumbling against the wind, the sack over his back. There was a smell of methylated spirit in the passageway.

FIVE

After the cannibal king tried to steal Africana, Joe was more careful. Before putting Africana's collar and lead on for the morning walk, he went out into the street to see if it was safe. Even if it was, he no longer led Africana past the shirt factory, because you couldn't be too careful. He also decided to brush up his wrestling in case it should come to that, so it was good luck that Shmule was just then in a period of intensive training.

Shmule had already beat Louis Dalmatian, who was, to tell the truth, a pushover, and the Stepney Thrasher was off with a broken collarbone. So Shmule's manager, Blackie Isaacs, who ran the gymnasium, thought it was a lucky opportunity for Shmule to do Turk Robert and Bully Bason on the quick, and have a go at the dreaded Python Macklin, who was anyway not in such wonderful shape, he heard, owing to his stomach ulcer proving troublesome because he couldn't leave fried food alone, not to mention the booze. It was Shmule's big chance and Blackie fixed for him to fight Turk Robert and Bully Bason in the same week—Bully on the Monday and the Turk on the Friday.

It wasn't so bad as it sounds, Blackie said, because Bully was being paid off to be disqualified in the fourth for persistent gouging. "Supposing," Shmule asked, "I only lose one eye, do you take half commission?"

"Suddenly," Blackie said aloud to himself, "suddenly our Maccabeus has got the wind up. I'm telling you," he told Shmule, "the Bully is being paid off—just keep your eyes closed and scream—it's too much to ask for a five-pound purse?"

As for the Turk, he only had two tricks, a deathly rabbit punch and a back-breaking full-Nelson. "You're up to that, kid," Blackie told Shmule. "I know you won't let us down by letting that dead-beat murder you." And he gave him a good rubdown.

Though he wouldn't talk to Joe about wrestling, except to say it was a mug's game, Bully and the Turk were on Shmule's mind all the time. Between stitching he weaved his head from side to side, and as he lifted the iron he would suddenly duck. All Joe had to do was watch.

The weather was cold, so by special arrangement with Mr. Kandinsky, Africana was sleeping in the workshop, and as the workshop had a double lock for insurance purposes it was safe. Joe could consequently pay more attention to the wrestling business than he could with Africana living in the yard. Someone might get into the yard by climbing over the backs of the houses, but you couldn't break in through a double lock for insurance purposes. Also Africana liked it better in the workshop because it was warm and there was nearly always company. He lay under the bench in the nest of off-cuts, looking with bright eyes from one face to another. He needed rest because he had a bit of a cold.

Mr. Kandinsky was worried, which didn't make things easier. He was first of all worried about his rheumatism, which was always worse in a sharp spell. He was also worried about Shmule and all this prize fighting. He was, into the bargain, worrying about a patent steam presser because with the work short it was getting to be more and more difficult to compete. And now there was the unicorn to worry about as well. "He don't look so good to me, Joe," he said. "A little animal like that should be full of beans, jumping and skipping, not lying about the whole day with hardly appetite for a lettuce leaf unless you beg him to take it." He bent down to Africana. "Go on then," he said, offering a piece of leaf, "get it down, it'll do you good. Oy—the roimatismus is killing me. And business so bad into the bargain."

Business was so slow that Shmule said could he spend a couple afternoons at the gymnasium, especially since he had the two fights coming off and needed all the training he could get, not that he would mind how long he worked if there was the work there, but like this even his finger muscles would be cramping up waiting for the next pair of trousers, not that he wanted to put the mockers on the business, far from it, but why should he sit here messing about making new patterns when they didn't have the work. "Do me a favor," said Mr. Kandinsky, "go and wrestle."

"Can I come with you?" Joe asked, and Shmule was so pleased to be going off he said Joe could, so long as he didn't talk too much and take his mind off serious matters.

Then, after telling Joe to be quiet, Shmule didn't stop talking all the way to Blackie Isaacs in Middlesex Street, behind Isaacs' fish shop which was his real business.

"You see," Shmule said as they walked round the back streets, "I got to think of all the angles. Take the Bully, for instance. He may take the duck in the fourth all very well, but suppose he doesn't? Also I got to think of my self-respect. If I can beat him fair, it's better, I don't care what Blackie says. So it's no good you saying don't worry because the Bully is taking a duck."

"I didn't say don't worry," said Joe.

"I got to keep after him whether he wants to drop out or not," Shmule went on. "After all, that's his business. He can be paid off if he likes, that's not my affair. If it pays him better, good luck to him, let him lose on purpose."

"Why does it pay the Bully better to lose?" Joe asked.

"You can't tell," Shmule said. "Maybe his manager put money for him on me and they got good odds because the Bully is an old-stager and they thought he would wrap me up with no trouble. On the other hand, supposing he don't get thrown out for gouging, and I'm taking it easy thinking, what the hell, no need to break my neck, and the Bully gives me a welt, I'm out. No, say what you like, no matter what, I got a fight on me hands. Then there's the Turk. I see him fight three four times. True he's only got the two grips, but never mind, you've only got the one neck, he's only got to break it the once, no more. And he's got a nice style the Turk, even if he is a bit past it. He must be turned forty."

"So old?" Joe asked.

"At least," Shmule said. "At that age you haven't got the speed, well you can't expect it, can you?"

"No," said Joe.

"But he knows a thing or two all right, all right, one or two tricks to give somebody something to think about and no answer back. I got to keep out of his way and watch out for that little opening then rush him and give him the lot. Otherwise curtains. Also I'm giving him half a stone, remember, and weight counts in the wrestling. Supposing he gets his knee into me gut, I've finished, had me lot. Just because he's got the weight. No good complaining then, is it? It's all right for Blackie. He don't have to fight 'em, but if he did he wouldn't be so pleased. Two in a week. I ask you."

"I ask you," Joe said, "I ask you."

"It's too much, Joe," Shmule said, shaking his head as they got to Isaac's fish shop.

"I ask you," Joe said.

In the shop they were hosing the fish down, being as it was late in the afternoon and still not sold out. Mrs. Isaacs who had a great mane of red hair like a lion and a hoarse whispering voice, sprayed the hose over the floor.

"Hello, Ham," she said to Shmule, short for Hammer. "Hello, sonny," she said to Joe. "Gonna wrestle him, Ham?" she said, laughing till she coughed.

"Hello, Hammer," said Miss Isaacs, who was also redheaded, giving Shmule a friendly smile. Sonia made a scene once because she was so friendly, too friendly Sonia said, to anyone in trousers, and Shmule a trousers-maker into the bargain.

" 'Lo, girls," Schmule said, "behaving?" He hitched his shoulders.

"Going to win for me next week, Hammer?" asked Miss Isaacs, with that smile. That was what Sonia called it, that smile. Miss Isaacs looked up from under her long lashes, and her eyes were a nice green-gray, very nice with deep red hair.

"For you alone, Reen," Shmule said.

"And is Sonia doing well with her weight-lifting then?" asked Miss Isaacs, looking down.

"Such a strong girl," Mrs. Isaacs whispered.

"Very nice," Shmule said.

"I do admire her," Miss Isaacs said. "Sometimes I wish I was a bit more developed myself," and she gave Shmule that smile again.

"This way, Joe," Shmule said.

"That Miss Isaacs has got nice eyes," Joe observed.

"I got no time for such things," Shmule said.

In the gymnasium, Blackie and Oliver, the second, were putting Phil Jamaica, the colored boy, through his paces. Blackie smoked a cigar and watched closely, grunting every time Phil Jamaica hit the bag. Oliver was a punchie and you couldn't knock him out, though if he hung one on you, you knew it. He was a porter when there was work, at Spitalfield's Fruit Market, and could carry eight baskets on his head at once. He helped out as second and would give anyone a fight for five shillings, hit him all you like. Now he was crouching by the bag, his fists following Phil's. The colored boy was covered with sweat and his eyes stared fiercely at the bag as if it might hit back if he wasn't careful. Blackie saw Shmule come in and waved his cigar.

"All right, Phil," he said, "turn it in." Oliver sat Phil down, puffing and blowing, and whispered into his ear as he rubbed him down.

"Good boy," Blackie said, when Shmule told him he was putting in extra training, "good boy." Shmule went into the little changing room at the other end of the gym. "Put 'em up," Blackie said to Joe, squaring off to him, "put 'em up and let's see what you're made of?"

Joe got into the proper position of defense and Blackie sized him up, still puffing at his cigar. Then Joe suddenly let go and punched Blackie all over his stomach, so that he swallowed some smoke.

"Turn it in, kid," choked Blackie, "I wasn't ready. See the kid?" he said to Oliver, "a champ in the making. Save it for Phil," he said to Joe, "he's in training."

"What your name, boy?" Phil Jamaica asked Joe. His eyes were not staring now, and he had his breath back.

"Joe," said Joe.

"Watch that old defense, boy," Phil Jamaica said, "you was wide open. You got to watch that old defense or you is cooked. Like this." He squared up to the punch bag again, shadowboxing it like mad.

"Easy, easy, Phil," said Oliver. "Easy, easy, boy, don't tax yourself, Phil." Phil whipped round and shadowboxed in circles round him. "Easy, easy, boy," Oliver said.

"Was you watching the old defense, boy?" Phil asked Joe.

Joe nodded his head.

"Now you show me, boy," Phil told him.

Joe took up the position of defense again, and jumped into action, weaving round Oliver while Phil Jamaica shouted.

"Box him, boy, box him there, boy."

Joe was puffed afterwards.

"I watched the old defense," he said.

"You're all right, kid," Oliver said. "Always lead with the right and follow with the left, one-two, one-two, like that. Don't forget, one-two, one-two."

"One-two, one-two," said Joe, punching hard.

"And keep up the old defense, boy," said Phil Jamaica.

"The old defense," said Joe.

Meanwhile Shmule limbered up. He wore crimson briefs with a white hammer in the corner, and as he lifted the weights his muscles stood up in great bands. Blackie Isaacs watched him, rubbing his hands.

"What a boy!" he said, "What a boy, Olly, what a boy, Phil! Run a couple of rounds with him, Phil. Take Phil for a couple, Hammer," he said.

Joe watched them wrestle for a while, but though they threw one another about, and grunted and puffed and shouted, beating the canvas, he couldn't see how it was done. First they walked round one another with their legs bowed and their arms bent. That was all right. Then suddenly one jumped onto the other, but it was usually the one who jumped first who finished up with his back on the floor grunting, while the other one twisted his leg backwards and forwards.

First one, then the other, the black man and the white man, and first a black grunt, deep and dark, then a white grunt, higher and lighter. And Oliver, the second, and Blackie Isaacs shouting first for Phil and then for Shmule, while the two of them twisted round one another on the floor.

While Joe was examining the gym, which was a big shed where they used to smoke fish in the days when it paid, and which still smelled of fish, Shmule won the bout. Joe didn't notice him winning, because he was trying to lift himself up on the horizontal bars, but his arms weren't developed enough. He knew Shmule won because Miss Isaacs was watching from the door, and suddenly there was a groan from Phil Jamaica, and a quick beating on the canvas from his hands with palms which were quite pink, and Miss Isaacs shouted out, "Great, Hammer."

Afterwards they had fish and chips in the frying tonight part of the shop, Blackie heaping their plates with great mountains of golden chips and fillets of plaice, all very good because the establishment used only the best frying oil.

While they ate, Blackie talked to Shmule about his two coming fights and what he had heard about how both the Bully and the Turk were finished.

"Get your scissors well up," Blackie told him.

"And watch the old defense," Joe told him. "Lead with the right one-two one-two."

As Joe took up the position of defense two chips dropped off his plate, one-two, on to Mrs. Isaacs's clean floor.

SIX

No one expected Shmule to lose his two fights, but at the same time, to win two fights in the one week is very good and you shouldn't expect it. Consequently when Bully Bason was disqualified in the fourth round, due to persistent gouging, and Shmule went the whole length with Turk Robert to win on points after a hard fight and fairly clean, everyone was delighted.

People kept dropping into the workshop to congratulate Shmule and ask him how it felt to be a champ in the making, and what he thought his chances were against the dreaded Python, and how their money was on him. It was just as well work was a bit short, otherwise it would have been held up and that means dissatisfied customers, which is very bad for business. So that if business is bad anyway and held up, at least you aren't losing goodwill.

"Nevertheless," said Mr. Kandinsky, "with the best goodwill in the world, a patent presser can still be a help, because in the long run people want good work, but they want it cheap as well, and how can handwork be so cheap?"

Business all over the East End was, as a matter of fact, a bit slow, and Joe's mother got a couple of days off, not that it was a holiday. She was piece-working at the milliner's and consequently didn't get paid if there was no work. But Madame Rita, her boss, a big fat man with very fine fingers, swore that it was often like that just before the spring started and the weather was, after all, extra cold for the time of the year. Without sunshine to wear them in, who wanted hats? All the rain and sleet would ruin a good hat, and in bad weather who anyway would be bothered to notice whether a customer wore a new hat or not?

Joe's mother had plenty to do at home. She ran herself up a dress on Mr. Kandinsky's machine, a green dress with a small red flower in it, and she made Joe three shirts and a linen jacket for the summer, if it ever came. The net result of all this being that Joe was at a loose end, because women don't talk much when they are making things, and there were so many people in and out of the workshop to talk to Shmule and Mr. Kandinsky about the wrestling, that he couldn't get a word in. As for Africana, except for his bit of a sniffle, which was only seasonable since most people were coughing and hawking and sniffing and sneezing, he was all right, although he still didn't want to play about much. Joe could play the Africa game silently, but it wasn't so real indoors, especially if you had to be quiet, and you did have to with so many people about.

Though Joe kept a careful lookout, there was no sign of the cannibal king. His spies must have told him that Joe was learning a trick or two, and knowing what was good for him, he kept away from Fashion Street. But you could never tell when he might strike, so Joe mounted guard three times a day at the doorway, well muffled up against the cold weather for the time of the year.

As it turned out it was just as well, because on the Tuesday he was sucking a bon-bon and thinking that he might as well go down and at least listen to other people talking, when he saw the cannibal king turn into the street.

Joe pressed himself against the wall of the passage and waited. Sure enough the cannibal king stopped when he got to the workshop, bending down to look into the window below the grating. He watched quietly for a moment. Then he stood up, took his nose between his fingers and blew it. Then he took a piece of paper out of his pocket and studied it for a while. Afterwards he folded the paper up carefully, took a last look through the grating, and walked on.

Joe watched him the whole time. That piece of paper was his plan for stealing Africana and the only thing to do was to follow him, find his lair, and tell the sweetshop man, the informer, who would then tell the police. As it was only cold and not raining, Joe waited until the cannibal king was a bit ahead, and followed.

All the way along, Joe watched the cannibal king carefully, ready to take up the position of defense at a moment's notice. But the old man didn't look back once, which showed how cunning he was, trying to make Joe think that he didn't know he was being followed.

Once he sat down on the curb for a short rest, and Joe turned to look into the window of a magazine shop where there were thousands of covers in full color. They showed horrible monsters about to eat beautiful ladies with torn dresses, and rockets going to Mars, the red planet of mystery, and boxers beating one another bloody,

and cowboys shooting and gangsters shooting and Huns shooting.
Joe was thinking that the pictures were exciting but not very real
because you never saw things like that in Fashion Street. He started
to think then how it would be if when he got back to Fashion Street
a whole lot of horrible monsters were trying to get into the green-
grocer's shop to eat Mavis, and her overalls were torn. When he
looked round, the cannibal king was gone, which again went to
show how cunning he was.

There was a little sunshine now, not much warmth in it, but it
made things look brighter, especially the small pools of ice in the
gutters. After looking round for the cannibal king for a while, Joe
began to carefully break the ice with his heel.

Joe had just found a small pool which was solid ice safe for skat-
ing on with the toe of one foot, when there was a great clanging of
bells. A fire engine rushed past, covered with ladders, hoses and
firemen in helmets, the brass everywhere gleaming in the cold sunlight, the engine bright red and glossy as it flashed past. In case the
fire was nearby, Joe ran off in the direction the fire engine had
taken.

Joe ran a long way keeping a sharp lookout for fires everywhere,
but it was no good. The fire engine had disappeared. It's always
the way with fires. You never see them, because they're tucked away
somewhere you never dream could catch fire, like the one just round
the corner that time when some curtains caught alight. Joe heard
the bells and ran all over the place, but when he finally went round
the corner, there was the engine with all the firemen standing about,
and a lot of people watching, but of course the fire was out.

Joe sighed. He could tell from the way his stomach felt, that it
was dinner time, and since the old cannibal was nowhere to be seen,
he might just as well go home. He would have gone straight home,
except that he noticed the big chocolate advert over the railway
bridge and being so near, thought he might as well have a look at
Itchy Park to see if any flowers were coming up yet.

Itchy Park was an old graveyard which, though full up, had
hedges and a few big old trees. Flowers grew up round the graves

which were so covered with grass that without the gravestones and monuments you would think it was a real park. There were two iron benches painted dark green for your convenience, should you happen to be tired, and in nice weather old men used to meet there to talk politics, while mothers pushed their babies in prams, and children played Release round the graves. With its white stone pillars with iron fences between them, the iron all black and green, the stone all white and black and gray patches from the rain and smoke, it was like ancient Greece. In nice weather, a pleasant place for a short outing.

At Itchy Park the sun made the white stone pillars and whitened headstones shine like alabaster, and Joe dawdled between the graves on his way to one which, last spring, was covered with crocuses. He spelled out some of the shorter words which could still be read on the stones, because even if he didn't go to school yet, Mr. Kandinsky told him, there was no need for him to be ignorant. He stopped at the memorial with the split angel on it to see if it had split any more lately. It had only one wing and the tip of that was missing, so that if it did split there wouldn't be much of that angel left, and Itchy Park was already short of angels because they got knocked off so easily. Fortunately, the split angel was no worse, so Joe went over to the crocus grave.

Some of the crocuses were shooting and striped dark green leaves showed through the grass which was winter thin and short. One of the crocuses was quite large but it looked as if it would never flower and felt stone cold. In spite of the sun, blasts of wind cut through the graveyard like wet stone knives. It was no wonder if the flowers were frozen stiff, and the grass thin, and the angels splitting. Standing up to breathe on his fingers, Joe saw the cannibal king.

Why he didn't see him straight away Joe couldn't imagine, because he was sitting on one of the iron benches with his sack beside him, drinking from his bottle. If Itchy Park was his lair, it was certainly a cold one, although maybe one of the graves opened secretly and the king crept into it at night. Joe knelt down again behind the headstone on the crocus grave to watch.

Between taking long drags on the bottle, the king grunted and coughed, not a short dry cough like a dog, but a large wide wet rackety cough, as if his whole chest and stomach coughed with him. The choker round his throat opened and his neck showed loose skin red and raw. There was spit all round his mouth, and his eyes ran with water. As he drank and coughed he only looked like an old man in a graveyard with a bad cold in the cold time of the year.

Joe was creeping round the back to go home, when suddenly the cannibal king gave an enormous cough which shook his whole body so that his face turned purple. While he was getting his wind back, his face turned white making his beard look dark and thick. He closed his eyes and sank back on the bench, and the open bottle, which was still in his hand, dipped over so that some of the spirit poured on to his coat.

When he got home, Joe's mother and Mr. Kandinsky were full of questions about where he had been and how cold he was. Joe didn't tell them about the old cannibal king. It would have been too difficult to explain why he wasn't a cannibal or a king any more, just because of the cold.

SEVEN

The morning the spring came, Joe woke up in a circle of sunlight with a breeze blowing softly upon his face. Lying still with his eyes wide open, he listened to his mother's breathing, like the sea in the distance, a ship going to Africa. But because it was the spring, Joe agreed it was only a dream, and jumping out of bed ran downstairs without his slippers on to see if Africana had noticed the welcome visitor.

Africana was indeed awake, and so full of beans, you would never guess he didn't enjoy the best of health. In view of the weather perhaps it wasn't surprising, because with the sun you always feel full of beans and it's a pity to go to bed because you will never sleep. With the sun up in the sky ripe and heavy like a solid gold watermelon, everyone feels it will be a wonderful day, and sometimes it is.

In the yard, the stones already felt warm. The rotten wood fencing which oozed in wet weather like a crushed beetle, was dry as if washed up on a beach somewhere, near pirate treasure. A weed had grown in a minute of the night on the small patch of bare ground, which in the sunshine was earth not dirt any more. It might grow into a palm tree.

Africana, awake in his house, scratched at the walls eager to play. When Joe lifted the hook on the door he at once ran out. There wasn't time for a complete game, however, because Mr. Kandinsky came into the yard in his carpet slippers and quilted dressing gown, blinking, his eyes still creased up from sleeping. He sent Joe up at once to get dressed, and put Africana back in his house until after breakfast at least. As he ran upstairs, Joe felt his own face just below the eyes, but there were no creases. He guessed Mr. Kandinsky had more skin to work with.

Joe's mother's boss, Madame Rita, was quite right, there was more work going in the millinery once the worst of the winter was over. Before the spring arrived, women, like the crocuses in Itchy Park, felt it near, and began to peep round at hats. They were already, during the short spells of sunshine, looking into the window of Madame Rita's shop and saying that it wouldn't really suit me, Sadie, it's for a younger woman, and Sadie was saying but it would, Ada, it's just your style. The next stage was, they came into Madame Rita's and tried on the hats. They tried twenty hats with the brims up, then down, then sideways, then without the trimming, then with more trimming. Madame Rita watched them, his hands on his large belly, a soft smile on his face, a small black cheroot between his teeth. As they tried one hat after another, with or without trimming, he made little soft cooing noises. "Pardon me, lady," he would say eventually, "the brim up is more your style." With a push here and a push there he made the hats suit the faces they had to sit over. In the end the ladies sometimes bought the hats.

Consequent upon there being more work in the millinery, Joe's mother was kept busier and busier at Madame Rita's, putting on more and more trimming as fashion demanded, and though this is tiring, it is just what the doctor ordered for piece workers. But they have in consequence to hurry over breakfast. The day spring came, Joe and his mother had boiled eggs, and before she had her coat on, Joe kissed her good morning and ran down to the yard—so you can tell how he hurried if his mother hadn't even left yet, and she in such a hurry as well.

The reason why Joe was in such a hurry that morning was that in his sleep he had thought of a new game and wanted to see if it would work. One of the things about games is that unless you keep adding to them and working out new ideas, they get dull—not the games really, but you get dull in the games, and then they seem dull. And games like the game called Africa are worth keeping fresh, you must admit, so no wonder Joe didn't bother about such things as turning his egg shell over and smashing the other side of it. Sometimes there are more important things to do in life than just playing about with egg shells, and things like that have to give way to Africa. Anyhow, you can smash egg shells anytime, but you don't get a new idea every night you sleep.

When Joe's mother was leaving, she looked into Mr. Kandinsky's workshop to say good morning to him and tell him that she might be late, and not to worry. Mr. Kandinsky pointed to the back window and nodded. Looking out, Joe's mother saw Joe talking to Africana, and waving to someone a long way off. She thought how the back of his neck was still like a baby, delicate, with a little gentle valley down the center, because he was, after all, almost a baby with everything yet to come. How much they had to learn, what a terrible lot they had to learn. She ran away to Madame Rita's to trim spring hats for those who had already learned what suited them.

All that morning Joe and Africana played together in the yard which, due to the dry rotten fencing, had become a ship, old wooden walls. Joe was the captain and Africana on one occasion mutinied. He ran to the other end of the yard frightened by Joe shouting out, "Fasten your jibs and loosen your mainsails, you lousy lubbers," which is only what captains do say. That nearly spoiled the game, but they went on, after a pause for Africana to eat a cabbage leaf. They visited the South Sea Islands, where Joe drank coconut milk, which is quite like ordinary milk. Mr. Kandinsky brought it out for him in an enamel mug. They found pirate treasure just under the lavatory door, a small black pebble which, when properly cut and polished, would be a black diamond. Then at last they came to Africa and had a few adventures there, but suddenly Joe felt like a talk with Mr. Kandinsky. Africana's sniffle had started again so they hurried on to the lost city, met Africana's parents and Joe's father and came home quickly. By air, as a matter of fact, the unicorns growing large wings like geese for the purpose.

The reason why Joe felt like a talk was that though it was a nice thing to have a unicorn, Africana often didn't seem very interested in playing. Sometimes he sat down in the middle of a game and just chewed, which was certainly irritating, even if he did have a cold. Joe was worried too because Africana still wasn't growing much and his horn was so tiny it couldn't even grant small wishes yet. Joe once wished on it for his mother to come home at three o'clock and take him to the pictures, and instead she came home at turned six and cried because there was no letter from his father.

While locking Africana up, Joe practiced talking and spitting at the same time. It was a question of holding the spit loose round the tip of your tongue which you kept between your teeth, and blowing when you spoke. With a little more time, Joe would have it perfect, but where did they get those sandwich boards from? Joe went into the workshop.

"Where do they get those sandwich boards from, Mr. Kandinsky?" he asked.

"Where?" answered Mr. Kandinsky. "A question."

"From the kingdom of heaven?" suggested Joe.

"Only the religious ones," Mr. Kandinsky said.

"From the agency near the arches," Shmule said without looking up from a turn-up he was turning up. "I know, because Blackie Isaacs has got six of them going round with me on them versus the dreaded Python Macklin at the Baths next Saturday night. No wonder I'm worried."

"Shmule," Mr. Kandinsky cried, "you never said nothing."

"Can anyone get sandwich boards near by the arches?" asked Joe.

"You fighting the dreaded Python so soon?" Mr. Kandinsky went on. "How come you are fighting him? Him next to the champion and you a new boy in wrestling almost."

"Look," Shmule said, "Python is warming up, see. He's near the crown five, six year. Already he fights the champ five times. Four times he loses, once he draws. Now he wants plenty of fights, get into form and knock off the champ, who is boozing too much anyway, quick. Afterwards, plenty exhibition bouts with big money for a couple year, and buy a pub in Wapping. So with the shortage in class wrestlers, Blackie does me a favor. Also knocking off the Turk and Bully didn't help me. I'm a gonner."

"It's wonderful," Mr. Kandinsky said, "to think in my workshop a future champion. Wonderful."

"Wonderful," Shmule replied, "I got trouble, so by you it's wonderful. I'm a gonner I tell you."

"What kind of spirit is this?" Mr. Kandinsky asked sternly. "A nice carry on. I'm ashamed."

"You're ashamed. You should have the worry and you wouldn't have no time to be ashamed." Shmule threw his needle and thread down. "That bloody Python is going to break my bloody neck."

"Think how proud Sonia will be of you," Mr. Kandinsky said.

"Sod Sonia, let her fight the Python and I'll be proud," answered Shmule, and he picked up his needle and got on with his sewing.

"The sandwich boards, Joe," said Mr. Kandinsky. "The sandwich boards is an interesting case."

"Sod the sandwich boards," said Joe. "That bloody Python."

"Go to the corner and get three rolls," shouted Mr. Kandinsky in a voice of thunder and Joe ran out. "A fine attitude to life," Mr. Kandinsky told Shmule, his mouth turned down at the corners, which was always a bad sign.

When Joe came back he found that Shmule and Mr. Kandinsky

were not on speaking terms, except for essentials like "Pass the black thread" and "Give me the shears." Joe couldn't break the ice by talking about what was on his mind before he thought of the sandwich boards, because he couldn't remember what it was, so after dinner he went out and spent the afternoon helping Mavis in the shop. At least Mavis always thought it was a wonderful day. She let him serve Mrs. Abramowitz with a pound of Granny Smith apples, of which she was very fond. Of course Mrs. Abramowitz managed to pinch his cheek, sod her.

EIGHT

The day before Shmule's fight with Python Macklin, the workshop was closed. Shmule was getting into top shape down at Isaacs' Gymnasium and Blackie was giving every assistance, including sending out of his own pocket a case of bad whisky to Python, because even if it would be hell for the stomach ulcers, who can resist the gift of an unknown admirer? Mr. Kandinsky did have, to tell the truth, a couple of things he could have got on with, but instead he spent the morning at Shafchick's vapor bath. By permission of Madame Rita, Joe spent the morning down at the milliner's with his mother, which certainly made a change from all the bad temper and arguments in Kandinsky's workshop. Furthermore, the girls at Madame Rita's gave you sweets all the time, and had a completely different kind of conversation.

Joe's mother was the trimmer, and there was another girl called Sophie who was learning the trimming from her. There was the machinist, Mrs. Kramm, who was old and had a chest, and a pretty assistant from the shop named Ruby but called Lady R. Ruby was very nice to Joe but she treated the others, even Joe's mother, a bit haughty. As soon as she went out of the workroom they talked about her.

"What a fine lady, I don't think," said Sophie.

"Some lady, I should say, and what was she before?—a little snot-nose giving the boys eyes the whole time," wheezed Mrs. Kramm.

"She's very pretty," Joe's mother said, picking up a small bunch of artificial cherries. "And good at her job."

"That you can say again," Mrs. Kramm said. "That job she can do all right, I wouldn't wish it on my worst enemy such a job as she can do so well." She pressed the treadle of her machine so that the thread shot through the needle like lightning.

"Mrs. Kramm," Joe's mother said, looking towards Joe, "I'm surprised at you. After all, it's only a rumor."

"Oh no it's not, Becky," Sophie said quickly. "I've seen him after her behind the gown rail carrying on something terrible."

"Sophie," Joe's mother said, "the child."

"Here you are, Joe," Sophie said, "I've found a caramel in silver paper for you."

"Thank you very much," said Joe, because they were the soft kind with a nut in the middle, although he would rather have heard some more about Lady R and Madame Rita. But it was just as well Sophie stopped when she did because while he was taking the silver paper off the caramel carefully so as not to tear it, who should come in but Lady R herself.

"Becky dear," she said to Joe's mother, "could Joe go an errand? Would you go an errand, Joe sweetie, for Auntie Ruby, dolly?"

"Certainly he could," Joe's mother said, though Joe didn't as a rule run errands for dollies.

"Will you, dolly?" asked Lady R, bending down and putting her face right close to his. "For me?"

"All right," Joe said. Lady R smelled nice at least, and she had large brown eyes and a smooth dark skin and oily black hair very smooth and curled into a bun.

"Bless you, baby," Lady R said, and suddenly she gave Joe a fat kiss on his cheek, which though better than a pinch is still a nuisance.

The errand was to go round the corner and collect Lady R's genuine French calf handbag which was having its clip repaired. When he was coming back through the shop with the handbag, which was a sack of coal over his shoulder, he saw Madame Rita and Lady R behind the gown rail, and what Sophie said was true. Back in the workroom his mother got out her handkerchief and licked it and rubbed off Lady R's lipstick, which meant that it had been on his face all the time and he didn't know, which proves you shouldn't go errands for dollies.

"Don't lick me," Joe said.

"Keep still, Joe," replied his mother.

"If you lick me clean, you should lick Madame Rita, too, because his face is even worse."

"Oy," wheezed Mrs. Kramm, "the cat is in the bag. What goings on. For a respectable woman it's terrible."

After Joe had been cleaned up he went down into the cellar where there were a whole lot of old dummies, colored crepe papers, and boxes. Although he got filthy, it did allow the women to talk about Lady R, which is all women want to do anyway. For his part he got down to a serious game of Club Row.

He was being an Indian fortuneteller with a green remnant round his head, when he had a happy thought. He thought how the women wanted to talk about Lady R, and how Shmule wanted to win another fight although he had already won two, and how Mr. Kandinsky still wanted a patent presser, and how his father hadn't sent for them yet.

So, Joe thought, everybody is always saying I wish, I wish, and always wanting things. And straightaway he improved being a fortuneteller by having Africana with him. Africana wasn't very much bigger, but his horn was coming along nicely, just big enough for, say, five or six wishes.

Joe set out four boxes, on which he made drawings with a piece of flat chalk he kept in his pocket for emergencies. One of his mother in a hat, one of Mr. Kandinsky, one of Shmule and one of everybody else, including Sonia and Mavis. Then he led Africana, the wish-maker, to each box. After what was necessary was explained to Africana, he was very glad to bend his head so that his horn touched the drawing on each box. And that was how the wishes were granted. All this took a good deal of work, so it was not until Sophie came down to the cellar to call him for dinner that the job was done.

When he went upstairs he still had the green remnant round his head. Lady R, who was eating a saltbeef sandwich, waved a pickled cucumber at him and called him the Sheik of Araby dolly. If Joe didn't find something to do in the afternoon she would spoil everything, because she was that type. It was good luck that Mr. Kandinsky called in while Joe was eating his second jam sandwich.

As Mr. Kandinsky had spent the whole morning at Shafchick's vapor bath in Brick Lane, he looked very pink and scrubbed, but he wasn't angry about Moishe, which was unusual. He said to Joe's mother, "That Moishe, the cap-maker, went too far today. He got cooked." And he giggled and asked Joe if he would like to come round with him to the Tailors' Union, he had to tell them about how Moishe was cooked.

Moishe, the cap-maker, had a huge belly and was an old friend of Mr. Kandinsky. They argued all the time, and always met on a Friday at Shafchick's, where they would argue their way through the hot room, then the hotter room, then the hottest room in the world, and even while they were being rubbed down by Luke, the Litvak masseur, who only used the Russian massage whether you wanted it or not. Luke carefully made up his own bundles of twigs, holding them high in the steam to pick up the heat. He gave you a rubdown like an earthquake, then shook hands and said "Good health, Reb." He was a big man with a huge belly, and when he and Moishe stood together you could drive a pair of cart horses between them. They carried the argument through while they drank glasses of lemon tea to put the moisture back into their systems, although they had just gone to all that trouble to get it out.

Mr. Kandinsky's arguments with Moishe were mostly political, like Macdonald and Baldwin, which is the best man, or was the Tsar murdered or can you call it execution, or whether the Tailors' Union should run a sick fund or was it placing temptation in the way? In Shafchick's such arguments became heated especially in the

hottest room in the world, because at Shafchick's you can always
rely on the heat. They say that Shafchick was a great rabbi who
was so pious that Barney Barnato wanted to give him something,
so being pious he said what else but a vapor bath for the whole East
End, and that's what Barney gave him, and of course he became
managing director and did very well, so they say, but why not since
at Shafchick's you can rely on the heat, day or night. It comes glid-
ing out of a hundred small gratings slowly until the place is like a
stew pot boiling on the gas. No one bothers you, you sit in a deck
chair like Bournemouth or the Crimea, play chess, drink your tea,
argue, whatever your pastime happens to be. All the time you are
getting the benefit of the heat. Rheumatism is melted before it can
crystallize round the joints of your bones, veins becomes less vari-
cose, the lumbago and all creaks in the back are eased, and you get
a good rest into the bargain. And afterwards? Don't ask. You feel
like an angel walking through the green fields of Brick Lane. If you
wanted to, you could fly looking down upon the hills of East London, while everything is fresh about you, as in the morning of life.
You smell the *baigels* leaving the bake oven. Cart horses make the
streets smell like a farm yard, and the people about you have the
faces of old friends. Everything is so good when you come from
Shafchick's that once you get the habit you never regret it, even if
Moishe's arguments are so ridiculous they make you a bit short-tem-
pered. It is not a real short temper. It is a luxury to make you feel
deeper the joy of having lived through yet another vapor bath.

As they walked over to the Tailors' Union, Mr. Kandinsky giggled most of the time, and once or twice he stopped dead, looked
down at Joe and laughed out loud.

"How that Moishe was cooked," he giggled. "What a hot-pot."

The Union was in Whitechapel Road, and in the week there
were not many tailors there, but on Sunday mornings they filled
the room and spread out into the street, chatting in their long coats
about this or that, small groups of them for a hundred yards up the
Whitechapel Road. Sometimes a master tailor would come up and

say, "Have you seen Chaim? I got three days' work for him," and everyone would shout out, "Where's Chaim? Here's work for him." The Union room itself was dirty, with dusty windows on which someone had written with a finger, "Up with," but they couldn't decide who, so there was no name. The wooden plank floor was smeared with rubbed out cigarette ends, and the only decoration on the walls was the black and red poster which said, "Wrestling Saturday Night," with pictures of Shmule and Python Macklin on it. A young coat-maker who happened to be temporarily unemployed was making up a small book at a table below the poster.

At one end of the room there was a trestle table with a big brown enamel teapot stewing on it, a quart bottle of milk, and a plate of rolls and butter. Behind the trestle Mrs. Middleton, the caretaker, stood, cutting rolls, pouring tea, and talking Yiddish with some old tailor who, like Mr. Kandinsky, looked in to hear what was happening in the world.

At another trestle table, which had benches along both sides, two men were playing dominoes. As Mr. Kandinsky and Joe came in, they finished a game, and the bones clicked as for hands smoothed them over for the next, for domino games go on for ever. Two other men drank tea from big chipped enamel mugs they carried in their overcoat pockets.

"So white gold is by you cheap stuff, rubbish?" one said.

"Who says rubbish," the other replied, "platinum is better, that's all."

"Platinum is good enough for you," said the first, "you're sure?"

"Another cup tea, Missus," the other said.

"You didn't pay for the first two yet," Mrs. Middleton answered.

"You short of platinum maybe?" the first said, putting sixpence on the counter.

Mrs. Middleton filled the cups up with black tea, and sloshed milk on top. "Why Mr. Kandinsky," she said, "what a surprise." She always told her friends that Mr. Kandinsky was a real gentleman.

"Mrs. Middleton, my dear," Mr. Kandinsky said, shaking hands with her, "what a pleasure to see you. So well you look, ten years younger. How's the boy?"

"He's in the signwriting now," Mrs. Middleton said proudly.

"A good trade," one of the men said.

"Very artistic," said the other.

"You know," Mr. Kandinsky said to the men, "that boy when he was twelve could draw anything you like, a pound of apples, a couple oranges, a banana, anything."

"Maybe he should have gone in the fruitery," one of the men said.

"No," replied Mr. Kandinsky, "people as well, the King, politicians."

"Bastards," the other man said.

"A nice cup of tea, Mr. Kandinsky?" asked Mrs. Middleton.

"By all means with pleasure," replied Mr. Kandinsky, "and a glass of milk for the boy."

"Your grandson?" asked Mrs. Middleton. "Bless him."

"Nearly," Mr. Kandinsky said, "bless him."

While they drank their tea and Joe sipped his milk, which was a little dusty, Mr. Kandinsky asked the men how was business, and they said he meant where was it, it was a thing of the past, tailors were two a penny if you were throwing your money away because in a couple of months the tailors would pay you to let them work. Mr. Kandinsky said it was terrible, he was feeling it bad, but what could you do? And the men agreed, what could you do?

All the time Mr. Kandinsky was on edge to tell them how Moishe was cooked. He was leading up to it by saying how well he felt after a vapor bath at Shafchick's. One of the men liked vapor baths very much, but the other one thought they were bad for the system, like lemon tea, tasty but rotting to certain organs of the stomach.

"You," the other man said, "with a barrel organ in your stomach, you couldn't make more noise, such rubbish you talk. Vapor baths is proven by the best medical authority to be the best thing in the world for the system. Lords and ladies are paying fortunes to go to foreign parts, and why?—because they got vapor baths. And here we got in the East End one of the finest vapor baths in the world, where for practically nothing you can go and sweat first or second class all day long to your heart's content. He isn't satisfied. It's rotting the organs from his stomach, Mr. Platinum here." He spat on the floor.

"Manners," warned Mrs. Middleton.

"Anyhow," continued Mr. Kandinsky, annoyed at the interruption, "who's telling the story? You know Moishe the cap-maker from Cable Street?"

"The one who married his son to the daughter of Silkin, the wholesale grocer?" one of them asked.

"No, no," the other said. "Moishe is the one with the big ears who goes to the dogs." One of the men playing dominoes looked up and grunted.

"You know," he said. "Everything you know."

"You know better?" the man replied.

"You know," the domino player said again.

"So play," said his partner, who was winning.

"Anyhow," Mr. Kandinsky continued, "Moishe comes to the baths on Fridays and you think you can argue, but that Moishe is one to argue you out of business. Doesn't matter what you say, he knows better. Whatever it is, politics, history, business, anything, he knows better. I just come from Shafchick's and you know what happened?" Mr. Kandisky stopped to giggle again and to give the domino players a chance to look round from their game. "He just got cooked."

Naturally they all wanted to know what happened, so after laughing a bit more to drag it out, Mr. Kandinsky told them.

He and Moishe were talking about the slump and he said that if only he had a patent steam presser he could do all right, slump or no slump, because if you could do the work fast enough, it didn't matter if you got paid less, just so long as you kept turning it over, and if you keep working you can always make a living. Also with a patent presser you could take in pressing when the trousers were slack. At once Moishe says what does Kandinsky know about economical matters, leave it to the specialists who get employed to know these things, they take years of study.

"I been studying my trade with the goose iron for enough years," Mr. Kandinsky replied. "I know what's what."

"Kandinsky," said Moishe, "that's where you make your mistake. Do you know what is a price spiral with an inflation? You don't. Do you know we are dropping off from the gold standard? You don't. Do you understand the economical problem of today? You should worry."

"What is all this to do with making trousers for a living, if you don't mind a question?" asked Mr. Kandinsky.

"That's what I mean," replied Moishe, "trousers-making you know, but what else?"

"And what else am I talking about? I read plenty books in my time and now also, but leave that to one side, what am I talking about except trousers-making? I am saying a patent steam presser is what I need. I don't know what is good for my business?"

But Moishe went on and on about gold prices and unemployment figures. He read the financial column of the paper very carefully every day as a hobby, and he was enjoying himself, especially as there was a shortage of cap-makers and he had plenty of work.

They went into the heavy steam room, where you can hardly breathe or see at all. But in spite of that Moishe went on talking and talking from his end of the room, lying on the marble bench with his towel under him, talking and talking. So Mr. Kandinsky left him to it. "Let him talk to himself since he's the only one who knows what he's talking about," Mr. Kandinsky thought, as he went out for a massage.

He had his massage talking with Luke the Litvak about his brother-in-law, the doctor in the children's hospital, although, funny thing, no children of his own. Afterwards he sat down quietly in a deck chair in a second class cubicle. He drank a glass of lemon tea and read the paper. Then he settled down for a little sleep.

Suddenly, just when Mr. Kandinsky is dreaming he is picking

cherries in an orchard at home, and though the cherries are full and ripe, there is yet blossom on the trees, which is impossible but looks wonderful and the smell, there is a shouting, and he wakes up. There, the color of borsht and steaming like a pudding is Moishe, cursing him and saying what a thing to do, locking him in like that, and it's wonderful he's alive to tell Kandinsky what kind of a lousy dog he is.

"And what happens," laughed Mr. Kandinsky, "is this. I am so fed up with Moishe talking and talking, I slam the door of the heavy steam room, and it jams. I told him, is it my fault the door jams? It's the heavy steam from him talking so much. What's it got to do with me? You should have seen him, just like a stuffed neck he looked, stuffed with red cabbage. Luke and me laughed our head off."

The men laughed and said it should teach Moishe to argue the whole time, they must remember to ask him how he got cooked and how was his price spiral. Then they went back to their own arguments, which since Mr. Kandinsky was there, came down to the question who would win the fight tomorrow night. They placed bets with the man who was making the book, and Mr. Kandinsky said as it was a special occasion he would put a shilling on for Joe. The platinum man said to the white gold man, "Even if he don't win, I don't want to make a crust out of that lousy Python Macklin, who is, without doubt, one of the dirtiest fighters in the ring today. Also if Shmule wins, it's good for the tailors and we should all be behind him, even if he loses."

Joe put down the buttered roll he was eating.

"Shmule will be the winner," he said. They all looked at him in silence for a moment.

"Put another bob on, Hymie," said white gold.

"Out of the mouths of babes," said Mr. Kandinsky.

Just at that moment, one of the old men stopped clicking dominoes and said to Mr. Kandinsky, "Kandinsky, you want a patent presser? My brother-in-law, the one with the big factory."

"Big factory," the other man said.

"You got a bigger factory?" the first old man asked.

"So?" asked Mr. Kandinsky.

"He just got a new presser for his new factory, and he's chucking out the old one."

"It works?" asked Mr. Kandinsky.

"To look costs nothing," the old man said.

"So I'll look," replied Mr. Kandinsky, and patted Joe's head.

Joe was very pleased, especially when you remember that Africana wasn't really with him in the cellar at Madame Rita's. It may have been the green remnant, because you can never tell where an odd bit of magic is going to turn up, so why not in the cellar of Madame Rita's. Joe thought they had better get home quickly now, because it might start to happen any minute.

The first thing Joe did when they got home was to go into the yard and thank Africana. He put his arm round his neck and kissed him gently on the head, next to his horn bud. Africana coughed and his head jerked up and hit Joe's jaw, making him bite his tongue.

NINE

The following day the weather was cold again. It was going to be one of those springs which stops and starts, unable to make up its mind whether to stay or not. One moment the stone streets were pink and bright in the sunshine, and the next they were gray and dirty again, the sun sunk away somewhere behind a million chimneys on a million slate roofs. But though Saturday morning brought no quick pools of sunlight and the Kremlin, a disused shirt factory, looked blank and dead in the gray light, no one bothered, for they were all impatient for the evening. Once the evening comes, what does it matter how bright or dull the day has been? So far as the evening is concerned, all days are bright, and tomorrow can be still brighter. Hurry along tomorrow, a brighter day, and for an overture, let the evening bring great moments of life such as the spectacular fight between the Aldgate Hammer and the dreaded

Python Macklin. And for the sake of tailors everywhere, let the tailor win.

Shmule gave Mr. Kandinsky four seats in the second row for Joe and his mother, Sonia and himself. The fights didn't begin until half past seven, and Shmule's bout came up an hour later. Mr. Kandinsky was going to get them there in good time for Shmule's fight but he would in no circumstances hear of them seeing the fights which came before.

"We are not," said Mr. Kandinsky, "savages to go and watch the gladiators fight and to enjoy the struggles of people we don't know. Shmule is our own boy, so we must encourage him, not have a good time while other people get broken necks. If it wasn't for Shmule fighting we would never go, not in a hundred years." And even Sonia, who enjoyed wrestling even if she didn't know the wrestlers—and she knew most of them, of course—had to wait round the house talking about her trousseau with Joe's mother until it was time to leave.

Africana was shivering. Joe tried to make him comfortable in his house, which had had so many bits and pieces tacked on to it through the winter that it looked like a wooden patchwork quilt. It was a shame that animals weren't allowed at the wrestling, because if Shmule did win it would be Africana's doing. Joe promised to tell Africana everything in the morning and anyhow Africana's cough was bad. He wouldn't take Gee's Linctus, even on cubes of sugar, and what with the break in the weather making it treacherous for bronchial complaints, it was just as well for Africana to stay at home. Joe told everybody that Africana wasn't very well. Being the first dressed, he went out to have a word with Mavis on the subject.

The street looked quite different at night. Great deeps of shadow gathered in the corners of the Kremlin, and the small shops were warm with lamps. The baker's lamp was gas and spluttered, but Mavis's were electric and steady. On the street corner there was a barrow with a big naphtha lamp spitting away white and blue, and two large iron braziers with iron trays red hot on them, roasting chestnuts and baking potatoes. Someone stood by the barrow and

Joe was surprised to find it was the man who helped the Eel King on Sundays, so it looked as if with the coming of the night everyone became someone else. Even Mavis looked different, older and paler in the yellow light, with tired markings on her face, her flowered overalls dirty from where she had clasped bins of potatoes all day long. She was surprised to see Joe up and about at that time of night.

"You do look a toff, Joe," she said, "in long trousers and a jacket to match, a real toff. Where are you off to? You should be in bed."

"Yes, they are nice," Joe said, putting his hands deep into the pockets of his long trousers. "They have real flies, with buttons."

"I suppose old Mr. Kandinsky run them up for you," Mavis said. "He run up all my old dad's."

"You look a bit old, Mavis," Joe said. "The whole street looks sort of different at night."

"I am a bit old, dear, I reckon," said Mavis, "and with the end of the day you feel it more."

"You'll have to hurry because we're going soon," Joe said, and told her about Shmule's fight.

"I shan't come, Joe dear," Mavis said, "there's still a lot to do though no morning market to think about, and I don't think blood sports should be allowed anyway, and wrestling is a sort of blood sport. Would you like a nice apple?"

"Thank you," said Joe, taking a large bite of the russet apple she handed him. "What's a blood sport?"

"Where they hunt poor dumb animals," Mavis said, "for their sport, like the early Christian martyrs and saints that were thrown to the lions."

"You mean the lions ate them up?" Joe asked, thinking it was a good thing he never did get that lion cub for a pet.

"Yes, poor souls, limb from limb," said Mavis, sorting through the tomatoes.

"They must have been hungry," Joe said, taking another large bite of his apple.

"It wasn't them, poor dumb beasts, it was the sinfulness of their masters, and yet, Joe, they prayed for their torturers in the midst of their torment."

"What's torturers and torment?" Joe asked, although he really wanted to talk about Africana.

"Don't trouble your head about it," Mavis said. "Oh, what a rotton one," she added throwing a soft tomato into a box, where it burst juicily. "How's your little unicorn?"

"That's what I was going to tell you," Joe said. "He's got this bad cold on the chest and coughs all the time, and he's not interested in anything, and won't touch the Gee's Linctus, even on cubes of sugar. Do you think it's the consumption?" Mavis stopped sorting for a moment.

"He never was very strong you know, Joe. He was always a delicate little thing. This has been a rotten winter for the best of us."

"I know," said Joe, "Mr. Kandinsky has been getting terrible creaks down his back this winter, and I saw someone with a cough." He was going to tell her about the cannibal king that time in Itchy Park, but he didn't want to think about it. "Will you have a look at Africana, Mavis?" he said instead.

Mavis closed the shop and they walked down to the house. They went through to the yard, and Mavis wrapped Africana in a piece of blanket and brought him into the workroom. In the light from the naked bulb over Mr. Kandinsky's bench Africana looked pinched and sick, and Mavis's face was serious. While she examined Africana, Joe heard Mr. Kandinsky call from the other room and went to see him.

Mr. Kandinsky was walking about in polished boots, wearing a combination woolen vest and long pants.

"I can't find them blankety trousers," he said. "Can you imagine, Joe," he added, "a trousers-maker without a pair of trousers to his back. Here they are." Grunting he drew a pair of striped black trousers out from beneath the mattress and pulled them on.

Joe told him that Mavis was in the workroom having a look at Africana who wasn't at all well. Joe made his face serious like Mavis, the lips pressed tight together.

"That animal," Mr. Kandinsky said, "has he ever been not sick?"

"Maybe we should send him back to Africa, to his mother and father," Joe said.

"Africa?" asked Mr. Kandinsky. "What's with Africa?"

"To the other unicorns," Joe said, a bit annoyed because Mr. Kandinsky wasn't thinking.

"Oh my God, yes," said Mr. Kandinsky. "Africa. Maybe we should. Quite right. Have a wine cherry, but only one." Mr. Kandinsky's bedroom was almost filled by a big mahogany bed with two large feather beds on it. A huge wardrobe stuffed with clothes and books and remnants took up one wall. The other wall had a small fireplace choked with colored crepe paper. But in the corner was a small barrel in which Mr. Kandinsky made cherry wine. It was the best thing in the room, with a little tap and a mug hanging from it, full of soaked black cherries scooped from the bottom of the barrel, making the room smell always of cherries and wine. Joe took a cherry and put it into his mouth. He tasted the wine while the cherry was still on his lips. Then he bit through to the stone slowly so that the wine taste spread right through his mouth.

"So," said Mr. Kandinsky, "I'm ready. Just let me put on my watch. This was my father's own watch and chain, Joe. A real watch, with an albert. So, lead on, Macduff. Forward to the big fight."

In the workroom, Mavis was rubbing Africana's chest slowly, and talking to him in a whisper.

"Mavis," said Mr. Kandinsky, "nice to see you. You coming to the fight?"

"This animal isn't at all well, Mr. Kandinsky," said Mavis. She looked in Joe's direction, and moved her head.

"Joe," said Mr. Kandinsky, "you can take one more cherry yourself and take some upstairs for your mother and Sonia."

When Joe had left, Mavis said to Mr. Kandinsky, "This poor little soul's in torment."

"Oy," said Mr. Kandinsky.

"It's cruel to leave him," said Mavis, and she was suddenly very hard and determined. "It's cruel."

"What must be, must be," said Mr. Kandinsky. "But wait till we go."

"That man should never have sold it to him in the first place. How could it live in Fashion Street?" She stroked the little animal's head just where its stunted horn buds grew so close together as to seem one horn. "Poor little kid," she said. "I'll take it to the People's Dispensary."

"You're right," said Mr. Kandinsky with a sigh. "How can a kid like this grow up in Fashion Street? It's not strong enough. I'll find something to tell the boy."

Joe's mother and Sonia came down the stairs, still talking about Sonia's trousseau. She had a nightdress of pure silk and another one with Flemish lace neck and hem, a shame to wear them really, except in hospital.

Joe said good night to Mavis who held Africana shivering in the blanket. Mavis would look after him, and he was pleased to go into the dark street again. He hurried ahead of Mr. Kandinsky and the women, and only for one moment did he want to run back again to Africana.

"One kid," sang Mr. Kandinsky quietly, *"which my father bought for two farthings*. Good night, Reb Mendel," he said to Reb Mendel Gramophone, who stood, a little bearded shadow, at the end of the street.

Reb Mendel's gramophone on top of an old pram pushed its big cracked horn towards Joe and sang in a fast-high voice like tin, *"Eli, Eli, lamah azavtani."*

TEN

In the Whitechapel road it was all bright lights and crowds of people, smart as paint, taking a Saturday night stroll after working the week as machinists and under-pressers and cabinet-makers.

They queued at the Roxy for the second house, two big pictures, while an acrobat turned somersaults in the road for pennies, and sang *Any old iron,* jangling a string of real medals. They crowded into restaurants for lemon tea, and swelled out of the public houses waving bottles, their arms about each other's necks, their children waiting at the doors with glasses of lemonade clasped to their narrow chests. They walked slowly along, bright ties and high-heeled patent leather shoes, eating chips out of newspaper, careful not to let the vinegar spill onto their new clothes. Arm in arm they walked, in trilby hats, brims down, girl friends with bright lips and dark eyes and loud laughter, mothers and fathers arguing together, calling to children licking toffee apples and taking no notice, old men talking quietly raising their eyebrows, knowing the truth of things.

Joe strode ahead of his mother, who chatted with Mr. Kandinsky, while Sonia dawdled talking to a girl with heavy penciled eyebrows and glossy silk stockings, out with her new fiancé, a bookie's runner and flash with wide padded shoulders to his blue double-breasted suit. Joe took giant strides past Russian Peter with his crooked beard and Russian peaked cap. Russian Peter usually had wreaths of garlic cloves and pyramids of home-pickled cucumbers on his barrow, a large box with handles mounted on two wheels, but now he had a tray with packets of sweets and chewing gum and toffee apples. Instead of calling out, "Cumber, knobbel, cumber, knobbel," as he usually did, he said, "Taffee eppls, taffee eppls," in the same high voice. Russian Peter's cucumbers were pickled by a special recipe he brought with him from Russia, with his peaked cap. Joe went back to ask his mother for a toffee apple. Sure enough, it had a special taste, strange, black glistening treacle.

They allowed plenty of time for the walk to the baths, which was just as well, because what with Sonia saying hello to all her friends and their new fiancés, and Mr. Kandinsky talking to this one and that, and different people asking Joe's mother how was his father, they would be lucky to get there at all. As it was, when they arrived at the baths, Joe heard a great roar from inside, and thought, that's it, that's the end of the fight, we've missed it. But they hadn't. It was still the last round of the fight before.

For the wrestling season, the swimming baths were boarded over, a relief to Joe who had been wondering how they could wrestle in baths. There were big lights over a ring in the middle, and you could make out the diving boards at one end, dim in the darkness, with canvas sheets hanging over them. There was no water beneath the boards though, because Joe dropped a small stone through them and there was no splash. It was like the railings over the pavements in the streets. If you made up your mind they were fixed, it was all right. People sat in rows, on seats in front and benches behind, while further back still they stood on wide steps, sitting on the floor in the intervals.

Men went round with trays selling hokey-pokey ice creams, roasted peanuts, and cold drinks, and there was a great hum of noise, which, during the fights, quietened down so that only one or two voices would be heard over the grunting of the wrestlers. Two wrestlers were tied up together on the floor of the ring, one of them grunting as he pressed down harder and harder, the other shouting out, "Oh, oh, oh, oh!" every time he was pressed. He wore a red mask but he was losing all the same.

Someone called out "Wheel 'em out," and someone else shouted "Carve up," and a red-headed woman screamed "Tear his arms off, Mask." All around people munched peanuts and drank ice-cold drinks out of bottles. As Joe sat down a man in a big coat started to eat a sandwich and a pickled yellow cucumber at once. At the end of the row where they were sitting, Joe saw Madame Rita and Lady R. Madame Rita had his arm round Lady R. He shouted "Chuck 'em out, they're empty," waving a cigar in his other hand. Lady R watched the wrestlers closely. Her eyes stared and her lips moved in a small tight smile, and when one threw the other, she clasped her hands together, breathing out hard between her teeth. Then, when they finished, she sank back in her seat and looked round with shining eyes at Madame Rita, who squeezed her shoulder in case she was frightened.

The end of the fight came while Mr. Kandinsky was buying them roasted peanuts. The bell rang, and one of the wrestlers, puffing and blowing, had his arm held up by the referee, while the other one still writhed on the floor. Half the people cheered, and the other half booed. The two wrestlers left the ring, sweating hard, their dressing gowns draped over their shoulders. One of them tripped on the ropes.

There was a good echo in the baths, although with all the shouting and laughing it was difficult to hear it, but sometimes there was a gap in the noise, people were suddenly quiet, as if getting their wind, and then one voice would ring out and the echo pick the words up and throw them back into the smoke and the smell of ozone. Joe would have liked to shout for the echo, but while it was all right under the arches, you didn't like to in front of so many people, and anyhow as soon as you decided to try it, the noise started again. "Wheel 'em in," they shouted. "Money back, get on with it." But nothing happened because it was the interval.

At the ends of the aisles St. John's men in uniforms with polished peaks and white bands sat looking out for people to faint, but no one did. Program sellers went up and down, shouting out that the lucky program number got two ringsides for next week. Madame Rita had two but bought two more, just to show off. The hokey-pokey men in white jackets did very well, and almost everyone was sucking orange and pink ice creams or drinking from bottles or eating peanuts, crunching the shells under their feet.

Then, just as the crowd was getting bored with lucky programs and hokey-pokey, and restless for the big fight to start, the M.C. climbed into the ring. There was a great roar, and though he held up his arms, it went on. He shook his arms, turning from one side to the other, and the dickie front of his evening suit opened a little. "Ladees and gentlemen!" he shouted, "your attention if you please, ladees, your attention, gentlemen, please."

The crowd quietened and the M.C. smiled. "For your entertainment, at great expense, Sam Spindler, the well-known harmonist, will entertain you." There was a groan as Sam Spindler, a thin baldheaded man in a Russian silk blouse with red ruching, and black trousers cut wide at the bottom but tight in the waist, climbed through the ropes with a piano accordion, all ivory and silver and red enamel, on his back. He bowed twice and played *Tiger Rag*, getting the tiger so well that lots of people threw pennies into the ring when he finished. Then he played a medley of songs like *My Old Dutch* and *Tipperary* and everyone sang, but when he stopped and got out a piece of wood, took his accordion off and started to tap-dance, the crowd started to boo. He had to play the accordion again, which was a shame, because Joe was interested in tap-dancing and liked to watch the arms and the legs bent at the knees and the little head jerks.

A lot more pennies were thrown, then someone shouted, "We want Python," and a whole crowd took it up. Another crowd answered "We want Hammer," and soon you couldn't hear Sam playing at all. He stopped and looked down at the M.C.'s seat with a worried expression on his face. The M.C. came up and thanked Sam, who was picking up his pennies. He spread out a big poster on the floor and started to read out the program for next week, but the noise was so great he gave up. He beckoned towards the dark door through which the other wrestlers had passed after their fight. A little wiry man in shirt sleeves and blue braces came bounding up the aisle, and leaped into the ring. After him marched the wrestlers.

First Shmule, in a crimson dressing gown gleaming in the light, with Blackie and Oliver bustling round him. A man leaned over to pat his back as he passed, and when he sprang into the ring there was quite a big cheer. Shmule bowed towards the cheers and looked proudly at the small group who booed. He waved to Joe, and Joe waved back. Sonia blew kisses and Mr. Kandinsky said, "A fine boy, good luck to him." Then Shmule started stretching himself, so as not to lose a moment's development.

After him came the dreaded Python with his manager, a man with a square blue jaw, like polished rock. The Python wore a black silk dressing gown and a white towel round his neck, and he towered above the seconds dancing round him. He climbed into the ring, not so full of spring as Shmule but with one powerful hitch of his arm. There was, true, a bigger cheer for Python, but Shmule's friends booed hard, Joe hissed like a goose, Sonia shouted out "Carcass meat," and Mr. Kandinsky said "What a bull."

The M.C. introduced Shmule first. He called him the white hope of Aldgate, the sensational young former amateur championship contender, a clean-fighting local boy, and so on and so forth. All the while the Python was baring his teeth and growling and shaking his fist at Shmule's supporters. Shmule slipped out of his crimson dressing gown and now his muscles rippled in the ring lights, his spotless white hammer shining like a star against the crimson briefs. Oliver and Blackie clustered round his corner with towels and pails and a chair for him to sit on between rounds. They looked worried, although after all that saying he was a gonner, Shmule looked as if nothing could ever frighten him. There was a fresh feeling about him, as if he felt there were so many tailors expecting him to make a good fight, especially with the trade being so up and down, and so much unemployment, they lent him the strength they had been saving for work.

The dreaded Python Macklin was very angry. He strained like a fierce bulldog at the rope, just waiting for the bell to sound to throw himself on Shmule, tearing him limb from limb like the Christian martyrs, just as Mavis said. The black hair on the Python stood up in fury and he ground his teeth together. When the M.C. pointed in his direction and called out his name, famous contender for the championship of the world, and veteran of the ring all over Europe, the Python drew himself up and the muscles on his chest and back were swollen with pride and power. He grinned, his teeth clamped tight together, and when the red-haired woman screamed out, "Murder him, Py," he stared at her as if he was hungry and she was a juicy steak.

"A forty-minute contest," the M.C. shouted through his megaphone, "of eight five-minute rounds, for a purse of not ten, not twenty, but twenty-five pounds."

He drew the two men together and whispered to them, the Python sneering, Shmule looking serious. Mr. Kandinsky said again,

"Good luck," and then the bell rang. In the sudden silence it echoed well.

Joe sat with his seat tipped up to see over the head of the man in front. This man had a head like a smooth watermelon with a bit of hair round the edges, pasted down with oil as if painted. As soon as the bell rang he started to talk slowly in a gruff voice like a gate swinging on rusty hinges in the wind. The woman next to him had gray hair permanently waved and never spoke, except to say, "Have a nut." The man was very helpful to Joe because he was an expert and explained the whole fight, hold by hold.

At first the wrestlers circled watchfully round one another looking for an opening. The man with the painted head said, "You watch, Em, he'll be on to him, just give him that opening, watch, it's coming—no, hold it, now—no, he missed it, he's waiting to put the scissors on him."

The Python prepared to spring on Shmule, who stood quite still waiting. Then, as the Python bent his legs to jump, Shmule stepped aside and Python fell on his face with a heavy slap.

"He missed him," said the man with painted hair, and even as he spoke Shmule leaped onto the Python, catching both legs below knee level in the crook of his arm, and pulling sharply.

"Ouch!" shouted Python.

"Ouff!" said the man with painted hair. "He got the old calf-lock on him."

The Python shook himself like an alligator, and one of his knees slipped free and bowled Shmule over. The Python caught hold of Shmule by the foot and thigh and prepared to throw him, but Shmule pressed into the canvas with both hands, and heaved his body into the Python's ribs like a battering ram. The Python reeled into the ropes, and the bell rang.

Shmule turned to his corner, but the Python came after him. The crowd roared with one voice, "Look behind you!" Shmule turned sharply, and the referee jumped in front of Python, and forced him to his corner. The Python was furious and pushing his seconds off the ring, he picked up his chair and punched his fist through the seat.

"Phoo," said the man with painted hair, "what a round, the dirty bastard turning on him like that after the bell, the dirty great bleeder."

"Have some nuts, Fred," the permanently waved woman said.

"The swine," said Sonia with tears in her eyes, "did you see that?"

The seconds rubbed them down and waved towels while the wrestlers spat into pails, and breathed deep and even, glaring at one another across the ring, listening to their manager's advice. The crowd wasn't shouting, "Carve up," any more. They could see it was serious. The bell rang for the second round.

The Python at once shot from his corner, his fingers crooked to seize Shmule, his race rigid, calling the muscles of his body to attention. Shmule crouched like a panther, waiting.

"He's giving him half a stone," the man with the painted head said. "He's got to play a waiting game, let the Python use hisself up, then come in quick. Ahh!"

The Python had his arms about Shmule and was hugging him like a bear. Shmule's arms were pinned to his sides, and he couldn't move. He twisted to one side then to the other, but the Python shortened the hug, working the grip of one hand upon the other wrist slowly up his arm. Shmule's face twisted with pain.

"Let him get out of that one," the man said. Sonia clenched and unclenched her hands, and Joe's mother looked away. Mr. Kandinsky was breathing hard, but Joe just stared, wondering what Shmule would do now. The crowd was shouting, "Finish him, Python!"

Then Shmule moved his hand up and down in fast little movements against his thigh, and the referee jumping about watching saw the sign, and told Python to let go, the Hammer gave in. But Python wouldn't let go, and Shmule bit his lips in agony. Now the crowd shouted against the Python but that didn't help Shmule. The referee and all the seconds jumped on to him to tear him away, and the bell rang.

Blackie and Oliver helped Shmule to his corner and gently

rubbed him, putting wet towels on his face. The crowd was furious with the Python, but he didn't care. He shouted back at them, showing off his muscles and asking if any one would like to try them. "Filth!" Mr. Kandinsky shouted, but poor Shmule looked pale and his eyes were closed.

"He's a dirty fighter," the man with painted hair said, "but give credit, he's got a grip like iron, the bleeder."

"Get us some more nuts, Fred," the woman replied.

Blackie and Oliver were working hard on Shmule, who breathed deeply, the color coming back into his face. By the time the bell rang for the third round, he seemed as good as new.

"But you can't tell," the man with the painted head said, "he could have a couple ribs broke clean and he wouldn't know till after."

"Has he got a couple ribs broke?" Joe asked.

"God forbid," Mr. Kandinsky answered, "God forbid."

Blackie and Oliver must have told Shmule not to waste time, because he came out fast and made straight for the Python who, being pleased with himself, was a bit careless. Shmule clasped his hands together and raised them for a rabbit punch, but he was too late. The Python crouched away, out of distance, not careless any more. Then a look of pain suddenly crossed Shmule's face, and the Python grinned and came in to attack, his hands low.

"He's hurt," Sonia whispered.

"He's hurt all right," the man in front of Joe said.

But what a surprise. Shmule suddenly leaped forward and caught the Python a great crack on the jaw with his left fist. The Python looked surprised and fell down.

"No boxing," the crowd yelled.

The Python started to get up at once, but Shmule was on top of him, his knees to either side of his stomach, his hands firmly planted on his shoulders, pressing them to the canvas. As he pressed he strengthened the grip of his knees. The Python groaned, shouted. He jerked and jumped and twisted, but he couldn't throw Shmule off.

"He can give it," the man said, "but he can't take it. Go on, boy, do him!"

The Python beat the floor with both hands and Shmule let go at once.

"Good boy," the man said.

"He should give him the same as he got," Sonia said, "why should he fight him clean?"

The crowd cheered Shmule, but the Python wasn't hurt as much as they thought, because as soon as Shmule broke away, he leaped to his feet. Not fast enough though. Shmule wasn't so green now. He didn't stop watching the Python for a second, and he saw him tensed to leap. Ready for him, he caught the Python another crack on the chin as he came up. The Python went down with Shmule on top of him, but he was saved by the bell.

"That's more like it," the man said, "he's got the old Python on the squirm, proper."

"Get us some nuts, Fred," the woman said.

"Fancy an ice?" the man asked.

"Some nuts, Fred," the woman said again.

"How's the boy doing now, Sonia?" Mr. Kandinsky asked.

"He's all right," Sonia said, "another round like that and he'll win."

"We're winning," Joe told his mother.

"That's good," she replied. "It's awful to see their faces."

In the fourth round the Python set out to finish Shmule off. He tried all the fancy holds, the Indian death lock, the flying mare, the cobra, but Shmule was like an eel, he didn't stay still long enough for the grips to take.

"He's using his speed now," the man said, "let's see the Python catch up with that."

But the Python couldn't catch up with that. After a couple of minutes the crowd started to laugh, because the Python lumbered like a great ox, while Shmule danced circles round him, cracking him on the back and chest every so often. Now the Python was on his guard against face blows, and being careful made him even more clumsy.

He was furious with the crowd for laughing. He looked at Shmule through slit eyes wanting to murder him.

"Let me get my hands on you, laughing boy, that's all," he growled.

Then suddenly Shmule nipped in close, his foot jabbed out, and the Python fell heavily on to the canvas, his arms round Shmule's leg. But as he fell Shmule struck the Python a heavy blow to the stomach, and pulled his leg free.

The Python held on to his stomach with both hands. His head came forward. His neck bent towards Shmule like a beast to the slaughterer.

Shmule folded his hands together as if to pray. He lifted them carefully aiming, brought a rabbit punch with all his force clean on to the Python's neck. The Python slumped forward over his hands. Shmule stood back, watching. The Python didn't move.

"Cold meat!" someone shouted.

"Hammer!" all the tailors yelled.

"Hammer!" shouted Joe.

The Python was out cold.

ELEVEN

It was the latest night ever. It was late when Joe and his mother and Mr. Kandinsky left Sonia at the swimming baths waiting for Shmule, both of them to follow on later. It was late when they got home, but no one suggested that Joe should go to bed, because it was, after all, an occasion. Joe said it was only fair to bring Africana in since he had been such a help, but Mr. Kandinsky said, "Leave him sleep. Tomorrow is also a day."

Joe's mother lit the gas fire in the kitchen, and put the kettle on the stove to make a cup of tea. As they waited for the kettle Mr. Kandinsky told them about the patent steam presser which, only four years old, he could buy for practically nothing from the Grosvenor Garment Company in Fournier Street. With a bit of patching up, tighten a few screws, a good repadding job, scrape off the rust, a coat of paint, it would make a first-class presser, good as new.

Now Mr. Kandinsky didn't have Shmule to worry about any more, he could concentrate on the steam presser again. In fact, now that Shmule had actually won the fight, it seemed unreasonable to Mr. Kandinsky that he shouldn't have the presser.

"A chance like this, Becky," he said, "doesn't, after all, come up every day. A chance of a lifetime. He would take thirty pound for it he said, but I know better. He would be glad to get twenty pound as well. After all, all the big firms can buy new pressers, what do they want with an old machine four years old, rusty, dirty? And whose got thirty pounds who isn't a big firm? Believe me, he would be glad to take twenty. And yet who's got even twenty?"

"Shmule has got twenty-five pounds because you heard, the winner gets twenty-five pounds to himself," Joe said.

Mr. Kandinsky looked thunderstruck. He slapped his forehead with his palm. "You're right, Joe," he said. "Shmule has got twenty-five pounds."

Joe's mother looked over from the stove where she was pouring boiling water into the teapot.

"Shmule must buy Sonia a ring before anything else," she said. "It's a shame otherwise."

"That's true," Mr. Kandinsky said, pursing his lips. "Quite right. Mind you, if Shmule was to come along to me and tell me, I bought the steam presser, what about a partnership, I would tell him straightaway, certainly. But naturally Sonia must have a ring. Only this other way she wouldn't just be a girl with a ring marrying a young fellow, a worker in the tailoring. This way she is marrying a guvnor, a partner in a business, and what is more, a growing business. Because I tell you, Becky, with a patent steam presser we can take in so much jobbing, we can make a living from this alone. Still, Sonia must have a ring. Maybe it is the only chance Shmule gets his whole life, but doesn't matter. A ring is important."

Mr. Kandinsky was very upset. It was selfish of Sonia to stop

Shmule becoming a guvnor. Mr. Kandinsky pressed the lemon in his glass with a spoon. Joe sipped his milk, wondering what Africana would do about this. Then they heard voices on the stairs.

Shmule and Sonia came in arm in arm. Though he looked tired, Shmule's eyes were bright.

"I couldn't get him away from there," Sonia said. "They all wanted to see him."

Mr. Kandinsky gripped Shmule's hand.

"Good luck to you always," he said, "good health, and every blessing."

Joe's mother said, "It was awful to watch, but you were marvelous, Shmule, marvelous. Only don't let him do it any more, Sonia. You mustn't do it any more, Shmule. Buy Sonia a ring now, and finish with the wrestling."

"She's right," Mr. Kandinsky said. "It's for the beast of the field."

"You know what he told me round one?" Shmule said. "He told me to lie down in the seventh, I could share the purse with him. That's what he told me."

"That Python," Sonia said, angry, "he wanted Shmule to lie down."

"When I tell him I am fighting clean he says he'll ruin me."

"You hear," Mr. Kandinsky said to all of them. "You hear what kind of a business this wrestling is?"

"It kills you for real development of the body beautiful," Sonia said.

"No good for the muscular tone or the efficiency," Shmule said. "Still, I can give baby a ring."

Sonia hugged him.

"I want to talk to you with a serious proposition," Mr. Kandinsky said, clearing his throat and holding his hand up for silence. "Namely, now that you got a bit of capital, and I am, after all, the truth is the truth, an old man. Namely a partnership deal."

Shmule looked more dazed than the dreaded Python the last time he was hit. Sonia hugged him again.

"Baby," she said, "you hear?"

"But," continued Mr. Kandinsky, and he explained that Shmule would have to bring with him a patent steam presser.

"Thank you very much," said Shmule, "for a hundred eighty-seven pounds a patent presser. Not two?"

"Don't grab," Mr. Kandinsky said, "listen a minute." He told him about the second-hand presser over at Grosvenor Garments.

"You think he would take twenty?" Shmule asked, stroking his lip.

"Take?" answered Mr. Kandinsky. "He would drag it out of your hands."

Sonia didn't say anything. Her face couldn't make up its mind whether she was pleased or not. It was a difficult decision.

"Let me speak to Sonia a minute," Mr. Kandinsky said. "Sonia," he said, "here you are a young woman in the bloom of her beauty, a perfect mate for life with this Maccabeus here."

Sonia blushed and looked at Shmule.

"Two years you have been patient," Mr. Kandinsky continued. "Listen, Sonia, this is important. Two years you have lived on the word of this man alone. No ring to bind the promise, so that sometimes other people, busybodies with big mouths, who didn't know what kind of girl you are, they said, 'Look at Sonia, no ring. What kind of an engagement?' " Mr. Kandinsky paused.

Sonia's eyes were full of tears as she listened. It was no more than the truth. She had been marvelous, it was true.

Mr. Kandinsky continued. "Sonia," he said, "they didn't know this boy, what a fighter he is, how clean and honest, and what a worker, no one to touch him in the entire East End. Him they saw tonight. Now they know what he is. And you saw him, too, what he will do for you, to get you a better ring than any girl in Novak Blouses ever had."

"Gay-day Blouses," Sonia said tenderly.

"Gay-day," Mr. Kandinsky repeated. "But something else no girl in Gay-day ever had. You know what it is?" He pointed to Sonia to answer the question. She shook her head.

"They didn't marry a fellow who was, already, so young, a guvnor in his own business. That's what they didn't have."

Mr. Kandinsky made his last point in a loud voice, his pointing finger sweeping round the whole world to find another girl who could say she had done better than Sonia.

"Now, Sonia," he continued after a moment in which Sonia squeezed Shmule's hand. "I ask you straight out. Which is better, such a husband, a champion, a guvnor, with the world in front of him. Or a fiancé, works for Kandinsky, the Fashion Street trousers-maker, wrestles Saturday nights to make a few pounds, he might be able to get married one day to a girl at Gay-day Blouses with a big diamond ring? Don't answer me," he went on as Sonia opened her mouth. "Think first. It is in your hands, his life, your life, I don't want to influence you. Drink a cup of tea and think."

That was how Mr. Kandinsky made Shmule his partner, and though everyone was pleased, they said Joe should be in bed.

TWELVE

The next morning was fine and sunny. When Joe woke up he heard the horses clopping over the cobbles, and good trains rattling from the arches. The first thing he thought was he must tell Africana. He dressed quietly, and leaving his mother to have her Sunday morning lie-in, ran downstairs.

Mr. Kandinsky was already at work, and Joe shouted good morning and rushed into the yard.

"Good old unicorn," he shouted out to Africana, but there was no rustle from Africana's house. The house looked like a pile of old boxes waiting to be chopped up for firewood, desolate. Africana was gone.

"He's gone," Joe shouted, running back to the workroom, "He's gone, Mr. Kandinsky, he's gone."

"What?" said Mr. Kandinsky. "Who's gone?"

"Africana's gone, he's just gone," Joe cried, and how would he ever bring his father back from Africa?

"Let's have a look," Mr. Kandinsky said. "Let's keep our head and look."

They searched the yard carefully.

"Let's look in the house again," Mr. Kandinsky said.

"It's empty," Joe replied, tears coming fast. "Can't you see, it's empty."

"Let's look all the same," said Mr. Kandinsky.

He searched through the bed of remnants.

"What's this?" he said. He bent down and picked up something. It was a gleaming golden sovereign. He handed it to Joe.

"What is it?" asked Joe.

"Come inside, Joe," Mr. Kandinsky said. "I will tell you."

"He's gone," Joe said, the tears still there.

"Come inside," said Mr. Kandinsky, and he put his arm round Joe's shoulder.

"You know what this is, Joe?" he asked, giving him the sovereign. "This is a golden sovereign. And what has happened is plain as my nose. You could see yourself that unicorn didn't do so well in Fashion Street, ailing the whole time, no interest, miserable the whole day. So you know what he's done? He's gone back to Africa like you said he should. But just to show it's nothing personal, he left this golden sovereign on account of that magic horn worth five thousand pound."

"Ten thousand," said Joe.

"Ten thousand pound I mean," continued Mr. Kandinsky. "Meanwhile, keep this for luck."

"He won't come back," Joe said.

"Maybe not," Mr. Kandinsky replied. "Unicorns can't grow in Fashion Street, but boys have to."

Joe went upstairs slowly, rubbing the golden sovereign between his fingers. There was a small rough piece broken on top of it but otherwise it was like the coin on Mr. Kandinsky's father's watch chain, which made two golden sovereigns in the house.

When his mother came into the kitchen, her face blanched with sleep, Joe asked whether two sovereigns would bring his father back. It was the only thing the unicorn had forgotten to arrange. With the sleep still on her, she didn't know at first what he meant. After Joe explained carefully, she said yes, it was a great help, and they would find his father's return passage money somehow. They would never go to Africa, it was a dream, but he would come back to them, he would come back soon. Next week she must see about Joe starting school. He was growing up learning nothing about life.

Joe rolled the sovereign on the table thinking that if all the pets he had ever had were in the yard now, he could charge people pennies to come in. They would cheer and throw more pennies when they saw Africana's shining horn stretching high above the slate rooftops.

After breakfast he went into the yard to play, although he had no special game in mind. For a little while he missed Africana but soon he thought of something. In the end, it brought him safely to Africa.

MAKE ME AN OFFER

ONE

AS FAR AS I KNOW IT STARTED WHEN I WAS ABOUT ELEVEN.

One Sunday my mother made some sandwiches for us and my father took me to the British Museum by tram. We got shilling all day tickets, which meant we could go anywhere in the world so long as we went by tram. So that we went a very long way round to the Museum and as soon as we got there we ate the sandwiches sitting on the bench by the Easter Island statue. They were chicken sandwiches and we couldn't look at anything until we had eaten them. Then we went to the Egyptian Room which was my father's favorite and he showed me the man in the stone tomb. He was crumpled up with his skin stretched very tight and the color of kippers. To tell you the truth, he made my mouth water because at that time I was always hungry.

We looked at the Assyrian bulls and some Phoenician glass and quite soon I saw the Vase. Afterwards I went to the Museum often and I found a lot of things there, but I always went to the Vase first. I always went to see it again before I left. I used to watch it carefully waiting for it to move, and once it did very slightly. I had my own way of looking at the Vase. First I looked at one side for a while; then the other side; then I walked round it from left to right; then I walked round it from right to left.

Once or twice in bed at night I worried about whether it was quite safe. Maybe someone was waiting until the doors were closed to steal it. I gritted my teeth to think of it lying in pieces on the floor. Once I opened the window of my room and looked out over the small back gardens. It was a warm summer night and I could smell the stocks my mother planted. The air was deep blue and very solid, and I thought suddenly that the Vase was solid night carved with figures of pure light. Then I became interested in chemistry and made a bench to work on in my room. I filled the room with chlorine once and another time I blew my eyebrows off in the lavatory and my mother gave me a Steedman's shock powder. The last time I saw the Vase I had a plan worked out for stealing it and I hung about for a whole day almost. Then I left the Vase for half an hour to have a look at the Prehistoric Room and it was suddenly closing time and my plan had gone wrong because there was a guard standing right behind me.

I didn't ever completely forget about the Vase though. I wrote a prize essay in the School Christmas Contest about it. *In 1594 in a sepulchral chamber beneath the Monte del Grano a small hill near Rome, the ashes of Alexander Severus and those of his mother were discovered. What happened to the ashes no one can say, but the urn containing them passed first to the museum of the Capitol, thence to the Palace of the Barbarini. In 1770 a Scottish antiquary in Rome, one James Byres by name, acquired the urn. In 1782 Sir William Hamilton, Ambassador to the Court of Naples, bought it for £1,000. The Duchess of Portland bought it from him secretly, and after her death the Duke of Portland purchased it at a sale of the late Duchess's private museum in Whitehall. In this way the urn containing the ashes of the Emperor Alexander Severus and his mother became the Portland Vase. . . .*

My father kept the essay, but soon after a boy at school whose fingers and clothes were always stained yellow with picric acid introduced me to the study of alkaloids. We kept nearly twenty different alkaloids in old tins, and he distilled a new one from violets which he called Violene. We wrote a paper about it and I bought a large glass flask to put it in. I don't believe I thought again of the Vase until years afterwards when my father brought home a black and white Wedgwood copy of it. It was a modern copy and not very good. I was buying at the auctions for my father at that time, and he asked me to find out when the first Wedgwood copies were made. I went to the British Museum to find out and as soon as I got there I

went to see the Vase. I walked round it once or twice, then I went to
the ceramics department and asked to see the Wedgwood copy. They
stood over me while I looked at it. They moved a little closer to me
when I touched it, and when I picked it up the curator gave a little
scream and his short beard jogged up and down.

I went home and told my father that his Portland was no good,
like his Constable painting and his Nuremberg cup, and for the first
time in years I thought about the Vase. The glass one which had
held the ashes was an urn all right. It was wonderful but in the end
it was only complete if the ashes of a dead man and his mother were
in it. But the Portland a potter named J. Wedgwood made in 1789,
that was a vase—a real vase, perfect and complete and alone. And
after that I always looked at Portland Vases to find a first one.

I suppose all this must have had something to do with my becoming a dealer in English pottery, but I can find all kinds of other reasons. What does it matter anyway? I never found a first Portland. I
collected all the books relating to Wedgwood, and many magazines
and news cuttings. I carried one cutting about with me in my wallet
until the folds rubbed through. It was a piece from the *Morning
Chronicle* of 1886. "Stolen from the collection of Mr. Daniel Drage.
Three salt-glaze pew groups valued at £650, a pair of 15-inch
Whieldon tortoise-shell glaze standing figures valued at £300, and
an old Wedgwood green copy of the Portland Vase. The Curator of
the Wedgwood Museum at Etruria tells us that there is no known
record of the great Josiah ever having made a green Portland copy.
The police are investigating the crime and doubtless the thief will
be detected when these famous and rare items of English pottery
are offered for sale. Mr. Drage's collection, an expert writes, is worth
in the neighborhood of £4,000 and is one of the finest in the world.
Mr. Drage was on the Continent at the time of the burglary, in
which entrance was effected from the garden behind the house."

Once or twice that green Portland gave me a bad time; or it could
have done if I had believed in it. And yet Old Drage knew the stuff
well. Dealers still like to say they have something from his collection. And yet no matter how well you know the game, you can be

wrong. But I liked to carry the cutting around with me as a sort of magic charm. If Josiah had ever made a solid green jasper Portland, I wanted to see it before the close of business.

I met a man once in the tearoom on Liverpool Street Station. He was a short, thin man with a marked curvature of the spine which made him look as if he had a bad pain, and when he swallowed his tea he wrinkled his face up as if it tasted like epsom salts. I said to him the tea was too strong, and he told me how the tannin coated your stomach and turned the delicate membranes into leather. "I should only drink milk," he said. "Milk is soothing to the delicate membranes. It nutrifies the stomach without straining it. You got to soothe the membranes," he told me.

I told him I liked milk, and he stopped fighting me. We had another cup of tea and soothed the membranes for a while longer. He was a button manufacturer, and in twenty years he had sold more than seventeen million buttons. "Put side by side maybe they would circle the world," he said. "Who has the time to do it?" I asked him, and he agreed sadly that it wasn't worth while. "But," he said, "don't misunderstand me. There is a great future for buttons." He pulled me closer to him, and dipped his hand into his waistcoat pocket. Then he showed me the only solid gold button with a two carat diamond in it in the world.

I was like that man. I wanted to believe there was a future in pots, and I thought of that future as a green Portland. I was looking hard, and finding a fair living, but pretty soon I would have to start drinking milk five times a day to soothe the delicate membranes.

TWO

That evening we had just stopped wrestling with the right way to bring up children, and given the baby a bottle. He liked it all right, and even let go of the teat for a moment to laugh. His soft yellow hair was flat across his great forehead, plastered down with tears. But his smile was full of satisfaction and triumph. He'd pulled it off once again, and was getting to feel infallible. I knew how he felt. I felt the same way when I managed to run something at the auctions —run it so high it was no use any more to whoever bought it. We laughed back at the baby, but he was busy now dragging on the teat. He had his hands gently placed on the sides of the bottle, and his eyes were already glazed with satisfaction.

While we were there we had a look at the other boy. He was curled up with his knees almost touching his stomach. The bed-clothes were kicked away and his pajama trousers had slipped down over his backside. We covered him up and he murmured "Black man" and turned over. Black man was his favorite game at the moment. He liked to play it on his own for an hour or so every morning, wearing nothing but the belt from his blue dressing gown weaved around his waist and loins.

My wife said, "He's breathing through his mouth again."

"How else should he breathe?"

"I'll give him some drops tomorrow."

"So long as he breathes," I said. "Let's eat now." The baby still had his eyes open, but he'd stopped drawing on the bottle. He hadn't needed it. It was just that he liked to feel he could have it. I certainly knew how that baby felt about life. It was a wonderful feeling, and it didn't happen very often. For my part he could have a whole bar next to his cot and just take a nip whenever he fancied it.

I hadn't eaten much that day. I had to get out early to catch a dealer in Baker Street before he went out buying. He was the brother-in-law of a man who had some tri-colored jasper cameos I needed. The man had decided not to sell to me. He was rich and temperamental, and it hurt him in the heart whenever he thought someone might be making a profit on him. But the brother-in-law was poor, and the rich man made a charity—his only charity—out of letting him take things on approval from time to time. The brother-in-law would get them for me, but I had to get to his basement shop before he started out on his rounds. I drank two cups of China tea without milk or sugar, kissed the family all round, fixed the boy's conductor's hat so that he could see me to the gate, and went off.

Lunch had got lost somehow between an auction at Phillips, Son & Neale in Blenheim Street, and an appointment with a big American dealer back at the Shop. I got what I wanted at Phillips'. I bought a yellow and white jasper Portland Vase and a pair of basaltes vases. I gave Mrs. Toshak, the interior decorator, three pounds on the vases for not bidding against me, and I got back to the shop just before the American arrived. He turned out to be a soft-spoken Baghdadi with a big pasty-faced American in tow as bookkeeper.

"I can spend fifty or five hundred pounds," he said with a sad smile. "Don't let us argue over price—name it and I will say yes or no. Is that all right?"

"Have the five hundred ready," I said, "I wouldn't insult you by taking less."

In the finish it wasn't quite up to scratch. But it was four hundred we needed—who doesn't need four hundred?—and I went home satisfied. My wife was vaguely surprised to hear that grown men could spend so much time and subtlety and money on vases, but she was impressed by the degree of the folly. And I was just about ready to put myself round the lamb stew she had in the oven when the baby started growling. Then when that was all settled and my stomach was beginning to sob for a little sustenance, the telephone rang.

I said to my wife, "Don't put it back in the oven—I don't want to lose any time when I get back," and went out to the phone. I picked it up and a voice blared at me.

"You don't want your coal."

"No," I said.

"We've run out of coal," the voice blared on.

"Have my coal, Mr. Sparta," I said.

"Good boy, Charlie," the bear answered. "You'll order it tomorrow."

"That's it," I said. And then it came to me like all the best ideas, out of the middle of nothing, into the middle of nothing. "I wanted to see you about something, Mr. Sparta," I said.

"You know where I am," the bear grunted, "so come up and see me." I went back to the kitchen with a smile on my face.

"Put it in the oven angel. I've got some business to do with Sparta."

"Charlie," she called as I opened the door, "ask him if I can keep the big pram in his toolshed."

I don't know where Abe Sparta found his name but he certainly was a self-made Greek. Maybe it was the poet in him which made him pick out Sparta for a name instead of Lwow—maybe he had a classical education. Whatever it was that made him my landlord I respected it. It isn't every Odessa lumberman who can stay out of prison long enough to become a respectable dealer in timber. Abe was a clever man all right. I had the lower part of the house which was damp, and he was upstairs, away from it all, and safer from bur- glars. It gave the old man palpitations every time he used those stairs, but it was certainly safer from burglars. He had a long-stand- ing affection for large items in silver-gilt—Victorian pieces, angels with and without cherubs, *putti,* festoons, devices, motifs, fruit, flowers and dead game. Impressive stuff worth about four shillings an ounce—but to him, civilization hallmarked with elegance. Back home a family with a pair of thin silver candlesticks was respectable. Sparta was just a homely boy at heart.

He was a big, broad, curving old man with a heavy moustache and down-turned eyes tucked away among grizzled eyebrows. He spoke a rich cockney flavored with Yiddish phrases and gestures, and though he was well into the seventies now he still couldn't resist a little business. I think the only reason why he bought this old Re- gency house was that he had nothing to do one day and was just pok- ing around doing it when he saw the place was up for sale. He walked around tugging at this and that. There were little terraces and porches all over the house then and it settled him when he found they were made of lead. Lead was fetching £117 a ton. I think he cleared his purchase money on the lead, and though the place looked a little bald, stripped of it all, it still had a certain quality about it. It was on a hill in a hundred yards of old houses which hadn't been developed yet, and the whole place had an atmosphere which made up for the damp. I'd like to think well of Sparta's feeling for beauty—but it was the lead all right. It's amazing how little lead makes a ton. I had tried to talk to Sparta about other things, the weather and the garden and life but he only rose to business. If you said to him: "That was a nice little deal today," or "Heard about a good sale next week?" some sort of animation would crease up his forehead and bring a little luster to his eyes. I was looking forward to seeing that lovelight now.

The position was this. A man I know in Chelsea buys gilded frames. He burns the frames and collects the gold and somehow it shows him a living. Now, when he's looking for frames he sees other things—bits of china, carved mantelpieces, and so on, and so he's in a position to put you on to a good thing now and then, if dropping the odd fiver doesn't give you gallstones. I'm no philanthropist but I believe in friendship, and in this case my belief in human nature has been justified on several occasions. I nearly got a pair of Chelsea birds through him once. I was young at the time and I took an older dealer along with me—an expert he was—to have a look at a load of china an old woman had cleared out of the attic. It was junk all right. I could see that and was counting the pieces to reckon them at a bob apiece all round. Then I dug out these birds—raised anchor mark, right as rain, just a little chipping on the leaves.

"What have you there?" screams this experienced lunatic.

"Just a couple of old birds," I said. The old woman had looked up with a slight gleam in her eyes.

"You fool," he said to me—he was calling me a fool. Then he turned to the old lady who looked as though she had just conceived, so brilliant was the light in her eyes. "Madam," he said, "these birds are Chelsea and very valuable. I will give you two hundred pounds for them."

I wanted him to drop dead more than I have ever wanted anything.

"Gord," the old woman said. "If you'd have said fifty bob you

could have had 'em. I'll send them up to London to my nephew who
works in a solicitor's office. They must be worth a fortune."

He looked at me with the wide-open eyes of a moron. It suited
him perfectly. I left him there still looking. Maybe he's still there.
It breaks my heart to think of those birds.

I had only just got into the shop the other morning when this
friend rings me. I was reading the fifth letter that month from an
old gentleman who had an original copy of the Portland Vase. It
had been in his family for years, and he didn't really want to sell it
unless he got a very good offer. I could just see the slightly insane
smile of subtlety on the face of the provincial dealer who wrote that
letter. I wrote a polite note offering him a fiver just for fun, and
then the phone rang. I let it ring for a while to show my independence, and then picked it up.

"You still after Wedgwood?"

"Yes."

"Well, come over and see me."

"Who are you?"

"Fred here, you know. Frames."

"Yes, Fred. What have you got?"

"Nothing. But I know where it is."

"All right, I'll be over."

I saw him later that morning. His shop was in a mews, and he was
fitted in neatly at the back between two high stacks of frames. I
crawled over to him and he told me all about it without wasting his
valuable time on vulgar pleasantries.

"This place here is a break-up job—period house—hundred
rooms—Sir someone-or-other, Christ knows. Whole room plastered
in Wedgwood, big, small, everything, all Wedgwood. You want it?"

I made it clear that I wanted it. I said, "Maybe."

"No one knows about it—got the catalogue up in the country."

"Let's have a look," I said, without enthusiasm.

The catalogue was one of those amateurish plush jobs a small
country auctioneer gets the local printer to dream up when he acci-
dently gets his hands on something good. They even spelled Wedg-

wood wrong. But it was certainly a lot of Wedgwood. I gave him a couple of pounds on account and went off with the catalogue in my pocket.

When I got back to the shop my manager was selling a Civil Servant a pot in black and white jasper. "In fine sunlight," she sang, "these colors will look delightful—black and white jasper is something we often send out to India—it's so civilized looking among all that Oriental stuff." The Civil Servant remembered he was civilized and took it. She came bounding up to the office five minutes later. I let her tell me all about it so as not to deprive her of one of the few real satisfactions in a dealer's life. "So I said to him, 'it looks wonderful in bright sunlight,' " she went on.

"Did you ever see it in bright sunlight?" I interrupted, and threw her the catalogue.

"Can't they even spell Wedgwood right?" she asked.

"How do you reckon it?" I asked.

"How can you say," she answered, "who'll be there?"

That was the whole point. That was why I was letting my dinner get dried up now. That was why I was going to talk on an empty stomach.

I went up to Abe Sparta's flat. The door was open and I could hear him hawking in the sitting room. His wife was drying the dishes in the kitchen. She dropped one as I knocked on his door.

"Break up the rest," he shouted. "What good are they? Come in Charlie. The plates she breaks. Have you got any plates in your shop? Bring them along. She'll break 'em. Sit down."

"That's a nice big fire," I said.

"Don't forget the coal. You want a cigar?" He knew I never smoked a cigar, so I didn't put his back up by taking one now.

"Sit down," he grunted, hunching closer to the fire.

"I got something good today," I said, lighting a cigarette.

"So that's all right about the coal then—I can rely on you."

I was taking it too fast. It was only manners to talk about the coal for a while. "You burn a lot of coal," I said with admiration in my voice.

"More than a hundredweight and a half a week," Sparta said with pride, looking up at me with a challenge in his eyes asking me to call him a liar. "Nearly two hundredweight," he rasped, spitting into the fire.

"It's a lot of coal," I suggested.

Honor was satisfied now, so he leaned back and said in what passed with him for a friendly tone, "*Nu,* Charlie boy—what's the excitement."

I gave him the catalogue, and he spent the next two minutes skimming over it. Then he gave it back to me.

"The break-up boys will be there."

"Yes." I agreed.

"So this paneling will fetch its price."

"I don't reckon the paneling."

"So what else is there to reckon?"

"I'll pay two and a half for the Wedgwood."

He made a swallowing movement and moved his lips silently. "That's about as much as the paneling's worth. What will you do with the paneling?"

"Sell it to you," I said.

"How are you going up?" he replied.

"By train."

"Find out the trains, Charlie. I'll come with you."

As I ate my dinner I worked it out the way Sparta saw it. If I said two hundred and fifty for the Wedgwood, he reckoned three hundred and fifty. If he said two hundred and fifty for the paneling, it was worth twice that. Maybe it sounds complicated to you but sparing the technical details it means we could both see a profit in the deal.

My wife was ironing a new shirt of mine.

"Take the bones out, honey," I suggested.

"It's your dinner—you take them out," she said.

"Out of the shirt collar I mean."

"Did you ask him about the big pram in his toolshed?" she answered.

"No," I said.

"I don't know what you put bones in the collar for, anyway," she grumbled, fiddling with the shirt.

"In my trade you have to look smart," I said.

THREE

That night I dreamed my father sold the lease of my shop and bought a two-and-a-half year lease on a shop in Jermyn Street. He paid £2,600 for it and the rent was £465 inclusive. I came back from the country, and a new shop front was already installed. There was no room for anything except jewelery. I hate dealing in jewelery.

"The rent's cheaper," he kept saying.

"Who cares about the rent," I screamed. "I need a place I can turn round in—I'm a big boy now."

It doesn't sound like a nightmare, but I woke up with sweat on my forehead. The bedclothes were over my face, and for a while I kept on looking into the window of that little shop and screaming. Then I reached out and put my hand on my wife's thigh. It was warm and I wanted to go to sleep again with my hand there, but she jerked away suddenly, as if I was a roadsweeper trying to feel the brush texture in one of the paintings at Wildenstein's. For two seconds I could have cried. There's nothing so lonely as the middle of the night with the floorboards creaking and the feeling about you that you're out of business. I reached up to switch the light on, but the lights in that shop had been on and the dark was more restful.

I was alone all right, just as she was alone in the middle of whatever business kept her asleep. The baby was working out his next deal. The boy was alone scheming out the next move in Black Man. Maybe only Abe Sparta was awake like me.

The floorboards somewhere creaked for what seemed like an hour. Maybe he was lifting his legs out of bed. They would feel like lead—cold and dead—but not worth £117 a ton. In his sitting room the fire would be out and the warmth in the air worn off. I reached

out and felt round for the flask of water on the bedside table. I drew
it over and felt for the mouth with my lips. But the water had
a dusty, stale feel to it.

I got up to make tea—I poured the tea into a glass and squeezed
some lemon into it. When you walk around in the middle of the
night, it takes a while before you can really say you're thinking about
anything particular. Your eyes look downwards, and if there's a paper on the table you follow the words out meaninglessly. It was the
paper of the day before yesterday. A story on page three told how an
important contractor was in trouble over an army surplus sale which
had been knocked out. Someone said it was tantamount to robbing
the country. "It is a practice which is as much criminal as unpatri-
otic." About as criminal as the income tax collector assessing you
for next year on the profits he thought you made the year before last.

The knock-out is not something I have much to do with. I don't
have to mix with such people. I am a specialist. This means I have
so little money that I can only deal in one thing—but it also means
that in that line I can buy and sell higher than anyone else. My father taught me to specialize.

About twenty years ago my father was a marketman. He had a stall
with shutters in a semi-enclosed market in East London. The rent
was twenty-six shillings a week, and he was down as a general dealer
because he didn't know what he was going to sell. There were two
reasons for this. One was he didn't know anything about selling.
The other was he didn't have any money. He used to borrow five
pounds from a man called Segal on Monday, and on Saturday night
he used to pay him back seven pounds. Now the whole of my father's
economic life was constructed on the principle of meeting Segal. He
tried buying cheap cutlery in the Houndsditch and found he
couldn't meet Segal. He bought fancy goods and found he owed Segal more money than he had stock. He tried some attractive boxes
of handkerchiefs and ties and bowler hats. But Segal was disappointed in him. Then he became a specialist.

For ten shillings a lot he bought ten lots of odd army boots. He
brought them back from the sale room and filled up the shop with

them. My mother went home in tears to fry roe for dinner. Then he stood in the middle of all those odd boots and started sorting them into pairs. Then he covered the whole stall with pairs sorted into sizes and started to sell them at two-and-sixpence a pair. That week he met Segal and hurt his feelings by not taking a fiver for next week. He was a specialist and out of the clutch of common usurers.

What a week end that was! He bought my mother the largest box of liqueur chocolates she had ever seen. He bought us all presents and he was laughing all the time. He sat at the table after dinner with his tea getting cold in front of him, and put his head in his hands and laughed till he was shaking all over. His hands had the black from the boots ingrained in them and they looked terribly strong. After that he always specialized. It was something different every week, but whatever it was the place was full of it. And always it was something the poor wanted and always it was cheaper than it had ever been before. One week it was blacking for grates—then it was perfume and we were spraying all the old women with it—then it was women's hats and we all wore them. Once it was iron tonic, and my father stood in his shirt sleeves showing his muscles and joking with the women while they bought it. Once it was a cellar of old claret bought at threepence a bottle. Everyone was tasting it and buying it instead of invalid port. It was just as good. And all the detective force came round to tell us we needed a license to sell it and buy a few crates.

When I started in business on Saturday afternoons selling foreign stamps on a corner of the stall, I already knew how to specialize. I used to buy Foreign and Colonial mixture in small sacks at a place in London Wall and put it into small packets at a penny and three-pence. My father financed me to begin with, but it never worried me to meet him on Saturday nights. We used to have a cup of tea and a cheese cake at teatime at the coffee stall in the corner of the market, and discuss business prospects. "You should always specialize," he would say. "We're specialists," I used to answer. "What else?" he would say, and start to laugh.

I was thinking about my father and wondering why I should

dream he was a bad business man. Between sipping my tea, I drummed on the table with my fingers and hummed a tune quietly.

> *What is it that makes you eat*
> *Bananas and cat's meat?*

It was a little thing my father had composed and which he used to sing when he was worried. He pronounced "eat" as "it" and "it" as "eat"—so it rhymed. He also made three words of "bananas"—so it scanned. I never read anything which had the poignant truth of that poem.

It worried me especially that I should be worried just now when things were going so well. My speciality had moved from foreign stamps to Wedgwood. I was once asked to chair a ring. It was like the top of a short ladder.

Here I was getting ready to go for a trip into the country to try to buy a whole room in the sort of house you pay half a crown to be shown round on a wet Saturday afternoon. With Abe Sparta I might even buy it. And I was worried. It was never having anything to do with the knock-out that worried me. I was used to going to the auctions for my one or two lots and either buying them or making them so expensive they weren't profitable any more to whoever bought them against me. After a while the trade got used to seeing me around whenever there was Wedgwood selling. They left me alone on the whole, or just ran a little way to show spirit and left the bidding before it cost them too much. In bidding you have to have a sense of how far the other man is going to go. It isn't as difficult as it sounds. You can be fairly certain that if you bid twenty-eight, the man behind you will go thirty. But if you bid thirty he'll think twice and let you have it. You have to watch the tens—most people think in decimals.

It's a funny game, this dealing. Nothing's worth anything until you sell it, and then it's worth whatever you can get for it. You can't get anything at all unless you have the goods, so you have to buy them whether you know you can sell them or not. Everyone reckons goods differently—some dealers can't leave bronzes alone, or

ormulu. There's an old short man with a great face like a pasty
baby, and thick glasses pressed into his bulbous nose, who can't leave
bird's-eye maple alone. When he sees bird's-eye maple a sort of lust
grips him. His hands tremble and his eyes turn inwards as if he had
some little shrine there on which bird's-eye maple was the only permitted sacrifice. He bids on and on, and he gets it. He used to man-
ufacture bedroom suites, and now he pays the price by having to
buy them all back. It's like those souls in hell you read about who
have to go on doing just what they did in life. I've often watched him
shaking away there as if he was praying. You don't know whether to
laugh or be sick. Everyone runs him. The auctioneer trots him like
a high-stepping racehorse pacing an old gray work donkey. And
when he's finished he wipes beads of sweat off his forehead with his
shaking fist all knotted up like a baby rubbing his eyes.

But all buying is like that. You get the bit between your teeth
sometimes. Your heart pounds away like the first time you made
love to a woman and you were frightened and couldn't do it properly. You suddenly have to have a big Sèvres vase or a collection of
netsukes. And afterwards you feel as if you had passed a test—only
it wasn't an intelligence test. Or you've come through the onset of
a dangerous fever. Then you look at the figures you've scribbled in
the catalogue and see just how much weight you've lost.

More often, though, there's no feeling in it. The Sèvres vase is
worth just so much to whoever buys it. Everyone wants it. And that's
where the knock-out comes into being, born out of the ingenuity
dealers have always given to the problems of survival. Seven dealers
want it—one buys it. The seven meet and auction it again between
themselves. Whoever gets it puts the extra money into the kitty and
it's split seven ways. He can still make a profit on it, and everyone
else makes their expenses. Who's to make laws for how a man should
make a living? Life makes him a dealer and then he has to deal.
Dealing's all anarchy—everyone's his own boss, he spends his own
money, and goes bankrupt in his own way. Dealing is buying and
selling—sometimes buying cheap and selling dear—sometimes buying dear and selling cheap. Everyone's after the dealer to make him

pay a little more for what he's buying. Everyone wants to buy from him a little cheaper than he's selling. He's made money a hundred times, but he's lost it sixty. If you want to be unpleasant about it, dealing is sordid, and the dealer a whore. But you won't pretend that whoring isn't hard work or that it doesn't supply a need. We don't have to be in love with the customers. We just have to take him upstairs. Anything after that is a cultural question. I'm no better, nor fundamentally different from the girl trading on Birdcage Walk on a wet Saturday evening. When things are bad, my standards and my prices also go down. But I want to do a better class of business if I can. Everything depends on it. First we look for a way of making a living, an existence. Then we find we have a standard of living. Then we learn about better standards, always further and further away from a woman crying into the frying oil on a Friday night. Are you trying to tell me that all this isn't progress? If you don't like dealing, try to do without it. You'll manage all right. But leave dealers and people who like to deal with them, leave auctioneers and knock-out men and profits and losses alone. It's a philosophy. You can have a different philosophy if you like but you can't alter this one.

So I agree with the knock-out, but I don't work it. But here I was on to something new, and a knock-out might be the only way. I was reckoning on someone being there for that room, and I wanted to buy it when it was knocked-out. I wanted to sell the timber paneling straight away to Abe and clear the Wedgwood plaques as profit. And already it seemed to me I was being too clever. It worried me to be too clever. It felt like I was asking for something to trip me up. Supposing I took the room after the knock-out and Abe wouldn't take the timber. I would have to sell it to someone else quickly. I didn't know how to price it—I didn't know how to sell it. And I didn't have the money to play with, anyway.

It all came to that in the end I didn't have the money. And this Wedgwood room was something for a Wedgwood specialist to get a touch of fever about. Already I was thinking about how much profit it would make and how long it would take to clear it and how I would offer the plaques. A little more thinking and the detail about not having the money wouldn't stop me. I could feel it coming on. I had to have it.

I drank all the tea in the pot. I felt tired with working it out this way and that. When I thought of coming back from the country with a few pounds in my pocket over my expenses and not a piece of Wedgwood to show, a feeling of faint sickness came into my stomach. My head felt empty now, and I was hungry. I cut some bread and cheese and made a sandwich. I read a copy of Joe Miller's Jest Book while I ate. I had bought it that day from a runner for twenty-five shillings. The covers were missing and it was bound in a piece of brown paper. I found three jokes I had heard at the Palladium a couple of weeks back. They still made me laugh, and after I'd eaten another sandwich, I thought I felt better and went back to bed.

I got under the blankets quietly but my wife sighed and turned round. "What's the matter?" she croaked.

"I was hungry," I said.

"What's the time then?" she said. It was four o'clock.

"Nearly tomorrow already," she said faintly.

"I might go out to the country tomorrow," I said as if to make conversation. "I said I might go out to a sale for a couple of days."

But she was asleep again. Women don't worry like we do.

FOUR

I left early the next morning, just as soon as I could get through reading Dan Dare to the boy. My wife still acted a little as if she was asleep and talked about having a woman to tea with a little boy from up the road who was always hitting his baby sister. The baby was in his high-chair carefully putting a spoonful of tomato pulp into his right ear. His eyes were alight with discovery when I kissed him goodbye on the top of his head just above where it hadn't quite closed up yet. I could feel his pulse with my lips. The boy escorted

me to the garage and backed me out like a policeman. He told me
to wait a minute and put a policeman's hat on to do the job better.

I switched the lights on in the shop, glanced through the post,
locked the door, and drew some cash out of the safe. Then I left a
note for my manager, looked up the route, locked the shop, and
went back to the car. The telephone was ringing when I left, and I
thought there goes my big chance of buying something really good.

I hate driving. I never can believe that I really control the machine under my hands. Why doesn't it rush up on to the pavement
and do a little window shopping? Why doesn't it throw me into the
nearest lamppost? But I couldn't waste the day by traveling down
by train just to view. If I went by road I could make a few calls
and perhaps buy something here and there. I was going partly to
show myself that it wasn't so important after all. I wanted to get
over to it and take a quick look and tell myself it was Victorian and
forget it. Then I could tell Abe Sparta it wasn't worth thinking
about, and I wouldn't have to bother about finding the few hundreds my enthusiasm might cost me. That's what I wanted, but
there was no point in losing opportunities. I might as well buy anything worth buying while I was out.

I was taking the car out of Regent's Park by the Hanover Gate,
and noticing as I always did when I passed that way that there
was a pair of overlay lusters in the lodge window, when it suddenly
seemed essential to go back to the shop. I might have forgotten something. Maybe I would think of something I ought to have remembered when I got there. I went round the roundabout, and drove on
thinking hard. I shot the lights and an old woman on the pedestrian
crossing looked up with an amazed face and nearly fell over backwards. I passed her with about three yards to spare but she had been
looking forward to getting run over ever since horse-drawn buses
had come off the road. I nearly passed a shop but noticed a campana-
shaped vase in pale green out of the corner of my eye, and turned
into the curb.

The lady of the establishment was hopping round in circles like a
hobgoblin trying to make up her mind how much she could ask for

the vase, and I was wondering whether like her I had forgotten to shave that morning, when I decided against the vase at any price. Her dentures chattered so brightly that I wanted to whistle the *Danse Macabre*. Her face went the color of putty, leaving two blotched spots on her cheeks and two dark holes where her eyes ought to have been, and her lips trembled with irritation as I turned out of the place. I still couldn't remember what I had forgotten. The green vase was just an attempt to distract my attention, and I wasn't going to be put off.

I drove straight on to the shop. My manager was entertaining an Australian when I arrived, and she looked at me with the blank lack of recognition which meant it was a difficult sale. I went into the office and played with some consular invoices which were lying on my desk. She came in after a few minutes with her eyebrows raised.

"What brings you home so soon?" she asked.

"Anything?" I said.

"No—he wanted to see what would happen if he came in," she replied. "There's something about Australians which makes me think about little jugs." I sympathized for a moment or two. There are people who come into antique shops looking for little jugs and they are very tiring to handle. It's best never to have a little jug on the premises. It only causes discord and it's never little enough. Or it's too little.

"Don't buy any little jugs," I cautioned her, "it'll only cause trouble."

"I thought you were going to view that house," she said, "I never buy little jugs."

"I remembered something," I answered.

"What?"

"I forget."

"Too many exciting afternoons at the auctions."

"You're a manager, not a wet-nurse," I reminded her gently.

There was nothing wrong with me that a good stroke of business couldn't put right. It was just that I was doing my best to keep a level head. You can't know what it means in this trade to get the smell of a large collection into your nostrils. You hear a rumor— you creep around after it—you speak to this one and drop that one and cut the other one in on a percentage. Then suddenly one bright morning when you've told yourself that the winter is over and the spring season is going to start, you hear: "You know that collection?" You start up like a hound seeing a rabbit as big as a horse. "Yes." "Burckhardt got it." It's like falling into a pit. You say "I should worry," and you do.

Or you watch and wait and the time comes and you go after it. Its all been valued to the last halfpenny of profit. They want you to buy it, but they don't want you to have any blood left afterwards. You buy it high, and already the taste of it is sour. You hold it and hold it. Pay rent to house it, pay rates, pay income tax, pay and pay until the sight of all those bits of paste and pottery sickens you. Or yet again, you buy it so right that business is good for the rest of the year. Why shouldn't it be like that?

I was disgusted with myself. To hell with it, I thought, it's only another deal. It's only another little back-yard farce—me and a lot of other mongrels scrapping over a dustbinful of bones. In the end none of us would get them. All the old bones would, sooner or later, be cased up carefully and shipped to America. We lucky dogs got a little chewed up marrow for our trouble; the bigger animals on the other side were the real red meat eaters.

For years now the whole British antique trade had been singing *Passing By* to its best goods. The country was a canal zone, and the canal led straight to the bottomless reservoir in America. We were just an old curiosity shop where the junk could be dragged out endlessly to the quaint accompaniment of a lot of anecdotes about the Duke of Clarence and this is the original Malmsey barrel a little worm-eaten, and how the Dowager Lady Dripping would be only too pleased to let you have her last tiara for a carton of Camels and six pairs of Du Pont nylons.

The Americans gave us their good hard dollars and took the lot, the big and the small, the right and the wrong, the Waterford chandelier and the bisque figure of a girl holding her skirt up. They took it away and built rooms round it and then houses round the rooms. It became part of their culture, and why go to Europe when all the best pictures, sculptures, and genuine handmade toasting forks are already in our American homeland? It was just darling, even if an occasional social misanthrope did call it conspicuous expenditure.

Once they had our bric-a-brac as a privilege and paid through their eyes, ears, and noses for it. Now they bought it as merchandise in bulk, while we threw the profit away in riotous living in the provinces finding the next shipment for them. I was glad Joe Duveen didn't live to see something he started through to the bitter end—an American wholesaler knocking a dollar a time off the price of six Doulton chamber-pots in the Portobello Road. Joe was the last of the great nose-specialists. The dealer today was an old-fashioned bird of prey, a pterodactyl with more teeth than goods; about as adaptable as a four-horse chariot, he had all the chances of survival of a flying pig. In twenty years time the few survivors would spend their lives buying up transfer-decorated lavatory pans for export— the latest fashion in wall lights.

You are a member of a dying profession, I told myself. You can either lie down and die, emigrate to America, or take a correspondence course in selling shoelaces. All God's chillun got shoes, and there might still be room in the industry. I told myself to think it over and then give me a ring any time between eleven and twelve on the first Thursday of the month, if I wasn't too busy buying Wedgwood rooms, that is.

To hell with it.

FIVE

When I came round the next day I found myself driving along the North Circular Road at fifty-two miles an hour. It was a fine bright day and I bypassed the calls I should have made. By midday I was nearly there. I stopped just once to have another look at the map on the back of the catalogue, took a left fork on to a minor road, passed through a small village which looked as if it didn't know the steam engine had been invented, drove past a long high wall, and stopped at a large pair of gates. They were worth about £120 and closed.

I rattled them for a while but they didn't seem to notice. Then a man in shirtsleeves crossed what used to be a lawn dragging a tree branch behind him.

"Hey, George," I called.

He looked up, not all at once, but drawing it out so as to make me think George wasn't his name.

"Can you spare a minute?" I shouted to him.

He put the tree down gently so as not to bruise it and walked over carefully. When he was right close to the gate I asked him if he had the key.

"Not locked," he said.

"Bolted?" I asked.

He thought it out for a while, drawing his hand over his brown cheek so that it left a dirty mark.

"Yes," he said.

"Does ten bob unbolt it?" I wondered.

He moved faster than he had since the free beer came up last haymaking.

I didn't want to waste time admiring the view. I didn't look at anything except the door of the house he told me was open. I pushed it hard and it creaked back slowly. It led into a stone corridor. I crawled around for twenty minutes before I found the room. I walked into six dining rooms, three sitting rooms, four parlors, and another half dozen different kinds of rooms, but there wasn't anything to make it seem worth while. Then I pushed open a pair of large mahogany double doors and walked into a room the size of Olympia. Wherever I looked there were Wedgwood plaques. My legs froze for a minute, and then I lifted them up and threw myself in.

A deep frieze of blue and white plaques large enough to be called bas-reliefs lined the walls. The light in the room was good, and I stood in the middle and counted them. I stopped after fifty-six and began to calculate what I should pay for them. Then I stopped calculating because the figures were beginning to frighten me. Someone had been pecking away at a light bracket on the wall and had left a ladder there. I grabbed the ladder and climbed up to get a closer look.

The plaque I was looking at was a Sacrifice to Pan. I rubbed some of the dust off with my hand. The surface had a slightly oily feel to it, a soapy texture. The figures were here and there a little mistaken in their poses and two of the bacchantes looked as if thy had suffered serious amputations. The Pan himself had a face like an old goat you milk, not an old goat you run away from. But I could be wrong. I shifted the ladder to the other side of the room and climbed up to have a look at a Sacrifice of Iphigenia.

Now I couldn't be wrong. The Wedgwood Iphigenia was modeled by Paccetti in Rome under Webber's guidance. The dozen or so figures in it have the rhythm of a field corn when the wind touches it. In this one the figures looked as if they were leaning on one another to save falling off the wall. The Iphigenia bowed as if she had a bad crick in the neck, and if Paccetti had seen it he would have gone into the ice-cream business.

Every so often you just have to face life—look it square in the eyes and say: "You win!" This was a time like that. I got off the ladder so as to say it in greater safety from the middle of the floor. I told those plaques they were a surplus broker's stock of grade ten French fakes. Then I went out of the room, my cheeks blushing with disappointment. I walked about ten yards up the passage and then came back. Nothing had changed except that I could now see at once they were fakes. I swore aloud and left them there to fool someone else. As I walked out of the house I counted the money I was saving, but I still felt as if I had just made a substantial loss.

Outside, the gardener was sitting on a tree trunk eating his lunch. I sneered at him. By rights he should have given me my ten bob back, but I wasn't going to be petty about this. I walked down to the gates wondering if anything had happened that morning at the shop, and telling myself the country air was doing me good. I didn't want to have any more expensive conversations with the gardener, so I went up to the lodge door and knocked a couple of times. I waited and then knocked again. I still waited and noticed that the gardener was watching me.

"All right," I shouted to him, "I'll buy it. There's nobody in. Right?"

He shook his head to save the wear and tear of saying "No," and I walked over to him.

"He won't open up," he said.

"Will ten bob make him?" I asked. "Or is he in a big line of business?"

"No," my friend said, "not even ten pounds would. He can't walk."

I was saved the trouble of asking him to tell me the whole story, because the idea of the man in the lodge not being able to walk seemed to encourage him.

"Terrible thing—can't walk at all hardly—shakes like a leaf he does—can't talk even—old groundsman here—hasn't walked for years."

"Hasn't talked either?" I asked.

"Hardly," he said, and tut-tutted his way back to the log-rolling. He turned back once, "Girl looks after him—redhead she is."

I went back to the lodge but this time I didn't knock. I went round to the back door and walked in. It led into a shabby little kitchen, the kind of place which wouldn't stand up to a really good meal but made you think of porridge gone cold and cabbage water being saved for soup. A deal table was covered with a piece of American cloth rubbed through at the edges. A lightly boiled egg mashed on to a saucer and a mug of milk half empty waited for someone to come and clean them up. It looked like the old man couldn't eat or drink either. I walked straight through into the parlor.

Sleeping in a deep leather-covered stuffed chair was a small old man. His mouth was open and he had no teeth. His breath came out in uneven shuddering gusts and his eyelids were only half dropped over his eyes. I could see their whites. I had to remind myself that you couldn't breathe if you were dead, because he seemed to be breaking the rule. Then while I watched he shook all over and started to wake up. But he stopped shaking suddenly and with his mouth closed tight now he went to sleep again.

I wasn't the man's doctor so I thought about leaving him to die quietly, when I noticed out of the corner of my eye something which made me remember. I went over to a Victorian what-not in the corner of the room and picked a piece of pottery off the bottom shelf. It was an old salt-glaze pew-group with the heads of both figures missing and a crack running across the base. For a while I didn't remember very clearly, and then as I stood there I suddenly knew that I had to find a pair of Whieldon figures somewhere. I poked about but I didn't find them. I didn't find a pair. But I found one, a beautiful fifteen-inch figure with a repaired head.

As I stood holding it in my hands I knew that the old man hadn't died. He was awake now and keeping one eye closed, he was watching me carefully with the other one. It was pale blue and full of water, but it seemed steady enough. Then he opened his mouth to speak and his eyes started to blink like a morse code transmitter. He got a few grunts out, but I pretended I didn't speak the language.

"Nice weather for the time of the year," I said. "Just having a look round the estate."

He tried to get up and even managed to raise himself about three inches. But he sank back.

"You wouldn't happen to have a Portland in the house?" I asked him.

His eyes stood out like boiled sweets. "A green Portland." He tried to stand up again, and once more he fell back.

We were just beginning to get to know one another, when I saw a red-headed girl in a yellow jersey go past the window.

"See you soon," I said to the old man and slipped out of the back door. I heard him muttering and grunting to the girl as I left.

On the way home I told myself I was beginning to need a rest. A week at Bournemouth perhaps, at some quiet home for incurables.

That night I re-read some of my Wedgwood cuttings. I kept trying to avoid it but eventually I put them all away, and dug out that old tattered one which had been in my wallet for such a long time. "Three salt-glaze pew-groups, a pair of Whieldon figures, and an old Wedgwood green copy of the Portland Vase."

Except for two pew-groups, one figure, and the vase, I had located Mr. Drage's lost collection. I started to tell my wife the whole story.

"And what then?" she asked.

"Then I took up flower-arrangement in a big way," I told her.

That night I dreamed I was arranging flowers in a large green vase decorated with a cameo of a girl with red hair.

SIX

Nothing much happened the rest of the week. I was wondering whether to have a black edge printed round the note-headings when a lunatic came into the shop and with terrible intensity proceeded to buy portrait medallions. It so happened that we had a lot of portrait medallions, and the man was certainly a lunatic for he bought the lot. When he had them parceled up, his features relaxed and a little blood came into his cheeks. I could see it had been a hard fight, but he had won, and the cost was nothing to reckon against the blessed relief he had gained. It was like having an ulcer lanced. The poison was all drained away and instead, he had a fine collection of medallions. Maybe one day they would start to poison him. Then he would get rid of them as quickly as possible and take to some other form of collecting. It takes all sorts to make a business.

On Saturday, I did an itinerant jewelry dealer a turn. He made a sideline of gold and dollars and I told him about someone who had offered me some dollars earlier that week. A legitimate trader hasn't much time for these little subtleties of business life, but this man was so cunning he often outsmarted himself just to keep in training.

He was the sort of man who got no satisfaction out of making a hundred on a straightforward deal, but a slightly illegal pound or two put him into a frenzy of excitement. When I told him about the dollars he started to sweat and his eyes turned into small flints behind his pebble glasses. He pushed his hat off his forehead, and couldn't get away fast enough. He left his suitcase behind, he was in so much of a hurry. It contained only about five hundred pounds worth of stuff, but making a few more pounds made him forgetful.

Sunday was a wet day. The boy and I built a stall out of some lathes and an orange box. We tacked a piece of red lino to the counter, and used an old twill sheet to make an awning. Then we found some chocolate cigarettes and some tins of sardines to sell to each other. We maintained the balance of trade all right, but business wasn't so good and by tea time we were playing cowboys instead. All day long the baby was shuffling about the floor using a cunning technique he had invented as an excuse for not walking.

"Will that child ever walk?" my wife asked.

"He's saving his energy to eat with," I suggested. I had to admire that baby. He kept busy organizing the place, and without wasting a moment in idle talk, he managed to create enough work to keep a whole family employed for a week. At this rate he could take over the business in six months. A chairman of Great Universal Stores in the making.

That evening I was just about to have a good idea when I fell asleep on the settee. When I woke up my tongue was like a piece of *anitco rosso* soaked in Parazone. Then I went to bed and couldn't sleep. Not sleeping was becoming a habit with me, and I began to wonder why. While I was still wondering I fell asleep, so maybe I had broken the habit.

Monday, the first caller was the dollar collector.

"A fine favor you did me," he whispered in a hoarse choked voice.

"Anytime—you would do the same for me." I wasn't paying much attention. Then I saw he was unhappy.

"What's the matter?" I asked him. "Did you lose on the deal?"

He did. There were tears in his eyes as he told me how he had bought the dollars for £140 and taken them straight to his contact. They should have brought £150, but the contact held them up to the light and shook his head.

"They were wrong," the man cried, and he seemed to be all rolled into a ball like a hedgehog without any spikes on him. He tore the notes out of his pocket and threw them up into the air.

"They're wrong—counterfeit—all my years in the trade—what can I do?"

He was distraught, and I genuinely felt sorry for him.

"Look on it as a business loss," I suggested gently. "Sometimes you make, sometimes you lose—that's business." But he was suddenly calm, and a sort of stupid kindness had settled over his face like a warm woolen blanket.

What now? I wondered. And then it came. As I had introduced him to the girl with the dollars, shouldn't I take half the loss? He didn't want to suggest anything, but how should he know whether the girl had made a separate arrangement with me? He wouldn't have taken the dollars, only I recommended the party and he knew me so well. And if not a half, perhaps a quarter. Why should he stand the whole loss? Weren't we friends? All right! He would settle for whatever figure I liked to name. He couldn't say fairer than that.

It was funny and I had to laugh a little.

"You have some funny ideas," I said to him. "Call in any time and we'll have a laugh together."

His mouth opened and the smile left his face. His eyes were large now and innocent with tears. I gave him back his suitcase. It was funny and ridiculous, but it wasn't a good start to a day. After the little man left, I felt irritated and worried. It was his own fault and it had nothing to do with me, but I wondered what it meant. Business makes you suspicious. You look for signs everywhere, signs and lessons and morals. You may say that a little greedy man losing his shirt has got nothing to do with me. But you can't be sure. You can't be too careful. You can be too clever. You can't be clever enough. It's a bad look-out.

On the Tuesday, a taxi came to pick us up at eight o'clock. Sparta had a heavy old coat on which made him look like a draped wall. He had had trouble ungumming his eyelids that morning, and when he talked it was like the bark of an old wolf and didn't mean anything except that he was there. I felt lively enough for a man who has spent the best hours of his night drinking lemon tea, and we didn't say anything until we got to the station. I paid the taxi and got the tickets. Abe Sparta always gave you the impression that you were his foreman, and when we got settled into a compartment he ordered me to get some papers; said: "Bloody cold here," blew his nose on a large khaki handkerchief, and sank into his big coat.

On the platform I had a feeling someone was watching me, and I looked around to see who it was. I could see no one I knew among the depressed morning faces. Picking up a couple of papers, I turned back to the compartment, when a husky voice called out, "Here, Charlie!" It was a voice like half a dozen wrought-iron hinges rusting on an old gate. There was only one voice in the trade to match it. Turning round I saw the voice had no real competition. It was the man himself—Wendl, the break-up man. He had been an old-iron dealer in the days when my father had a stall, and many a big deal had passed between them, sometimes amounting to as much as thirty-five shillings. Now Wendl's was among the biggest of the break-up firms, but he was wearing the same green-cloth cap he had worn years ago—or maybe now that he was a big businessman, he had them greased specially.

"Hello, Mr. Wendl," I said, taking hold of a hand like a piece of old salted beef.

"How's your dad?" groaned the voice. "Must be years—no, I'm a liar—saw him somewhere or other, sometime or other—can't remember—getting too old."

"Not too old for business, Mr. Wendl?" and I walked him back to his compartment.

On the way down the train, I glimpsed Armstrong from Welkin Street talking to two men in the corner of a compartment. It was becoming quite a party. I wondered if I should find that my uncle was driving the engine. It would have been nice to feel that I had a friend in a position of responsibility. As it was, I sat down in Wendl's compartment with a feeling that my goose was cooked and the boys were reckoning on having it for lunch.

Wendl puffed and groaned as if he was stoking up for a race with the *Rocket*. It was alarming, but I could see that it was only his way of sitting down and I didn't worry too much. Even if he did burst his boiler, I had my own troubles. So I gave him enough time to get settled and then I came straight to the point.

"You're not going to the big break-up, Mr. Wendl?" I said.

"Why ask, Charlie boy, if you know?" he answered.

"It's certainly nice to see you again after all these years, Mr. Wendl. I'll tell my dad. He'll be pleased."

"But, I thought," went on Wendl, "somebody told me—I don't know who—maybe your old dad. How is the old bastard?"

"He's fine, Mr. Wendl. Just bought two tons of black pepper. You can imagine. He's very happy," I said.

"So, as I say: what's in the break-up for you? Me, I'm a break-up man. Sashes, cornices, mantels, architraves, the bricks from the garden wall—I reckon them. But you! You going into break-up business?"

It wasn't that he was worried. His interest was ordinary human interest. He wanted to know whether I would be bidding against him. I went straight into what was becoming my routine.

"Look, Mr. Wendl," I said. "I deal in English pottery."

"Nice class of trade," said Wendl, nodding his head and with a faraway look in his eyes, as if he was giving the matter his earnest consideration. He was thinking how much he liked buying houses and pulling them down, and how pleased he was not to be in a nice class of trade.

"There's a room in this place," I continued, "with a lot of Wedgwood in it."

Wendl held up his hand as if to stop me committing an indiscretion.

"You mean the paneled room?"

"Yes."

The old man was silent for a while sucking on his teeth. Then he smiled as if I was his young grandson asking for a trip to the moon. He would have given it to me, only he wasn't in the shipping business. He spoke kindly.

"Look, Charlie boy," he said. "It's a nice room. Old pine, no rot, no faking, nice linen fold. Everybody wants it; like gold dust."

He sank back as if he had told me more than he should.

"All I want is the Wedgwood," I said, with a slight break in my voice.

"For my part," wheezed Wendl, "you can have it."

"That's all I wanted to know, Mr. Wendl," I said, as I got up to go. "Well," I said, "my dad will certainly be pleased to hear you're looking so well."

"Wedgwood you can have," he repeated, like God giving the sea to the fishes.

"By the way . . ." I was nearly out of the compartment but I leaned back. ". . . who do you think's on the train?" I asked.

"Not the Chief Rabbi?" said Wendl.

"No," I said. "Another friend of the family: Abe Sparta." I was out of the compartment, but I could feel the jolt as Wendl sat up.

"Who dug up that old bastard?" he croaked. "The old cow-son thinks he can follow me? He should drop dead, the rotten thieving. . . ." He might have gone on a little longer, but this was just about where I had come in, so I left him talking to himself.

There are certain enmities in the trade which have no origin. A dealer who lives in one place hates a dealer who lives in another place. He doesn't know him out of the salerooms—whether he's an orphan; whether he's got children; whether his wife died giving birth. It isn't another human being he hates. It's another dealer. Maybe it's like two stags meeting. They fight because otherwise they wouldn't be stags. They don't think or count the cost, or ask what it means. The blood runs into their heads and flecks their eyes and their tongues go dry, and they fight.

Sparta and Wendl had come up fighting one another. They would fight over the paneling, and one of them would get it while the other walked out with a white face and a racing heart, cursing himself for giving in and determined never to let it happen again. I didn't know who had beaten who the last time they met—they kept out of one another's way because even strong stags don't look for trouble—but whichever it was, I would be the first to congratulate him. After a battle, while the heat was still high, money meant nothing. Whichever bought the room, I would get the plaques at my own figure. And after all, they were good fakes, those plaques—they had a price. The two stags had a hyena on their tails.

By now, I was enjoying the situation. It was very funny and very clever and I was laughing to myself as I went up the corridor back to my compartment. "You're a clever boy," I told myself. "Let the best man win and me as well."

The train had started now. I passed Armstrong's compartment with a silly smile on my face, and he must have seen it because he called out: "What are you so pleased about?"

I turned back. "Hello, Armstrong," I said. "It's my sunny disposition."

He as a tall, very thin, very long-faced man, who always wore the same mud-colored suit. His eyes were like oil, dark and dead, and he had a hand like a cold fish ball. He was an interior man, but that didn't stop him creeping into everything else, inside or out. He'd been in the game a long time and there wasn't much he missed. It never made him happy. He soaked up a fair amount of Scotch every day, but it only made his face longer and his hand more dead. I was willing to try again, but I would never get fond of him.

"Come in," he said. "We want to speak to you."

I wanted to tell him it was only my first offense, and he shouldn't be too hard. He should let me off with a caution.

Inside the compartment, two smiles were fished out from the bottom of their spleens by a couple of American friends. They put them back quickly to save wear and tear.

"Sit down," said Armstrong, the magistrate. "Meet Mr. Mindel and Mr. Sweeting from the States. This is Mr. ——, I can never think of your name, Charlie—but Charlie is a bit of a specialist in his own way."

It was a great buildup, and Mr. Mindel was pleased to meet me. Mr. Sweeting took a toothpick out of his gum and waved it at me, so I suppose he was pleased as well.

"Well," said Armstrong, "what do you think of it?"

Mr. Sweeting put the toothpick back. Mr. Mindel was looking at me through half-closed eyes and fishing for that valuable smile of his again. He nearly found it.

"A very nice compartment," I said, "but I must be going."

"Look, Charlie," Armstrong said, "I know what you're after, and you know me." I nodded that I knew him. "I wouldn't stand in your way in the ordinary run of things, but Mr. Mindel and Mr. Sweeting here haven't come all the way from the States for nothing, you know."

Mr. Mindel and Mr. Sweeting tried to look like a pair of early colonial pioneers. Their jaw lines almost emerged from their necks, but sank back through lack of practice. Their eyes were like steel and with a little more tempering would have thrown off a spark or two. But they still looked like a couple of dealers to me.

"No," Armstrong went on, "we want that room, Charlie. We're going to rip it out and pack it up and ship it straight out to California."

"We surely are!" said Mr. Mindel.

"That's right!" said Mr. Sweeting.

"So why?" pleaded Armstrong, "why waste your time, Charlie, and get nothing for your trouble? Leave it to us and we'll see you all right."

"Play ball with us," said Mr. Mindel.

"And we'll play ball with you," said Mr. Sweeting.

They were a wonderful combination and I could have clapped my hands with pleasure. I sat down next to Armstrong.

"That's the idea!" he said. "What the hell—we're all in the trade, aren't we—why should we fight?"

And in this atmosphere of jollity, I sat and talked about life with my three new friends—prices in America; the cost of shipping; how much Mr. Sweeting made; then how much Mr. Mindel made; then how much Armstrong made. I told them the story about the man who didn't speak for fifty years, and when he did finally stand up to say something, it turned out to be: "Life is a big fish." Everyone thought this a very fine saying, until the local teacher came right up close to the old man and asked him: "How can you seriously suggest to us that life is a big fish?" "All right," said the man, "so it isn't a big fish." And he sat down and never spoke again.

Armstrong brought down his little attaché case and gave me a piece of chocolate. Mr. Mindel gave me a packet of Luckies. Mr. Sweeting gave me some chewing gum and a toothpick. They would have given me the business if we weren't all dealers together. As it was, we were friends, only they were going to have the room, and I was going to be paid out.

"Don't think I'm being small-minded about this," I said, "but how much?"

"Don't be silly, Charlie," said Armstrong. "We're not dealing small—there's a clear pony in for you." He took out his wallet. "And you can have it now." He started to count out five fivers.

"Well," I said, standing up, "thanks for the chocolate and cigarettes, but I must be running along."

Armstrong looked hurt. "What's the matter, Charlie? Isn't twenty-five enough?"

"Look, Armstrong," I told him, "there's a lot of money in that room I'm not going to make, if I do as you tell me. Do you think it's enough?"

I took fifty after a little more friendly discussion and left after shaking hands all round. I mused on the idiocy of a life which tosses you money when you don't work for it, and a bellyful of promises when you do.

Back in the compartment Abe Sparta was asleep. I didn't wake him up. He had a hard fight ahead of him, and I wanted him to be in a fit state for it.

SEVEN

The position an hour before the auction was due to start was this. I had been paid fifty pounds not to bid for anything by Armstrong, Mindel, and Sweeting. I had an arrangement with Abe Sparta to buy the Wedgwood in the room from him if he bought the room. And if Wendl bought it, he was prepared to sell me the Wedgwood as well. But it wasn't Wedgwood, and if I got it all I had to get it at shipping price—for nothing. It was still two-to-one that I would get it for nothing, unless Armstrong made an arrangement with Sparta or Wendl. But dealers like Wendl and Sparta can ship as fast as they can buy, and they were too big to be both paid off. They were also too proud to buy and then go back with nothing except more money in their hands. After all, dealing for these men isn't just making money. It's a lot of other things as well—other things not so easily arranged—feelings having nothing to do with profit and loss accounts. But if the worst came to the worst, I could go back that night with a good day's wages for my trouble. It wasn't a bad break-up so far as I was concerned.

Sparta woke up a few minutes before the train was due in. He looked about him with a vacant expression as if trying to remember where he was. He looked at me once or twice without recognizing me, and then again. "Oh, that's where you are," he muttered. "Where are we?" We were coming into the station, and I suggested that it might be best if we get a taxi first and then something to eat. My stomach was self-supporting at the moment, and I wanted to make some small contribution—a dry cheese sandwich for example. The old man was still a little bit vague. "Leave it to you, Charlie," he said. Then he came round. "So long as we don't get there too late. No," he went on, "we'd better get straight there and see what's happening. Says here in the catalogue light refreshments will be obtainable."

As we walked to the taxi Sparta looked back and saw Wendl a few yards behind. His face went the color of borsht.

"That old bleeder Wendl. Did you see him?" he growled. "Follows me about the old rat."

"Here's the taxi, Mr. Sparta," I said.

He got into it still cursing Wendl. I saw Armstrong and his friends get into another taxi but I don't think they saw me. Wendl didn't take a taxi. He was the sort of dealer who knows all the bus services and isn't ashamed to save money by using them. He passed us as we got into the taxi and I said in a loud voice: "A lift? Well, yes thanks, Mr. Sparta, it's very nice of you." But Sparta wasn't interested. "You see that mean old bastard, Wendl? Wouldn't take a taxi if he had to go on his hands and knees."

It was an untidy countryside with a lot of trees looking very underfed, and grayish grass which no self-respecting cow would give a second look at. We passed a few blank-faced farmhouses, one of them a decayed Jacobean relic with a large muddy field in front of it. Some sick looking cows were stuck knee-deep in the mud, but no one worried. Abe Sparta showed no interest in the rural scene except once when we passed an open-shaft iron ore mine.

"What's that?" he asked, and when I told him, he replied: "That sort of business is all right for Wendl, he's an old-iron man. But I'll tell you something for nothing. The timber round here isn't worth a light for cutting. I never did see such a miserable lot of overgrown weeds. Trees, you call 'em?"

He glared at me like I was selling trees. Then we came up over the crest of a hill and below us we could see the gables of a fine house. Sparta had the driver stop for a while so that we could admire the view. We got out of the car and stood by the road looking down on to the house, and we didn't say anything.

The morning was just getting into its stride, and the place had a look of having been there for ever. The stone toned into the colors of the fields, and the house sat there as if it had grown up with the hill. Sparta was staring down at it all and I was telling myself how there wasn't a dealer in fine things who could help responding to beauty. I felt a glow of satisfaction when Sparta said quietly, "That, Charlie, is a very fine house—a very fine property." He was quiet again except for a sigh. "Yes," he said, "it's a beautiful house. It would be nice to have the breaking of it." Nothing could stop him being an Odessa lumberman. He loved trees but only when they were chopped down.

We were coming to the house now and Sparta leaned forward in his seat. We drove into the grounds through the iron gates. Now a board saying SALE THIS DAY was tied to the gatepost. I noticed a little smoke trickling out of the chimney of the lodge, and I thought I caught a glimpse of a vase on the mantel over the fire, but maybe it was a mirage.

The house itself seemed larger than before. Four Corinthian columns formed the center entrance. The wings swept round on each side to form a crescent. It must have been magnificent in the old days, but murder on the feet—the sort of place where you need a bicycle to get from the sitting room to the nearest lavatory. Now the façade had that diseased look which means the break-up isn't far off. A lot of stucco trimming had cracked away revealing the brick beneath, but whoever bought those bricks would certainly have to work to drag them out. That place had been built. Built like a monument to stand up for a long time. It would have gone on standing up, too, if it wasn't for the demolition dealers. It wouldn't have done anyone any good, of course, and in a hundred years or so it would have disappeared, but it would certainly have stood up for a while longer than the determined men who were, even now, getting their tackle ready to tear it to pieces.

The main doors were open today and inside it was dead cold with that bitterness which only large, long-empty houses have. I put my collar up and followed the old man to the room. On the way we passed some sheet lead which had been ripped off the roof. Sparta stopped and stared at it. "You see that?" he said. "The bastards have pinched the lead already—lead! You know how much lead there is there?"

I said, "No."

"A lot—a lot." The old man shook his head at the criminal idiocy of a world which entrusted lead to people other than Sparta. He rapped here and there on the walls as we went along, just for practice.

We walked round to the room. The doors were open today and as soon as we walked in, Sparta began to examine the paneling. The plaques were still there and they looked terrible. The ladder was still there, too, but I noticed that all the light brackets had disappeared. Sometimes trifles do walk before an auction begins. I climbed up the ladder to make it look real. When I came down, I nearly tripped. It depressed me to be on top of so much cheapness.

I tapped the pocket with the ten fivers in it as I walked back to Sparta.

"What do you think of it?" I asked him.

"All right," he said.

"I only want the Wedgwood if it's cheap," I told him. "Wrong color."

"You want it cheap?" he said, still bent over the paneling. "Don't we all?"

"I was just telling you, Mr. Sparta," I said.

"Don't worry, Charlie," he said. "I'll manage."

As I left the room, Armstrong and the Americans came in.

"How do you like it?" Armstrong said.

"You buy it," I told him. "It's good."

Then I went to the refreshment room for that sandwich.

EIGHT

The position when I took my first bite of the cheese sandwich was this. The auction had just started. I didn't want to buy a thing. Wendl wanted the paneling. Sparta wanted the paneling, and Armstrong wanted the lot. I looked at my watch. I could be back by the early afternoon, but somehow I wanted to see the thing through. I wanted to know whether anyone else would see that the plaques weren't right, and I didn't want to miss the big fight either. I finished my coffee and ordered more. There were two or three local dealers hanging about, but no one I knew. Then Wendl came in and sidled over to me.

"Have a cup of coffee, Mr. Wendl," I said. "Warm you up."

"Does Abe Sparta want the room?" he answered, as I handed him the cup.

"As a matter of fact he does, Mr. Wendl."

Wendl took a long drink before he spoke again. Then he asked me to come into the garden for a breath of air.

The canteen was in the old kitchens, so we went out the back way towards what used to be the stables. Wendl shuffled along.

"We walking home, Mr. Wendl?" I asked him.

He didn't answer until we were about fifty yards from the house. His voice was pitched so low that nearly all the rasp had left it, and it sounded almost gentle.

"Listen, Charlie," he whispered. "I'm one of your dad's oldest friends. I knew you when you used to sell stamps on the corner of your old man's stall. I want you to do something for me."

"You know I'd be pleased to do anything I can for you, Mr. Wendl," I said.

So after telling me what Sparta had done to him over the past twenty years, he finally came to the point. He didn't want to bid. Sparta was only there to make him pay. I should bid for him. Of course, he would look after me.

My ethical position was deteriorating fast. I had been paid not to bid by one—I had cancelled a joint arrangement to buy with someone else—I had decided not to buy for myself—and here I was being asked to buy for Wendl. If I bid after agreeing with Armstrong not to, it would be bad for my reputation and I would have to give him back ten fivers I had grown fond of. If I gave him back the fivers and bought for Wendl, it might be worth more than fifty to me, but Sparta would be annoyed—and he was my landlord. But if I *could* bid, it would be the funniest deal of my life.

The room was lot number 178, and it didn't come up till after lunch. That gave me an hour or so to think of something.

"Look, Mr. Wendl," I said. "Mr. Sparta is my landlord. I haven't got a lease and I have a family to keep sheltered. I think he might not like it if I bid against him."

"I'm ashamed of you," Wendl said, "for being frightened of a great ox like him. Come on, Charlie—you'll do me a turn?"

"I'll see you in about half an hour, Mr. Wendl, and let you know," I said.

"What's so difficult you should have to think it over for so long?" he croaked after me, but I was already back at the canteen door.

There was Armstrong drinking Scotch with the Americans. He said to me with misery in his voice, "Lovely room, isn't it?" It must have been his third double, and it was beginning to depress him.

"Sparta's mad about it," I said.

"Who? Abe Sparta?" he asked, swallowing the rest of his drink.

"Yes," I said. "He wants it badly."

Armstrong gathered his friends to him. "This isn't so good, boys," he said. "Sparta's a hard man to do business with."

Mr. Sweeting said, "Yeah?"

Mr. Mindel didn't say anything.

"Just thought I'd let you know, " I said.

"Very nice of you, Charlie," Armstrong said with sincerity in his voice. "I appreciate it."

"That's all right," I told him, "you've been fair to me and I want to be fair to you. Did you see Wendl was here as well?" I added.

"Wendl," Armstrong explained. "He's not interested in paneled rooms. He's strictly demolition."

"He happened to mention he could use a paneled room," I said. "I think he's always wanted one and he loves the Wedgwood in this one—thinks it just makes it."

"It sure does," said Mr. Mindel. "I sure want that room." Armstrong blinked his eyes in irritation.

"Well, you're out anyway, Charlie," he said with an edge of threat on his voice.

"That's right," I said, "it's all yours—and Sparta's—and Wendl's. Goodbye."

"Just a minute, Charlie," Armstrong called, "don't be in such hurry always. You know Wendl, don't you?"

"Very old friend of the family," I said.

"What about Sparta?" he asked.

"Even older friend of the family."

Armstrong looked at his associates and then gave me a long straight glare. "Can you fix something?"

I shook my head. "No one can fix those two old dogs," I said. "Certainly not me. Why don't you ring it with Wendl? He might be interested."

"Will you speak to him?" Armstrong asked.

I said I would and went back to find the old man, feeling that at least my fifty was safe.

Wendl agreed without a struggle. He didn't want to have to fight Armstrong's friends as well as Sparta.

"Will you bid?" he asked.

"I don't know yet, Mr. Wendl," I said. "I'll tell you." I thought for a while. I looked at the catalogue and then I went off to find Sparta.

I searched through the rooms until it felt as if my feet had taken frostbite. The auctioneer was carrying the bidding with him from room to room, and he sold a nice piece of rotten cornice molding for ten shillings as I passed him. He was a big, fresh-faced man with riding breeches and high boots, and he looked as if he'd like to get back to the pig market. I couldn't blame him. He was surrounded by a small crowd of stunted local demolition boys who looked as if they would garrote him for sixpence. The pigs were more generous.

I found Abe Sparta out in the grounds looking up at a fine oak. He had an abstracted look on his face whenever he looked at trees.

"Not gone yet, Charlie?" he said.

"No," I said, "I thought I'd hang around and see what was happening. I just spoke to Mr. Wendl."

"What did the grisly bastard have to say? You know, Charlie," he ran on, "you should be careful who you mix with. He can give you a bad name."

"He hasn't come for the room," I said, "I know that. Well, I'm off now, Mr. Sparta. See you tomorrow." I walked towards the gate.

"Hey, Charlie!" the old bear shouted. "Come back a minute." I came back a minute. "So what does he want?" Sparta said.

"He didn't say, Mr. Sparta, but he asked me when lot 206 should come up."

Sparta took his dog-eared catalogue out of his pocket and licked his thumb. "Here it is," he said, "lot 206: the painted metal stairs finely wrought and so on."

"Yes," I said, "that's it."

"I'll just have a look and see what the old bleeder's up to," Sparta said, and he scuttled back to the house.

When he buttonholed me a quarter of an hour later, his face was gray with suppressed excitement.

"He wasn't far out, the old bleeder," he said. "You know what those stair rails are made of?"

I didn't know.

"Lead," Sparta whispered, "and it's not catalogued."

"I thought it might be something like that, Mr. Sparta," I said.

"Charlie—you've done me a good turn." He gripped my shoulder hard as if I had just saved his little boy from drowning. "I won't forget."

"What about the room, Mr. Sparta?"

"To hell with the room," he said. "Who wants a pine room?"

"I might buy it myself if it goes cheap," I remarked carelessly.

"You have it, Charlie, I won't bid against you. What do you think of that cunning old bastard letting me think he wants the room?"

"Well, I hope you get the stairs, Mr. Sparta," I said.

"Thanks, Charlie," he said, "and Charlie, tell your wife of course she can leave the big pram in the shed."

"That'll please her," I told him, and I went back to business.

By lunch time the situation had clarified. First and foremost, I was in the clear. Then, Armstrong and Wendl were going to ring the room. Sparta wasn't interested, but only I knew it. He wasn't going to leave those stairs until they were sold. I had to laugh. I had picked on the stairs just because I reckoned a metal merchant ought to be interested in metal, and because Sparta always thought of Wendl as a metal merchant. If Sparta got them and they were lead, good luck to him. If Wendl didn't get them and he didn't know they were lead, it wouldn't hurt him. I was squared with Armstrong, but they were giving me a share in the knock-out because I was going to do the bidding. Now there was only the question of the local opposition, the possibility of there being a high reserve on the room, and the danger of the auctioneer trotting the bidding. Even a pig seller knows how to pick imaginary bids out of the air if his ten per cent is suffering.

There had been no excitement so far in the bidding. It was all routine stuff, and everyone was talking about the room and trying to guess what it would fetch. I couldn't see anyone who looked like a buyer though, and it seemed we would have it pretty well to ourselves. I wanted to find out if it carried a reserve. I introduced myself to the auctioneer.

"It'll be the room you're interested in?" he said, after looking at my card.

"You certainly sum things up quickly," I said to him. "I did come down to buy the room. It would have been very nice if it had been right. Still, that's how it is in this game. You never know until you see it."

He looked puzzled. "You mean to say it's not right?"

"Not a piece there that's right," I repeated. "All French copies. If you had one of them out I could show you."

"Come along to the office, will you?" he said.

As we walked down to the butler's pantry which they were using for an office, he asked me: "You specialize in Wedgwood, do you?"

"That's right," I said.

He shook his head. Back in the office he had a broken plaque. He handed it to me. I turned it over and handed it back.

"If it was Wedgwood it would be solid. This is hollow. If it was

Wedgwood it would be dull. This is shiny. And anyway it would be impress-marked. This is junk."

"We thought it would fetch a lot," he said.

"It may," I told him, "there are plenty of mugs who don't know the difference. If you're lucky, there might be a couple here today."

"But it's no good to you?" he said, a little desperately.

"Only if it goes reasonable—not if the reserve is high. And not," I looked straight into his eyes, "not if it's trotted."

"We don't do that sort of thing in the country, you know," he said, hurt.

"I'm glad to hear it," I said.

"And nothing's reserved very high. It's all got to sell or be pulled down, you see—it's purely a demolition job—d'you see?"

I could see that he was frightened the London dealers would cry off in a crowd and his sale might go to hell.

"Well, maybe I'll hang around and see what happens," I said.

"Yes, do," he urged, "I'm sure it will be all right."

"Thanks," I told him. "I can see you're going to be fair about it."

I was getting to be a first-rate canvasser. Maybe I should go in for politics.

NINE

I communed with nature during the lunch recess. I took a glass of beer and a meat pie out into the garden, and sat on the trunk of tree down by the porter's lodge. I broke the crust off the meat pie and examined it. It was like a piece of heavy parchment, and I wondered what good it could do me to eat it. I threw it high into the air to see if it would take off. Then I took the solid wad of meat out and studied that, too. It looked like an old composition floor the damp had attacked. I nibbled a little of it just in the way of experiment. It tasted of nothing I wanted to put my finger on. The rest of the crust slipped away from it like a plaster mold, and I threw it in the same direction. It fell in about the same place and there was a scrambling noise as if it had started to dig its way back into the earth. Then a red setter jumped out of the bushes and stood stock still a couple of yards from me. Thinking that at least someone would make a profit on the pie, I offered him the wad of meat. He came up to it slowly, as if he had experienced this sort of disappointment before.

"Go on," I told him. "Eat it up—it's only another old red setter. Dog eat dog," I told him. "Eat it up. Enjoy it."

Then, because the dog still seemed uncertain, I tried to make a little polite conversation.

"How's business?" I asked him. "What do you think of the room?"

Then, because he seemed new to the game, I thought I'd take him into my confidence.

"Don't touch the room," I told him. "I know about these things. Don't touch it. It's dead wrong."

That seemed to convince him of my good faith, and he came up and licked at the meat.

"Yes," I told him, "you look like an honest dog to me, and I wouldn't like to see you go wrong on that room."

He took the meat into his mouth confidently now, as if he had earned it.

"You should give me the meat," I told him, "after all, think of the money I'm saving you."

The dog didn't answer, so I stopped wasting my valuable time on him.

A woman was standing by the bushes a little nearer to the lodge. She was wearing jodhpurs and a yellow sweater, and her figure didn't suffer by it. She had red hair, cut carelessly, and her face was pretty without being anything out of the ordinary.

"I don't mind you talking to my dog, but I'd be grateful if you wouldn't feed him," she said. "Drop it, Rover!" she told the dog.

But he wasn't going to give up so easily. He pretended to be deaf as well as dumb and finished the meat quickly in a great gulp.

"Sorry," I said, "but we were having a quiet little talk about business and he said he hadn't eaten since breakfast."

"Yes," she answered, "I heard. What makes you say the room is no good?"

I looked at her. "You don't look like a dealer," I said.

She laughed, and it was a nice performance—a low, long note which could shatter your backbone if it really tried.

"No," she said. "My grandfather was the groundsman here in the old days. He has the lodge. I look after him because there's no one else."

"Nice quiet life," I suggested.

The red setter was being a good boy now. He kept twining like a snake between her legs. It didn't seem to me that he was wasting his time.

"Won't you take a seat?" I asked her.

"It's lovely here, isn't it?" she said, sitting down.

"Yes," I said, "it's got a nice atmosphere of decay—and I like the way the herbaceous border's gone tropical and the trees haven't been pruned and the bushes haven't had a haircut in years. It's nice and wild, but the break-up boys will soon tame it. In three weeks' there won't be a wild strawberry left."

"It's sad, isn't it?" she said.

"I suppose so," I said. "Though it'll only fall down if it's left. This way at least someone makes a profit—men make a living—rents are paid and children get new toys and wives new hats."

"Are you going to pull it down?" she asked. "You don't seem like a demolition contractor."

"I'm glad you said that," I told her. "Destruction is foreign to my nature. I wouldn't harm a slate on its roof. I came for the room."

"And yet you say it's no good. I think it's very lovely, but I suppose you only care about its value."

She was beginning to treat me like a knocker—as if I was calling on her to see if she had anything to sell today madam. I glanced at my watch. It wasn't too late to begin a little course in aesthetic appreciation, and she was a nice class to teach.

"Now look," I told her, "I'm a dealer, and I care about what things are worth because that's the way I make a living. If I stopped caring, then I wouldn't make a living. You don't want my family to starve, do you?"

She laughed as if the idea was funny.

"People have different ideas about what's beautiful, and I wouldn't contradict a single one of them, but in my experience when something's really beautiful, it's also rare. If it's rare, there are people who want it just because it's rare. They don't care about its beauty. It's just something no one else has got so far as they're concerned. Or, it's an investment, or a way of hiding money from the income tax. But don't blame me if I sell to these people. I'm only responsible for the rarity and the beauty of the thing I sell. I'm not responsible for their reasons for buying it. If I only sold to people with a nice sense of beauty, I'd be president of a debating society, not an ordinary ignorant dealer. As for that room," I said, "there isn't a piece of Wedgwood in it. It's all fake stuff let into some nice paneling, and for my part it kills the paneling."

She looked depressed now, and I felt sorry I'd opened my mouth. It was better she should stay ignorant and go on seeing beautiful things. I might be doing a lot of harm by telling her the facts of life.

"What's the matter?" I asked her. "It doesn't belong to you, does it? What do you care how much it brings?"

"To tell you the truth," she said, after a while, "Grandfather is to get a little out of what the place fetches, and he needs it badly."

I looked at her and she blushed.

"I'm surprised at you," I said. "Here you are, telling me all about beauty, when what really worries you is what price it's going to fetch."

"It's not for myself," she snapped back. "I'm not going to make anything out of it."

"It's like that for all dealers," I said. "All they get out of it is the fun of the fair. The profit's to pay the rent collector and the milkman."

Now don't think I had forgotten what I was sitting on that log talking philosophy for. It's always nice to put over a good line of sales talk to a red-headed client, but this time I was setting the right atmosphere for breaking and entering the lodge again. And this time I would have my own guide.

"Look here," I told her, "I'm the only dealer here who knows the stuff's no good, and I haven't learned what I know in order to educate the masses. The room will fetch good money and Granddad will get his slops for another five years."

That cheered her, and she got up to go.

"Has your grandfather got any bits and pieces he might like to sell?" I asked her.

"Well," she answered, "he does have a few bits and pieces, now that you ask."

I was away now after the hare, and she didn't look like a pretty girl any more.

"I'd like to see them very much," I said. "You never can tell." I got up to follow her.

"I'm afraid Grandfather's asleep now," she said. "He suffers from agitans, and he's very ill and I don't want to wake him. Could you come this afternoon and then I can ask him? He can hardly talk, poor dear. But I can understand him."

I could come and we said goodbye with lots of smiles. I saw her to the door and shook hands with her to make her feel that we were already in business together.

As I turned to go, I could have sworn that there really was a vase on the mantelpiece. I didn't want her to see me looking through the window, so I walked back to the house. But I could have sworn there was a vase over the fireplace.

TEN

The arrangement was that I should buy lot 178. The little crowd following the auctioneer around had been belching its way through indigestion and a few dismal lots which were the overture to 178. Then when they came into the room, a hush fell over the assembly as if they were in chapel and cared for that sort of thing. Armstrong and the Americans were out of the way looking unconcerned in the far corner, but I could feel their eyes drilling wormholes in my back. Sparta wasn't about. He was frightened the stairs might walk, and he wanted to keep on their tail. Wendl was over by the window picking his nose as if nothing else mattered. I couldn't see anyone who looked like a bidder, and for a moment I entertained the dealer's old hope that maybe he'll buy on the first bid. Lately I've only seen it happen with a bundle of rotten curtains and a Britannia metal plate-stand, but it could happen here, too. I wondered if the girl in the yellow jumper would come to watch, but she wasn't about.

The auctioneer was giving a short speech on the history of the room and how fine it was and how lucky we were to be buying it. Just as he finished his story and said "Now, gentlemen, shall I say five hundred to start?" the girl came in. I bid him fifty just to show how much his sales talk was worth. She looked fresh and small—a flower on a rat-infested rubbish dump.

The auctioneer was speaking after the slight murmur which followed my bid.

"Now, gentlemen, I appreciate a joke as much as the next man, but let's have a serious offer, if you please. The whole room, mind you, including these magnificent Wedgwood plaques."

He caught my eye as he said it and threw me a roguish twinkle. But no one bid.

"Speak up," he shouted. "A serious bid, if you please."

"All right," I said, "sixty."

Then he looked over my shoulder and said, "Seventy, am I bid? Thank you, seventy."

I couldn't see who was bidding. Either someone was having a go while the figure was small, or he was trotting.

"Eighty," I said.

He took another bid from behind me.

"Ninety," I told him.

Then we bid in twenties.

At two hundred and forty we were still bidding, and my hands were sweating. At three hundred I stopped to get a nod from Arm-

strong. I looked round. There was a slight buzz around the girl over
to the right. As I looked, she nodded her head.

"It is yours, madam," the auctioneer said gallantly.

She was bidding against me. Why? Who for? What was all the
talk about back on the tree trunk? Maybe I should have let her
teach me the business. Wendl now gave me four quick nods.

The auctioneer was saying, "Going, at three hundred," and leer-
ing at me.

"Three fifty," I said, to show I was serious and glanced over at the
girl. Her expression meant nothing. It was just a dish cover, and no
one could say what she had on the dish.

She ran me up to four twenty and then turned on her heel smartly
and walked out without a word.

"Thanks for your help," I called after her neat, cunning little
figure. "That'll be enough now, sir," I said to the auctioneer.

"I think so," he said, with that happy leer, and knocked it down
to me.

We met outside. "Not such a bargain," Wendl said.

"Leave it to us, if you like, Wendl," said Armstrong.

"Let me finish, Mr. Armstrong, if you please," answered Wendl.
"I was going to say, not such a bargain, but what can you do?"

"All right then," Armstrong said irritably. "Let's find an empty
room somewhere, knock it out, and get home."

I could see he was dying for a drink. Wendl had stopped picking
his nose, but he looked as if he was still thinking about it. Mr. Sweeting had come to the point where only chewing his toothpick would
quiet his nerves. Mr. Mindel kept bleating, "It's a lovely room. It
sure is a fine room," as if he was trying to sell it to himself.

For my part, I couldn't stop wondering about the girl. Even if it
wasn't my money I was throwing away, it still hurt me to be run. I
would rather have left her the room. What the hell could she do with
it anyway? Maybe she wanted it to put the vase in—if she had a vase.

We found a room in the servants' quarters not much bigger than
a large cage. We made a ring, all of us bidding, me with Wendl, and
Armstrong with the Americans. Wendl put the room up at four

twenty and bid another ten. We went round twice in tens, making another hundred on the price. Then we went round once more, putting another fifty on. Then Wendl bid a hundred more. He didn't want to waste time messing about, he said. That made the price two hundred and fifty more. Then Mindel got very excited.

"We want that room," he snarled—if a sheep can snarl. And he bid another hundred. He seemed to forget we weren't playing stud poker, although Armstrong was looking worried. The price was now three hundred and fifty more, and it was enough. Wendl looked unhappy and said: "All right, you can have it."

"We'll pay out back in town," Armstrong said.

"No," said Wendl, "we'll pay out here before Charlie transfers the lot."

"What's the matter Wendl?" said Armstrong. "Don't you trust us?" He didn't like the room so much now.

"I trust you," said Wendl, "but business is business, so let's get it settled."

They paid out Wendl in cash for both of us, two-fifths of three hundred and fifty—one hundred and forty pounds in new fivers.

"All right, Charlie," he said, "transfer the lot to these gentlemen," and we all trooped down to the auctioneer's office.

Afterwards Wendl said to me, "Charlie, greed is a terrible thing. Just think what that room cost those men because they were greedy."

He gave me forty and put the rest back in his pocket.

"So you made a crust today, Charlie?" he said. "Remember me to your dad," and he went off to catch the bus back to the station. I asked him did he want to buy anything else in the break-up, and he said sadly: "It's taken care of, Charlie, don't worry."

He hadn't given a damn for the room. He had bluffed good money into his pocket out of the pockets of Armstrong's friends, and that was all he wanted.

I went back to have another look at the room. For all that money, it looked worse than terrible. Armstrong and the Americans were running about measuring it up and telling one another how lucky they were to get it.

"Wendl certainly caved in," Armstrong said to me, for the benefit
of his friends.

"Yes," I agreed, "there were tears in his eyes when he left."

ELEVEN

It was three o'clock and the position was that the party was over and
I had ninety pounds in my pocket. Like Wendl, I didn't care a
damn for Wedgwood rooms. All I wanted to do was to go to every
break-up in the country. In two years I would be able to buy enough
Savings Certificates to settle down quietly and live on the interest.
But I wasn't really serious. I knew that it was a fluke. It would never
happen again like this, and on the whole, I wasn't sorry. There's a
lot of luck in business, but it would be terrible if there was nothing
but luck. It would be demoralizing, and the competition would make
life impossible. There are a lot of lucky people about and every one
of them would be a dealer, and if that happened, who would there
be left to sell to? The trade would go out of business if it was all
luck. There had to be something else as well. What it was I didn't
know, but it had to be something.

I was sorry the girl in the yellow sweater should have treated me
like that after our talk, but I was going to take her at her word and
see what her poor old grandfather had besides agitans. I walked over
to the lodge after telling Sparta I'd be back for the taxi at four. He
was too interested in the stairs to worry about me. Looking at his
glazed old eyes it seemed to me that he didn't have very long to live.
He couldn't think of more than one thing at a time, and thinking
about that one little thing took up all the breath and blood and life
he had left in him. He couldn't have been much older than Wendl,
but he had used himself up faster and with endless, senseless fury,
while Wendl paddled along saving money on bus fares and quietly
never missing a deal. Sparta was almost a hulk. It just wanted another cold winter or a really bad deal to put him out of business.
All that silver-gilt up in his safe would come out, and while his wife

looked at it through red-rimmed, sightless eyes, maybe it would cross her mind that the fire was burning low and they were out of coal again.

As I walked over the untidy grass and the muddy drive down to the lodge, I was inclined to be philosophical. What did it mean, anyway, this break-up, or anything else for that matter? To begin with, it meant people dying alone and so quietly that no one noticed it until probate was granted. But even that wasn't the beginning. It started with a man living. He put a few stones together and crawled between them. Finally he built a house with a hundred rooms and into every room he put a thousand bits and pieces to look at and think about. He was just about to explain exactly what all these bits and pieces amounted to, when, unfortunately, he died. They were lost—it couldn't be helped. The man's life was in them and when he died they had nothing left to live for—until the dealer came along and gave them meaning for the lives of other men. The dealer was the ringmaster in a dream circus—he flicked his catalogue and presto, another routine. As for him, the dealer, the Autolycus of the auction rooms, he never owned a thing in his life, and he knew it. The objets d'art, the objets vertus, the bijouterie and the pots, they all passed through his hands and into history. Who knew better than he that nothing is given, that everything passes, the woods decay? He was the ultimately human being. He resigned himself to making a profit. Whether or not grandfather had a vase worth buying and selling was the only question.

I knocked at the door of the lodge, and after a couple of minutes it was opened. It was the red-head, but she was wearing a dress now. It was a light dress of a brilliant blue color and for a moment, after that red and blue hit me between the eyes, I could find nothing to say. She smiled at me as if auctions couldn't be further from her mind, and said: "How nice of you to come. I was just about to make a cup of tea. You will have one, won't you?"

I said yes, I would have one, and she led me into the small parlor.

The old man was sitting by a small bamboo table in front of the fire. He was bent over the table, smaller than life. A little dull white hair was plastered carefully over his skull, and his face was shrunken and very pink. His eyes stood out like marbles, and swivelled a little when he spoke. The only way he could stop his hands shaking was to keep them on the table. He couldn't move very much, and every time he opened his mouth, I thought the effort would spin him out of his chair.

I could see that conversation was out of the question until the girl came back, so I told him what a nice little place he had here, and how nice it was out, and what a nice girl his granddaughter was. He gulped every so often and I took it to mean that he agreed with me. But until the girl came back, I didn't take my eyes off the vase standing on the mantelpiece. When she did come back, it was difficult to know which to watch. If the vase won, it was only on points—points of information with which I happened to be familiar.

It was a Portland vase about ten inches high, and generous in its proportions, decorated with a pure white cameo on which the shading was as delicate as the carving on an antique gem. The side facing me showed Pylades, the rope dancer, approaching the daughter of the Emperor lying on her sickbed with Cupid flying over her, and Galen, to the other side, bearded and very stern, pointing out that the only trouble with the princess was that she was sick of love. It was the usual Portland story, but this time it was told with so much genius that my heart skipped a beat every time I looked at it.

And that wasn't all. The white cameo was laid upon a silk-smooth jasper of a green which had never existed before. It was the translucent green of deep sea-water, a green with more green in it than any other color, but with every other color there, too. And there wasn't a doubt in the world that it was an early copy—nothing later than 1795 could have had that precision and clarity, that quality of sheer genius which spoke to you clear from the other side of the room. And yet no green jasper Portland was ever made in the period. There's no mention of it anywhere. They were all black, or blue-black. First Portlands don't exist, and if they do, they aren't green. But this did, and it was the greenest green in the world.

I talked on to the old man about the weather until the girl came back with a tea tray with two cups and saucers on it.

"Grandfather mustn't drink tea," she said. "Now have you had a nice chat?"

I said, "Yes," and the old man gulped again, and she busied herself pouring out the tea.

"I was surprised to see you bidding at the auction today," I said.

"Wasn't it fun?" she cried, putting the tea-pot down.

"What did you want with the room?" I asked gently. "Are you going into business with your grandfather?"

"Mr. Pilkington, the auctioneer, gave me five pounds to nod my head at him until he waved at me. Wasn't it nice of him?" She was being very sweet about it.

"It certainly was," I said. "You cost my friends a nice packet." Pig-dealing hadn't hurt that auctioneer at all, I thought.

"Oh, good!" she said. "Grandfather—you should get a nice little present out of the sale—isn't that nice?"

Deaf as he was, the old man caught the sense of that and made a sudden jerk which almost knocked the bamboo table over. He put his heart and soul into it and managed to say "Good," but it was hardly worth the effort.

"I was very glad, too," I said. "I bought it for some fellows who would be very happy tonight if they knew their money was doing your grandfather good."

Then I talked about the vase and said what a pretty green it was.

"Grandfather had me fetch it out of the attic the other day. He wanted it left on the mantelpiece so he could see it all the time. I didn't even know he had it."

She let me pick it up, and I noted there was no mark on it, except for a small manganese pencil X on the inside rim. It was solid body and it felt like silk. The cameo in the base was the most perfectly gem-finished work I had ever seen.

"It's very pretty," I said. "Would your grandfather like to sell it?"

The old man was watching all this palaver very closely, keeping

his hands well on the table to stop them shaking. His eyes were practically out of their sockets, but only he and I knew why. The girl
was saying: "You wouldn't mind, would you, Grandfather? I knew
you would be pleased."

The old boy was doing his best to have a stroke. But she understood him and knew he was pleased.

"What is it worth?" she asked.

"Well," I said, "there are all sorts of vases of this pattern, but this
one is nicely made and I like the color. I might pay a very good price
for it."

The old man was shaking away, trying to tell her to throw me out.
But I held on to the vase and kept smiling. Ninety pounds had fallen
into my pocket that day. "I'll give you eighty pounds for it," I said.

When she recovered, she told the old man and he jerked for a
while, trying to tell her, "No."

"He's trying to say he's very grateful," she said to me, "Mister
. . . I don't even know your name."

"Drage," I said. "Name of Drage." I was looking at the old man.
He made a convulsive effort and rose up shaking upon his feet.

I counted out sixteen fivers, smiling at him the while.

"Thank Mr. Drage, Grandfather," the girl said.

He moved and pushed the table over, scattering the five-pound
notes.

"He's so excited, Mr. Drage," the girl said, and she put him carefully back in the chair.

I watched his eyes. It wouldn't have been impossible for him to
add murder to his crime sheet. As it was, what could he be convicted
of? Had he stolen the Drage items all those cold years ago? Stolen
them thinking, "A promising young man in service deserves a better
start—I'll pawn them and open a tobacconist shop." And did he
suddenly realize that now he had them, all he could do was get fond
of English pottery? Or had he gone in for a little quiet receiving and
found the goods didn't sell? Whichever way it was, what was he
worrying about? Now I had the worry and he had sixteen fivers to
buy himself a nice silver-plated coffin.

She found a box for me and I packed the vase up, carefully stuffing newspapers round it. She was very happy and couldn't stop thanking me for being so nice. She was a nice girl, and I could have spent a long time talking to her without getting bored.

"I'm sorry about bidding against you at the auction," she said, as I was about to go. "I feel very ashamed."

"Don't be," I told her. "You look after your grandfather always like that." After this shock, he was going to need careful nursing until he could work up enough energy to steal Mr. Drage's vase back again.

She had eyes, that girl, and lips, and the only color that would ever bring out the full beauty of her hair was the green of that Portland.

The whole jungle was never as green as that. The whole jungle which looked after the tiger, sometimes let the bird of paradise, the flash of light under the trees, take a quick flight round the festering mangrove swamps. Even if it has to finish up on a hat at the world première of a film about the fall of man, let the bird take flight once in a while. It won't alter anything, although even the tigers will give it a glance as it passes. It may not show a profit now, but one long dark night when there's only one good tooth left in his decayed jaw, an old tiger will think about it.

"Goodbye," I said to the girl, "and thank you."

"What for?" she asked, "you've been very kind." For one moment there was only a vase between us. It was a moment of deep sentiment, so I did my best.

"For having such red hair and such green Portlands."

She laughed on that long, low note again, and I kept a tight hold on to my box to stop the sound hurting the vase.

TWELVE

I got back late that night. I was very tired and happy in a sad kind of way. The hall light was on and the flat was quiet. I took the box into the kitchen and unpacked it. I put the Portland on the table and sat in front of it for a while, watching it silently. I made some tea then, and ate a piece of cherry cake I found in a tin. Then I drank tea and watched the vase for some time. I didn't think about anything. I just looked. Then I put it away in the sitting room, and turned the bath on. While the bath was running I went back to the sitting room and looked at the Portland again. Then I had a bath slowly and nearly went to sleep in it. I took another look at the Portland before I went to bed.

As I got into bed my wife stirred and woke up. She switched the light on.

"Is that you, Charlie?" she asked faintly.

"No. It's Abe Sparta," I said.

"You're late," she said.

"Yes. It's been a long day."

"What did you do?" she asked, yawning.

"I sold a room. Then I didn't buy it. Then I did. Then I sold it again. Then I bought a green vase."

"Is that all?" she said. "It sounds very tiring."

I pressed down into the pillow. "No," I said, "it wasn't tiring. Just a little confusing."

"Is it a nice vase?"

"It's nice."

"Well, that's good then. I'm going back to sleep now. Goodnight."

"Goodnight," I said, kissing the back of her neck. "Oh yes," I remembered, "Abe Sparta says, of course you can put the big pram in the shed."

She sat up. "Now that is nice of him," she said. "Why didn't you tell me before?"

"I kept it as a surprise," I said.

I turned round to go to sleep, but I kept wanting to go back and look at the vase again.

About two o'clock, I got up. I put the vase in the middle of the table. Then I looked at one side for a while; then the other side. Then I walked round it from left to right; then I walked back again from right to left.

THE MENDELMAN FIRE

ONE

THE FIRST TIME I DID HIS ACCOUNTS FOR MORRIS MENDELMAN HE had a second-hand clothes shop in Cable Street. He was going out with Hettie at the time, Redhaired Hettie we called her, the daughter of Sam Finkin who had the grocery.

That time Mendelman wanted the accounts made up properly with debit and credit and balance carried forward and net profit, so that Finkin would think it was worth Hettie's while to go to the Roxy with Morris and half a pound of chocolates every Sunday night. I ruled the paper out specially in red ink while Mendelman watched.

"Put in a couple more columns," he told me. When it was finished it showed that Mendelman Clothes Co. was owed two hundred and eighty-three pounds by sundry debtors, owned assets valued at more than six hundred pounds, and there was forty-two pounds in cash into the bargain.

"Independent valuation," Mendelman told Finkin.

Finkin liked the balance sheet very much, and in seven months Mendelman and Hettie were married with a house in Dollis Hill and a walnut bedroom suite bought and paid for by Sam. The wedding reception was at Margulies Dining Rooms by Leman Street. I had a table with Mendelman's brother, the one with the shirt factory. We had a long talk about whether it was better to be a company, and he asked me to call on him. The smoked salmon was piled so thick on the plates, the Master Tailors' Union could have made sandwiches for a week.

At that time it was fashionable to be a company, and my prices for making a company out of anybody were the lowest quoted. Nearly everyone you met was a company director. My clients would tell one another how their companies were getting on. One year I had six companies in Sclaters Street alone, but most of them lapsed and I arranged the liquidations. It wasn't that my clients had anything against being companies. It was disagreement between the directors. "My co-director is nagging my life away," they used to tell me. "Ever since my wife became a director," the chairman of Alf's (Pickled Herrings) Ltd. told me, "she won't stay in the house; every day she comes to the shop and helps me. I can't stand it." The whilst I made a living. I could make a company for twelve pounds and liquidate it for five. The fees of Leo Botvinnik & Associates were the lowest ever.

On the other hand some of the companies I made did very well. Abrams & Berkoff Limited which became A & B (Girls-wear) was famous all over the country. United Metal Brokers, which I made for fifteen pounds including the name, would have been a great thing if Lippmann hadn't been silly about the income tax. And Mendelman Clothes Co. Ltd. proved a good thing too. Morris always kept with me; though I say it, he could never have got on otherwise. His ideas about bookkeeping were as clear as a plate of barley soup. When he started exporting to South Africa I used to send a clerk over to his warehouse every month. He was a good boy, that clerk, inter-B.Sc. mathematics, but even he said that for Mendelman's accounts you needed a slide rule which hadn't been invented yet.

But Mendelman was never worried. He did some fairly large deals in army surplus uniform trousers and overalls for the Kaffir trade, but he never knew whether he was doing well or not. For him the only deal which meant anything was the one he was doing now. "You still have fifty gross to sell, Morris," I would tell him. "But this is different," he would say; "there they are throwing at me; you want me to count like an old woman? Who counts?"

Morris was one of the first surplus men to sell by post. He started with a quantity of army jackknives in a boys' paper. He wrote the advert himself.

Look, Boys!!!
A real jackknife at last!!!

Combined tin-opener, screwdriver,
stone-remover, and three razor-sharp blades!
A shilling postal order brings you a pound jackknife!!!

There was a little drawing of a knife with blades sticking out in all directions. After the jackknives, he sold boots, denims, dubbin for football boots, handy metal boxes for bread or tools, stewards' drill jackets for light summer wear, and a special compass which fitted round the wrist and was suitable for scouts and guides. But mail-order was too slow for Morris. "You want me to spend my life opening envelopes with sixpenny postal orders in them like a post-office clerk?" he said, and left his cousin in charge of the mail department while he went to South Africa to start a Kaffir business.

When Morris Mendelman went to Africa, Hettie already had Rosa. A wonderful picture they made together, both with deep red hair and white skin like marble, and blue eyes. Rosa was a year old, and Hettie cried every night for a month before Morris left, and for another month afterwards. Morris told her he would send for the two of them in a few weeks, but Hettie thought Africa was a big jungle full of lions and tigers and that if Morris went there he would get torn to pieces before he sold a single garment.

"Hettie," Morris told her for the hundredth time, "South Africa is just like London only hotter. They got big cities with good Kosher restaurants, and everyone is so busy making money selling clothes to the Kaffirs that even if a lion and a tiger was to come they wouldn't even see them. Anyway, everybody carries a gun and if that lion shows his nose, straightaway it is like a firework show at the Crystal Palace, a thousand bullets shoot him dead and teach him a lesson. What you want Hettie, I should spend my life loafing about Whitechapel Road saying "Good shabbos, Mr. Pincus," while the world is passing me by like an old baigel woman?" But Hettie went on screaming and crying and going back to her mother three times a week with Rosa in her arms.

After he had booked his passage, Morris came to me. "Leo, make me an Africa company," he said. "You are the biggest company man in the world and for special business like this I must have a special company. I will write and tell you how I am getting on and you will make up some books, and Hettie and Rosa will come out for a nice holiday, and when we come back we will all be rich like Solly Joel and Barney Barnato and I will bring you a diamond as big as a fish ball for a present."

"But Morris," I told him, "who will look after the mail business, which is, after all, very good, and your only real money coming in? You are not Rothschild, Morris, you can't go to Africa and make a business straightaway. And to leave Hettie and your lovely baby."

"Leo," he answered, "make me a company. Mendelman is also somebody and I am doing it for Hettie and Rosa especially, Rosa shouldn't grow up like we did, worrying, worrying, with no joy for living. You want me to be ashamed in front of my daughter when she grows up and tells me, 'Daddy, why did you never send me to Cambridge college and let me learn to play piano and be a lady?' I couldn't stand it, Leo. Make me a company and good luck to everybody." So I made Mendelman Exports Co. (London) Ltd., and a few weeks later Morris left smiling, after kissing Rosa and Hettie a hundred thousand times and shaking his cousin's hand every time he said once more how well he would look after Hettie and Rosa.

What actually happened in Africa I didn't hear until many years afterwards. Morris wrote home every week telling Hettie he would send for her and Rosa soon, and what a wonderful country it was, and how well he was doing. He wrote to me a few times, telling me I should come out to a land where you didn't have to blow your nose all day long, and could I see his cousin and find out why the money he was asking for didn't come.

I never did like that cousin. He was a tall, broad man, very strong in the wrist, with a long, bony face all gray with small gray eyes and strong glasses, very quiet and religious, always wearing his hat when he ate, and walking everywhere, even ten miles, on the Sabbath day. Morris was a short, broad man, tending to fat even in those days, with bright brown eyes and his mouth always puckered up to laugh. He laughed until the tears came into his eyes, and with Morris you laughed too whether you liked it or not. The cousin never missed a synagogue service in his life, while Morris even on the Day of Atonement used to spend most of the time talking to someone outside about Charles Kingsley's *Hypatia.*

"What a marvelous book, you should read it. I learned English from this book." He had always a new book to be enthusiastic about. For a long time he told me every week to read Sir Humphrey Davy's *Salmonia.* "You read it and you think, all right, it's about how to catch salmon. But you're wrong. It is really about life. I will lend it to you, Leo." His favorite book was Wolff's *Bokhara,* although Wolff was a proselyte. He would quote too from *The Vicar of Wakefield* in a singsong—"When a lovely woman stoops to folly." But the cousin, although he was a very pious man and never read anything except Rashi's *Commentary* and the *Gems from the Talmud,* I could never like him.

I went to see him to ask why Morris hadn't received the money. He shook me by the hand and said I should sit down. He didn't pass the time of the day or ask me how things were. He said, "Morris is very rash. The mail-order business is not so good. We have large stocks. Everyone is selling mail order now. We are not getting many orders. Look." And he showed me the orders for the past few weeks. The business had dropped to a few postal orders for lines which were mostly out of stock.

I wrote and told Morris, although I couldn't understand why the business had fallen off so quickly. It wasn't until I was going through Mendelman's accounts for that year and noticed that a firm called Excelsior Products had been buying very heavily from Mendelman Clothes that I realized what had been happening.

"But you have been selling these things at a loss," I said to the cousin.

"What can I do?" he answered. "I have to keep going and we have no capital, only this enormous stock, and only Excelsior will buy. We have no mail orders to speak of. What can I do?"

I checked up on Excelsior Products Ltd. and the next day wrote to Morris to tell him that his cousin had been selling Mendelman stocks for practically nothing to his own independent company. I think the cousin was transferring the mail orders to Excelsior as well. He was a very pious man, but I never liked him. I asked him how he could do this to Morris and still pray without choking himself.

When Morris came back from Africa he was very brown and had lost weight so that his suit looked as if it was slipping off him. For weeks afterwards he and Hettie would sit and look at one another by the hour with eyes full of wonder. It was as if they had both been in the shadow of death, and had seen death itself looking into their eyes, which now were full to the brim with love to make them forget. They watched Rosa stumbling about and Morris would keep picking her up and kissing her, and then Hettie would cry and kiss him again and again. And there they would stand, kissing one another and crying together, with Rosa between them laughing.

Morris wasn't interested in business all that time, and when I tried to talk to him about his affairs he would look at me as if he didn't understand what I meant and say, "What difference does it make? You know I think Rosa will be very musical. Yesterday she sang 'Baa-baa black sheep' all through." It was no use talking for the time being. The cousin had left Mendelman's as soon as he heard I had sent Morris the money to come back. The Exports company was bankrupt in Africa, and Morris had left it just in time. As it was, he had lived the last months working as a potboy in a public house and sleeping on the floor behind the bar. "They gave me a wonderful free lunch on Saturdays," he told me. "Once a week I ate like a lord." But he didn't talk very much. "You should read a book called *With Buller in Natal*. It is very exciting," he said.

Then one day he walked into my office in the Clerkenwell Road. His sunburn was beginning to wear off but he was still tanned enough for his eyes to flash like diamonds. They were certainly the only diamonds he ever got out of Africa.

"That lousy, filthy, rotten, bleeding, stinking bastard my cousin, he should drop dead, he should take a cholera, he should rot. You know what he has been doing? He has been robbing Hettie and Rosa. That's what." He walked up and down the office.

"Did you just think of it, Morris?" I asked him. "Didn't I write to you in Africa, that land you remember where nobody blows a nose, and tell you about that bandit? He has stolen your business." He turned on me angrily.

"That I forgive. That I don't care. I can make another business. I will buy him and sell him a hundred times." Then he told me that he had just heard from Hettie how she had called at the office more than once for money and the cousin had told her there was none. She had borrowed from a friend, a few shillings to buy food.

"And that hyena, he would steal the business and not spare her a few shillings to buy bread." He wept hot tears of rage as he spoke. He screamed as if hot irons were tearing his flesh. He cursed and swore, and I sat there quietly until he had finished. What was there to say? He was full of hate and at the same time full of love. This way he left his hatred in my office and went back to Hettie with his love.

Within the year Mendelman's son Jacob, named for his dead father, was born. Mendelman was happy, although what with the worry and the fear and then, suddenly, so much love, like the sea running upon a small island of sand, Hettie was very weak.

It was a bad spring, that. Every week it suddenly broke into sunshine and the crocus bulbs in the graveyard we called Itchy Park began to peep through. Then a wind like a wet stone knife would cut through the air so that the sun fell away out of sight, and the paper in the gutters rattled like tin, and the crocuses were frozen stiff. A lot of people took the flu that spring. It was a special flu which left you in a couple of days if you were strong. But Hettie was weak, and it killed her. Then the baby pined for a day or two, taking no food, and one bitterly cold morning it stopped crying and Morris found it dead in the pink cot Hettie had bought, expecting another girl. May they find their place in peace.

TWO

All this was a long time ago, and besides, the past is finished. Better forget it and be done. Except no one ever forgets. It's a funny thing and you will perhaps laugh, but I think I could remember every company I made in those days when Morris was starting and I was a cut-price accountant. Although if you were to give me a thousand pounds, I couldn't tell the names of the firms I audit today. Of course, if suddenly the telephone rings and it is the income tax collector asking about this one or that one, what did they spend on advertising last year, I remember at once. But it doesn't mean the same thing. There is nothing for me to get excited about. I won't starve if I don't remember. Then it was different. Sometimes I had to collect five shillings advance fee from an old client. You might think that bad for business, except that everyone likes to own an accountant, more than a performing dog even. Also, believe me, they were saving money by employing Botvinnik & Associates.

You might have thought that after Hettie died Mendelman would have been finished, walking about like a man made of clay, not caring that there were stains on his jacket, not seeing anything except that face in which the eyes had gone like two hard-boiled eggs, not hearing anything except the whisper of a voice getting fainter every day. But no one can guess how trouble will take a man. The day after Hettie was buried he told me to put Mendelman Clothes into liquidation, and start forming Rosa Products. The creditors were paid off at six-and-eightpence, and Morris was left with five hundred gross of soiled raincoats, small sizes, on his hands. They had been bought in Hettie's name before he went to Africa, and the creditors couldn't touch them. He sold the house in Dollis Hill and moved into my flat. Rosa went to live with his sister who had no children of her own. He wouldn't have anything to do with the Finkins because they had told Hettie from the moment she married him that he was mad, and she should wait and see, he would finish up in the gutter.

The first business Rosa Products did was to sell by mail order five hundred gross of ladies' raincoats in bottle green, nigger brown, black, and bronze. Mendelman set about the new business like a man possessed by a dynamo. Rosa Products put out more adverts and handled more lines in the next twelve months than any three of Mendelman's competitors put together, including the cousin at Excelsior. Once that pig got the swill bucket all to himself and gorged himself, he found out that you needed brains to fill it again. He went on offering lines that Morris had brought in, but every time he added something new he lost a little more stolen capital. He would try to sell woolen underwear in the summer and cotton frocks in the winter, and no matter how hard you pray, that is bad salesmanship. Morris kept an eye on Excelsior and one day he told me to ring his cousin up and say I had a purchaser for it.

"Listen, Morris," I told him. "I don't want to buy even a gold sovereign from your cousin for half-a-crown."

"Phone him, Leo," he told me. We bought it for the price of the stock, our valuation. Morris made me buy it in my name, and then told me to offer his cousin five pounds a week to stay on as manager. He accepted, and the next month Morris went over to the Excelsior warehouse, while I phoned through to explain that Mendelman was the final purchaser.

Morris walked straight into the office and sacked his cousin that day. When I saw him later, he told me about it.

"His face was gray like stone when he saw me, and I thought how much better he would look dead than Hettie. With him, death would be natural. But she should only have lived." As a rule he never mentioned her name. I suppose he went with other women, but I don't think he cared whether they lived or died. With him, in his heart, it was only Hettie.

In the years that passed Mendelman worked often with Botvinnik & Associates. He made money, lost some of it, and made more. Then he took an order from some tin-pot South American government for thousands and thousands of bell-tents. At that time you couldn't give bell-tents away—they were all that old model, dark and only useful if you didn't want to breathe very much. How Morris arranged the deal, I don't know, but it made him. What did they do with all those tents, I wonder? The important thing is that Morris delivered them and was paid, and the money was good. Quite soon afterwards the government which bought the tents was liquidated, and the new government offered them back to Rosa Products for practically nothing. So Morris went over to South America to look into it, and when he came back he had sold the tents again to an American oil company. He also had orders in his pocket for the new government for a whole lot of other rubbish. After that if Mendelman walked down the street, he would pick up a five-pound note. Luck is like that. She has no time for the unlucky—but let her do you a favor once or twice, and she's got no time for anyone else. For Morris, for the time being, there was nothing she wouldn't do.

He bought his big house in Wimbledon in those days.

"I paid for it with rags. You want me to fill it with rags?" he said, when I suggested that perhaps he didn't need antique Chinese silk embroidery for the curtains. He made that house, a rambling high Victorian villa, into a palace. He put in a big library first of all. He had a dealer in Charing Cross Road buying first editions for him all the time. He read them all and whenever he came across another book he liked he phoned the dealer and told him to get a first edition.

"That dealer is no good," he told me one day when I was at the house looking at the books. "I read a book by Ovid the other day and he can't find me a first edition. Very good book. You must read it. I will lend you my copy." But as a matter of fact, Morris never lent anybody a book. Even when he was reading a book himself, he used to make a cover for it out of brown paper. He was very fond of books, but he spent a lot of money on other things too. He liked Chinese blue and white porcelain and had some large vases which I understood were worth a lot of money and extremely old, although they looked brand new to me and anyway too big for a sideboard. But such things never interested me. I am more a man for science. I believe that in our lifetime it will be possible for men to fly to the moon. I used to tell Morris that men will discover new worlds in space.

"Tell me," he would answer, "what will they find there? More trouble. More misery. More things to fight over. More madness. The more flesh, the more worms. Will they live for ever if they reach the moon? Will they eat more than three meals a day, sleep in ten beds, read more than one book at a time? Leave me alone with your space and new worlds." He was very reactionary in a lot of ways, and I told him so. "I am a progressive. I am a mathematician, a scientist. You are not progressive, Morris, I am sorry to have to say. Mankind must move forwards, always forwards."

"If you will excuse the expression," he answered, "kiss my arse. Mankind—what is mankind? I know a few men, a few women. But mankind—pardon me—is this something new? You made it up in your accounts, perhaps? You will make a limited company out of it? I don't see it. I don't feel it. I can't speak to it, love it, hate it, want it, not want it. It doesn't exist, your mankind, and your progress is a lot of horse-shit. There are always new ways of passing the time, but the time passes all the same. It is the same life, the same death, always, for ever. The more property, the more anxiety. We are men, for God's sake. Let us live men's lives. Not arithmetic." How can you talk sense to a hothead who has read too much and isn't properly educated into the bargain? We were friends, but except when we made up the books of Rosa Products, we never agreed about anything important.

All this time Mendelman's Rosa was growing up. She was fine, that Rosa, growing more like Hettie every time I saw her, but finer, with clear white hands and such a skin you could tell she had never washed dishes. She was away at some good school Morris read about somewhere, in the country, where they had an orchestra and kept horses, and important writers used to go and speak to them, although what they could have in common with a lot of children I don't know. I believe they did hardly any chemistry-with-physics at all at that school, although it was very expensive. In this way Rosa became a young lady. She was going to go to Cambridge, if you don't mind, with an allowance of five pounds a week. Five pounds a week, by my life—as much as we earned in a month at her age. She was studying music as Hettie had wanted, but in spite of all that expense, she couldn't even play the piano too well.

"Either I am mad," I said to Morris one day, "or something is wrong. Rosa tells me that *Madame Butterfly* is no good, and she can't even play the 'One Minute Waltz' well on the piano. What then does she study at Cambridge?"

"My dear Leo," Morris explained to me, "you are out of date. Today it is all different. You listen to a tune and you think, ah, a pretty tune. But today they are not interested."

"So what do they want?" I asked him. "Suddenly a bad tune is good?"

But Morris didn't worry what Rosa was learning, so long as she had the chance to learn whatever there was being taught.

"Let her live," he said. "That is the only thing." So she became more and more educated, first coming to London to go to the Academy, and then running about abroad all over the place, Paris, Berlin, Madrid—so far you must go to hear music, the Albert Hall is not good enough.

Morris sometimes asked me to dinner when Rosa was home. He had a French cook-housekeeper at Wimbledon, with degrees, if you please, for cooking. She had a blue ribbon, two diplomas, another light-blue ribbon and a silver medal. "Such a good cook doesn't grow on trees, you know, Leo," he said. It's all very well, I told him. With so many ribbons she can dress her hair, but what sort of a stuffed neck can she make? But as a matter of fact, she was a good plain cook as well, and her stuffed neck was excellent. Her fish balls were very fine too, although my mother was also a great cook without having any ribbons. However, dinners at Morris's home were good, and when Rosa was home it was a banquet, nothing less.

After dinner Morris always asked Rosa to play for us. For some reason she was never very keen, and it wasn't the piano, because Paderewski never had a finer one. She played to us in the end, but to begin with you could tell her heart wasn't in it. Then Morris would go over to her at the piano and speak to her.

"You know, Rosa," he would say, "I am a pretty ignorant man. I don't know very much. But I know always whatever is in my heart, and if I haven't got a good understanding I can always say what I feel inside me. Sometimes what I feel is gone in a minute and other people say, 'That Mendelman. He is not genuine.' But when I am feeling it, it is true. If you don't feel any music, don't play it. Tomorrow you will again, and then you'll play marvelously. But now— what does it matter? Tomorrow is also a day and the piano won't walk and your fingers will be as quick, and your heart full of the music, and so you will play."

Other times Rosa smiled at him and laughed at me and said, "What shall I play you, Leo—'Softly Awakes My Heart'?"—because she knew that was always a favorite of ours. Then she was more like Morris' daughter. But those other times tears came into her eyes and she would say good night and go to bed. What was the use of pretending? She was different from Morris and her world was never ours. I knew it and Morris knew it, and Rosa worried about it and felt strange when she came back to us. But it was nothing to be sad about. This, I have always seen, is the way with children. They are suddenly grownups, strangers. You go to embrace them and they tell you, good morning, we haven't been introduced.

I am not a father myself, but I can imagine what it must feel like to see a fine girl grow up and think "She is my daughter and a flower among women." I can imagine how it would be to have a son and know that your name will go on being spoken in the world—have bad things said about it perhaps, but be mentioned by some with pride. Maybe to have one of your name do something great for mankind, something for which everyone will be grateful always. Botvinnik will be dead. His clients will go to other good firms, and if two of them meet they will say perhaps, "Pity Botvinnik left no one to carry on. You know what we used to call him—the Demon Accountant from Jubilee Street. But he is dead, old humpty-back Botvinnik. Is that why he never married?" And it will be true, for I would rather my hump remained a joke with my clients. It is not a present for a woman I love. But this is neither here nor there, except to tell you that I know how Mendelman loved his Rosa and I was sad to see her grow up so strange to him, although like him I was proud to see her so fine and well-educated.

And now I must come to the point where this story really begins. Now that you know about Mendelman, and something about his family and his business, I must tell you how he came to me one day to tell me that he had once again lost his fortune. Only this time he would not make it again. For he was going to die.

THREE

In 1930 the whole world noticed that there was a depression because a lot of very big people went broke and jumped out of office windows and shot themselves. Also nearly everyone was waiting for dole at the labor exchange, and business in the East End was completely credit. The explanation of depression is very simple. It is when the creditors who are giving credit suddenly turn round and find there is nothing to eat in the house. So they run over to their debtors to get a little on account. Except that they can't because the debtors finished their credit for last Friday night supper. Then everyone is depressed, and that is depression.

But all this started before the big people shot themselves in 1930. Already in 1926 and 1927 a lot of small businesses found there was nobody to sell anything to. And in August 1928 when Morris came to tell me he had lost his fortune, a lot of people were already scraping together enough pennies to buy a small pistol. Although in spite of that, I give it as my considered opinion that Morris had behaved very rashly. He should have taken more care than he did. But he could never be bothered with facts and figures. He thought that if you went broke it was because you had lost your nerve or your flair. You could talk to him about world trade cycles until you were blue in the face, he only laughed and told you the important thing was to live.

Rosa Products had long ceased to be just another small import-export business. Mendelman had become a manufacturer—one time it was novelties he made, then it was children's bicycles. Ever since he had been to Africa, and in spite of what happened to him there, he took every excuse to travel. On his travels he had picked up a contract to supply some special part for a sewing-machine company in France. It was only a small part, but it took a whole factory to make it. Mendelman took the contract for supplying the French firm, and it was going to be very big business indeed. He turned his entire capital over to it, put every penny he had into the new tools and machines. The factory was beginning to get its first order ready when the French company suddenly fell to pieces. There were trials afterwards and two or three went to prison, but a lot of people lost their money all the same. And Morris came to see me one hot afternoon in August 1928, months before the papers had it in headlines, to tell me his contract was worth nothing. He had thousands of sewing-machine parts which would fit no other sewing-machine in the world. Rosa Products was bankrupt. And he was going to die into the bargain.

That he was broke I could understand. It was serious, but from time to time you had to expect it. Also Morris was used to it, and had managed before, even in worse circumstances. But that he was going to die—that was serious. Except it was impossible. Mendelman, a strong, healthy man not yet sixty, why should he die? I told him he was simply worried, he would be all right again as he was all right before. Anyone can go broke, and besides, the house and furniture were in Rosa's name. We still had two small companies with assets which couldn't be touched. He would start again, that was all. What was all this talk about dying?

He let me talk and then he sat down and wiped his forehead carefully. The air in the office was thick and heavy. You took it down into your lungs but it was no more use than the air you already had down there. The heat hung on your skin like a blanket, and it tasted stale, like the air of a bedroom with no windows.

"Look, Leo," Mendelman said at last. "You are my friend, my old friend of many years. You know me, you knew Hettie, you know Rosa, you have watched her grow up. I am not making a joke. I will be dead before this time next year." He laughed. "Perhaps this will prove it to you," he said. "I just paid a heart specialist five guineas to tell me. And other doctors have told me the same for less money." I asked him if they could be mistaken. Even a specialist could make a mistake.

"Leo," he said, "this is not mathematics. This is an old worn-out heart that is no good to anyone. If it was a car engine you would throw it away. It is finished."

"But die—why die?" I asked, and I could feel there was no blood in my face, and I thought as I spoke that if you love a man this is how you feel. "Surely with modern medicine they can keep you alive —you can retire—lead an easier life. You will live for years more. Why die?"

"Leo, my friend," he said, "a man dies when he has to—not when he wants to. I will do my best to live, I assure you. But I think they are right, and that I will die no matter how hard I try not to."

What could I do? I am not an emotional man, but this was a great shock to my system and I couldn't speak because tears choked me whenever I opened my mouth. I just opened my mouth three or four times without anything coming out.

So I sat quiet and listened to the most dishonest proposition which has ever been put to me in my life.

"I want you, Leo, my friend," said Mendelman, "to listen to me till I finish—whatever I say, listen. Sit quietly there, light a cigarette. Maybe when I finish speaking I will drop dead. The heat when I go into the street will be too much. I will die in the Underground. So listen. Maybe I am already a man speaking from the grave. This is what I have to say.

"We are friends, Leo, for thirty years. We were boys together, running after the girls, having big ideas, working, hoping, dream-

ing. If one man ever can know another man, you know me—I know
you. Good. All this is very good. Good things have happened. Bad
things as well . . . although sometimes the good things turn out
not so good, and the bad things could have been worse. What does it
all mean? I don't know. Why? Because one minute it means one
thing, and the next minute something different. This is what life
is, and for this kind of monkey-business there is no accountant. At
the end it is neither profit nor loss. At the close of business there is
nothing—no more bargains, no more arguments, no more presents
for everybody, no more baked *kishka* to eat, no more lemon tea, no
books, no kisses. In a word, nothing. That's why a man must care
about life and living things. Most of all, he must love the life he has
made. That life is not what I have been and done. It is my child."

Mendelman paused and lit a cigarette from his case. He smoked
the old Russian ones in yellow paper, and he held the match between his brown fingers for a few seconds while it burned, drawing on the cigarette in the exact center of his lips, and looking at me
with pursed-up eyes. It was his last speech maybe, and Morris was
always a speechmaker. He was going to make it good. Already I was
forgetting everything else and getting ready to enjoy a real Mendelman speech, for he was a great talker, especially when you remember he was not even properly educated. When I was at Toyn-
bee Hall studying, he was already selling clothes. But how he could
talk, that Mendelman! He drew another deep breath through his
cigarette, and blew the smoke out in a long, thin cloud. Then he
spoke, underlying the points with the index finger of his left hand.

"Why do you think that everyone smiles when they look at a
child? Is a baby funny? Does he say something to make you laugh?
You smile at a baby because in your heart you are saying, this baby
will live when I am dead. My life will be in his life, a little bit, whoever he is, whatever he becomes. And you smile because you are
happy that life will go on. And with your own child, how much more
true is this? The man who does not love his children is dead and
has never lived, and they too will never live, and without love the
whole world dies. The only men who should be punished are those

who do not love. And already they are punished, for not to love is to tear your heart and your liver to shreds, like a wild dog in your stomach, terribly painful. Such men die screaming for another life, another chance. It is for them a heaven must be made, so that they leave a real hell behind them and pass into a world in which there is no more pain, no wild dogs.

"But I love my child, and so when I die I will not even notice it. I will not be thinking about it, only about living things, my things which still live on and on, always, somehow. Yet although they will always live somehow, a father must try to give his children every chance. He must help them, even if he is dead, to get on with the main business—to make living good, better than his life, so that the life of their children may be better again, and so better and better until from the first moment until the last, life is a joy and, as my father (may he rest in peace) used to say, a pleasure to God.

"Now Leo, you and I know that this needs money. This is the meaning of money, to smooth the way, so that a man's life is not wasted in always worrying, no time to read a book, to talk to friends. Who wants such a life? But how can there be a better life for men if they are poor? Poverty is hateful and terrible. We have known it before—no fire to keep us warm, no food but thin cabbage soup, no laughter in the house, only the endless nagging of tired women and the anger of defeated men. Against that existence I have made money, and given my child whatever she could be given, even you say something, too much. She will think nothing of money, you say. She will not care that it must be worked for. Good. She will be better for that. Rosa will have time to find out about better things, time to run after great ideas. Maybe she will catch them. Who knows? And if not, at least she would have tried, and this must be good. As for making a living—if he has to, any man will find a way to do that. And he will find a better way if he knows only about the best things. This anyway, is what I have always thought." Mendelman paused again, looking sad for a moment, and then laughed. "But," he said, "such a kettle of fish is life that now, all of a sudden, not only am I going to die, but I am going to be bankrupt as well."

He laughed again as if he enjoyed the idea, and perhaps he did, because Morris could talk himself into anything. The trouble with a good salesman is that when he is selling something he thinks it is the best thing in the world. Mendelman was the finest salesman I ever knew. Whatever it was, he could sell it. You took it home and opened it up thinking it was a new life in a brown paper parcel he had sold you, and when you found it was only a couple of khaki shirts, you thought, Well, even if it isn't a new life a couple of shirts is always handy, I could even make a profit on them. And you wanted Mendelman to sell you things again—always a new world going reasonable, always something you could use. This is what makes a good salesman. He must want to give you something which he thinks will do you good. The money you give him is just what he needs to go on living, to go on buying, to go on selling something to you for your own good. The bad salesman is the man who doesn't care, so long as he gets your money. And what good is he? Will you buy from him again? Let him drop dead, you will walk over his body, the jackal.

"Yes, Leo," Mendelman continued, "this is certainly the end of the business. Not only one end. Both." He smiled, and then suddenly the smile was gone. "But do you think I will do this to Rosa?" he asked. "You want me to die and let her think her father a fool and a failure? You want her to remember me from the depths of misery? Even if I was dead, my heart would burn. No, Leo, I can't do it, not even for you, my oldest friend. Not for the world."

He crashed his fist down on my desk so that the inkwell jumped, and I replied a little startled, "All right, Morris, all right, I wouldn't dream of asking you to do such a thing. You think I'm inhuman?" But still he glared at me as if I wasn't his friend.

"No, Leo," he said at last, "I have a plan."

It was always Mendelman's way. He talked to you about life. He frightened you a little bit, he made you cry maybe, he shouted at you. And then, at last, he had a plan. It was always his way. And there are, I think, worse ways of doing business.

FOUR

This was Mendelman's plan.

Rosa Products would have to go into liquidation when the French sewing-machine company folded up publicly. The assets of Rosa's were its machines, useless for anything except the one special job, its stock of sewing-machine parts, office furniture and so on and so forth. The lease of the factory premises of course, but in 1929 who was starting factories? The whole lot was worth nothing but its breaking-up price. The factory could stand there with a big sign up saying *For Sale,* and fall to pieces waiting for a buyer.

But it would take a couple of months before the French company was finished. And maybe a couple of months more before Mendelman's firm need go into liquidation.

Now supposing, only supposing with these new machines and electric dynamos and so forth, there was to be a fire at Rosa Products, and the whole lot went up in smoke. What would it be worth then? Fifteen thousand pounds fire insurance.

"But Morris," I told him, "that money would belong to the company when it was liquidated, would be used to pay off the creditors. And anyhow, a fire would be nice, but what can you do? Pray for lightning to strike?"

Of course, Morris agreed; the money was the company's. But at the same time, wasn't he the company, and couldn't he draw the money before publicly liquidating the business?

"Morris," I told him, "you are being silly. They would get that money back from you if they had to take it out of your pocket with torture, murder and assassination. What is all this nonsense? You, an experienced business man. I'm surprised."

"Of course," he agreed. "Only I wouldn't have the money. Rosa would have it."

"Now you are even more ridiculous," I told him. I was beginning to be angry at all this nonsense. "They would get it from Rosa too.

They should worry if your child starves. They want their money and they will get it."

"They won't get it, Leo," he answered. "It will be legally Rosa's money. No one will touch it. Listen again."

And he described an even more terrible plan. Professionally speaking, I have never heard such a shocking suggestion in my life. Listen to this and blush.

Mendelman was going to write a whole lot of letters to everyone he knew, all people who knew Rosa. In the letters he was going to say that Rosa was a woman of low morals, a loose-liver, no better than a harlot. It was terrible. And Morris was laughing as if he was at the Palladium, and by some chance hadn't heard the joke before.

Then we would arrange, he said, with our old friend Weiss the solicitor for Rosa to sue Mendelman for libel and defamation of character. And Mendelman would settle out of court for fifteen thousand pounds. He would pay it in cash, and then, no matter what anyone could say or do, Rosa would be provided for.

"Could it be more legal than that? Can you say it isn't a good idea?" Mendelman asked, slapping my shoulder.

"Not only is it a brilliant idea," I told him, "it is completely *meshuggah*. You are mad as a hatter. You had better lie down. I have got a headache myself." But I knew Mendelman was serious, and all I could hope was that he didn't want me to start the fire for him. In my profession, after all, there are certain ethics.

I was like the little man in the old story. Two big men are having an argument in the middle of the street. The little man stands between them. They become violent. One shouts. The other shouts. They raise their hands against one another. They scream at one another. All the time the little man looks from one terrible face to the other terrible face, his eyes getting bigger and bigger. Suddenly he can't stand it any more. "Leave me alone for God's sake!" he shouts. "Haven't I got troubles of my own?"

I wanted Mendelman to leave me alone. But I knew he wouldn't, although, thank God, he didn't want me to do anything except go and see Rosa and explain the arrangement to her. "You mean to say," I said, "you can bear to write such terrible things about your own lovely child? It is a monstrous thing to do."

"You are not an artist, my Leo," he said. "I am not saying anything about my child. I am making a drama, a story, and in this story there is an old dying man called Mendelman and he happens to have a daughter called Rosa. That is all. You are only upset because it is such a good story you think it is true when you hear it. That is how a story should sound. But it has nothing to do with life. It is not my Rosa I am talking about. I am making a business arrangement, that's all."

That night what with the worry of Mendelman and the heat of a long day, my hump was like an aching furnace. I always sleep on my left side with one pillow under my head and a larger pillow under my shoulder to stop me turning onto my back in my sleep. Years ago I worked this out as the best way, and always it has been good, and I have slept as well as you might yourself. But this night I twisted and turned, pushing the pillow about. The hump was so hot I couldn't breathe from the heat in the bed. My head was full of figures turning round and round very fast, and I was trying to stop them so as to add properly. But they wouldn't, so I got up to make a cup of tea.

While I waited for the kettle to boil, the figures in my head still turned round, but slowly this time. When I added them up they came to precisely fifteen thousand. That Mendelman, how often had I worried about his figures? How often had I woken up and straightaway thought, "Mendelman's books today." And yet, what else did I have to do? I poured myself a cup of tea sitting at the table, my dressing-gown round my shoulders and over my back. It didn't ache so much now, but it was still hot, so I let the dressing-gown slip onto the floor.

I drank tea and thought that a man is born from an accident maybe. A young couple, hot and clammy in the darkness, their eyes half-closed with wanting one another, their breath heavy and quick, their hands groping in the night for something certain. What do they know about life? What do they care? They want one another, they want to make love and then sleep quietly. They get up in the morning and the woman is thinking that she must make breakfast and clear up and do the shopping. The man is thinking he must hurry to the office and will Rosenberg ring today and yes he will take the lot at ten per cent less. Yet though they hardly look at one another, though they do not know it, they have carried another life into being. Quietly, quietly, life is beginning again, knowing nothing of them as they know nothing of it. And so she goes shopping and he goes to wait for Rosenberg to ring. And later on a man is born.

What gives it meaning? Maybe this little man is a messiah the world waits for. He may be the inventor of a different kind of internal combustion machine, using air as fuel, making mankind rich and happy. He may develop a new language for all men, invent a perfect accounting system, be the first man to step on Mars, discover a drug to end evil. Or he may be just another man who waits for Rosenberg to ring, and sometimes in the night gropes, hot and breathless, for another human body in the darkness. How should we know what it means?

In all the years I knew Mendelman I learned enough about him to know that he was a groper—a man born to make one try after another, make a company, lose a company, sell something, buy something, on and on. A man made to go on trying and to have children. He was a mistake, but that was what he had to do. I was a mistake, perhaps a mistake my mother never enjoyed, one she never wanted to make. I don't want to know. Mendelman's children, somebody else's children, what did it matter? I was glad that one of them was so close to me, become like my own. I was going to do something for Rosa, for her good and no other reason.

Gradually I began to feel very pleased with myself; my head stopped going round, and my hump stopped aching. When I went back to bed, I put the pillows right and lay down: I fell asleep at once and had no dreams.

FIVE

I was going to see Rosa. She was living in a hotel in Paris. Imagine.
Leo Botvinnik in Paris.

I didn't like the idea of going at first, but when I got used to it I
felt quite excited. From all accounts Paris was a fine city. Mendelman told me it was very nice, everybody sitting in cafés all day drinking sweet wines and talking, with very lovely buildings and a lot of
monuments and statues, and the wonderful smell in the streets of
beautiful women with perfume and delicious food cooking everywhere. "You will come back with a wife, I think, Leo," he said.
"Those French women are very fine girls. Be careful." He teased
me as if I was a schoolboy, and me two years older than him.

My chief clerk arranged all the papers, and the ticket, and wrote
down the trains in a notebook, with Rosa's address.

"How will I speak to everyone, Morris?" I asked.

"I have been all over the world," he replied, "and even if you
can't speak the language you can always make yourself understood
so long as you know what you want. Don't be a baby, Leo, a grown
man like you. Also, you could get a small book and learn French. It
would be useful to you. There are very fine books by Frenchmen.
Candide is very funny, and *Penguin Island* is also good. You must
always be willing to learn, so don't make difficulties. Just go and tell
Rosa what is to be done." So I went.

I was sick twice on the boat. The second time it was terrible. I
wanted to die. I was having a nice conversation with a traveler, a
man with a goiter, very intelligent, in the bar, and drinking a brandy
to settle my stomach. We were talking about whether there was human life on any of the other planets, and I was explaining that on
Venus men would have to live on ammonia gas instead of air, while
on Mars there was very little oxygen in the atmosphere. Then I
felt my face go white and I said excuse me and rushed down to the
gentlemen's lavatory, and got there just in time.

When at last the sea stopped throwing me up and down like a rubber ball and the boat was coming into port, I could hardly wait to get out onto dry land. How do sailors live in such conditions? Up and down, up and down. The sea is for fish, although steam is a great invention and no doubt ships were even worse before the gyroscopic balance was invented. They are still terrible.

It was no trouble on the train. They took my briefcase away and wrote in chalk on it and gave it back to me. The train was standing right there waiting, so good is the service. I found my seat, looked out of the window for a while and then fell asleep. When I woke up I was very hungry, but it was nearly Paris so I waited. I was going to spend the night at a hotel Morris knew. In the morning I would go by taxi to Rosa's hotel and speak to her. Rosa didn't know I was coming, but early in the morning I would be sure to find her in. After I had explained things to her I would catch a train, and come back—God help me—on the boat at night. But maybe if I slept it wouldn't make me ill again. This time I had a little cabin booked. I saw one coming over, very nice and comfortable. I would take three aspirins and drink a couple glasses of brandy very quick and sleep through it, please God.

The Paris station is very like Liverpool Street, except everything is different and in French. Even the lavatories have *Hommes* and *Femmes* on them. I learned a little bit of French studying the advertisement posters which are brighter than in London. You know what the French for motor-car tire is? *Pneu.* I looked it up in my book. *Pneu.* You could never guess it in a million years.

I got a taxi and said, "Bitte, hôtel ici," and showed the driver the name Morris wrote down for me. He understood after a while, and drove me there. If I spent a few months in Paris, with my mathematical training and interest in scientific things, and a language is after all a kind of science, I would pick up French very quickly.

At the Hôtel Weinberg it was easy. Even the porter spoke Yiddish —with a foreign accent but at least you could understand it. I met Mr. Weinberg the proprietor, who asked me how terrible business was in London. He showed me to a room on the first floor with a double bed, very comfortable, and said I could have dinner just when I wanted it. I might have been in my own home, except, of course, outside everything was French, the cars, the clothes. As a matter of fact, I did notice that the French ladies looked very attractive and smart.

I had dinner with Mr. and Mrs. Weinberg at their own table, but I didn't talk very much with the lady as she couldn't speak the mother language. But Mr. Weinberg asked a few questions for her. It seemed she was very fond of Mendelman, who she said was very spirited and full of charm—like she was talking about a dancer at the Russian ballet. Dinner was chicken soup with *creplach,* very delicious, some good *hamsche* fish, and roast veal, and then suddenly *tzimmis* and little golden potatoes and lettuces with vinegar and oil, all a bit different from home. But I followed the Weinbergs, eating everything separately with the same knife and fork, like a real Frenchman. Mrs. Weinberg, a lady about forty-five, buxom with bright eyes and a pretty mouth, taught me a few French words, like thank you and please. Afterwards I played *club yoss* with Weinberg until late, winning two hundred francs. I drank a glass of wine with my dinner and another glass afterwards. When I went up to bed, people were still walking up and down the street. Those Frenchmen don't care about sleeping.

In the morning some rolls and butter and coffee were brought to the door. I shouted out they should leave them there, then put on my dressing-gown, unlocked the door, and brought the tray in. After breakfast, Mr. Weinberg called me a taxi and told the driver where to take me. In no time at all, I was going to see Rosa.

But now, after it had all been going so smoothly except for the boat, it suddenly became difficult. At the hotel they didn't understand what I was talking about. I wrote down Rosa's name on a piece of paper and pointed to it and said "Où est la?" and they said she had left two weeks before to go to another hotel. They wrote the name down for me and talked a lot with the cab driver who was a boy Weinberg had told to look after me. They talked loudly, and

I thought, hello, it's going to be trouble, but it blew over and Moishe the driver said he would explain to me on the way over to another hotel.

It appeared that Rosa had stayed at this hotel for a long time, but that now she had a flat.

"Very nice," I said to Moishe.

"Who knows?" he answered, driving fast. He nearly knocked people over three or four times, he didn't stop for lights or sign what he was going to do—a real Frenchman. I was glad when the drive was over, I can tell you. On the way we passed what must have been the biggest fountain in the world, making even Trafalgar Square look small.

At the address we found a note saying in French that Rosa was having breakfast round the corner. How could she know I was coming? And why leave me a note in French? It was very mysterious.

We drove round, and I got out of the car. The sunshine was very bright now, and I blinked for a while looking up and down the tables on the pavement outside the café. Then I saw the sun on her red hair shining like copper. I called out to her, "Rosa, Rosa, look who has come all this way to see you!" She looked up at once.

"Uncle Leo!" she cried. "What are you doing here?" She stood on the pavement in the sun, her skin very white, in a pretty green dress, looking so beautiful that I was very proud everyone should hear her call me uncle, even if they didn't understand English. She was with a man, but I didn't notice him until she bent over for me to kiss her cheek which now was pink with a blush. Then I sat down and we asked one another questions for a while. How was her father? What a long time it had been! What was she studying now? And so on and so forth as people do when they are a bit uncomfortable. At last I got to the point.

"Rosa," I said, "I must speak to you very seriously, and alone, if this gentleman can be left for a while. Perhaps it would be best to go back to your flat." She spoke in French as good as a native to the man, who stood up and bowed when we left. In the car I remarked:

"A very nice young man. Nicely brought-up. You can tell without speaking to him." But she didn't answer. Maybe she thought it was none of my business, and of course she was right.

The flat was high up in a narrow house, and when I got my breath back from climbing about a hundred thousand stairs, I carefully explained what had to be done, and laughed as I showed her the draft letter Mendelman intended to send around. "My daughter Rosa has broken my heart. She is no better than a whore, though it kills me to say it. God forgive her." While I laughed like a jackass to make her feel at ease, poor Rosa turned very pale. Then she cried as if her heart would break, while I still sat there like an idiot telling her again and again that her father didn't mean it—it was only a techncality so that he could provide for her. I hadn't told her yet that Mendelman was, without technicalities, going to die. She went on sobbing, her whole body heaved as if breaking in pieces.

"Rosa," I said at last—for there was no other way—"Rosa. Your father is dying. Soon he will be dead. He wants only to help you. Try to understand and help him so that he may die happy. You are clever, you know how things are in this life. Try to help. Be sensible."

Then, like a woman, when I gave her something to cry about, she stopped crying and stared at me with red eyes out of a gray face.

"Tell me," she asked quietly, "what is wrong with him? What can be done for him? Something must be done for him. I must go home." She stood up as if to go home at once.

I was sitting in a low armchair and what with my hump and my belly it takes me longer to get up than most people. Rosa stood with a window behind her, her figure like a silhouette. She had always been a slim girl, but now she had lost her figure a little. Suddenly I knew why she wept. I cursed myself and Mendelman's schemes together.

"Rosa," I said quietly. "Rosa. I think you are going to have a baby. Is this so?" She turned her face towards me and nodded, her lips pursed up tight.

"But I love him, Uncle Leo," she cried. "I love him so much. I am glad to have his child. It is right for me. Only how could father say such things? Could he know? Tell me, Uncle Leo, do you think he knows, and that's why his heart is weak?"

Of course not, I told her, he isn't a magician. It was just his luck he happened to think of such a thing, such a ridiculous scheme, which he would never have thought of if he hadn't been sure it was impossible. Furthermore, what was there to cry about? All right, the baby was started a little early, but that can happen as well. She could get married and then everything would be fine.

It is my luck to say the wrong thing in such circumstances. I should be a diplomat, so carefully I put everything. Anyone else would have known that she was crying not because she was pregnant—sooner or later most women expect that. She was crying because the man— that man she was having breakfast with—was already married.

"But he loves me," she said. "We would marry if we could. But his wife is a terrible woman. She hates his work—he is a wonderful composer, Uncle Leo, really wonderful—she hates me. She hounded me out of my hotel. She hates every decent, wonderful thing, everything that makes him happy she hates." And in the same vein for a few minutes.

It was for this man that she stayed in Paris. Her work? She didn't care about her own work. She only wanted to help him, to do what she could for his genius, help him as a wife helps a husband, as a woman helps a man and an artist.

It was a whole performance, I can tell you. You wouldn't have thought a Cambridge girl could be like that. Which only goes to show that education is a waste on a woman. As soon as they fall in love with a man, it all goes to hell. But it wasn't for me to tell her how to live. What do I know anyway? Maybe he was a genius. Maybe it was right for her to have his child. Maybe they would get married. Although when he got married before wasn't it the same thing, all this love and forever business then as well? But this is the sort of thing you must never say to a woman. This time it is always different. Thank God, I remembered and didn't argue with her.

But so far as Rosa was concerned, Mendelman's plan was a wash-out. Now all I had to do was to go back and tell him about Rosa, and—God forbid—he would have heart failure on the spot. What was I supposed to do—The devil take me for a certified lunatic to start with Morris in the first place. It was a mad idea from the start, and now I would go mad as well, not being able to tell Morris why it couldn't be done this way, and having to find some other way of making sure Rosa's bastard had a good schooling. Excuse me putting it this way, but I was very upset.

Anyhow, we went back to the café where Rosa's friend was still sitting looking very sad. When he saw that Rosa had been crying he turned on me with an angry face, and said something very quickly to Rosa. She answered him, and with a lot of hums and haws he said to me, "This is a terrible thing. Her father is to die?" So she at least had enough sense not to tell him about Mendelman's plan.

We had lunch together. They were, I could see, very much in love. When their eyes met he grew more handsome and she looked more beautiful. They loved one another all right, and so, I suppose, it was certain that they would have a baby sooner or later. Although you would think that with a Cambridge education it might be different. But no, women are alike in that. As a matter of fact, no one has ever mentioned it, but I am sure Hettie herself, even with her strict background, I think even Hettie was a little bit pregnant when she married Mendelman.

I don't know what you do when you have to think something out carefully. Some people eat a big dinner and go to sleep as if they could dream up an answer. Some pull their noses and play chess, some go for a long walk as far as Finsbury Park perhaps. I knew a man who used to read algebra whenever there was anything on his mind. For my part I walk round the room whistling. I don't think about what I am whistling, but if I should happen to notice, a hundred to one it will be an aria, and this isn't surprising because I am particularly fond of grand opera. I was finishing my coffee in this little restaurant we went to for lunch, a nice little place not unlike Soho, and Rosa was talking to Albert, as his name turned out to be, only with the "t" not pronounced, when suddenly I noticed that I was singing under my breath, "All the Flowers Awaken."

"Did you say something, Uncle Leo?" Rosa asked. I cleared my throat and spoke to the two of them, chattering there like a couple of sparrows with nothing to worry about except which direction the cat was coming from.

"I think the time has come, Rosa and Albert"—and I said it with the "t" because this was no occasion for flighty nonsense—"the time has come for us to consider what is to be done. What are we going to do?" I repeated, to bring home the point.

Rosa looked as if she was going to cry again, and Albert looked down his nose as if he would rather make jokes with Rosa. But it was no good. All that nonsense there is a time and place for. And there is a time for action as well. I was going to bang my fist on the table, but I thought it would draw too much attention, and it was a small table anyway. I went straight into a consideration of our problems.

"The point is this," I said. "This is the point. You, Albert, have to get a divorce at once, and then you have to come home with Rosa and get married." To hell with it, I thought, and I really did bang my fist on the table. All the plates shook, and everyone looked round at us, and Rosa's eyes were like saucers, but I didn't care. There is a time for action. This was it.

A pity I am so quick to suggest what is good for people. You should have heard the talk, the tears, the argument this way and that. The while I know it will be Botvinnik, chartered accountant and man of action, who will have to see Albert's wife and come to suitable arrangements.

And that was how it turned out. Albert took Rosa off to kiss her better, because though kissing causes the trouble in the first place, people still go on believing that it can also make everything well again. And I am left, I can't say carrying the baby, but anyhow with another slip of paper with the name Mme Jocaste Barré, rue Lepin 16. All I have to do is find the address, speak to this woman and tell her she should give Albert a divorce at once, because our Rosa wants him. How could she refuse? Such a reasonable request, it happens every day and Rosa being such a nice girl, what wife would object?

I could kick myself, such a complete fool I am for getting into places where I have no business, such a busybody I am, such a big-head. My father—God rest his soul—used to tell me, "Every man has his own proper measure of trouble; but you will have a little bit more, because everyone else will kindly give you a piece of theirs, such a nice fellow you are." He was right except that I am not such a nice disposition, only I get bored because everyone else is worried and I am getting on with my work, and life is very dull if there isn't something to worry about. But believe me, you don't have to encourage people to part with trouble. You hardly know them before they are crying and asking your advice and the next thing you know you are driving out to see their wives to ask them for a divorce, Rosa would like their husbands.

Moishe drove me out to this rue Lepin in the afternoon. His business must go to hell because he hung about waiting for me all day long, and twice I saw him refuse to take a fare, smoking cigarettes and reading a sports paper. When we went to lunch I thought he would go, but he was outside waiting for me. He said when I came out of the restaurant with Albert and Rosa, "So, what now?"

I would like to have been able to tell him.

SIX

That Albert, he had certainly worked his way up from nothing. Here he was, engaged, in a manner of speaking, to our beautiful Rosa. And here I was, trying to talk business to his wife, who was absolutely no class at all, except such a low class I wouldn't like to be seen with, although in the way of business it goes without saying there is no class distinction.

To such a woman as this, Albert (with or without the "t") was tied—with a great bush of black hair, greasy, knotted, wearing trousers (not a garment for a nice sort of girl) and gypsy earrings, not at all inappropriate because she had these dark features like Carmen, and was so nervous, smoking the whole time, I expected her to start dancing the habañero any minute.

It turns out, in spite of looking so foreign, Albert's wife is English, from a very nice family in Croydon. She comes to Paris, she tells me, to learn the painting business. What with girls coming to Paris to learn music, and painting, I am surprised there are still girls left in England. What is more, I don't care what you say, all this Boheme business is very nice in the opera, but it's a different matter when it happens in your own home. Still, let Jocaste's father send his accountant to Paris to get her out of trouble. I have enough problems with our own Rosa.

I didn't mince words. I said straight out to the lady, perfectly frankly, "I am representing a big legal concern in London. There is a small matter of a will. But first I must ask you something." I could see from this studio, filthy dirty, the stove out, the table covered with used plates, that "Jo" (as she signs the paintings stacked up against the wall) is not what you might call a popular painter. I decided to work in the dark on the proposition that a little money doesn't come amiss, even if it sometimes means selling a husband. In this, human nature is the same for artists and others. Jocaste was straightaway interested. As soon as I mentioned a will, she started to smoke very fast till smoke came out of her ears and it looked like her hair was suffering from what we scientists call internal combustion.

So I explained that Albert inherits a certain amount, not too large, but still useful, of money under this will. "How wonderful," she said. "Yes," I told her, "it would be a marvelous thing for him —only now the money goes to the Dogs' Home at Battersea." I reached for my hat and started to walk to the door.

"One moment," she cried. "Why must my Albert lose this money, not to mention myself? I am getting ready a little exhibition of my paintings, which will cause a great furor if only they can be seen, but of course I need money to arrange the gallery."

"I always thought the gallery paid you for pictures," I said to her, because one should not lose an opportunity to learn a little about the technicalities of another kind of business.

"Formerly," she explained to me, "formerly, this did happen, but nowadays there are so many artists chasing so few galleries, the boot is on the other foot in a manner of speaking. But why does Albert's money go to a dogs' home?"

I could see she was very interested, so I explained that this eccentric uncle of Albert's doesn't like women, on the principle that all his life he can never leave women alone, and consequently has suffered a great deal. Therefore he wishes Albert not to get married, and (and I quoted from the will) in the event of Albert so doing, the money is going to the Battersea Dogs' Home, where only dogs will benefit from it; and this doesn't include any bitches at all, so against women is Albert's uncle.

I was about to leave when the girl said to me, "Is there nothing can be done to break this inhuman will?"

I sighed and sat down to explain to her how sorry I am, but the damage is done; she is Albert's legal, married wife, signed, sealed and delivered, and that's all there is to it. It is too late to change the uncle's mind.

"One moment," she said, "I am not quite so signed, sealed and delivered as all that."

"Madam," I told her, "I am not the kind of man to come between husband and wife. You are legal married, and that is good enough for me." And I made to leave again.

"One moment," she cried. "This is a great sacrifice to me, but I will tell you the truth." Good God, I said to myself, she is not going to tell me that Albert is illegal married twice, an illegal bigamist?

Then she explained how these two, young, romantic, go on a honeymoon down in the South, and they enjoy the honeymoon so much they decide to get married; and this arduous duty was performed for them by the parish priest down there. Naturally this information can only depress me, and I put my hat on again and told her good

afternoon. It was finished, and I knew it. "As I say," I told her, game
to the end, "you are legal married, so the money goes to the dogs."

"Not so fast," she said, a calculating look on her face. "In France,
you must be married civically to be legal. This we didn't bother to
do, so I am not, in law, Albert's wife, though it breaks my heart to
tell you."

Highly delighted, I struck a deal with her on the spot, paid her
the cash after a little bargaining (and this girl, though an artist, was
no piker when it came to making a bargain) and I got back as
quickly as Moishe could drive me in his taxi to tell the children the
glad tidings.

Then we celebrated the mysterious ways of destiny, though between ourselves I don't think it was destiny at all, just sheer artistic
carelessness, and on principle I don't approve it. Nevertheless, I returned to London very satisfied with myself. A pity only we account-
ants do not have a trade newspaper in which I could announce how
resourceful, nay, inspired, the firm of Botvinnik & Associates is in a
crisis. Except, of course, it is not professional to advertise in my profession.

SEVEN

Back in the office everyone is running about like the fire is upstairs
and not in Mendelman's factory at Watford. Mendelman's fire assessors, the insurance assessors, inspectors, policemen, the whole
world is knocking at the door all day long. Mendelman has been telling everyone "Botvinnik has the figures"—"Botvinnik knows everything"—"Ask Botvinnik." Where is Mendelman all this time? The
weather is very hot and he is sitting in a madeira chair with a glass
of lemonade with ice in it, at Bournemouth at a very good hotel
where every meal is a banquet. So I let the clerks in my office run
about making up accounts and figures for the assessors, and the
other assessors, and anybody else who wants figures.

The paper from yesterday is still lying on the doormat at my flat. The headline says FIRE AT WATFORD, then a little bit smaller, but still big enough, FACTORY DESTROYED, then underneath a little paragraph which says that a fine new light-engineering industry has been wiped out over night just at a time when we need all the industry we can get.

I phoned through to Mendelman at Bournemouth. After a lot of waiting and asking for Mr. Mendelman to a girl, then to another girl, then to a man, then to another woman, Mendelman answers the phone.

"Well, Leo," he asks, "how is my beautiful Rosa?"

"Beautiful, Morris," I tell him. "She is very happy and is looking more lovely than ever."

"Yes," he says, "she is a fine girl. Did you like Paris?"

"I liked Paris very much. Do you know the French for motorcar tire? *Pneu.* You would never guess it in a thousand years."

Morris laughed.

"It is a very funny language but pretty, and everybody talks it over there, so what can you do? Is everything arranged?"

"Morris," I said, "Morris, I have only just got back. I am not the prophet Elijah a fiery chariot is waiting to take me everywhere as quick as you can say Jackrobinson."

"Well, of course, Leo," he answers, "naturally, of course. Don't worry, Leo, I know you will not waste time because you are an intelligent man and you know some things have not got long to wait."

"How are you feeling, Morris?" I ask him.

"I am having a glass of cold lemonade under an umbrella on the veranda. It is very nice and hot here. But I am very upset."

"Your heart?" I ask him.

"Yes," he says, "my heart gave a nasty jump when I heard my factory at Watford was burned down. But what can I do? I am a sick man, Leo."

"Just have a good rest, Morris," I tell him, "after all you are insured just in case this kind of thing should happen."

"Of course," he answers, "but, Leo, a man builds a business, a new industry, and this happens. You think it is a judgment?"

"Who knows?" I answer.

"Well, anyway, you will see to everything?"

"Yes, Morris," I say.

"Goodbye then, Leo. I am reading a good book. Bewick's *Birds*. The things birds can do. You would be surprised."

"I am always having surprises even without birds," I tell him.

To tell you the truth, although there was a great deal of excitement and running about, coming and going, telephone ringing, accounts, more accounts, it wasn't very different from usual. It was a bigger fire than we were used to, but what difference did that make to us? When you are an accountant it doesn't matter what the figures are so long as they balance. Botvinnik and Associates have always balanced, and why should they do any different this time? A man is a professional man first and foremost, then afterwards he is a father, a lover, a friend. For the time being I was only a professional man, an adding machine which drank lemon tea and could talk. I did my part, and in a few days it was all over and Mendelman's claim was going through. But although Mendelman was enjoying himself in Bournemouth, I still had my troubles.

I couldn't go and see Mendelman and tell him his libel plan was no good. How could I say to him, "Morris, you have written your daughter is a whore, and believe me, you are right?" Because legally speaking what else was she but an adulteress, a harlot some lawyers would say, although, of course, she wasn't taking money, only for love. But love is something respectable people like to read about. When it happens they can become very nasty indeed. A love-child is just another bastard all of a sudden, and look at the fellow's poor legally married wife, and the girl took him away, and all this sort of thing. It is strange because romance must always lead to these other things. After all, love isn't just looking into a pair of eyes. But when it becomes serious so that you would expect people to say "If they weren't really in love they wouldn't act like this," what happens?

Everyone is furious, and there is no end to it. In this life it is safer to make a mistake in your accounts than to fall in love. Love is very dangerous. It is the most dangerous thing in the world almost. Look at Napoleon with that Josephine. A lot of good she did him. And Caesar with Cleopatra. You would think a man with his experience would know better, but no. I seem to remember that she actually had a child by him; although, of course, in those days it was nothing even for a Queen.

But Mendelman, in spite of being philosophical about these things if they happened to other people, wouldn't be so pleased if he heard it was happening to his own beautiful daughter. He would drop stone dead, and that would do nobody any good. So, I had to think of something; me of all people. It shouldn't happen to a dog what was happening to me. And what is more, Mendelman so liked his libel idea that he would be very upset to give it up.

I have known him in the past do the same thing. There was the time when he bought all that shaving cream from a company which went broke. He decided to put new labels on and sell it as hand cream. He liked the idea so much, he insisted on doing it, although by the time he had taken the old labels off and printed new ones and put them on, the whole business showed a loss. He was Mendelman. He had to have a label in five colors.

I think he liked this idea in the same way. It was going to be difficult, but now I was so worried about Rosa I had to find a way. After all, it could have been my daughter who had got, God forbid, into trouble. I know it isn't a nice thing to say, and if anybody else said it I would be very angry. But couldn't it happen to anybody's daughter? Of course it could, and we might as well face the fact. And don't tell me you know a good man for abortions. How could you ask a girl like Rosa to do such a thing, kill a baby from a man she loved? It was a terrible situation but a way out had to be found. It wasn't the end of the world, a girl having a baby.

I thought for a long time, even while I spoke to other clients, even when I added up long columns of figures, how I should manage this business. What I decided to do may not have been very clever, but if Mendelman had told it to me I would have believed it, and better I couldn't do. I would tell Mendelman that Rosa being such a refined lady, due to her education, and moving in good-class circles on the Continent, she couldn't possibly have a libel like that against her. Her friends would never speak to her again. That was it, and even better. I would tell Mendelman that Rosa was friends with very fine important people and if the newspapers got hold of a story that she was being in a libel action, even if she won, even if it never went to the courts, they would think she wasn't good enough for them. Furthermore, and this was the fundamental part of my thesis, Rosa was engaged to a very nice boy of good family, and such a story would spoil everything, all her chances. She would lose the man she loved and become an old maid. And why? Because Mendelman was being so stubborn, he had to have a libel action with her. It was just conceit on his part. He wasn't thinking of Rosa at all. That poor girl, what a father to have! He would make a joke out of her, a terrible thing to do. Did he hate her? Didn't he care what happened to her life? It must all go for the sake of one of his crazy ideas? I was getting furious with Mendelman, when I remembered I wasn't talking to him. I was talking to myself in the office, and the chief clerk put his head round the door and said "Did you call, Mr. Botvinnik?" It was a wonderful idea.

When I left the office I was feeling happy. I had been in the jaws of calamity, but I had solved the whole problem. First the wife business and now the libel nonsense. Rosa would be all right. Mendelman would not drop dead. Everything was fine. It is the scientific training. It comes out with the right answer just when you have given the problem up. You can say what you like, but you can't beat a real scientific mind in a crisis. What is more, I even had an idea for providing for Rosa. After all, you must admit it would be terrible for Mendelman to go to the trouble of burning his factory down for the creditors.

EIGHT

Morris came back from Bournemouth looking brown and so well that for a moment I wondered whether it could be true that he was a man with death in his waistcoat pocket. His eyes were bright, and his face tanned and he wore a light tropical-weight gray suit very nicely cut, and a straw hat, like a tobacco planter. He came into the office and waved his brown-paper cigarette at me.

"Did you enjoy yourself in Paris, Leo?" he said.

"I told you on the phone to Bournemouth," I replied, "it is very nice, but there is no place like home. Incidentally," I added, laughing, "do you know the French for motor tire?"

"You told me on the phone," he said, "how is Rosa?"

"Marvelous, I told you," I said.

"She agrees to my plan? You must admit, Leo, it is a marvelous plan."

"No," I said.

"What do you mean *No?*" he said. "No what, no who, Rosa says no, you say no?" He got excited very quickly, that Mendelman.

I explained to him very tactfully that Rosa was engaged to a promising composer, and everything would be ruined if we went ahead with his plan.

"And to tell you the truth, Morris," I added, "I for one am not sorry, because I think it was a very brilliant but if I may say so, a slightly mad idea. Also these great ideas sometimes backfire."

He was quiet for a moment. His lips moved two or three times, little movements which didn't mean very much. He finished his cigarette and stubbed it out.

"All right," he said, "what shall we do instead?" and I could see that if someone was to come into the office now and put his own crazy idea up to Mendelman he would have laughed his head off. "I never heard such a stupid idea" he would say. He had dropped it, and already it seemed to him impossible that such a scheme should ever have been suggested. That was the kind of salesman he was.

Then I put to him my own suggestion, a simple professional plan, not brilliant, not flashy, not poetic, but it would do the job he wanted done.

My proposal was simply this. That Rosa should become a partner in Botvinnik & Associates. We would make up a partnership agreement, and Mendelman would pay me say five thousand pounds in return for Rosa's interest in my firm, and we would guarantee to Rosa an income of five hundred pounds a year. How we would get the five thousand was more difficult. We could predate the agreement and try to make Mendelman's debt to my firm a first charge upon his business. We could even have Rosa Products issue Botvinnik & Associates with a debenture to that amount so that it became a first charge on the firm. Then when the insurance claim was paid, Botvinnik would have to be paid out before anyone else.

"Why not make it for ten thousand, Leo?" Mendelman asked. "Why not aim high and pay Rosa seven hundred and fifty a year?"

"Because my dear Morris," I said, "we are not doing a deal together for a hundred gross trousers. My business is not worth ten thousand, but a half share in it could be worth five thousand, and we must be practical about this and stick to the facts."

I think Mendelman was more relieved at my suggestion than he seemed. He accepted all my points. A man comes to an end with everything. Everything has its end. A gambler can get tired of cards, so tired that ace, king, queen, jack in a hand means nothing to him. A glutton sooner or later will sicken at the thought of food. A woman can have too many diamonds. A Don Juan too many women. The more flesh, the more worms, as Mendelman used to say, Mendelman, a business man who had lived through enough businesses. He was tired of arguing and scheming. He was glad for me to take over the problem.

"So you will look after Rosa," he said.

"Yes," I told him, "I will be very pleased to do so, but apart from all that, you are after all buying a piece of my business for her."

"That is so," he said, "it is all being done on a businesslike basis. Business, after all, is business."

"Absolutely," I agreed, "also what have I to work for anyway—this way Rosa will benefit from my meaningless life."

"This is what makes life something," he said. "Well, and what about my fire? Does it go through all right?"

"It appears to be going through very satisfactory," I said. "How did it happen?"

Mendelman laughed, sat back in the chair, lit another cigarette, and told me.

"You shouldn't smoke so much in your condition," I said.

"You are wrong, Leo," he said, "it is in exactly my condition that it doesn't matter. I could smoke all day and all night, through my ears as well as my mouth, and it wouldn't make much difference. But who wants to smoke as much as that? Anyhow, let me get on with the story."

Mendelman was always a good judge of human nature, and when it came to burning down his factory this power of judgment served him very well. Everything depended on his night watchman, because, after all, if the night watchman was actually watching at night no harm could come to the factory even from its owner. This problem Mendelman had carefully considered.

He had always taken a great interest in his employees. He was godfather to seventeen children and always gave good christening, wedding, and Christmas presents. Some thought that Mendelman interfered too much in the affairs of his employees, and the night watchman himself was just such a case. He had been employed for over two years about the factory as an odd-job man, and very efficient and reliable he was, although well past retiring age. Mendelman used to talk to him for a half hour whenever he visited the factory. Philosophy and religion they used to discuss together, and being as the night-watchman was a Scottish Presbyterian, they got on very well together, almost always agreeing. Sometimes they disagreed, and then the Scotsman would threaten to leave. But Mendelman used to beg him to stay, and perhaps give him a small rise as a proof of his good faith. "Fergus," he told me often, "is a good, clear thinker. His ideas on making a republic out of Scotland are completely sound. What is more, if Scotland was a separate country it would have many business advantages." Mendelman would always continue, "Fergus has only one fault. He can't leave the girls alone. If a girl should come past him, straightaway he is an octopus with sixty-three hands. All after the girl. It causes bad feeling."

What caused especially bad feeling was that for some reason girls liked Fergus with his hands. He was an old man, and yet from what Mendelman told me, I think some of those girls went out of their way to turn their bottoms in his direction, if you will excuse the expression.

"What?" I said to Mendelman, "such an old man to still be after the girls?"

"Leo," he answered me, "with some old men things are even worse than with boys."

Anyhow, through this Fergus the factory was burned down, and this was just an example of Mendelman's great luck, for it was certainly through no interference on his part that the fat girl got pregnant.

This fat girl, you might say, was sure to get pregnant in the end. A girl who spends so many dinner hours in the disused shed on the other side of the lot should expect that. But it must have been a great surprise to her when Fergus put the finish to her nonsense. When Mendelman heard about it he didn't bat an eyelid. "All right," he said, "let Fergus marry the fat girl. Sometimes it happens this way round." That's how broadminded he was with other people. But Fergus didn't want to get married. The fat girl cried and cried, until Mendelman was absolutely sick and tired of the whole business. "Look Fergus," he shouted, "I am absolutely sick and tired of this whole business. Either you marry the fat girl, or by my life, you can go."

"Good afternoon, Mr. Mendelman," said the Scotsman.

"Just a minute, Fergus," Morris called after him. "Don't be so hasty."

"Pardon me, Mr. Mendelman," Fergus replied, "you cannot talk such words to a freeborn Scot, so with your leave, I'll be off." Eventually Fergus agreed to stay. But only if he got a change of job. He agreed to marry the fat girl, but only if he got the night watchman's house. He got them, and was married. From which it follows, that on the night on which Mendelman called at his factory intending to burn it down, the night watchman was not there. Where was he? Where do you think? He was in bed with the fat girl.

Now Mendelman's factory before he took it over was the Bigga Balloon Co., specializing in all types of rubber goods. Taken over with some warehouse equipment were several boxes of balloons and suchlike. What with these and the night watchman it was certain that the factory should burn. But you have to admire the artistry with which Mendelman managed it.

Other men might have been satisfied to soak some old rags in petrol, set fire to them, and trust in God. Not Mendelman. He carefully installs paraffin central heating radiators a couple of weeks before. Then when he passes by the factory late that night, he takes a can of paraffin out of the storehouse, and a dozen balloons from a tea chest. These he fills with paraffin. He ties them together with thread soaked in paraffin. Then he sets light to the thread and leaves.

He heard five or six muffled pops as the balloons touched off. "I didn't know it would work," he said, "so you can imagine how happy I was when I heard them. Pop, pop, pop."

"Pop, pop," I said. "What terrible risks you take, Morris."

"I must admit," he answered, "perhaps I am a little bit of a fire-raiser, because I enjoyed it." What can you do with such a man?

"But I went to all that trouble for nothing," Morris concluded. "Now Rosa will be looked after by your firm, and——"

"Please, Morris," I said, "if you don't like my ideas get on with your own, but please don't expect me to take any more interest in the entire affair."

"Don't get so blown up, Leo," he said, "keep your sense of proportion. I realize you have done the best you can." I would have been rude to him, except that he went on without a pause, "Now we must plan an extra-special wedding for Rosa and her boy. When are they to arrive? We will invite five hundred couples and eat caviar out of ladles."

"I think they would prefer a quiet little wedding, Morris," I said.

"Do you think five hundred couples is enough?" he answered. In a matter of ten seconds I was helping plan a tremendous wedding. Oy.

NINE

I am sorry to say that this wedding never took place. In another way I am not sorry, because although the plans (it was to be a proper occasion) were all fixed, Mendelman had not taken into consideration one small fact. It is a beautiful thing to see the confidence a father can have in his daughter. Mendelman arranged for the ceremony and everything, and not once did it occur to him that there might be, let us say, a technical objection. For my part, I kept trying to think of diplomatic ways to tell him, but who can be diplomatic about such a thing? Albert was a lovely boy, but he just happened by some ridiculous oversight, to be a Catholic.

When Rosa and Albert came back from Paris, Mendelman arranged a quiet dinner for the four of us, and you could see that he really had taken a fancy to Albert as a son-in-law. After the dinner, Mendelman insisted on the young couple going to an opera he had bought them tickets for, because he thought it was the right thing to do on such an occasion. After they left, he explained to me that he liked the boy so much he didn't want to have him around too long in case he started to discover his faults.

"Now, Leo," he said, "we can sit here and drink brandy and smoke cigars——"

"You smoke too many cigars," I told him.

"—And talk about old times, Ah, Leo," he said, "it's a marvelous thing to see your family provided for. They should be very happy, those two. At least, what I mean to say is that when they fight, they should enjoy making it up afterwards, which is the true test of marriage."

Mendelman took his brandy glass and warmed it gently with his hands as he left the table and made himself comfortable in a deep leather chair by the fire. I sat in a smaller chair opposite. "Well," Mendelman sighed, "it has been not such a bad life. It's a pity you didn't see that fire, Leo. It really was something. You would have enjoyed it. I am going to tell you now," he continued, "the truth about life. This is the truth——"

Then the telephone rang, and I went to answer it.

It was my chief clerk. All the evening, he had been trying to find me, he said. The inspectors for the insurance company were not satisfied with Mendelman's claim. "They sounded a little upset, Mr. Botvinnik," he said.

"You should send them from me, Harris, in the morning," I told him, "a big bunch of flowers." Then I went back to Mendelman.

It is a pity the phone didn't ring a little later, because then Mendelman would have told me the truth about life. As it was, I had to work it out for myself. Mendelman, with the bowl of brandy cooling in his hands, and a smile on his face, my mad friend Morris Mendelman was dead.

I removed the cigar, which had fallen onto his jacket where it had already burned a small, perfectly round hole.

"Mendelman," I said to him, the tears slowly running down my cheeks, "the truth about life is——" But like Mendelman, I forgot the point. So I just cried for a while instead.

A VILLAGE LIKE YOURS

THE FINEST PIPE-MAKER IN RUSSIA

MY GREAT-GRANDFATHER WAS CERTAINLY THE FINEST PIPE-MAKER in Russia—or at least in that part where he lived. Not only did everyone worth noticing buy a pipe from my great-grandfather, but even landowners and the owner of the large timber business in the next village came to him for their best pipes even if they sometimes smoked others made by inferior craftsmen. And so my great-grandfather was a very famous man indeed, for, although you can live your whole life and only hear of Napoleon when someone digs up a French coin or an old rusted saber, you cannot smoke a good pipe without remembering who made it, and you wish him many more years, so that he can go on making you pipes, although, of course, my great-grandfather's pipes were not such bad workmanship that you needed perhaps more than two in a lifetime. But you would be pleased for him to live a long time, anyway. Once, however, my great-grandfather made a bad pipe—and even then he made it bad for a good reason. He was the finest pipe-maker in Russia and would never have made a bad pipe without having a very good reason.

It happens that this pipe was bad because of what took place on a Sabbath morning. Not that my great-grandfather made the pipe on a Sabbath. I would not like anyone to think that of him. Any pipe made on a Sabbath morning—it goes without saying—is not likely to draw well after the Sabbath has gone out. And my great-grandfather was not the man to make pipes at any time except when a respectable man should make pipes. No, my great-grandfather was not in his workshop on this particular Sabbath morning. He was in the synagogue with the other men of the village. Where else would he be? But it had to be on this particular morning that somebody

191

should want to make himself a nuisance by coming to my great-grandfather for a pipe. My young grandfather was not at the synagogue. If he had been thirteen yet and confirmed, he would have been there. As it was, he was sitting in my great-grandfather's workshop laying with a chisel and a piece of wood. Suddenly my great-grandmother rushed into the workshop, calling out: "So where are you, Yankele? Why don't you answer? Put down your father's tools. What do you mean on a Sabbath morning playing with tools? Run quickly to the synagogue and tell your father he should come home straightaway."

My grandfather was young, but he was not so young that he did not know my great-grandfather to have a big, heavy hand all hard with working wood. So he did not rush out like a mad person straightaway to do as my great-grandmother had asked. Instead, he thought for a moment, and then he said: "Supposing I go and tell my father he should come home. What will he say? He won't say anything. He will give me a clout on the head. On the Sabbath he doesn't want to know about the house. Only if it's burning down should you try to fetch him from the synagogue." Which was true, because my great-grandfather was a pious man. He used to say: "If God has given us six days, can't we spare him one?" And who could answer him? There was no answer. Everyone stood dumb.

But my great-grandmother said: "Yankele, if you don't hurry to the synagogue and bring home your father I will give you such a clout on the head you won't argue any more."

This made my young grandfather think: If I stay here, I get a clout on the head. If I go to the synagogue, I get a clout on the head. At least let me get away from the nearest one first. But he looked obedient and said to my great-grandmother: "All right, but what shall I tell my father so that he won't give me a clout on the head? Why should he come home right away? The house isn't burning."

My great-grandmother could see that what my grandfather said was reasonable, so she answered quickly: "Outside is waiting a lord with a big carriage with horses and a coachman, and he wants father to make him an extra-special pipe."

Not many lords came to my great-grandfather's workshop. "If they are satisfied with inferior workmanship, it is their own business," my great-grandfather used to say. So that when a lord came my great-grandfather was bound to be very excited. My young grandfather was also excited, and rushed out to see the carriage and the horses and, of course, the lord himself.

The lord was in the kitchen sitting by the stove. He was a big man, with a lot of furs on him, and he was sucking a thick cheroot. My young grandfather could see he needed a pipe badly and told him: "I am going to fetch my father, who is the finest pipe-maker in Russia, to make you a pipe."

And the big man said, "Good. Here is a sixpence for you. Run quickly." And to my great-grandmother he said, "Have you any vodka in the house?"

My grandfather ran out of the house without even putting his hat on. It was snow everywhere, you understand—real heavy thick snow covering everything, not like in this country, where an inch is a lot, but real heavy thick snow. When it melted, sometimes you could find a cow which had been lost all the winter, or sometimes even a drunken man last heard of months ago. But my young grandfather was very strong although he was not yet confirmed, and he was thinking of the boiled butter-beans he could buy at school with the sixpence, so he ran over the snow like a wolf, and the cold did not bother him.

Still, the synagogue was two miles away, and before my grandfather got here he stopped running, and when he stopped running he began to think of how (without letting himself in for a clout on the head) he could ask my great-grandfather to leave the synagogue. When he got there he still had not thought of a way, so he went up to my great-grandfather, who was praying with a big shawl round him, and he touched his hand and waited. Then my great-grandfather, who was a very big man indeed, looked down and smiled through his beard and nodded his head and went on praying. He thought my young grandfather had come to the synagogue to be with the men praying, and said to himself, "Perhaps he will be a student and a teacher after all. Perhaps he will turn out to be a credit, although he is developing late."

But my young grandfather was feeling very nervous with his hand in his pocket fingering the sixpence which the lord had given him, because he suddenly remembered that he would get a clout on the head even if it was only because he had taken money on the Sabbath. After a while he looked up at my great-grandfather again and said quietly: "My mother wants you to come home."

My great-grandfather was very surprised, and replied: "What?"

My young grandfather looked away and said even more quietly: "She wants you to come home because someone wishes to see you."

My great-grandfather looked even more surprised and was also beginning to look angry. He blew through his beard: "What? Yankele, on a Sabbath morning you come to synagogue to bring me home to the house? What does it mean? I will give you a clout on the head."

My young grandfather knew to expect this, so he had already moved a few yards away, and he answered: "A lord is waiting by the house. He wants you to make him a pipe. He is a lord with a carriage and horses and even a coachman. And he is wearing a big fur coat."

But my great-grandfather still looked angry and surprised. It had never happened before, this being sent messages at the synagogue in middle of the Sabbath morning to come home and make a pipe. Well, what could you expect from a woman and a boy not yet confirmed: but this was too much already. He chewed his beard and said: "A lord is waiting? Well, and why shouldn't he wait? Tell this lord he must wait for my lord. And leave me alone on a Sabbath morning, Yankele, or I'm telling you I will give you such a clout on the head you will never forget it."

My grandfather was already out of the synagogue. He ran for a time, but because it was two miles back to the house he began to walk and think of how he could tell the lord what my great-grandfather's message was without getting maybe the hardest clout of all.

He saw the lord walking up and down outside the house, and he was breathing out big clouds of steam like the horses, which were also breathing out big clouds, but the lord's clouds were even bigger than the horses'. The lord was walking up and down with his hands in fur gloves behind his back, so my grandfather went first to the closet which was at the bottom of the piece of ground on which my great-grandfather kept my great-grandmother's cow, Masha, and his own cherry trees. He hid his sixpence under the seat, and then called out to the lord what the message was and quickly ran back to the closet. My grandfather heard the lord shout at my great-grand-mother: "Well, then, must I wait a month for this pipe-maker? Is he a lord, or am I? Must I wait until the thaw? Well, must I wait all day?" And the lord got into his carriage and his horses pulled him away to the inn at the next village, which was on the other side of the hill.

When my great-grandfather arrived back from the synagogue he greeted my great-grandmother, and the next thing he said was: "Now, Yetta, is dinner ready yet?" And then he asked: "Where is that Yankele? And what did he want? And don't you know any better than to send him for me on a Sabbath morning? What do you mean?" When my great-grandmother explained to him he said: "Aha! So the lord is getting tired of his bad pipes. When he tries everybody else's pipes and finds out how bad they are, he comes to me. Aha!"

Then in the afternoon, when my grandfather had come out of the closet, he was taken with my great-grandfather to the next village, to the inn. The inn smelt very strong. "Faugh, faugh," said my great-grandfather.

All the peasants who spotted my great-grandfather greeted him with respect, because they knew he was the finest pipe-maker in Russia and a credit to the neighborhood, and besides that, he was a very big man, who had beaten a drunken peasant once who shouted after him in the street.

The lord was drinking in the inn, and when he saw my great-grandfather he shouted: "Well, are you the pipe-maker? Why do you keep me waiting? Are you a bigger lord that you can keep me waiting?"

My great-grandfather answered him: "Sir, if when you are in the army your general calls for you, you go?"

The lord drank a glassful of vodka and replied: "Yes, of course you go. In the army when a general calls you, you go."

My great-grandfather continued: "And how long do you stay with your general?"

The lord looked at my great-grandfather with an unpleasant look: "So you have not done any military service? What do you mean, how long? When a general calls you, you don't ask how long. You stay there until he tells you to go away."

My great-grandfather paused. All the peasants were standing around looking at him as if they were dumb, and my young grandfather knew that they thought he was a clever man because he was getting the lord into such a deep argument. My grandfather had heard the argument before and this time he did not think it so clever. Why argue with a lord? With a peasant, yes; with my great-grandmother, yes; with the rabbi even, yes; but with a lord—it was like arguing with a policeman. But my great-grandfather was completing the argument: "I was called by my general," he said, pulling his whiskers, "and I had to stay until he told me to go."

All the peasants looked at one another, and the lord drank another glass of vodka, and my grandfather thought: it is a very fine thing to make arguments, but with a lord I don't think it is so clever.

Then the lord drank still another glass of vodka, whereupon he shouted: "All right then, all right. Well, then, I want a pipe, a specially good pipe for a present for a prince. You hear, a present for a prince. It must be a good pipe, the best."

My great-grandfather looked down his nose, and he made some more argument: "My pipes are all the best. Would you be coming to me for a pipe if it wasn't the best?"

And my grandfather thought: arguments, always arguments he's making.

The lord went on: "Very well. This one must be better. And, most important of all, it must have a carved eagle on the bowl. It is no good without a carved eagle. It is for a prince, and he must have an eagle, otherwise it is no good."

My grandfather expected more arguments, but, instead, my great-grandfather said very quietly: "Very well. With a carved eagle it will be good, otherwise it is no good. Right."

"Yes," said the lord. "It must have an eagle, and I want it tomorrow."

Now my grandfather really expected arguments. Sabbath was not yet out, and the lord wanted his pipe tomorrow! When could it be made? To make a good pipe takes a long time. My great-grandfather liked to make a pipe in his own time. You said to him one day: "Moishe, you know I would like a pipe." And he would say: "Yes, a good pipe is a very good thing." And two or three months later when he met you in the street he would say: "Here you are. Here is a pipe you will like."

But for this lord a pipe had to be made with an eagle, otherwise it was no good. "All right," said my great-grandfather. And he sat up all night to make a pipe with an eagle carved on the bowl.

When in the morning my grandfather went into the workshop, he saw the pipe lying on the bench. It had a fine eagle carved on it, with big wings curling down to the stem, and the wings were made up of Hebrew letters carefully carved to look like a row of feathers.

The lord came early with his coach and horses, and he came in and saw the pipe and paid my great-grandfather what he asked— twelve rubles—and he liked the finely carved eagle very much. He gave my grandfather another sixpence, and now my grandfather was fingering two sixpences in his pocket.

Afterwards my great-grandfather said to my grandfather: "This lord must have an eagle carved, but the pipe is not so important. He knows what one of his generals can do, but my general is not so important. All right, then, I have given him a pipe I should wish my worst friend. Two, three years a pipe like this could last"—my great-grandfather knew when he made a bad pipe because he was certainly the finest pipe-maker in Russia—"and I have carved on it the Prayer for the Dead. How long can a prince like that live, anyway?"

But my grandfather thought: for two sixpences I can have boiled butter-beans every day for a year.

THE LAW-BREAKER

At the school to which my grandfather went there was no privy. At least there was a privy but it was attached to the synagogue which the village millionaire had given to the community, and it was always kept locked except on Saturday when of course it was required. But at the back of the schoolroom there was a big piece of ground, and when a boy raised his hand in the middle of a difficult text the teacher used to say: "All right, then, all right, go into the yard. I am waiting."

The teacher, who was called Yaacov, was a short fat man with a black dusty beard which was going gray perhaps though you couldn't see that because of the dust. He could only read a book by holding it up close to his face, but he never needed to look closely to see if my grandfather was reading wrong, because Yaacov knew everything by heart, and anyhow my grandfather normally did read wrong. On a Friday, Yaacov went round to all the fathers of the boys he taught to collect his teaching money. He used to make it a little more or less according to who he was collecting from, and when he was teaching a boy for confirmation he added a little for the extra strain on his voice and for writing the special confirmation discourse which was spoken by each boy. It was worth the extra, too, because Yaacov was a clever scholar and every confirmation speech was a little different, although there were the usual thanks in it to the boy's mother and father and to Yaacov as well, who was always called in these speeches "my learned and respected teacher, the scholar Yaacov ben Yitschok."

When Yaacov himself went outside to the yard he left his oldest son (the one with pimples and long side curls) in charge. This son was his cleverest and, though very ugly, was regarded as a good prospective match being as he was so clever and had such a good business head. When his father went out he would unfold a paper which came to him from Moscow every week, lay it on the table in front of the class and offer the older boys a read of a column for a farthing. It was no good expecting to read more than one column for a farthing because he covered up the part of the paper for which you hadn't contracted, and if your eyes moved over to it he shouted out, "Breach of contract—another farthing." Usually he sold at least three or four columns to different boys while his father was outside, and in this way made quite a nice profit on his papers, as well as out of the butter-beans which he boiled at home and brought to the school to sell to the boys.

Why his father was always so long outside didn't bother him. The longer Yaacov was away the better it was for the newspaper business. All the other boys to didn't mind how long Yaacov was out in the yard. They read the paper, held fighting competitions, and ate the butter-beans which they had been sitting on all through the lessons. As they used to wrap the beans in their handkerchiefs before sitting on them it was quite all right. My grandfather got a clean handkerchief every Saturday morning.

Now often my grandfather watched Yaacov in the yard standing in one corner for a few minutes then moving lower down the fence and standing there for a few minutes, then moving lower down still and yet again standing there for a few minutes, then at last moving across the yard to another corner. He thought that this was a very unusual and impressive business and sometimes back at home he would pretend he was Yaacov in the yard and shuffle from one corner to another muttering to himself. Soon he became very good at being Yaacov, and one day at school he took some friends into the yard and without warning began to shuffle from one side to the other muttering all the time.

All the boys laughed very much and kept on asking him to do it again. They said he was certain to become a teacher because he was so good at being Yaacov, but he said no, he would sooner be a soldier even than a school teacher, a sentiment with which most of them agreed. After this it became his favorite way to make the boys laugh at school when Yaacov wasn't looking. Once when the clever son was busy arguing with an older boy about whether he had been reading too much of the paper or not, my grandfather with great daring followed Yaacov quietly out into the yard. Five other little boys followed my grandfather. As Yaacov shuffled from one place to another my grandfather shuffled after him and after my grandfather shuffled the five little boys and then they quietly returned to the classroom. They found this so funny that afterwards whenever Yaacov went out back, grunting to his son to meanwhile look after the class, they followed him out and shuffled after him, and Yaacov never knew because he always concentrated so on his work. The boys even looked forward to school, until at last as they trooped out after Yaacov, Yaacov's son saw them and shouted to his father, and Yaacov turned and saw them for the first time, and chased them in, but he only caught my grandfather, who was the smallest. Then he made my grandfather read a very difficult place in the Pentateuch, getting him to explain the part where it says: "Thou shalt not baste the kid in the milk of its mother."

Now my grandfather knew that this had something to do with eating or not eating but he couldn't remember which. After sitting there with Yaacov breathing down on his face for some minutes saying: "Well, then? What, what? Come on, then, you learned one, tell me," he admitted that he did as a matter of fact find it a bit difficult to recollect. Then Yaacov shouted, "Oho! To mock his teacher is not hard for him, but to learn is too much!" And he gave my grandfather a very hard knock with a book on the back of his head and told him to get outside and go home to tell his father why his learned and respected teacher refused to have him in the class.

My grandfather ran out of the class crying, which was the only sound heard for some while, because Yaacov stood in front glaring at them all, and no one dared to say a word or whistle or make even the slightest noise by breathing too hard.

My grandfather stopped crying quickly after he left. Even more quickly he decided he certainly wouldn't go home to catch trouble from my great-grandfather, who being a pious man would certainly be very annoyed with my grandfather for making a nuisance of himself to the teacher. So my grandfather sat down in a ditch by the side of the road—as it was summer it was very dry and warm—to think over the whole business. While he was thinking he found a spider running from under a stone so he caught it and kept it in his hand till he made a small hole surrounded with stones. Then he put the spider into the hole and pushed it about with a piece of straw, making it go in different directions.

All the time he was doing this he thought about how Yaacov had hit him, and for no reason at all. Did all the boys laugh or did they not? Everyone laughed, he was a public entertainer, and yet Yaacov hit him. Anyhow, there had been others following Yaacov all over the yard, so why should my grandfather get the blame? And as for my great-grandfather, he always sided with the teacher. He believed anyone who said my grandfather had stolen some Hungarian plums or had knocked off somebody's high hat, which he had, but still. My great-grandfather said my grandfather was only good for a soldier, and that if the Army came to collect him they would only get thanks and a couple of roubles from my great-grandfather.

Everything he did was wrong. No one cared about him except to give him a knock on the head or to shout at him. And how should he know why a kid should never be basted in the milk of its mother? Who wanted to baste kids anyhow? If he was a soldier he would show that Yaacov. Throw his skullcap into some mud, and then put dead rats in his house. And he would carry money on Saturdays, swear in Russian, and get drunk like Bonifas the Cobbler. He would even eat meat and drink some milk with it!

When my grandfather suddenly thought of that he stopped pushing the spider about. He thought of it again, wrinkling his mouth as if tasting the two foods together. Or what about some roast liver with butter—why not eat them together? He swallowed hard, sat up in the ditch and made a decision. If everyone said he was a no-good, very well then, he would show them they were right. And my grandfather jumped up out of the ditch and ran home.

When he got to my great-grandfather's house he stopped at the gate. Then he went round the back, tiptoed through the yard so that no one could hear him, and before going in, looked through the kitchen window to see if my great-grandmother was cooking. The kitchen was empty, so he walked quietly in and opened the cupboard where food was kept. On one shelf were all the milk foods, buttermilk and milk from my great-grandmother's cow (which was called Masha) and cheese and butter. My grandfather put his finger into the butter and brought out some of it. Then he put most of it back because he thought that, after all, he only needed to eat a little of it with liver. Then he looked over the other shelf where there was cold roast meat, some boiled fish, and some pieces of chicken liver which my great-grandmother was keeping for her husband's supper. He took a small piece of liver, looked round quickly, and ran out of the house.

My grandfather ran right away from the house, up a hill where there were still trenches from where soldiers had come past a long time ago before even my great-grandfather was a boy, leaving behind them only a few coins and sometimes a bone and of course the trenches.

When he got to the top of the hill he sat down again to think, but first putting the small piece of butter on to one bundle of grass and the piece of liver on to another. He thought of everything everyone would say when they heard what he had done. Then his hair stood on end as he suddenly remembered a fact. All the boys, even some of the older ones who had been confirmed, always said that if anyone ever ate milk with meat something terrible would happen, not only to that person but to the whole village a calamity would happen. My grandfather looked down from the hilltop. In the village, lights were already on in some of the houses. He saw a light go on in the baker's house just behind his shop where you could get fresh white rolls, and in his mind's mouth he tasted the crisp bread. He watched a light go on in his uncle Yossef's house and remembered that his uncle Yossef always gave him some money every Chanuka. But he thought again of my great-grandfather and of Yaacov, and feeling very angry he quickly put the butter with the liver together into his mouth, and swallowed them, thinking: serve them right.

Even as he felt the mixed taste go from his tongue he felt sorry. He was sorry because he was already beginning to feel slightly sick, but also because when he looked down towards the village he knew that something terrible was certain to happen to everyone there because of his sin which he had just sinned. Yet more than anything else he was sorry because he remembered Yaacov saying that anyone who ate meat with butter was certain to die young. And wasn't my grandfather young? The more he thought about it the less pleased with himself did he feel. Groaning quietly but proud that at least he was the only boy in the village to die in this particular way, he lay back in the trench and waited.

It drew darker and darker. All the time the dew fell heavier until all the grass around my grandfather became soaked. There was some long grass over his face and some drops of dew fell off from the top of the blades of grass suddenly, and ran down the side of his nose and he jumped up thinking his last moment had certainly come. But it hadn't, so he sat down again leaning his head against the side of the trench, thinking how sorry my great-grandmother would be, even if he had sinfully eaten liver with butter.

Then my grandfather fell asleep but he didn't sleep for very long. In less than half an hour he woke up because it had grown very cold and he wasn't wearing his overcoat. As soon as he woke up he felt hungry, and as soon as he felt hungry he remembered he was dead and couldn't eat. So he got out of the trench and saw that the village was still there and realized that he was a demon or something. Then he felt his face and found that although it was wet with dew it still felt like his old face, and on top of everything else he really was very hungry. He thought the whole thing out. If he was dead, could he be hungry and yet not eat? Was it a punishment? On the other hand maybe God hadn't seen him do the sin? Perhaps God didn't care? Maybe God was too busy to watch my grandfather the whole time to make sure he didn't eat liver with butter? In which case my grandfather could get away with all kinds of little sins. He might carry a mouse to synagogue in his pocket on Saturday. My grandfather felt suddenly very strong. He stood up to the top of his height, very straight. Then he ran down the hill, very pleased with himself.

When my grandfather got back to the house, my great-grandfather looked up and saw there was something different from usual in the face of his son. He had never seen my grandfather look so pleased after coming back from school. Neither had he ever known him home so late. Usually he was home too early, running back as soon as he could get out, never wanting to stay and listen to the older boys discuss reverent problems. So my great-grandfather smiled at him and said:

"You are late, my son. Have you been learning for so long in the school?"

My grandfather, still looking very pleased, thought he'd try a little lie and said that he had. My great-grandfather wondered if perhaps he had been wrong about his son, that the goodness and the intentions of God were impossible for any man to be assured of, and he asked my grandfather what he had been learning. The only thing my grandfather could now remember was the piece from the Pentateuch about basting a kid in the milk of its mother. This he expounded to my great-grandfather, explaining that it meant that no one should eat liver with butter, and that if they did they would certainly die young.

My great-grandfather was so pleased at my grandfather's knowledge, he offered some of the chicken liver my great-grandmother had prepared for him alone. But my grandfather said no, he couldn't eat the father's own food like that, he would rather take some fish. And my great-grandfather thought this was certainly a miracle and that Yaacov was indeed a great scholar, and my grandfather would surely grow up to be a pious man and a teacher. My grandfather was thinking for his part, that he would be terribly sick if he ever ate liver again, even without butter.

THE DAY AUNT CHAYA WAS BURIED

One Sabbath my great-grandfather was singing some verses of the service which belonged to the cantor. The cantor sang loud. My great-grandfather, who had a very strong voice, sang louder still so that one or two men in the synagogue felt uncomfortable and wished that Reb Sholem Pinsk the beadle would arrive and quietly request my great-grandfather to let the cantor earn the few pennies he was paid.

But where was Reb Sholem? This was really a question to ask, for where should a beadle be on Sabbath morning if not in synagogue. Then, suddenly, like an explosion, in ran Reb Sholem waving his spectacles in one hand and his praying-shawl in the other. He rushed up to my great-grandfather (who was singing even louder) and pulled at his coat. "Why shouldn't I sing?" asked my great-grandfather. "What sort of a cantor does he think he is anyway? My own cow can sing better." Reb Sholem pulled his arm. "Listen," he wheezed between coughing and spitting for he was an old man to have been running so fast. "Listen," he grunted, "the bronze horse at Nevel has been blown up." "What?" cried all the men around, "The bronze horse at Nevel? You don't say so?" they said.

"I'm telling you," shouted Reb Sholem Pinsk, "The bronze horse standing in the market place at Nevel has been blown up."

The cantor was taking advantage of the disturbance to get through a few verses without assistance. But what was the use since everyone was listening to Reb Sholem. The cantor stopped singing and called out in his rich voice, "Reb Sholem, why should we care whether the bronze horse at Nevel is blown up or not? This is the Sabbath and we are at worship. What do we care about the bronze horse at Nevel?"

"He's right," said my great-grandfather. "He can't sing, but what he says is true. What do I care about the bronze horse at Nevel. I already have enough worries of my own," and he began to sing again where he had left off before.

"He's right," said all the men. "*We* should worry about the bronze horse at Nevel," and they straightened their praying-shawls and went back to their seats.

Reb Sholem pulled at my great-grandfather's coat again even harder. "Believe me," he said, "you should be worried. We should all be worried."

"You should have no false gods, even a bronze horse, Reb Sholem, especially as you are, late on shabbos or not, the beadle," called the cantor severely.

"God forbid," answered Reb Sholem, "let all bronze idols be blown up. But—" and again he pulled at my great-grandfather's coat, "not by your youngest sister Chaya."

"What?" shouted my great-grandfather. "At least he has stopped singing," thought the cantor.

"Your youngest sister Chaya has blown up the bronze horse at Nevel," repeated Reb Sholem. "God help us," whispered my great-grandfather and walked straight out of the synagogue. "Now perhaps I can sing without an ass braying," thought the cantor.

When my great-grandfather arrived home he was greeted by the sound of crying and voices all asking different questions at the same time. The family was gathered around Aunt Chaya asking her questions, and weeping for her, and so worrying the poor woman that, true as she remained in principle to the Revolution, she was beginning to wish she had never learned how to make bombs, nor how to throw them, particularly in the direction of, for example, bronze horses. But everyone was silenced by my great-grandfather shouting, "Hold your tongues, you geese, or I will give you something to cry about. You understand me?" Then he continued politely, "First you must understand, my dear Chaya, that we are very pleased to see you." Everyone shouted out, "Certainly," "I should think so." "Naturally."

"Be quiet," my great-grandfather shouted. He turned again to his young sister. "Chaya," he said in a solemn voice, "Chaya, I have always said to you, make your own decisions and go your own way, for if you must associate with riffraff then it must surely be God's intention and it is not for me to interfere. But now you have done some terrible thing and although God certainly knows what you have done and why you have done it, I do not, and if it is not troubling you too much I should like to hear the entire story." And my great-grandfather sat down in his chair, in which, of course, no one else was sitting.

Aunt Chaya was a little woman even at the best of times but when my great-grandfather stood beside her they looked like a big gander and a little goose. She had never been a great talker but you could see from the way her eyes moved quickly like a pair of small fish, that she thought a great deal. So she stood there in an old torn black dress, with a red ribbon in her tightly curled black hair which always looked freshly oiled, and told them how she happened to blow up the bronze horse at Nevel.

The revolutionary party Aunt Chaya belonged to was not very large, but Aunt Chaya had been a member ever since she was a girl. In those days a few of the less religious youngsters from the village used to go in couples, the boys with red handkerchiefs tied round their necks, their arms round the waists of the girls, the girls with red ribbons in their hair, into the woods, there to listen to one another's speeches, and to sing revolutionary songs, and also, to be frank, to make love. One Sunday afternoon, Chaya, a young girl at the time, followed them into the wood, hid in a tree nearby, listened, watched and learned. Then she came down from the tree and said that unless they let her become a member she would tell all their fathers what the Revolution really meant. So they let her join although she was so small and so young, but soon they began to respect her. She had a genius for hiding revolutionary pamphlets. She became secretary of the group, and once when the police came to the village to see if there were any deserters from the tsar's army about, Chaya hid a broken pistol which a party speaker from Lutzen had given her. She hid it in an earth closet and all the brothers and sisters in the party said what a genius she had for organization. But when Chaya left the village and the others had all married, and the boys blew their noses or carried their dinners in the red handkerchiefs, and the girls used their red ribbons to tie their aprons, Chaya began to learn other things. She even went on missions and because the party remained so small, became a very important person indeed.

I am telling you all this so that you shouldn't be surprised that Aunt Chaya, small as she was, should be chosen to throw the bomb at Peter Petrovich Minsky. But now I expect you want to know something about Peter Petrovich as well, for there is no end to people's curiosity. So.

Peter Petrovich was a clerk in the recruitment office at Nevel. When the recruits were brought in, Peter Petrovich pulled his thick moustaches, stared through his steel-framed spectacles which contained only plain glass but which made him feel important, and asked questions. "Your name is what?"—"You were born where?" —"Your father was what?" Naturally a man who asks so many questions is a great nuisance.

Aunt Chaya's party had just decided that the only way to be noticed was to become a great nuisance just like Peter Petrovich. There he was, a very small official indeed, but if it wasn't for Peter Petrovich there would be no recruitment office, and if there was no office there would be nowhere for the recruits to go to, and if there was nowhere for the recruits to go to, they would have to stay home in their villages, and if they stayed at home they wouldn't be in the tsar's army, and then the tsar would have no army, and there would be nothing to stop the revolution. If it wasn't for Peter Petrovich there would be happiness for all and a picture of Aunt Chaya in every village in Russia, but there was Peter Petrovich sitting every day in his recruitment office, pulling his mustaches, looking through his plain glasses, asking questions and sending men into the tsar's army. It was unbearable that such a man as he should stand in the way of the revolution, and the party decided it wouldn't put up with it any longer. Peter Petrovich was to be blown up one morning as he went into his recruitment office. The morning was better than the evening because there would be more people about and this would make the bomb-thrower harder to find. It would also save another day's lot of men from the tsar's army. What was more natural than that Aunt Chaya with her record and reputation should be chosen to throw the bomb. Though my great-grandfather was against fighting except sometimes with fists like a man, believe me, he (we all) would have been insulted if Aunt Chaya had not been chosen.

Now the recruitment office of Peter Petrovich Minsky stood in the market place of Nevel, and in the center of this market place there also stood a large beautiful very old bronze horse. Tell me how many towns do you know where they have a bronze horse? You agree, not every town in the world can turn round and say "We have a bronze horse standing in the market place." And the bronze horse at Nevel was certainly a horse to end horses. There it stood in the snow and in the heat, covered with ice or covered with dust, always at the center of Nevel for everyone to see and admire. It pranced up, waving its forefeet in the air, its mane blew all over the place, its tail was long and thick, its thighs were enormous, its eyes were wild, its nostrils wide open, its teeth bared, its lips covered with spume. Why, you could almost hear it neighing, you could almost hear its hind feet stamp the earth, and any minute it might run you over and leave Nevel behind in a cloud of dust. No wonder the citizens of Nevel were proud of that horse, for whoever you are it would have given you pleasure to see it. You would have taken your cap off to the town of Nevel and agreed that it was a very fine town indeed.

Peter Petrovich Minsky passed the bronze horse every day as he crossed the market place to his recruitment office. Every day he walked past the horse without so much as a look at it, staring straight ahead through his glasses, counting up, no doubt, how many good men he would throw to the tsar that day. For all I know he got a commission on each man, per head, you might say, like cattle or sheep. Nevel could spare such a man and nothing more might have been said if only Aunt Chaya had been a little more careful. The fact is that in spite of her quick bright eyes she was a little bit longsighted. Certainly Peter Petrovich must have been very annoyed at losing all his hair, especially his moustache, and of course his glasses were completely destroyed, and his office overcoat torn to shreds, but he himself was still alive after the bomb was thrown. But the bronze horse, Oh, my goodness, the bronze horse had really left Nevel in a cloud of dust. And when the dust cleared there was nothing to be seen except its hind feet. Everything else was spread all over the market place. A cabbage seller was knocked out by one of the front legs, a stall of cakes was upset by its head, everything was in a terrible state, and the bronze horse had left Nevel for good. You can imagine how everyone felt about Aunt Chaya. Peter Petrovich they could manage without, but the bronze horse, who could forgive?

So it was with great enthusiasm that the police from Nevel began to make inquiries after Aunt Chaya. And, she said, it was only a matter of time before they traced her to the village. "And to my house?" asked my great-grandfather. "Exactly so," replied Aunt Chaya, her eyes darting about the room looking for policemen.

Everyone started to shout and ask questions again and, naturally, my great-grandmother was crying. "Well," said my great-grandfather, "let everyone be quiet. We are all in great danger and I must think carefully. But what, first of all, is that terrible smell?" Everyone turned round and sniffed, and my great-grandmother cried out, "It must be the cat. She is dead you know."

At this moment who should run in but a friend of my young grandfather's, a boy with a very long nose and side curls, who was, in spite of being pious, a terrible liar. "Listen," he shouted, "a whole lot of police are arriving on horses. Which is your Aunt Chaya who blew up the bronze horse at Nevel?"

"Oh, my God," cried my great-grandfather, "it is too late to do anything. Hide under the stove Chayele quickly, with the chickens, and perhaps they will not see you. What a terrible smell," he went on, "where is this dead cat?"

Now though it was really a bad smell, my great-grandfather was sorry to see the cat gone like that, for it was a good cat and had lived with the family for a long time, catching rats sometimes as long as your arm. All the children played with it and it hardly ever bit them except when rats were short, and this wasn't often because there were plenty of rats at all times in the village. It was not a cat to die so easily, brought up like that, to a hard life with few comforts. But what had happened was that by dying this cat actually saved eight lives. Now I expect you had better hear all about that before I finally explain how Aunt Chaya was buried.

It is a strange thing that among all the foods which the true believer may not eat you do not find mushrooms mentioned. And yet on the other hand it is not such a strange thing, because the rabbis must have known how good a pot of mushrooms can taste, and how they make a change from soup and potatoes. My great-grandmother's mother was very fond of a dish of mushrooms, so fond of them in fact, that in the season, in spite of being a very old woman—you can tell how old, she was my great-grandfather's mother-in-law— she would go down to the meadows and look around for perhaps two or three hours for mushrooms. In those days there were really mushrooms, not like now, the size of a pinhead, but big as saucers, big as plates some of them.

One morning the old woman was searching in some new fields, slowly walking along talking to herself, and looking carefully about —but she couldn't find her mushrooms anywhere. "So," she said, "now they are taking from me my only pleasure. They take from an old woman a few mushrooms nobody wants. Nobody wants me. Nobody looks after me so they take away my mushrooms." As she got ready to cry a little she suddenly noticed a whole dinner of mushrooms under some trees. "My prayer has been answered," she wheezed, "there is a God who cares for the old and will never see them want."

What wonderful mushrooms they were, bigger than ever before, and golden yellow like rich butter! Home she took them talking all the time and feeling like an angel. She skinned and washed them, flavored them just so, and left the pot on the stove to cook while she sat in a corner and saw that no one took them away. But she was tired by the excitement and so much talking to herself, and fell asleep in no time. When, suddenly, there was a noise and the old woman woke up, it was already too late, for the cat had knocked the pot down and was eating the mushrooms up as quickly as she could swallow. How the old woman swore at the cat, and kicked it, and threw things at it, but it was too hungry to notice. Without moving it finished the mushrooms and then, leaving the old woman crying her eyes out lamenting the misery of being old and weak, the cat walked into my great-grandfather's workshop and went to sleep and died from fungus poisoning in one of his biggest and warmest tool chests.

So it was that this famished cat saved the old woman's life—such as there was left of it—as well as the lives of her grandchildren, because, naturally, she always gave them a few spoonfuls of her mushroom stew. And how everyone in the house knew it at last, for when my grandmother had seen the cat lying dead in the tool chest, and had said "Aach," and closed the lid hoping somehow it would disappear. It did not disappear. It was smelling to the highest part of heaven which brings us back to the story of how Aunt Chaya was buried.

It turned out that this little liar, who, you remember, came rushing in shouting, "The police are coming," was telling the truth for a change. In next to no time the police were in the house, and everyone stood around with their mouth open, saying "Sir" because this is the only way to make sure that a policeman doesn't take you to prison. Only two policemen came into the house but believe me, when you've got a hunted criminal hiding under the stove with the chickens, even two policemen are no joke. Furthermore outside could be heard the voices of a whole regiment swearing and laughing and telling dirty stories to one another.

One of the policemen must have been a general almost, for he was covered from head to foot in gold braid and gold lines and gold tassels. He had an enormous mustache—much bigger than

Peter Petrovich's—and he kept his helmet on, which my great-grandmother thought was very nice of him, it being the custom in an orthodox house. The other policeman was less well-dressed but much fatter. He took his helmet off and called my great-grandmother "Dear lady" and she didn't like the look of him at all. My great-grandfather just said good day to them, and beckoned all the children to leave the room.

The first policeman looked round the room and wrinkled his nose. "Do you smell something unpleasant, Ruspensky?" he asked. The other replied, "I do, Peter Ilyitch. Are you the brother of the revolutionary Chaya?" he snapped at my great-grandfather.

"It is a deathly smell, Ruspensky," said the other policeman, "I believe——"

"Don't say it, Ruspensky," answered Peter Ilyitch, "I think you are right." He turned on my great-grandfather and said sternly, "There is something dead in this house is there not?" And truthfully my great-grandfather replied, "There is."

"And where is your sister Chaya, the red cow?" asked one of the two (I don't know whether Peter Ilyitch or Ruspensky). Praying silently my great-grandfather said, "She has been dead these two days and in this hot weather, you understand. Please let me take you to the body so that you can arrest her, because if what I hear is true then she deserves to be sent to Siberia whether she is dead or not."

The two policemen were crossing themselves again and again. "Peter Ilyitch, we should never have come into this accursed place. We shall be cursed for ever—already I have a pain in my belly," said Ruspensky.

"We must inspect the coffin, Ruspensky, or we cannot make a report," replied Peter Ilyitch. "Take us to it," he ordered my great-grandfather.

When he had led them into his workshop, praying all the time, my great-grandfather said, "Here is the coffin and accursed mortal remains of that devil's cat. There is truly a curse on them but perhaps you would care to inspect them?"

Now you must understand that the atmosphere in the workshop

was really unbearable. The cat had been dead for maybe six or seven days in very hot weather, and there it had stayed, for business was too bad for my great-grandfather to bother to go into his workshop. And since it would be terrible bad luck, the last thing the police wanted was to examine my devilish Aunt Chaya's mortal remains. "No," he said, "unnecessary. She smells dead enough, the witch. God—the pain in my belly is becoming terrible," and he pushed Peter Ilyitch out of the house. "Arrange to bury that malignant tomorrow, you," he shouted to my great-grandfather. "Certainly, my lord," called my great-grandfather, "with pleasure." And he wiped his forehead on his sleeve.

Aunt Chaya remained under the stove throughout her burial. Very quickly it was whispered round the village what had happened, and naturally everyone was pleased to attend the burial service the next day. The cat in the tool chest was carried up to the graveyard with the whole village following behind my great-grandfather and three others carrying the box. The cantor was here and sang the whole service beautifully without a single interruption from my great-grandfather. Everyone wept, and after the last shovelful of earth had fallen they all shook hands and wished my great-grandfather and mother long life.

Meanwhile Ruspensky and Peter Ilyitch stood by on their horses. They both had headaches because the brandy at the inn where they stayed the night was so bad, and Ruspensky still had a terrible stomach-ache and knew he was accursed.

Everyone said what a pity it was that Aunt Chaya had to miss her burial. As for the cat, believe me, it was entitled to become a saint if we had such things. Anyhow it must surely have had the finest funeral any cat, believer or otherwise, has ever had anywhere. Even in Pinsk I bet they don't look after cats better.

A FOOL IS ESSENTIAL

In a village there has to be a fool. Where everyone lives on top of everyone else there has to be someone with whom even the most foolish action will go unnoticed, someone, we will agree, who is more stupid than you or I. In my great-grandfather's village, anyone could always consider himself better off and more gifted than Simcha the Golem, as they called him. When someone was annoyed with his wife's cooking he could always laugh at the thought of what Simcha had to go through with his shrew of a woman. When the rabbi said something which my great-grandfather might nod his head against, at least Simcha took it for the word of God. So that quite certainly Simcha was a fool, as stupid as if his head were made of clay, but although everyone agreed that he was a fool, the son of a fool and the father of fools, they still liked him, because in a small village a fool is essential. He gives everyone a feeling of self-respect. "At least I am better than Simcha the Golem, the fool, the clay-head."

So, besides being a convenience for the village, what good was Simcha? If he wasn't bad it was only because he couldn't think of anything wrong to do, and after all, what we consider so good in a good man is the fact that if he chose he could be as evil as he is good. And everyone is grateful about it, because not being evil he doesn't steal your goods, interfere with your daughter, hurt your cow, or cheat you very much in business. But Simcha, oh, Simcha, you could never call good like this. He simply wasn't bad; he wasn't anything. But as sometimes happens with a man like Simcha, though his head was thick clay, his shoulders were an ox's, his legs as solid as the two trees behind the synagogue, and his hands so knotted with strength that he could straighten a horseshoe as you can bend a pin. And through this gift he made a living.

If you had a heavy parcel Simcha carried it. If a wagon was stuck in the mud, when in the spring the snow and ice were melting,

Simcha would move it. If you were building a house and collecting
wood for it, Simcha would cut down the trees as if they were sap-
lings and carry the wood there for you. Every day he worked like a
beast except Saturday, for on the Sabbath he went to the Synagogue.
When he got there Simcha stood behind all the other men just
watching and watching, his eyes moving from one face to another
like a bird's. He listened for as long as there was anything to listen
to. When everyone sat Simcha crouched on the floor, when they
stood up, so did he, and when some old men in the front row started
to snuffle and grunt "Sha, sha," to boys who were making a noise or
other old men who were discussing too loudly the right and wrongs
of some affair, Simcha would stand up at the back there, glare
around at everyone and shout "SHA, SHA, SHA." When everyone
turned to look at him he grinned and blushed and sat down again,
for he was, in spite of his size, somewhat shy.

Though Simcha could never pray for himself he got very near it
by crying his eyes out and beating his breast harder than anyone else
in the synagogue. When he beat his breast it made a hollow sound
like a copper drum, and his tears fell like heavy rain drops upon his
fists. He forgot to follow the actions of the men in all things but
went on beating, beating, crying, crying like a child all the time. Did
Simcha know why he was so upset? He didn't, but if so many good
men were miserable then he had to be miserable as well, just as
when they were happy shaking hands with their neighbors, the
rabbi dancing with the scrolls in his arms, hugged closely to him,
Simcha danced and made noises as if he too were happy. This was
Simcha, a fool, a fool in a village like any other fool, harmless and
with a body like iron, a servant to everyone.

Now this Simcha lived in a filthy hut with a woman who had no
dowry. She was cross-eyed, her wig was never clean, and she hated
everything. She hated Simcha most of all. So why did she marry him
then? A wife should at least not hate a husband. But who else
would have married her? She waited as long as she could and then,
cursing all the men in the village, she married Simcha. What could
he do to protect himself? When she spoke to him, he grinned. She

went on speaking and he went on grinning, until she managed to grin back, making her cross-eyes smaller and stretching her mouth into a thick red worm. Simcha was finished. She married him, and he made a hut out of pieces of wood which nobody wanted and took her to live there, although after a few nights he began to sleep in the open again, except when the weather was too bad, not because he wanted to insult her but because in the hut he couldn't breathe.

Every day of the year you could hear his wife cursing Simcha the Golem. As the years passed her only pleasure was to stand in the door of the hut with her children climbing around her, all cursing Simcha at the tops of their voices. But still he went on working to bring them a few kopecks, and still he always looked surprised when he gave them to her and she cursed him for it. People sometimes gave him a little more when they thought of his sorrow. He thanked them as he always did, gave the money to his wife as usual, and she cursed him again. She never grinned at him any more. Perhaps it was an accident that she ever did.

If Sholem Pinsk wanted above all to go to the city of Pinsk where he pretended he had already been, if the rabbi wanted above all to be visited by an angel, if Yaacov the teacher's son wanted only to print something in a paper, then it is reasonable that Simcha should want something also. You would see him sometimes sitting by the road smoking tea leaves wrapped in newspaper. He pressed the leaves together into the shape of one of his own thick fingers, wrapped them carefully, and smoked them, a dreamy look on his face, staring at the road yet seeing nothing but what—what is the dream of such a fool? Tea leaves he collected every day from the inn, straight from the big urn where tea was always brewing. He dried them in a little heap on the stove and put them in his pocket. As he left the inn he watched men smoking their pipes quietly and the same dreamy look came over his face as when he smoked his own newspaper cigars by the roadside.

Once when Simcha was drying tea leaves on the stove my great-grandfather came into the inn. He sat down with a glass of brandy, for it was a market day and he had sold one or two pipes. He got out

his own pipe, one which he had made when he got married to celebrate and to soothe him. He filled it with tobacco from a leather bag,
and sat smoking quietly. Then he noticed Simcha was staring at him,
and he said:

"Good day to you Simcha. Have you made a good meal?"

For how else can you talk to a simple man other than about the
things that mean something in his life? Yet Simcha did not reply. He
stared at my great-grandfather for a while, then suddenly stood up
and left, his face black and miserable.

"What have you said to Simcha?" asked a man.

"Nothing at all," replied my great-grandfather. "He is surly, a
surly fool. Whenever he sees me he looks like that. Have I got the
evil eye?"

"What do you expect from a fool?" replied the man.

Yet Simcha had no ill-feeling for my great-grandfather. The sight
of a pipe always made him sad, and the sight of a pipe-maker smoking his own pipe, a pipe which made all others look small and badly
carved, made poor Simcha more miserable than a regiment of cross-
eyed wives, more weary than twenty wagons of corn, more black in
the face than insults, more cold through his whole body than the
darkest winter. Because he did not understand any of these things
Simcha simply accepted them when they came, but a pipe—ah, a
pipe he had wanted all his life, so that the mere sight of my great-
grandfather's pipe made him feel sick and empty. Desire came suddenly upon him and he felt weak in his guts.

As Simcha smoked his tea leaves quietly by the roadside he
dreamed of a pipe. Pipes filled his mind and his dream was happy,
until all other pipes were cleared away and a pipe of my great-grandfather's making lay in the mind of Simcha with nothing else at all.
Simcha moved his fingers stroking its warm bowl. His thick fingers
moved gently as if handling a moth.

So in the life of Simcha, which was simply one thing after another exactly as it happened, this was the only misery. And things
grew worse with him. When he lay down at night he looked up at
the sky and it was nothing to him. He carried bigger packs, he

pushed more wagons out of the mud, his children spat at him, his neighbors laughed, yet he, he thought only of a pipe. He talked less and less for "pipe" was the only word he wanted to say, and to what purpose? But he spent as much time as he could near my great-grandfather's workshop watching, always watching. He saw the pipes being made, and as the stock piled up Simcha rejoiced. But as the pipes sold he grew sad, so sad he would not work but lay on his back all day moping. The taste went out of his newspaper cigars. His life went out as all men lit their new pipes and sighed their contentment.

My great-grandfather wasn't blind. He saw Simcha watching him, but he went on with his work. If a fool wants to watch, let him, it was none of his business. But after a while he had to admit that his shaping and carving were not as good as they had been. He cursed his tools, he hit my young grandfather for no reason at all, yet still as he bent over his bench he felt the blank eyes of Simcha the Golem watching him. His blood began to boil in his veins, his neck grew red, his eyes became bloodshot. Then one day when in the hot sunshine Simcha just stood looking and looking not saying a word, my great-grandfather swept everything off his bench, and with a shout threw down his tools.

Simcha stood still, but his eyes were suddenly full of tears. He rushed up to the bench and searched all around it muttering to himself and crying.

My great-grandfather shouted, "Are you satisfied now, you great fool? Are you satisfied? Standing there loafing, looking with big cow's eyes all day long. Are you satisfied?"

Simcha said nothing. Then he found the broken bowl of the pipe my great-grandfather had been working on, and his tears fell like rain as he held the two pieces together.

"Simcha," said my great-grandfather more quietly. "What is the matter?"

Simcha opened his mouth, holding the pieces out towards my great-grandfather. His lips tried to make words and his tongue went in and out, but he said nothing.

"Tell me what's wrong Simcha. Are you in pain?"

"A pipe—a pipe I want." Through the thick lips came a voice as small as a little cat.

"Take one then, Simcha, you should have spoken before. Have one, certainly, any one you like," said my great-grandfather.

Simcha looked down at the broken pipe in his hand. He wiped his face with his fist. The pipe was carved with a bull's head; you could mark out its fierce eyes and its nostrils, and the powerful muscles of its thick neck below the bowl.

"A bull," said Simcha, and he turned away and went and sat by the roadside. He placed the two pieces of the broken pipe on the grass together and without looking away from them took a packet out of his pocket. He opened the packet, took out tea leaves and newspaper, and rolled a cigar as thick as one of his own stupid fingers.

"Have a good pipe, Simcha, have one of these," shouted my great-grandfather.

Simcha looked at the bull's-head pipe on the grass. He put the cigar between his lips and lit it without ever looking away from the two pieces of the pipe. His face looked just as the rabbi's face would look if suddenly an angel came up the village street and told him that next year it would be in Jerusalem.

THE PORTRAIT

Not very many strangers came to my great-grandfather's village, but when it happened everyone knew and avoided them, not that they felt unfriendly, but because usually strangers came from the police or the army or the tax collectors, and who wants to talk to such people?

So it was when early one spring, just as the snow and ice were beginning to disappear, a stranger arriving in the village walked about all day trying to start conversations, without anyone answering more than "Yes" or "No," and sometimes even less. Now this stranger carried a box on his back, and wore his beard trimmed close to his face. He was a big man, too, and what with his red neck and the black beard he looked like a bull. He walked about the village the whole day, sometimes pulling out a book to write something, and smiling at people when they unsmiling hurried past him, until at last he began to feel that perhaps no one liked him very much. Just as he came to this conclusion he happened to be walking past my great-grandfather's workshop.

My great-grandfather bent over his bench working a piece of wood into the shape of a pipe bowl. Though he didn't look up, he saw the stranger, and furthermore, he saw the stranger take out his book and write something in it. As he wrote, the stranger looked up every so often at my great-grandfather's workshop until my great-grandfather decided that even if the man watching him was a tax collector he should at least know what he was going to get into trouble for. So he put down his chisel, and went outside.

The stranger watched him as he walked up to the gate slowly. My great-grandfather considered meanwhile which would be the best way to address the foreigner. Should he call him plain "Sir" or "Your lordship" or what? But before he could decide, the man ran up the path towards him shouting. He clapped his arms round my great-grandfather and shouted right in his ear:

"I have searched Russia for this face!"

And the stranger embraced my great-grandfather before anything could be done to stop him, still shouting, "My God—this is the face I have been looking for!"

By this time my great-grandfather realized he was dealing with a madman, so doing his best not to make things worse by seeming not to want the embrace of the man, he got himself out from his grip, and walked back a few paces. The madman stood there with his arms stretched out, a stupid smile on his face, looking like a bull smiling, and he said happily:

"I never expected to find such a face in such a village as this, never."

Though he didn't quite see why a face as his shouldn't be found in his own village, my great-grandfather decided not to argue with the madman about that. Instead he said to him, "If you don't mind my asking you, what are you embracing me for?" To which the man replied, "I have always known this face in my mind. Only now for the first time I have seen it."

Which made my great-grandfather think, "Who wants to argue with a madman?" Though he said, "Well, I'm glad you like it, but if you don't want to buy a pipe now I'll go back to my workshop." And he turned to go back into his workshop.

Before he could walk more than two or three yards the man rushed up to him and shouted again like at first, "You must let me have it!"

By now my great-grandfather was getting a little annoyed, because he was always a man with a quick temper. Once he lost his temper with anyone it was not such a good thing for that person. But still he kept polite and said to the madman:

"Please. You only just now said to me that you liked my face and you didn't want to buy a pipe. Now you want it. Either you want to buy a pipe or you do not want to buy a pipe. I don't mind which." And he pushed the man's hand from off his shoulder.

But the madman wouldn't go. Again he said, "You must let me have it. You must give me your face."

This was altogether too much for my great-grandfather. He turned away saying, "Please do me a favor and stop making jokes with me. I am a poor man with work to do." And he walked away quickly.

Yet still the madman—he must have been really mad—wouldn't leave him alone. He shouted—he was always shouting—"I only mean you should let me paint a picture of you."

My great-grandfather, who had never seen a picture of himself, stopped with his back towards the madman—who was perhaps not so mad after all. He thought of a picture of himself which everyone could see and recognize and point at and say, "Look at that! Isn't it him to the very life? You know who that is? He is the finest pipe-maker in all Russia." Why shouldn't there be a picture of him? After thinking which he turned round and asked, "Why should you want to paint me? And how much would you charge?"

The madman, who was (as you can tell) really an artist, answered very quickly, "Believe me, my good sir, it would be a pleasure and a privilege for me to paint your portrait for nothing."

Which made my great-grandfather wonder whether there was something else behind it after all. But when he told the artist, "I wouldn't be able to have a painted image made in my own house. I'm a religious man, you must realize," the artist said, "You shouldn't worry about that. I will paint the picture here in your own front yard and everyone in the village shall see it, and then with your permission I will take it back to the city for other people to see."

So my great-grandfather said to himself, "If people want to see my painted picture and this madman wants to paint my picture, why should I make so many people disappointed? After all, this madman is no fool. Hasn't he picked me from among everyone in the village?" And he replied to the man, "All right then. I give you my kind permission to paint me."

To which the artist answered, very excited, "Thank you, thank you. Let us begin now."

My great-grandfather, never having had his portrait painted before, said, "All right, then. Paint." And he turned for the third time to go back into the house. But the artist explained to him that he had to sit still for a while, and after a lot of fuss they brought out a small piece of wood for putting the paints on, and all the other things which he used for painting. There were so many of these things I haven't got the time to tell you all about them. But what does it matter? However many things there were, they were needed for painting my great-grandfather's portrait.

The artist, who was a quick workman, finished the painting in a couple of hours, and all the time my great-grandfather kept asking him, "Well, is it finished? How much longer?"

But the artist was so polite and told him so many times that this was the face he had been looking for everywhere, that my great-grandfather sat more or less still the whole time, thinking about how the village would be surprised, and what the rabbi would say, and how jealous Reb Sholem Pinsk would be that the artist had not asked him if his face could be painted. Of course, my great-grandmother was also there, standing near my great-grandfather hoping that the artist might be painting her into the picture as well. As for my young grandfather, he had run round to all the houses telling them what was happening, so that more and more people crowded round the artist as he sat on his little stool painting. My young grandfather stood in the front of the crowd shouting out, "Now he's painting the nose. Now he's painting the eye." And so on until the artist had finished, when my grandfather shouted out, "Now he's finished!"

Then the whole crowd, which had been watching very quietly, breathed out together, and no wonder, because the painting was the first one which had ever been made in the village, and what do you think? It looked exactly like my great-grandfather even to the eyes, one of which was brown while the other was blue. Reb Sholem Pinsk, however, was speaking in a loud high voice, saying, "Such excitement over a little picture like this! In Pinsk everyone is painted, not little like this, but big—almost as big as a house."

But no one took any notice because Reb Sholem was the only one who had seen pictures in Pinsk or anywhere else, and no one believed that he had been to Pinsk anyhow.

When my great-grandmother saw the picture she was at first very upset because she wasn't in it. She said, "How could he leave me out? Wasn't I standing there right beside the bench?"

Still, when she saw all the other women looking at the picture first up close and after from a little distance away, she decided it was indeed a proud moment for her. She stood beside the picture for the whole time it was in the yard with the crowd around it, smiling to everyone and bowing her head as if she had painted it herself. Oh, there was no doubt about it, the picture was very fine indeed, although my young grandfather was in the back yard having a fight with a boy who said it looked like the Tsar Nicholas himself. Everyone agreed the picture was a wonderful likeness except Reb Sholem, who kept asking, "Will anyone tell me whose picture this is? It is no doubt a very fine likeness, but surely it is no one in this village."

However, who listened to him? They were all standing around my great-grandfather waiting there to shake him by the hand, to congratulate him and wish him long life. Everyone told the artist how clever he was, and the rabbi asked him if he wasn't grateful to God for such a gift to be breathed into his hands, to which the artist replied that he most certainly was very grateful. Then Reb Sholem asked him how much a man could earn in the city making pictures like this, to which the artist replied, "No money could buy a picture like this."

My great-grandfather smiled, and poured out brandy for everyone, while my young grandfather looked round to see if any more of the boys felt like saying the picture was a bad likeness.

Well, the artist stayed in the house of my great-grandfather that night, as guest of honor, though the picture was left in the workshop because, as the rabbi pointed out, even such a good picture as this was in a sense a graven image and could not be kept in an orthodox house. My great-grandmother made a special borscht which was so thick it could be cut in slices, and there were plenty of potatoes as well. After everyone else had gone to bed, the artist stayed up talking with my great-grandfather. They finished another bottle of brandy, though what they talked about I do not know, because my grandfather was asleep on top of the stove at the time and consequently did not hear, and therefore was not able to tell me.

The next day the artist went. Everyone saw him off from the village. Afterwards they spent days talking about what an honor it was for the village that my great-grandfather had been painted. Pity the artist took the picture away with him, wrapped up in cloth my great-grandmother cut from one of her best petticoats. A picture like that could only be wrapped in the best. It was nice too that after the artist had left and my great-grandmother looked about the house, she could find nothing missing, which may have been because she had hidden away the silver sticks for the candles used on holidays and Friday evenings, and there was nothing else to steal in the house except the hens, which she then counted and found all present. It was, however, this artist and what happened to the silver candlesticks which he did not steal that brought the great shame of his life on my great-grandfather. This shame was not to fall for several months, but it did fall, and when it fell it was a very great shame indeed.

What happened was this. Later on, in the same year as my great-grandfather had his portrait painted, my young grandfather was sent to the market to buy some fish cheap. This market was held in the village over the hill where they were celebrating a holiday called Lent in which for some reason or other everyone goes crazy and eats fish the whole time. There was therefore a lot of fish on sale. Though there were also stalls with fruit, vegetables, and even a few selling spindles—which they make out of soft wood which grows in the forests near my great-grandfather's village—and a stall with toys. Still almost all the stalls sold fish. Which means, since the peasants can catch their own fish, that it will be sold cheaply. So my young grandfather was sent over there to buy some fish, although when he returned out of breath and red in the face, he had, strange to say, brought no fish with him. When my great-grandmother asked where the fish was, he couldn't answer he was so excited and out of breath. Even when she asked him for the second time, "So, where is the fish, you little loafer?" he still found it hard to reply, though in the end he managed to answer, "In the market there is a stall covered with pictures of my father." At which my great-grandmother could hardly believe her ears. She put on her best shawl, and told my grandfather, "If this is only one of your stories I shall see to it that you are sorry for it. Telling your mother stories!"

But he replied to her, "Come and see for yourself then. I am telling you—a stall is covered with big and small pictures of my father." And he led my great-grandmother back to the market at a terrible pace.

When she got there my great-grandmother walked through the crowds looking all round, my grandfather following eating an apple which he had found near a stall which happened to be selling apples. When he was about to eat the core, my great-grandmother stopped, turned round and said to him, "Can I see this stall with pictures anywhere? Am I blind?"

My grandfather was so annoyed at not being believed the whole time, he threw away what was left of the apple-core—there was very little—swallowed what was in his mouth, and shouted, "How do you expect to find it? Are you leading me or am I leading you? If you will only let me show the way instead of running everywhere like a squirrel, I will show you this stall with pictures of my father on it." He was very annoyed.

Then he ran ahead so fast that my great-grandmother had trouble keeping sight of him. At last she saw him stop at a little stall at the end of the market. She hurried towards it promising herself she would see he had some of the nonsense knocked out of him even if he had told her the truth for a change. But she stopped before she got up to him. She stopped because on a large banner hung across the stall was a big icon. And the face of the icon—God should have forbidden it—was the face of my pious great-grandfather.

She was even more shocked when on coming closer to the stall she found that *all* the faces of *all* the icons on the stall were the face of my great-grandfather. Big icons or little ones, there was no difference in the faces, and each one of them had the name of a different saint written underneath it, though of course they were not different saints, they were all my great-grandfather.

Well, my great-grandmother blushed for shame. That a pious man like my great-grandfather should have a thing like this happen to him! She didn't wait to ask the orthodox man who kept the stall any questions. She ran straight back to the workshop to tell my great-grandfather, though she remembered to shout as she passed my grandfather that he should buy some fish.

While his mother was away my grandfather went back to the apple stall to see if he could find any more apples. On the way he met a friend, and they decided that my grandfather should find apples while his friend asked the peasant whose stall it was how much he would take for six pounds of apples. After they had done this, the friend explained at length to the peasant that the apples were too dear, they went to a quiet part of the market and ate the apples which my grandfather had carried away in the legs of his trousers which were tied at the outside with string.

Meanwhile my great-grandmother was explaining what she had seen to my great-grandfather, who was (as you might expect) struck dumb by the news. He was unable to think, so full was his mind of big and small icons, all with his face painted on them. Then he saw with his mind's eye Reb Sholem Pinsk holding these icons close to his face to see them properly, then looking round and laughing and rubbing his hands, telling everyone in the world about this great shame that had fallen upon my great-grandfather. After watching such things in his mind for so long that my great-grandmother thought he was never going to answer, he pulled on his coat, and rushed out of the house without a word.

My great-grandfather hurried to the market, found the stall and stood dumbly looking at the icons. While he wondered what to do, my grandfather was still eating apples with his friend, and already they were beginning to feel slight pains in the stomach though they still went on eating. My great-grandfather at last decided that all he could do was buy the icons and bury them. He was about to speak to the orthodox man who kept the stall when the man said to him, "Haven't I met you somewhere, in Lutzen perhaps? I seem to know your face. Yes, yes, it is Mendel the Carrier, surely."

My great-grandfather said no, he was not Mendel the Carrier. He was in fact a pipe-maker, and he would like to buy all the icons on the man's stall. The man looked in amazement and said: "What should an orthodox man with such side curls be doing with all these images, and anyhow, can any man be so religious as to want so many icons?"

My great-grandfather said to him not to mind, that he wanted to make presents to all the peasants who were his customers, and that the man should make him a fair price for all the icons. Well, naturally they argued for a long time, the man explaining that he had paid a big price for them but that's how he was in business—he always paid too much for his goods, still, seeing as my great-grandfather was such a generous fellow he would only ask him for six rubles for the whole lot complete.

"What? Six rubles? Am I made of money?" inquired my great-grandfather.

The man said all right, it was a terrible loss to him but he would take five rubles, he said it was robbery but he would take three rubles and a pipe. All my great-grandfather had to do now was to find three rubles, and from where was he going to get so much money? A man can work a whole week and keep a family on a ruble so where was he going to get three rubles from? There was only one man who could spare so much money in the village—Asher the Moneylender, but you think Asher was a moneylender because he was fond of giving people money? No. Asher always had to have something of yours as security before he could give you any money, and what had my great-grandfather got which might be a security for three rubles? I have already mentioned them. He had a pair of silver candlesticks for the Sabbath and for holidays.

Now a man may sell his animals or his piece of land or his cherry trees. He may even pawn his book if he has one, or his wife's beads or anything else he likes, but he may not pawn his silver candlesticks. He may not pawn them because they are not really his. They belong to his father, and to his son and to his son's son, and how will he keep the sabbath without his candlesticks, where will his wife put the candles so that she can light them when the sun goes down, and everyone can sit around the table, and say prayers, and eat supper with the candles burning on the table, and people passing outside seeing the light from the candles and everyone looking forward to worshipping God and doing no work the next day? Obviously a man can't pawn or sell his silver candlesticks. Without them his carry-on can fall to pieces. But in spite of this my great-grandfather was thinking about pawning his candlesticks. He asked himself which was the greater shame, to do that or to be in every peasant's hut under false pretenses as Saint This and Saint That. While he could work to get back the candlesticks, what could he do to make up for being a saint under false pretenses in the peasants' huts?

So he regretfully wrapped up the candlesticks in his coat and went out to pawn them, leaving my great-grandmother crying in the kitchen. He knew Asher never spoke about who came to him for money, but the whole way over to Asher's house he saw himself on pieces of wood hanging up in the corners of cottages all over Russia with lights burning in front of him and peasants praying to him. Believe me, it was far better to pawn the candlesticks, even if it was the greatest shame that ever fell upon my great-grandfather.

After he had seen Asher the Moneylender and argued about how much the candlesticks were worth, been offered a ruble, then two rubles, he finally took three and a half rubles, promising to pay Asher back four—because this after all, was how Asher made his living—my great-grandfather rushed back to the market where the orthodox man had already tied up all the icons into a big parcel. He gave the parcel to my great-grandfather and said to him, "For such a man as you who will spend money to make the peasants happy, I have a special gift." And he handed him a little crucifix which he swore was made out of wood from the original cross.

All this time my grandfather was still with his friend and as they rubbed their stomachs they said what rotten apples the peasants sold, and how they made a mistake to bother to steal them. My great-grandfather didn't notice them but took the parcel home, putting the little crucifix in his pocket. He took the icons into his workshop to wait until night came when he could bury them. All the while my great-grandmother still cried in the kitchen, lamenting the loss of the candlesticks, for how could my great-grandfather ever pay Asher back, and why had such a shame fallen upon the family and upon the whole village?

All day my great-grandfather would not eat. He spoke to no one and did no work. At last he came to the conclusion that somehow or other he must get his money back for the icons—he simply couldn't afford to bury three rubles and the family candlesticks. But how to do it? He thought and thought and at last came to a solution. He sat up all night carving small faces out of soft wood. Though they weren't very good likenesses of anyone you could see they were faces. These he nailed onto the icons, and then packed the whole lot up again. He would take them the very next day to the market, and sell them—a brilliant plan of campaign.

Which is what he did. But when he got to the market and set out the icons, none of the peasants fancied them. My great-grandfather stood there with my young grandfather, feeling more and more certain he would never get back the candlesticks, my great-grandmother would cry in the kitchen for years without stopping. He got so tired of waiting to sell an icon, even one, that he went off for a glass of brandy to help him forget his troubles. He drank two or three brandies, but with each drink he only felt his troubles more and more. He began to sing a song to cheer himself up, but in spite of the fact it was a drinking song and consequently very happy, he began to cry a little, the tears dropping onto his beard. At last he decided he was wasting more money sitting there drinking only to get more miserable. He left the inn and found his way back to where my young grandfather was looking after the icons.

When he finally got there my great-grandfather rubbed his eyes in amazement. What should he see but my young grandfather lying on the ground sleeping with not a single icon left. My great-grandfather knew at once they had all been stolen, he had done right to get more miserable. It was his great bad luck to have only such a boy as my grandfather to leave in charge of things. He pushed him with his foot, shouting:

"You fool, you! What have you done with all the icons? You have let them get stolen while you sleep."

My young grandfather jumped up and shouted right back, "What do you think this is, then?" He shook his pockets and they jingled like mad. Then he took money out of them and gave it to my great-grandfather.

When my great-grandfather realized that the candlesticks were saved, he wept over my grandfather and blessed him, and finally asked him how this miracle had happened to them. My grandfather explained.

"I hung the icons upside down one by one. A religious peasant may not see a saint treated like that. They bought to save them from being hung upside down."

Still weeping my great-grandfather thanked God for such a son and went at once to Asher the Moneylender.

But at the same time, although everything came out all right in the eleventh hour, it was a shame on the family that even for a day the sabbath candlesticks should be in pawn.

THE DEVIL AND THE COW

Naturally my great-grandmother had a cow. Not that it was in any way a particularly good cow. It never won any prizes, it sometimes didn't give so much milk, one of its horns had got knocked off, and it would never come when it was called. It was an ordinary cow, a cow like any other, and when my great-grandmother went out at night to call, "Masha, Masha," (because that was its name) she might hear a noise somewhere, of something kicked over, but whether Masha heard my great-grandmother is another matter, because she never answered.

She wandered about all day and at night wandered still, into other people's yards, the street, a plowed field, all night through, yet never tiring. Sometimes you would see Masha slowly walking over the hill. Those nights it took hours to find her again, and it was no use calling. As a further aggravation, this cow often went up to the ruin on top of the hill and stayed there all day.

You might say, "All right, then, it was an annoying cow. What do you expect from a cow?"

But then you will have missed the whole point. It was an annoying cow, agreed, but going up to the ruins and loafing around them all day and night is too much, because, you understand, there was a devil up there.

This, of course, is the reason why my great-grandmother's cow gave so little milk. Not because she had a hard time being driven about the place all day, or because she never got enough to eat, but because two or three times a week she went up the hill to the ruins, and while she was there, the devil milked her. So you will perhaps now agree that Masha was going too far, for who was going to climb a hill simply to be pushed down by a devil? No one would go after Masha.

No one, that is, except my great-grandmother, for she had to cook dinner every day, she had to find something to eat, and for this Masha was essential.

My great-grandmother used to ask the rest of them, "Has anyone seen this devil? What does he look like? Like Sholem Pinsk, maybe? Or like your father when he was drunk last time?"

And so she went out every evening to find the cow, and even if it had gone up to the ruins she climbed the hill slowly, calling, "Masha, Masha." And though it happened she went up the hill many times to bring Masha back to the house, my great-grandmother never once saw that devil.

But that is not to say there was no devil to be seen. The time came when even my great-grandmother discovered that the devil was actually there, although even then she didn't exactly see him. Why should the devil waste his time showing himself to my great-grandmother? The devil is too busy to spend his time showing off to anyone who happens to walk up a hill looking for a lost cow. He lived there because he had a very good reason. If not, why should he waste his time at the top of such a little hill when there were so many mountains he could have chosen?

This devil could, in fact, have stayed wherever he fancied, like any other devil, but he chose the hill because of the ruins that were at the top of it. And it was not only the ruins that interested him, but what was hidden in them. Somewhere in those ruins was buried a treasure worth more than the whole village, more than Pinsk, even.

No one knew what this treasure was exactly, but it had been hidden in the ruins for many years, and since every one said that there was a treasure, there certainly must have been one.

You might wonder why if there was a treasure no one tried to find it. After all, it's something, the chance of finding a fortune and living in a palace for the rest of your life, with servants around you and nothing to do except drink lemon tea and eat chicken all day long. And, naturally, several people had thought that it wouldn't be such a bad thing to find a treasure like this. But then, there was always the devil protecting it.

What is more, everyone knew the treasure could only be discovered at midnight by the light of a full moon. Why, they were unable to say, but that it was so no one questioned. Who would bother to invent such a ridiculous story? It was obviously true, and no matter how much someone wants a fortune it's not worth his while if it means being eaten by a devil. Even a dead lion is worth only the value of his skin, and believe me, not many people are buying lion skins these days.

So this was the situation—at the top of the hill there was a ruin, and in this ruin there was a treasure, and over this treasure there was sitting, or sometimes, maybe, standing or dancing—after all, a devil is a devil—a pretty dangerous devil. Anyone who thought of trying to find the treasure thought first of the devil, and then went out to earn an honest living instead.

For most people it would have been enough to know all this. Most people can be relied upon to act sensibly if they know that it will be a lot easier for them if they do—after all, a devil is a pretty good warning. However, sometimes you come across a man who just won't learn, and then there's no use talking. You must simply take no notice of such men. When they say, "I think I'll go up to the ruin and take the treasure," you simply reply, "Good luck to you. You should have a nice night for it." And then go about your business.

There is such a man in every village and this man is not necessarily large. In my great-grandfather's village he was small and thin, and although he lived in an orthodox village he wasn't orthodox but lived there because he had inherited a piece of land. This man was a carpenter and his name was Igor.

Igor never swore. He drank very little, yet he was certainly the most reckless man in the village. Sometimes he turned very quiet. Then suddenly he would disappear, coming back a couple of days later with a few dead wolves. Once he came back after a week with a bearskin.

One night this Igor dug up the whole of the village street without saying a word to anyone. Suddenly one morning he was found standing there, with the whole street dug up. Being a reasonable man he put all the rubbish back when it was pointed out to him that the road being dug up made it difficult for people to pass. That was the sort of thing he used to do, yet in spite of this, everyone took him their trade, when they happened to need a coffin. Igor made good plain coffins of a seasoned wood which did not, like your cheap coffins, rot away in no time. Igor's coffins would last you a lifetime.

Mind, sometimes you felt uncomfortable meeting him, for as a result of measuring up so many people for their coffins, he always looked you up and down, working out how much timber you would need, and that sort of look makes you feel a little cold, particularly if lately you haven't been feeling too well.

This Igor may have been reckless when he dug up the village street for no reason at all, but, at least, there was—if the constable was not around—no danger in that. But when he suddenly came into my great-grandfather's workshop and said, "I think that I shall go and find the treasure up on the hill," it was something different. After all, what man, even if he is very strong, can hope to do well against a devil? A man is a man, and when he starts interfering with his betters, his chances of doing good business are worth a blown-out egg.

But that is what Igor said, and my great-grandfather could see he meant it. So after drinking a few glasses of brandy together, they shook hands and Igor went off to wait until the moon came up.

That very night my great-grandmother's cow decided to loaf about as usual. Still Igor wasn't a man to worry whether a skinny old cow was either here or there. He did what he had to do, regardless of cows and other people.

That night he took a few more brandies as he put the finishing touches to a beautiful coffin he was making for a small, very square, fat man he had studied with interest for some time. It was a good coffin and was sure to come in handy. When he had finished both the coffin and the bottle of brandy, he went out to the foot of the hill.

At the same time my great-grandmother was calling from her yard, "Masha, Mashkele! Where are you, darling?" She knew the cow never answered, but she also could be stubborn.

Igor went up the hill, and once or twice he thought he heard someone calling, but he didn't look back. He went straight up towards the ruins and settled down to wait on a bank of grass with bushes growing on it, for midnight to come. My great-grandmother called out again after the cow, "What are you doing, then?"

This time Igor heard. He stood up, all on guard. Again she cried, "Well, why do you wait you beast?" Igor shouted back, "You are the beast, you old devil."

Now, when my great-grandmother heard a voice reply, she realized something unusual was going on. Masha the cow never answered, she never cared who waited for her, and here for the first time, a voice replied to my great-grandmother, calling her an old devil, into the bargain.

My great-grandmother was not the woman to stand for insults. At once she shouted back, "I shall flay you alive, you dog!"

And this made Igor—who was a little drunk—remember what he had heard about the devil. Igor felt, for the first time, afraid. Nevertheless, he was determined to find the treasure, so he climbed quickly up the wall of the ruin and began to feel around the top of it with one hand, while holding onto the stones with the other.

My great-grandmother was by now beginning to worry about Masha, and she shouted as she walked up the hill, "Where are you, little skinny beast?"

At this insult Igor—who was, you will remember, a little thin man—turned round to shout back, and saw, just below him, a single horn sticking up, and a great face with a dribbling mouth looking at him. At that very moment my great-grandmother shouted, "I shall make you sorry you climbed up there."

Now Igor was more than plain worried. He knew he was as good as dead. Wondering if they would bury him in the square coffin he had made for the fat man, he fell down into the long grass crying out, "The devil is eating me!"

My great-grandmother could tell from all this racket that there was someone on the hill, and even she felt a little afraid. Then suddenly she saw a black shape charging towards her, because, just for a change, Masha had decided to move in the right direction for once.

My great-grandmother turned and ran, thinking that even if it wasn't actually the devil chasing her, a good woman couldn't be too careful, and whatever it was, she didn't like it. She ran all the way back home, and locked the door, waking everyone up.

My young grandfather looked out from on top of the stove where he slept. "The devil played monkey tricks with me," cried his mother as all the chickens flew out from under the stove, kicking up a terrible fuss.

My great-grandfather looked very grave when he heard the whole story. "You, running about the countryside all night like a madwoman shouting out, 'Masha, Mashkele,'" he said. "You should be ashamed. I suppose now you'll believe clever men who say there is a devil here or a devil there? Have a little respect in future." And he went out to collect Igor's mortal remains.

When Igor told him how he had seen gold and jewels shining in the moonlight, my great-grandfather asked him if he had perhaps managed to bring a little away. He was very disappointed when he heard that just as Igor was about to reach out for the treasure, the jealous devil pushed him down and spat on him.

But as he wisely observed, "At least it proves there must certainly be a treasure up in the ruins. For if not, why should the devil push you down? The devil is not a person to waste his time pushing people around for no reason."

Igor sadly replied, "If there was not a devil I would have got the treasure. A poor man can do no right."

As for Masha, no one knew what became of her that night, though she came back the following day. My great-grandmother noticed she didn't look as pleased with herself as usual. Of course she still gave very little milk, but it was welcome. And of course she still refused to come when called. But after this my great-grandmother said she didn't care. For her part, the cow could loaf around the ruins every night if she liked. She could stay there and be roasted, for all my great-grandmother cared.

BONIFAS THE COBBLER

Bonifas the Cobbler died when my grandfather was six. He died drunk in a puddle. That is to say, his face was in the puddle though the rest of him was lying across the road. And the rain came down for two or three days, and no one went out very much, and those that did said when they saw Bonifas in the road, "That drunken peasant Bonifas! Let him get wet, the pig."

And they walked over him to wherever they were going, but if they had tried to wake him up they would have been unlucky, because he was dead.

This Bonifas was a big peasant, very strong, with hands which could bend a horseshoe straight, and though he was always drinking too much, he was a good cobbler. If you went to him and said, "Look here, Bonifas, I would like a good pair of boots before the next holidays," he would very likely be a little drunk, and then if he didn't try to beat your head with his hammer, he would laugh a great deal and keep clapping you across the back, and dribble onto his chin, which was even worse because he was still likely to hit you with his hammer. Or he might pick up a horseshoe—there were always a few horseshoes about his workshop for the purpose—and insist that you bet him a few kopecks he couldn't bend it straight. It was no use telling him he was maybe the strongest man in Russia, that he could bend anything he wanted, he still insisted, which cost you money for nothing. Of course, you could always refuse to bet, but it was advisable not to because he would shout, "Oho—you call me a liar to my face! Where is my hammer?"

In this way then, Bonifas made a good living with which to drink himself to death. But it was not only drinking that killed this Bonifas. It was his behavior when drunk. He would stand in the middle of the village—and it wasn't his village either, because he lived over the hill in the other place—he would stand there shouting out terrible things while everyone who listened observed, "That drunken peasant Bonifas, may his entrails shrink, may he die in a ditch" (which is exactly how it turned out in the end). Then the good people went to bed shaking their heads at the fate which they knew would overtake Bonifas, but making sure the shutters on their windows were locked all the same. But not for some years did anything overcome him. He just went on drinking two or three whole bottles of vodka before he became drunk enough to notice. After a while it took four or five bottles of vodka. It was about then that Bonifas became worse in his behavior than anyone could remember, and not long after that, he died.

One morning it was discovered that the graveyard had been desecrated. All the stones were knocked over, and everything kicked and dirtied. The earth, loose from the rain which had been falling endlessly for the past few weeks, was piled up. When the beadle (who was also the gravedigger) Reb Sholem Pinsk came to the graveyard that morning to measure up a grave for a good friend who had asked for a nice piece near the synagogue (so that everyone could see his name) he was amazed at the sight. He was a pious man although somewhat shortsighted, and when he first saw the graveyard that morning he thought the dead had risen, and began to imagine he had been chosen to announce the Messiah. But when he realized at last what had actually happened, he ran into the village shouting to everyone he met. He went on running until he got to the house of the rabbi to whom he told the dreadful story.

The rabbi sat him down and gave him tea freshly poured, and got him to repeat the whole story. Then the rabbi thought for a long while, pulling at his white beard, and side whiskers, for he still had all his hair although being as he was old it was snow-white. The rabbi thought and thought, and sometimes he stopped pulling his beard to ask a question, but always he was thinking. Finally he said, "Come Reb Sholem. Let us go together to see what actually has happened."

Everyone was already at the graveyard, and when the rabbi arrived, began at once to ask him questions. But he just stood there quietly pulling his beard, till Reb Sholem began to feel a little impatient with all this thinking and pulling white beards.

"If this had happened in Pinsk," he grumbled, "we should already be doing something, not standing about like a lot of old women, pulling our beards."

He was at once silenced sternly for his lack of respect, and the rabbi was just about to make a wise observation when there was heard shouting, and down the road came running two short, sturdy, clean-shaven men wearing leather aprons. My great-grandfather remarked correctly, "It is the two brothers Grigor and Saba from the other village, whom I know because they make my boots."

These two brothers were, you understand, cobblers as well as Bonifas, although they didn't drink so much, and never insulted the rabbi, or stood about swearing and cursing. In spite of this they didn't get as much trade as Bonifas, simply because although they were good men they were bad bootmakers, and also because if you didn't go to Bonifas fairly often he came to you, and then there was likely to be something broken. My great-grandfather, however, had always said, "That drunken dog will never make my boots, and if he comes shouting around here, he'll be lucky to get away with a chisel through his neck." He always went to the brothers Grigor and Saba for his boots. As the brothers came running up they shouted about the graveyard, telling everyone that Bonifas had torn up the tombstones and dirtied everything, and straightaway they made themselves a few more clients. The rabbi pulled his beard and replied, eagerly, "I am not surprised. This was in my mind. This Bonifas is a malignant."

Now that they had evidence as to who had desecrated the graveyard, the rabbi said he would go and make a formal complaint to the constable. He went to get his high hat and frockcoat, first telling Reb Sholem Pinsk to clean up the graveyard, which was, after all, what he was paid for.

My great-grandfather and my young grandfather went back to breakfast, my great-grandfather complaining in his deep bass voice, "Make a complaint to the constable! And what will the constable do? He will go and have a drink with Bonifas, that drunken impious dog Bonifas." To which my young grandfather replied, "Why doesn't someone simply hit Bonifas very hard?"

My great-grandfather thought this remark over, slowly rubbing his nose meanwhile. My young grandfather ran on into the house and by the time my great-grandfather arrived, three fresh rolls had already been eaten.

Although it had not rained for a few hours, it started again as my great-grandfather drank his third glass of tea. When he had finished it, he went out saying he had to go to see Grigor and Saba about a new pair of boots. Now when the father says he is going to see about a new pair of boots you mustn't question him, although you may know that new boots have only arrived two weeks ago. So my young grandfather didn't contradict, but simply thought he could play the entire morning. Which was not, as it happens, true, because at that very moment my great-grandfather decided he should crawl under the stove to clean out from the chickens and bring out the eggs if any.

As my great-grandfather had truly said, all the constable did was go to see Bonifas, get drunk with him and then stand in the rain shouting curses even worse than those normally used by Bonifas himself. My great-grandfather on hearing the accursed pair quietly prayed "May the rain burn their lips away." But the swearing continued, it rained more heavily than ever, and they still kept their lips. That night something happened worse even than the grave-yard business.

Late that night only the rabbi was still awake, his lamp burning, studying. He sat quietly reading while outside the rain fell and a high wind blew. But the rabbi didn't hear what went on because he was studying so hard, and anyhow he had heard wind and rain often before, so why should he now after so many years start taking notice?

But suddenly there was a beating at the door and a rattling at the window. The rabbi looked up as the window was broken. Glass fell all over the room, and through the hole came stones and muck which fell mostly on the rabbi's white hair and beard. With the rubbish the wind rushed in blowing rain everywhere, and with it all a string of curses from that drunken Bonifas who had been outside swearing loudly against the wind as he watched the rabbi study quietly his holy book.

The rabbi wiped his face and called out of the window, but listening for an answer, heard only the wind whining like a devil, so very sensibly, he stuffed some rags into the broken window, cleaned up the mess and went to bed.

The next morning my great-grandfather and everyone else heard of all this, though none of them heard that Bonifas was at this moment lying with his face in a deep puddle of water near the grave-yard. Later that day Reb Sholem Pinsk called round to tell them. Whereupon my great-grandfather hoped, "Perhaps the water will put out the fire in his head."

Several people who had to travel that road saw Bonifas lying there and also thought that a little rain would do him no harm. In the end he lay there for three days, until the rain stopped, with no one doing anything but look down their nose as they hurried past thinking Bonifas was a fool to lie in the damp for so long.

It was the constable, the friend of Bonifas, who while walking down to the village to see what he could collect in the way of presents for looking after everyone so well, found the cobbler lying in the road with the puddle deep about his head. The constable, recognizing Bonifas, laughed and called to him, then kicked and prodded him. But he didn't move. After kicking him a little more the constable pushed the cobbler over onto his back, whereupon he saw that the face of Bonifas had altered to an unusual color and was bloated with water. The constable now realized that Bonifas was dead, and as he went into the village to announce the discovery felt like a high official. Although he would miss drinking brandy with Bonifas, he would enjoy finding someone to blame for his death.

So he went into the village and announced the death and asked questions, receiving from all the answer that Bonifas had been struck by lightning because of what he had done to the graveyard and to the rabbi. The constable sent in a report which someone wrote out for him, and everyone waited for officers to come from a town fifteen miles away. As for Bonifas, he was left on a pile of timber near the graveyard, where he lay without anyone bothering about him for four days. On the fourth day the officers arrived, including a doctor who had a very good name as a surgeon.

This doctor had earned his good name by curing some cows of a disease which no one had even known them to be sick with. Then he was called in by the biggest landowner in the district to look after his son who was very ill. By chance the boy lived, and this further developed the doctor's name. When he arrived with the other officers, the whole village knew about it and waited around the pile of timber where the body of Bonifas had been lying for four days. The officers walked about with the constable questioning everyone who had not given him a present lately, while the great doctor examined the body. He could see that Bonifas was dead even without listening to his heart, but he listened to make sure.

Just then my young grandfather managed to climb out of the barn where Yaacov the village teacher had locked all the boys while he went off to watch the officers. My grandfather being the smallest had been lifted up by the other boys to a narrow window in the loft of the barn, but once there found he couldn't lift anyone else up, so he got through the window himself and ran off to see what was happening to Bonifas. When he arrived the body of Bonifas had been moved onto some planks of timber, and Yaacov was busy being questioned by the other officers. This was mainly because he had never given the constable a present. Why should he? Had the constable ever given him anything? Anyway my grandfather was pleased because his teacher was too busy to notice him as he squeezed through the crowd watching the doctor listen to Bonifas' heart. The doctor concluded that Bonifas was dead because his heart had completely stopped. He adjusted his pince-nez, and it was soon after this that my grandfather had the honor of assisting at a brain operation.

When the doctor discovered it was safe, he decided to operate on Bonifas' brain, because he had never operated on a brain before, and also because there was a large bump on the head of Bonifas which seemed to be quite unusual. He got out a knife and cut round the skin, and then he got out a saw and began to saw through the bone. Everyone standing round nudged one another, saying, "Have you ever seen such a wonderful doctor?" When the doctor sawed right through the bone, they all cheered and he turned round and bowed slightly. Then he took off the bone cup of the head of Bonifas and handed it to my grandfather who was standing right there in front. My grandfather held onto the bone cup while the doctor looked at the brain of Bonifas, in which he seemed to find nothing that interested him.

As he stood there my grandfather thought how jealous the other boys would be when they heard how he had helped the doctor. When the doctor at last took it back he wasn't sorry because it was heavy, but he was pleased so many people had seen him hold it, in case the other boys called him a liar when he told them.

Then the doctor made a dart for Bonifas' stomach. He made two long cuts in it and moved away quickly. Everyone else moved away quickly too, because at once the whole place was full of the smell of brandy and vodka and rotten food. The doctor called away the officers who were still asking questions, and told them he was ready to make his report. Then he turned to the crowd and shouted that Bonifas had died because brandy had burned his stomach away inside, and that was all there was to it. He told the officers to tell the constable to get the body buried, after which formalities everyone went away saying that Bonifas had got what he deserved.

When my grandfather arrived home he found my great-grandfather talking to Grigor and Saba. After he had told them what had happened my great-grandfather got out a bottle of brandy and poured out three glasses full. Then Grigor and Saba shook each other by the hand. As they drank their brandy my young grandfather kept saying that brandy had burned the stomach out of Bonifas. But my great-grandfather replied that Bonifas had died for different reasons, and they were all good, both from the religious and from the commercial points of view. And he raised his second glass of brandy to Grigor and Saba who were delighted to be the only cobblers—though clumsy ones—in the entire district.

GOOD BUSINESS WITH
SENTIMENT

A LIFE IN ART

WHAT IS THE USE OF PRETENDING? PELK KNEW, EVEN AS A BOY, EVEN in the moment of exultation when the head of the art department shook him by the hand and said, "Cooper might have painted that sheep's head," he always knew that however right his hand might be, his temperament was wrong for a successful life in art.

For Pelk dressed somberly and was quiet. His habits were regular, his ideas conventional. Color, even in paintings, worried him unduly. He preferred his personality to be pale as a ghost. And while the Academy was completely discredited by violent young men whose pictures were robust with color, Pelk painted away regularly and without excitement, working like a mathematician to make the view on the canvas precisely equal to the view he looked at.

After a few years Pelk still painted on in spite of his job with a frame-maker. He had patiently grown a moustache hoping to balance his recessive chin and large eyebrows. Strangely enough it gave his face a certain authority. People began to notice his serious unsmiling eyes and grew to respect his suggestions for framing. Several important clients always headed their instructions "Attention Pelk." He might have made a career as an understanding frame-maker, and he would have been satisfied. But Life will never let well alone and one day Pelk received a note on beautifully engraved note paper asking him to call on Mr. Marmourian at his famous gallery in Bond Street.

As Pelk wandered over the crimson carpet looking at the fine eighteenth-century paintings with genuine appreciation, he was

246

surprised by Marmourian himself. The great dealer had been stand-ing just behind him for some seconds before he spoke his name.

"Pelk," he said in his slightly throaty way, "Pelk, is it not? The clever frame-maker who truly cares for what he frames. What is your opinion on this little Fragonard you find so intriguing?" And with that confidence of the timid when invited to speak about his soul's delight—and there is not a solitary timid soul which does not have some secret delight or other—Arthur Pelk spoke of the lit-tle painting with thought and love and clarity.

When he finished, a faint blush glowed to either side of his mous-tache, and Marmourian shook him by the hand and then dashed a tear from his eye as he led the way to his private office. "It is exactly as you say," he said. "You have truly understood the picture. If I were a client I would have bought it—yes, yes, I could not have re-sisted."

When Pelk left the Marmourian Gallery it was as a newly en-gaged salesman, six pounds a week plus commission, to start in a fortnight. "You are in the greatest profession of all, my Pelk," the dealer had said, "for if a man paints well it is God's gift—but to sell pictures a man must really work." Pelk was certainly frightened, but the prospect of living henceforward on intimate terms with dead and undisputed masters gave him confidence, and within three months he had married a rather nice girl whose artistic interests had never ventured beyond barbola work.

And this is really all that happened to Arthur Pelk for thirteen years. His knowledge increased—his salary grew—his commissions were substantial—his timidity was concealed by a moustache and eyebrows which were recognized in the world of art. But he re-mained a secret painter. And, thirteen years after his introduction to Marmourian, Arthur Pelk was distressed to realize that some-where inside him that old juvenile desire to be a recognized artist still fluttered its imprisoned wings.

Immersed as he was in successive vogues for the various dead painters who become, every four or five years, the only fashionable masters, it was inevitable that a simple-minded craftsman like Pelk should be variously influenced. When the slight landscapes of the Frenchman Coutet were keenly sought after (Marmourian having bought a vast collection of works by this obscure little Toulouse genius well beforehand), Pelk discovered one evening that his hand and brush were automatically following out the style of Coutet. In fact, four hours produced a very passable Coutet indeed.

And so it was with Pelzner and Pieter de Wint, Gerhart Ister and Charles Bicking. Every minor master to be handled by the Marmourian Gallery became so well-understood by Pelk that his brush unfailingly emulated their strokes. He found that he was a perfect painters' medium (or possibly ghost). His first real victory, though, was when Marmourian, while taking a cocktail with the Pelks, glanced at one of Arthur's little seashore paintings and said, "A good eye, Arthur, you have—a pretty little Boudin, I think. But to buy for yourself—is not ethical, my dear Pelk." This chance mistake in identity at once set the vanity of the old student fluttering away like mad in Pelk's breast.

It so happened that at the time when Pelk's vanity was fluttering, collectors were becoming much interested in that charming artist Constantin Guys. After his thirteen years in the trade Pelk could easily understand the salability of the delightful pen and wash drawings. Reasonably enough everyone suddenly wanted parasols and top hats, the freshness and immediacy of the Guys sketches, the atmosphere, the delicacy. . . . Pelk had no difficulty in selling at ever-increasing prices every Guys the talented Marmourian could lay his hands on. It was just as easy for him of a Sunday afternoon, inspired by some fine antique cartridge paper, to draw some of the prettiest Guys sketches Marmourian had ever seen.

No one will believe (though it is a simple fact) that Pelk had no motivation other than suppressed artistic vanity when, one dull winter morning when Bond Street was swathed in a fog to depress even Whistler, he carefully slipped seven of his Guys-style sketches into the folder reserved for that artist. Yet everyone will have to believe that Pelk acted in this way without the desire for illicit profit.

For he made no false entries in the books—absolutely no money passed into his hands.

It was a quiet day and Pelk spent it in secret delight at having found his true place in a master's folder. He proposed to leave his drawings there for a few hours—perhaps even show them to an unimportant client or two, and then take them back home to the spare room where he worked. But every eye seemed to be upon him whenever he made a move to retrieve his drawings from the Guys folder. And not a single client entered the gallery that day.

Pelk hung about long after his usual time for leaving, and still it was impossible for him to retrieve his work. He planned a dozen different attempts on the folder. Each time he heard in his mind's ear the throaty voice of Marmourian, "Caught you red-handed, my Pelk—stealing from me—your employer—your friend." "But they are mine," Pelk would cry. Who would believe him? He left the drawings where they were and hurried home.

The next day Pelk found a few moments in which to take out the folder. Sure enough he heard the throaty voice of Marmourian, introducing to him a pale gabardine-draped gentleman—"the greatest collector of Constantin Guys in America—in the World." The American smiled and held out his hand. Marmourian patted Pelk on the back as a promoter might pat his prize heavyweight. Pelk wanted to scream and cry "I'm ill, I'm ill." But the American was already studying the drawings in the folder.

For twenty-five minutes Pelk, his blood like liquid ice, excelled himself. He used every device in his salesmanship, every word in his vocabulary of hyperbole, every gesture of the hands, the shoulders. Persuasion, intimidation, flattery, all failed. The only drawings the American would buy were Pelk's own poor imitations. He held in delicate fingers a Guys of ten ladies in a row all with parasols —it was the best of Pelk's efforts. "The best I have ever seen," he said. "I will take it, and this, and these." And he left only one small Pelk, alone with thirty-three authentic drawings.

After Marmourian had received the check (and the price was

really fantastic, for the pound had only recently been devalued),
the great dealer turned to Pelk. "My clever Pelk," he said in a
broken voice. "You are the greatest of us all. These new little things
—I even forget I have them—they must have cost practically nothing." Which indeed was true. But what could Pelk do? He accepted
the praise and the extra commission and went home to sit moodily
cursing his vanity and his skill.

He looked about him at the well-furnished sitting room of the
new house his commissions had given him. That delightful little
Louis Quinze *secrétaire*—it reminded him of a small Watteau, won-
derfully authenticated, he had handled. That Meissen inkstand—a
Corot had given him that. Art had served him well, as a loving hand-
maiden serves, while he—he had betrayed her. And her consort
Marmourian also he had betrayed. For what? For a little itching vanity—the unexpired portion of his boyhood dream of fame. What
was he after all these years at the elbow of greatness—A copyist. A
vain, untalented, slinking, cowardly copyist. And—my God!—a
forger too. The hair on the back of Pelk's neck felt electric. The
cold dead hand of horror gripped his heart.

Nothing in the range of human feeling can equal the misery of
the timid man who realizes that he has destroyed the only defense
his timidity has ever devised. The little bits he had prized so greatly
now seemed to Pelk resentfully out of place. His own work—those
quiet evenings with the brush and pen in the spare room—looked
at him askance, as if the authentic works were shouting from a thousand galleries, "How dare *you* trace *us*—perfect lines by real masters!" And night after night Pelk tossed and turned in torment as
he fell through a brilliantly sketched maelstrom (rather like Leo-
nardo's torrents) while the voices of a myriad *objets d'art* screamed
"Shame, shame."

So it was that Pelk, his eyes dark with worry, his back bent, his
hands shaking, went through the polite routine of mortgaging his
house. The bank manager gladly accepted Mr. Pelk's life insurance
as further collateral. Was there anything else he could arrange for
Mr. Pelk? There was no limit to the overdraft he might have—pro-

vided there were suitable securities. A few hundred safe Industrials —"We might as well add those. Good morning, Mr. Pelk, good morning." Such was the extreme to which Pelk was forced by artistic conscience. For he knew there was no alternative. He had to buy—buy with hard money—buy back those damn' creations of his over-eager imitative hand.

So it was too that after protracted negotiations through one of Marmourian's competitors Pelk purchased back his own drawings, changed only by the addition of the impressive stamp of a famous American collection. Pelk was penniless but his peace of mind for a day or two was beyond the understanding of those mere art dealers who lack honest feeling for authentic and original art. It was sheer bad luck that someone had to tell Marmourian that the drawings had changed hands again at an even more important price than he had obtained. And it was a tribute to Marmourian's knowledge of one of the most complicated and secretive trades ever devised by cupidity that within forty-eight hours he knew Pelk was the purchaser.

"My Pelk," he said in sorrow. "You underhand dog," he cried in anger, thinking of the profit he believed Pelk was about to make. "I take you—I make you," he wept. "I break you," he screamed. "How many times have you cheated me?" After thirteen years Pelk's integrity had completely triumphed. But he was up to his eyes in debt. And he was no longer Marmourian's star salesman.

Pelk surveyed the situation in the gloominess of the spare room that evening. His wife was busy with her barbola. He had tried to lose himself in the practice of his art, but it was useless. By some peculiar quirk of the mind he found himself in his distress painting after that unfashionable Victorian academician Cooper—a sheep's head like the one he had been so fatally complimented upon in the promising days of his youth. "But by God," said Pelk aloud, "it is exactly like Cooper—a little stronger if anything." His Guys sketches were, after all, thoroughly authenticated. And naturally every other collector in the world would hear of them and lust after them.

A man in his despair has a single moment of vision, like the pano-
rama a drowning man is supposed to view in the moment before
complete submersion. Pelk had the courage to believe in his vision.
Once again his house is his, once again he is solvent, while the trade
says again and again, "You know Pelk, of course—how does he find
them? Coutets, Pelzners, de Wints, Gerhart Isters, and Bickings.
And Guys—of course, Pelk is the specialist in Constantin Guys."

TOO MUCH MAN

Lenny runs this salt-beef bar, The Roll-Mop, near Windmill Street.
Whenever I am round that area I drop in for lunch whatever time
of day, because Lenny is a fellow who carries a good twenty stone.
This makes me feel like Gary Cooper. I am also highly partial to
salt-beef.

The Roll-Mop does great business because the truth about selling
people food is you should look like you enjoy it yourself and want
them to get the same fun out of life. This Lenny does with his big
fresh fat face, in which the eyes, nose, and mouth are set with a
strong delicacy as tasteful as his menu. Sometimes there are ten of
us pretty fat men with a lickerish tooth for delicatessen in The Roll-
Mop at the same time. But believe me, though we are packed tighter
than roll-mops in a bottle we are all feeling very slim because there
is good old Lenny bigger than any of us and proud of it.

"Have another lutka," he philosophizes, "try the strudel. Take another vienna. Don't worry—how many times do you live anyway?
And if it knocks five years off your life, so you will drop dead with a
good flavor in your hollow tooth." This spiel helps morale and it
doesn't do business any harm either.

And that's how it was, a long, delightful gorge without conscience
—till the rot set in. The rot was called Renée and she was in the
front row of the show round the corner.

Of course, The Roll-Mop was headquarters for a lot of the girls
from around, including many from the different theatrical produc-

tions which are such a colorful feature in the Shaftesbury Avenue
vicinity. But though Lenny was prone to a laugh and a joke and
maybe even a slap now and then here and there, the actual rot itself had never before set in to his slightly enlarged heart-works. Certainly—the occasional friendship, but never like this Renée performance.

I first saw Renée on a Tuesday morning about eleven when, happening to pass that way, I dropped into The Roll-Mop for an early
lunch. The bar was empty except for good old Lenny talking with
(and this was unusual) sad brown eyes and a serious worried expression on his usually joyous chops to this strawberry blonde, or
maybe the color her hair was dyed is called pink champagne. She
stood a bit less than average height but with a more than average
build on all sides and with big eyes and, it goes without saying,
longer than average legs. What you might call a pocket Venus if you
can afford to carry such things in your pocket.

"But why not, Renée?" Lenny was saying as I came in. "We can
have a marvelous time. It's a first-rate occasion and the eats will also
be first-rate, not to mention the band, which is a specialist in South
American." He swayed his hips a little, clicking his teeth and flicking his fingers gaily.

"I can't," said Renée, looking embarrassed at me. "Serve the gentleman," she continued as Lenny's face collapsed into depression.
"I have to pop now for rehearsal."

As she popped both Lenny and I watched her.

"Seems a nice class of girl, Lenny," I said.

"She's real class, Wolfie," he sighed. "What can I give you,
Wolfie, the usual?"

He sliced me the usual, sighing. He sighed as he put mustard on
it, and as he slipped a pickled cucumber onto the plate sighed yet
again.

"Business so bad, Lenny?" I asked him.

"What's business against a happy life?" he answered.

"I thought you was married," I replied through a mouthful of
the best salt-beef in Soho.

"Me? Never," he said, "and it looks like I never will."

Then, with tears in his eyes he told me. "The truth is, Wolfie," he said, carving off a little slice of beef and popping it into his mouth sadly, "the truth is I embarrass her. Not me personally, but the weight—the weight is an embarrassing thing for her. I read somewhere a famous writer says inside every fat man is a thin man screaming to get free. First time in my life, Wolfie, I can hear him screaming."

I finished my sandwich but the second half didn't have the taste —not with Lenny mooning around slipping bits of this and that into his mouth so miserably.

"Listen, Lenny," I advised him, "if she can't appreciate you through all that blubber, she's not worth breaking your heart over."

"Don't tell me," he replied, "tell my breaking heart."

How can you enjoy delicatessen served by a lovesick salt-beef slicer? I wasn't the only one. Within the next few weeks The Roll-Mop's business dropped off. Fat men like me just don't enjoy the disapproval of eating that radiated from Lenny like heatwaves off freshly cooked pastrami.

Also Lenny was getting the sagging look of an empty salami skin that tells you a man is murdering his gluttonous metabolism by enforced starvation. No more the big fat smile of encouragement as he cut your sandwich. As for lutkas—they were right off the menu.

"You look like you're wasting to death," I said to him one afternoon as I chewed a late lunch more out of nostalgia than enjoyment.

"I'm down to eighteen stone," he replied, a sad pride lighting his sallow features. "Renée says if I take off another few stone maybe she will reconsider things. The weight was an embarrassing thing to her."

"You already told me," I reminded him. "I think you are up the pole to throw away your business and your substance for a dollface who makes such demands. There is nothing in history that says a fat man can't be a husband."

"I am now trying the banana and milk diet," he replied. "Next month I go on to a vegetable juice torture which is guaranteed to produce startling losses. Tonight Renée has consented to come to the pictures with me, so it's an occasion. Unfortunately, it turns out, the film is with Burt Lancaster, also a very slim man. Still, I'm making progress."

This progress Lenny finally completed after working through a raw potato diet, an all-meat régime, a fortnight session devoted exclusively to acid fruit, and a five-day stint on nothing but glucose. He was a pasty miserable fifteen stone when he told me that he was going to close the shop for a month's holiday at what is laughingly called a "health hydro."

"How's Renée?" I asked.

"Life is very difficult," he replied, "now she says I am not jolly like I used to be—a thing which she always very much appreciated in me. What can I do? I'm slim but I don't feel jolly. Thank God Renée gets on with my mother. That at least is something to be thankful for."

"Have a nice holiday," I replied.

Lenny told me that at that hydro they gave him the works with massage and sun-ray and infra-red and ultra-violet and various other rays which are hardly on the market yet. Also with vitamins, enzymes, and gland-extracts. Also massage, body-building, muscle development, and fresh air—not to mention a special juice from pressed mangold-wurzels which is the richest drink in something or other ever discovered.

"Give me the address," I asked Lenny, because he really looked in great shape when he got back.

Now he was sad, with his hair longer and his eyes big and brown and full of thought, and his mouth rather sensitive, as if he was easily hurt. And since he was always tall with the fat off him he looked real well-built, especially since his suits didn't look like tents any more. Even his personality had changed. He had a feeling about him like he was studying in his own mind the real meaning of life and was about to come to such a miserable answer you wanted to hug him to cheer him up. Not me, that is. I thought it was all a tragedy for the salt-beef business. But Renée, she was always in there hugging him. "Didn't I tell him he could change himself?" she chortled.

Needless to say they got married, although I don't know which health hydro the honeymoon was spent in because frankly the whole affair disgusted me slightly. I hate to see a fellow's nature put upon by a pocket Venus of whatever size. There are other salt-beef bars in Soho, so I went to them. But it wasn't like The Roll-Mop used to be.

One lunchtime I was in the vicinity of Lenny's place, so I thought for old-time's sake—why not? I looked in. I say look—but it was more like a squint, the place was so packed with fat men all knocking back salt-beef sandwiches by the gross. Surprised, I pushed my way through to the bar.

"Wolfie," greeted Lenny as he handed plates past a buxom pretty brunette who looked after the cash register. "Where you been? The usual? Go on—enjoy yourself. How long have you got to live, anyway?"

"You put on weight, Lenny," I said, because there he was back with more or less the same twenty stone he had before the rot set in.

"Listen," he said, "is it a better thing to be a bit on the plump side and contented or to have a figure and cry like Johnnie Ray the whole time?"

"Johnnie Ray?" said the buxom brunette, "I'll say. With that miserable look he couldn't keep the girls away." She punched the cash register steadily as she talked. "But a couple of months' real eating got him back to normal," she continued smugly.

"She took me to every delicatessen in town. And eat—I had to eat my best to keep up with her," added Lenny. "You know my wife Renée of course." He introduced me to the brunette.

"Didn't you used to be blonde?" I asked.

She shook her dark curls. Already she was getting the dewlapped look of the constant eater-between-meals.

Blonde is not really suitable for the eating business," she explained. "Lenny, dolly, you want more butter on your baigel?"

"You see," Lenny explained out of the side of his full mouth, "now we are married the weight is no longer embarrassing to her." He patted his enormous stomach. "What do we always say, Renée?" he asked.

She stretched out her hand and also patted. "What we always say is," she said, "if you got the right man, how can you have too much?"

LA VIE EN ROSE

"Jean-Louis is an efficiency expert, really, aren't you, Jean-Louis, an efficiency expert?" The dark girl with short legs like peanuts wriggled in her armchair.

Mrs. Pargeter, the grocer's wife, looked at Jean-Louis and thought how expensive all those fancy French cheeses were. But they bought them, so what could you say? A good bit of cheddar took some beating though, say what you like, you can't beat the old cheddar when it's good. Half the time you couldn't make out what they were saying. It must be terrible to be a foreigner.

"Yes?" said Mr. Pargeter, wiping his moustache gently with a dark-blue handkerchief. "Must be interesting work. Take the grocery for instance. In the grocery you have to be efficient, I don't care what you say, take any perishable goods for instance, if you order too many of them and you have miscalculated your public, why then, what's the net result? Loss, sheer gross loss."

"Please," said Jean-Louis, "a little more quick. I am in England four months. If you go a little more quick I am listen and do understand how you are speak."

"A little slower, Jean-Louis," the dark girl said. "His English is wonderful considering. I think he has done wonders considering."

She showed her teeth to Jean-Louis and wriggled again. He smiled winningly at Mrs. Pargeter. The grocer's wife smiled back thinking I'm not sorry that Dorothy left the shop when she did. Women with big teeth are always a bit that way although I don't say she wasn't a good cashier.

Mr. Pargeter was watching the dark girl cross her legs. Short but sturdy, he thought, these girls with strong legs take some beating say what you like. He laughed.

"Let us all share in your little joke, Fred," said Mrs. Pargeter with *that* smile. If she caught him pinching the Ramage girl's bottom again underneath the counter *she* would have a go too. "It's not fair to keep a good joke to oneself, is it, Mr. Payray?" Mind you, foreigners had nice smiles and a brown shirt with a brown tie to match gave them an air of you-know.

"Call him Jean-Louis, Mrs. Pargeter," said the dark girl. "In Paree one does not stand on ceremony, n'est ce pas, Jean-Louis?"

"Pé-ré, P, EY, R, EY, Pé-ré," explained Jean-Louis.

"Pay-ray, Pay-ray," answered Mrs. Pargeter, "I've got it."

"Ta-ra-ra-boom-de-ay," said Mr. Pargeter.

"Just call him Jean-Louis, he won't mind." The dark girl uncrossed her legs.

The marines was there, thought Mr. Pargeter.

"How about another drink? Drink, Mr. uh-pay——"

"Pay-ray, Fred. Fred has no grasp I'm afraid, though he's a wonder on figures." Mrs. Pargeter's temper was fraying a little.

Ay-ay, thought Mr. Pargeter as Jean-Louis crossed to the dark girl's chair and edged his arm round her waist. You can't beat it, Mr. Pargeter thought.

"Now what are we all drinking?"

"Plain Vermouth for Jean-Louis, isn't it darling, just the Vermouth plain?"

"I think you've had enough, Fred," Mrs. Pargeter said with that smile again. But Mr. Pargeter was asking the dark girl how she liked it, long or with less water than gin, take your choice. Pretending he didn't notice his wife's warning, he poured himself another large whisky.

"Well, here's all the best to all of us, and may we all get whatever we want in life." He drank half the whisky in the glass. "Good luck to us all," he said, "best of luck Mr. What-not, good luck, Dorothy, don't do anything I wouldn't do, all the best dear. Drink up."

They drank up, Mrs. Pargeter giving Mr. Pargeter the signal to slow down, Jean-Louis looking deep into the dark girl's eyes which tried to look back over the rim of the glass. His hand was on the dark girl's thigh. Mr. Pargeter caught the signal, and refilled his glass quickly.

"One last one for the road, my dear," he said, "last one, longest one. That's the ticket John-Louey," he added as Jean-Louis pushed the dark girl's glass away and kissed her full on the mouth.

"Well," Mrs. Pargeter said, "well, there is a limit." This is the last time that hussy comes into my house with her fancy men, and Fred looking at them as if they were a couple of rabbits, well, after all, well.

"Fred," she said sternly, "what's the time, Fred? It must be after eleven." She managed to get that smile into her voice, and it brought the dark girl to her senses.

"Look at us," she giggled. "Really, Jean-Louis, this isn't Gay Paree, you have to watch your p's and q's. I say, what a fright I must be looking. Oh, dear, Mr. and Mrs. P, whatever will you be thinking of us? I don't know what I shall look like in the morning."

Jean-Louis was bumbling into her ear:

When I took you in my arm
Je vois la vie en rose.

She pushed his hand away and stretched for her bag. Mr. Pargeter smiled as he reached absent-mindedly for the bottle. But Mrs. Pargeter reached it first and tucked it firmly under her chair.

The dark girl used a thin lipstick quickly, giving herself a neat outline which ignored her lips completely.

"I don't know how I shall look in the morning. I'm terrible getting up in the morning."

Mr. Pargeter leered over her compact mirror.

"It's nicer to lie in bed, Dorothy love," he said.

They watched Jean-Louis accompany his song with a few neat dance steps.

"He's always like that," the dark girl said proudly, "soon as he wakes up, bounces out of bed, full of beans."

"Well!" Mrs. Pargeter said. "Well!"

"So he says anyway, don't you, Jean-Louis?" the dark girl added blushing. "Up with the lark he says," she continued, looking away from Mrs. Pargeter but with a sly grin.

"Early to bed early to rise," said Mr. Pargeter watching the dark girl's legs as she stood up.

"Good night then," she added, "thanks for a lovely time. Come on, Jean-Louis, maintenant bonne nuit."

"What about one for the road?" asked Mr. Pargeter.

"Now you didn't have a hat did you, dear?" Mrs. Pargeter stated firmly as she coldly handed them their coats.

While she saw them to the door Mr. Pargeter had the presence of mind to get the bottle from underneath the chair and pour himself a stiff one. When the front door had clicked to she came back into the room. She didn't have that smile on her face.

"I didn't invent sex you know, Emily," he said, half truculent, half querulous.

But Mrs. Pargeter knew better.

NATURE'S WAY

The village in question creeps up a hill. This it has been doing for a long time but not yet long enough for the vicar's pamphlet *Crawlingtree: an historical retrospect* (privately printed in 1902) to have gone into a second impression.

Those afflicted with a sufficiently undiscriminating love of landscape may savor the quality of the Essex countryside from the brow of Crawlingtree Hill. And on this very brow they may further indulge their aestheticism by mounting to the roof of the combined shop and living accommodation of J. Scully, the local pharmacist. From this vantage point they will see scrub pasture declining towards a marshy pond, and let out to a local farmer at five pounds per annum, payable in advance. A small herd of cows of mixed origin browses disconsolately day after day upon the dry grass, or wades hopelessly knee-deep into the mud which surrounds the dark patch of water. Whether a cow has ever managed to get beyond the mud and savor two or three stomachs-full of that dingy liquor, seems, on the face of things unlikely. So that the whole herd might be expected to perish eventually from the combined effects of drought and starvation. But so persistent is the grasp upon life that apart from becoming bonier and bonier, the herd browses on. No one notices if it is ever milked. The farmer appears to have forgotten the whole matter. Presumably he feels it worth five pounds yearly in advance to get rid of the miserable creatures. Perhaps he has always wanted to be an arable farmer anyway. Whatever the case, the whole herd is painted in water-color (well after Constable) several times a year by the older girls of a local private academy, the least talented of whom is the red-headed daughter of J. Scully, local pharmacist. J. Scully's only other distinguishing characteristic is an obsession with regularity—a condition he has consistently achieved and maintained, skilled pharmacist that he is, by nightly potations of that common but unparalleled herb, Senna—which comes, as all know—in pods.

Such the landscape against which the saga of Safelax is set. And what countryside in the world could possibly be more constipated?

Now Mrs. J. Scully was a quiet efficient woman, a sleeping partner of her husband's in a very uneventful business, for Jim never quite matched his premarital ardor, and the Scully daughter remained the sole legatee to his home and its view.

But quiet woman as she was, Mrs. Scully had her demon. It drove her towards perfecting bread pudding (use up the stale loaf), beef broth (use up the bones), paper spills (save vestas) and similar virtuous economies. She never varied in her weekly household budget of forty-five shillings. "You can spend a little more from time to time if you like, my love," said Jim Scully occasionally. "You run your shop Jim," answered his wife, "and let me look after the house." He took it kindly and grew to enjoy the weekly bread pudding and regular beef broth.

It took only a very few years for Mrs. Scully to effect every possible economy in the management of her simple household. Her demon felt its honor to be satisfied. She was certain that there was no wastage anywhere, and yet she felt something more could be done. Between her household motions she would stop and purse her brow and press her lips together for a moment, only to dismiss her anxiety with a shrug and turn with familiar pleasure to the mincer. But one night as she lay in their vast bed watching Jim pour hot water upon the Senna Pods in the bowl on the pot cupboard, her eyes lit up and she sat bolt upright exclaiming. Jim turned with a pained expression on his face towards her, upset at the disturbance at a time when the least jolt to his arm might ruin the potation with too much water. "My love," he said, "is something wrong? I'm rather busy you know." "Don't bother yourself dear," replied Mrs. Scully. She smiled quietly and was quickly asleep.

The nearest Jim Scully ever came to losing his temper with his wife followed upon this strange nocturnal behavior of hers. He had been unusually busy the following day, for it was a dank November, and tubes were threatening to clog in the chests of the local inhabitants. Scully had a dozen times been disturbed in his reading, but he had supplied vapor rub and cough tonic with good feeling, and he had not noticed his wife's unusual trips into the shop from the adjoining parlor. It was when he had closed the shop for tea, and had actually sat down to a plate of pork sausage and mashed potato that he raised his head and sniffed deeply once or twice. Above the savory scent of the pork he smelt the familiar odor which presaged, for him, secure sleep. The house was redolent with the scent of Senna Pods. Startled out of his customary calm, Scully leaped to his feet and ran to the kitchen.

There stood Mrs. Scully in a cloud of aromatic steam, pouring an enormous black kettle of boiling water over at least six pounds of Senna Pods, a huge brown pile like autumn leaves in an enamel bowl. "Upon my soul!" exclaimed Scully. "What in the devil's name are you doing my love?" But Mrs. Scully poured on till the kettle was empty. Then she turned to him as he stood there fuming at her inhuman behavior to man's unswerving friend. "I'm troubled by the waste that goes on here, Jim Scully, night after night, with you taking fresh pods for your draught. Now I shall bottle this lot and you shall have a glass every morning and you'll see how we shall save in the long run." What use was it for Jim to try to explain that a great deal of his satisfaction lay in dropping a handful of pods in the bowl, boiling the water and pouring it carefully, night after night? What sense would the poetry of that make to a reasonable woman? He choked back his indignation and went into the shop to read leaving his tea untouched upon the table. Mrs. Scully scooped up the plate and slipped it into the oven. Then she set about bottling the liquor she had brewed in so crudely wholesale a manner.

Needless to say Jim Scully eventually felt hungry and returned sheepishly to eat his tea. There is not a married man who has failed to capitulate in similar circumstances, for no sooner does anger pass than appetite returns. And when he saw all the demijohns of translucent brown liquid lined up on a shelf he did feel, to tell the truth, a sort of satisfaction. He tried to calculate how long his supply would last. He wondered at the vast period of regularity those bottles represented. And although he poured his morrow's draught with a certain amount of trepidation and a definite sense of loss, he was delighted in the morning to discover that the liquor had lost none of its potency in its new economic form.

It so happened that Scully's neighbor, a baker who supplied the entire village and district with bread, had a piece of rather bad luck at almost the very moment that Mrs. Scully was pouring her large black kettle. This baker—his name is of no importance for in spite of the part he has unwittingly played in all our lives we shall not refer to him again—this baker then, had, for private reasons, agreed to do a friend a turn, and store six sacks of plaster of paris for him. The baker, as a matter of fact, had been proposing to whitewash his bakery for some time and a little plaster out of each sack would

hardly be noticed. It would probably do the job very well, and anyhow, he wasn't charging the man rent. But so secretive did his plan
make him that he completely forgot to mention the presence of the
sacks to his assistant. By the time the baker himself came down to
supervise that night's baking, two complete sacks of plaster had
been converted into bread. Fortunately they had mixed in well with
the flour and apart from the loaves being a little heavier than usual,
no difference was noticeable. "A little plaster's not going to do
them any harm—and as for him, he'll just have to take his loss in
bad part if he feels that way," the baker philosophically observed
to his apprentice. He was gratified to hear several of his customers
comment on how white the bread was. "It certainly won't poison
them—that's flat," he remarked to his wife. "All's well that ends
well."

The baker's error may perhaps be considered an example of the
way trade circulates and creates trade. Within twenty-four hours
Jim Scully was being disturbed in his reading by customer after
customer demanding "something safe." His remaining supply of
Senna Pods was exhausted very soon—and still they came. One after
another the demijohns were taken down, and ounce by liquid ounce
they were emptied. Furthermore the customers were delighted to
find that they could take the draught without waiting, without bothering to potate it themselves. Their urgency was great and they were
thankful. Neither they nor Scully realized until the entire stock
was cleared that, liquid ounces being somewhat heavier than the
dry herbs, the firm of J. Scully had cleared a little over four hundred
per cent profit on its entire stock of Senna Pods.

"Dear me," said Scully when he realized what had happened,
"what shall I do, my dear?" And then, with one of those swift, tran-
sient flashes of sheer feminine insight Mrs. Scully put her husband
on the road to fortune. "Make some more of course. Make some
more." And already she had the kettle on while she bundled Scully
onto his bicycle and sent him off to the next village to buy up the
local pharmacist's stock of Senna.

Once a human soul accidentally slips onto its right road, nothing can stop its growth. Most souls can only peep out once or twice before freeing themselves of the wearisome burden of the flesh, and yearn wistfully after their destiny. But let ambition and circumstance meet but once. The quietest soul will swell to gigantic proportions.

Thus it was that while Jim Scully preserved, though always now with some small irritable frustration, his regularity, and a smart young man encouraged the growing demands in the shop, Mrs. Scully brought the principles of household economy to bear upon what had started as pure inspiration.

Scully's fame spread quickly among the villages. It was exciting to think of a new cure being discovered in their midst by one of their own people. It seemed old-fashioned not to try it, and conservative to wait until it was merely necessary. A little peppermint oil was added. "It tastes so clean," said the customers. A little bromide. "And I sleep so well," they told one another. Night after night in the scattered hamlets men toasted their wives in it, while the enthusiasm of the ladies caused a serious drop in the local sales of invalid port. But man and wife slept secure knowing that the future's mornings would always, at the very least, start well.

As for the magical name itself, Jim Scully hit upon it as he served his first customer. "But what is it?" asked a careful lady who wasn't going to throw another bad pain after the first. "It's safe, madam. Take my word for it," replied Jim with habitual sincerity. "It's new, but it's natural. It's a safe laxative. It's Safelax, that's what it is."

We may hardly add how necessary it is to beware of imitations, and assure the reader that,

> SAFELAX, "Nature's Way" to health
> and regularity, may be had ONLY of
> J. Scully, Crawlingtree, Essex, one
> **shilling the large bottle.**

THIRTY-FIVE MINUTES FROM NOWHERE

A man called Woodrough woke at 6:55 on a hot summer morning surprised to find that his face was smooth with perspiration. It was light outside and the birds were chattering loudly into a day for them already well advanced. But Woodrough habitually awoke at 7:30, a habit which ensured—what with bathing, shaving, and dressing, and drinking one cup of tea only—his appearance on the broad pavement of Piccadilly precisely fifteen minutes after his assistant was due at the office in St. James's.

Woodrough was, therefore, on the particular day in question, thirty-five minutes in advance of himself.

Now Woodrough was a man to whom minutes spoke with the voice of all Time. For the adult years of his life Woodrough had been one of Time's virtuosos—a connoisseur, a collector, a dealer-doyen.

He accepted his position as only a third-generation dealer could, and he valued minutes in full appreciation of the fact that antiquity is a mere matter of time.

So that when Woodrough saw that he was thirty-five minutes to the good he at once applied himself to the problem of profiting from this unexpected advantage. He drank his tea and glanced at the paper, missing his wife's presence at the breakfast table.

Then walking out into the sunlight he was conscious of a slight feeling of discomfort—to call it danger would be to overstress Woodrough's feeling. It was simply that thirty-five minutes from nowhere are a temptation and an inconvenience as well as an asset.

Woodrough walked along Piccadilly with his usual unconscious assurance, only a little put out at not encountering the familiar nods from familiar faces.

He walked up to his office and was surprised to find the door unlocked. "Good Lord!" he said.

And then: "Good Lord, Symes. What are you doing here so

early?" Woodrough's assistant had looked up from the books spread out before him on the desk, and his face was a shocking mask of malevolence and fear. He glanced at his watch and looked back at Woodrough. "My God!" he said with a break in his voice, "you're early!"

Woodrough's system took the shock of Symes' consistent dishonesty with unexpected resilience. Yet a sort of dullness behind his quiet phoning of the police betokened irremediable loss of confidence, of trust, of money, of trade secrets. Symes had never seemed very concerned over his selling commissions and the memory of this too made Woodrough sad.

Afterwards Woodrough dropped in his chair behind the desk. His mind was still fussing over the thirty-five minutes he had saved and still not entirely consumed.

Not unnaturally, a businessman in his trouble turns to a woman. And not surprisingly, that woman is his mistress rather than his wife—for a mistress is a better investment for sympathy. Woodrough's Rose was sympathetically thornless. Towards her his spirit bore him, away, a four-shilling taxi ride away to Knightsbridge, at the opposite pole to business.

Woodrough felt tired as he fished out the key and slipped it into the lock. The door floated open silently on to the little hall of the flat and he walked in. It was quiet and sheltered from the sun and cool with the faintest touch of Chanel (which for Woodrough remained timelessly fashionable), and he stood quietly for a moment or two before turning into the bedroom.

But alas for the man of habit who tries to make thirty-five minutes on twenty-four hours! The cause of fresh bitterness snored beside Rose, his mouth open, and his face completely relaxed. She had failed Woodrough and it was more painful than Symes' betrayal.

For men who deal always in things of beauty know well how love ranks above art in price.

Woodrough turned away without a word while the strangers to his stricken heart slept on as if he were a ghost.

Then Woodrough in his misery walked fast towards St. James's, and as he walked he raged and through his mind the words of resolution turned again and again. "I will make more money—more money than Symes could steal. I will find another and another mistress, kinder than Rose and more faithful." Rose, O Rose, he thought. And he arrived at Christie's Auction Rooms in time for a most important sale of porcelain.

Without a glance at the red and sallow faces of his fellow dealers, Woodrough walked towards the table, the crowd clearing for him with that kind of awe which primitive men reserve for the possessed. And possessed Woodrough seemed to be, as against his friends, against reason, against the great Ring itself, he bid again and again in tens of guineas for lot after lot.

The auctioneer called out his name as the hammer fell. "Woodrough—Woodrough—Woodrough." They looked on him, those careful valuers for probate, with the mixed horror and envy which only the potency of really great dealers can challenge.

When it was over Woodrough left the rooms unaware of the thousands he had bid away for the Meissen birds and Wedgwood vases, the Chelsea birds, and the lot of mixed items belonging to an almost bankrupt dealer who was delighted to see them fetch so inflated a price.

Woodrough, exhausted, took a taxi home. Through his mind echoed the cry "Woodrough—Woodrough—Woodrough," though the auctioneer's voice was charged with uncustomary sorrow. There were tears in his eyes as he listened. But he felt the relief of bidding away a vast burden of agony.

Yet for all that he suffered Woodrough had still something to be grateful for. By the time the taxi reached his house and he had stumbled through the door he was too sick to notice his wife's hurried handling of the telephone.

She had found herself that day some half-hour to the good and was informing a very old family friend of their unexpected opportunity. What she felt about his early homecoming Woodrough would never appreciate. He retired to bed with the strength of his secure family life to succor him through a bout or serious blood pressure—which is, among dealers in *objects,* almost an occupational disease.

A HANDFUL OF EARTH

Moishe he was called, and because no one had ever thought to ask what his surname was, and because he had been selling secondhand records almost from before the invention of the gramophone, Moishe Music. His stall was in one of those short dead-end streets which lead off from Petticoat Lane like forgotten backwaters in a Venice in which the Grand Canal is two hundred thousand people sluggishly flowing between banks of bargains.

As you edged your way nearer to Moishe Music past the crated ducks cackling, the fish being gutted, the smoked salmon being sliced, and bare arms dipping into barrels for herrings and cucumbers, you'd hear Chaliapin booming through the cracked horn of an old gramophone, or Gigli, his voice just a little too high and a little too fast, chirping like a canary from behind a pile of red and green watermelons.

There was nothing on Moishe's stall later than Flanagan and Allen singing "Underneath the Arches." In other parts of the market you could bop and swing and jazz it any way you liked from big loud Tannoys. But here you had to stand close to hear Nellie Melba singing "Coming through the Rye." There they were in boxes, Jack Hylton and his Metronomes in quiet partnership with Carroll Gibbons, both at sixpence, and old red label classics marked down to a shilling a piece and looking like derelict hansom cabs.

Moishe was the dustman of music and I owe an astonishing knowledge of extinct music-hall numbers to his salvage work.

I used to stand among the collectors flicking over the old discs while Moishe plugged his best-seller for the week on the hand-wound gramophone—"The Song of the Flea" it might be, or "Softly Awakes My Heart." Slowly, carefully, considering all faults, the customers paid over their shillings and sixpences and Moishe stroked his gray-streaked beard as he slipped the coins carefully into an old-fashioned public-house till.

One Sunday Moishe was stalling-in while I still thumbed my way through a batch of early Carusos. "Take the lot at a shilling each," he said, "it'll be one last bargain for you. There must be twenty-five there—here, give me a pound for the lot."

Caruso never sang so cheap and who could resist—even if it meant stumbling home from the Underground like an overloaded camel.

"Next Sunday you won't see me here," Moishe said as he made a parcel of the records.

"Moving to a new pitch?" I asked, thinking the parcel will weigh a ton, and what do I want so much Caruso for anyway?

Moishe handed the Caruso glut to me. It weighed a ton and a half to be precise, and the secondhand string would never last out. Then Moishe fiddled inside his shirt bringing out a small, worn, purple velvet bag.

"For fifty years I carried this round my neck. From Russia. Through Poland—sometimes I didn't have luggage, but this bag I always had. And always, right from a boy, I swore I would take it back where it belongs. To Beth Zion."

What can a man carry around with him the best part of his life, in a small, worn velvet bag?

"Earth," Moishe told me, "a handful of earth from the Holy Land. Now at last I saved enough to take it back—exactly back to exactly where it come from."

Two or three weeks afterwards habit took me against the Petticoat Lane crowd towards Moishe Music's dead-end. When no reedy ghost voice crept above the watermelons, I remembered that he had emigrated for the last time in his life. I was sorry to see him go but at the same time glad to have lost the bad habit of carrying home heavy parcels of old scratched wax.

One Sunday, when we were expecting for supper half a dozen elderly relatives who wouldn't be satisfied with anything less than the best herrings, I took the long creep to the best herring stall in the East End—the only other feature of interest by that dead-end from where Moishe Music had emigrated. But as I trimmed my way through towards the barrels I had completely forgotten the difference between salt herrings without and with Melba.

Then, as an old brown woman with a black scarf round her head sliced the herrings with a quick snaky knife, a Russian bass started to boom out "The Death of Boris." I took my slightly leaking bag of herrings and pushed through towards it. Moishe was back in the music business.

There they were, the same half-dozen careful collectors sorting over the same tattered stock, while Moishe wound the same cracked gramophone.

"Did you put the earth back?" I asked.

"It's you?" Moishe shook my hand. "I certainly did," he explained, "and don't think it was an easy affair. When I got to Beth Zion the whole place was covered with concrete for a dam or something they're building there."

"So you put the earth back somewhere else?" I suggested.

"If you think," he replied, "that I am carrying around with me for fifty years a handful of earth from Beth Zion and I am saving and saving only to take back that handful of earth to Beth Zion, and when eventually I get to Beth Zion I am going to put that handful of earth somewhere else, then, let me tell you," he told me, "you are making a big mistake."

Instead Moishe Music had given everyone a headache with his handful of earth. He nagged so many officials that eventually they decided the quickest thing was to drill through the concrete at Beth Zion and let Moishe put the earth back. Then maybe they could get on building dams without interruption.

"Why didn't you stay, Moishe? Retire there—no?" I asked him.

"No," he explained, "the weather was marvelous the whole time, you can pick oranges in the garden, there's a few little political problems, but who cares about politics so long as we get Jerusalem in the end. And it's a marvelous country—but it's a country for young men to live in, not for old men like me to die in. Also, I don't mean this as a criticism, but you know what I mean when I say, well—it's marvelous there, but it's not the East End."

He put another record on the gramophone. Then as an Italian tenor started to tra-la-la-la his way through "The Barber of Seville," the bit every tenor always sings, Moishe fiddled under his shirt for a moment, and pulled out a new velvet bag.

"Earth," he explained, "from the Holy Land. I couldn't leave without a souvenir."

FIVE PER CENT OF PARADISE

It's my luck I should be in Badarabad with a large quantity of slightly soiled Union Jacks and assorted flags of the Empire in all sizes the week they get their independence. I also have with me a few other short lines, the St. George toast rack which takes four pieces of toast secured by the ridges along the dragon's back; a nice range of tartan tea cosies all clans; ten gross little camera with a little battery inside you press the button a light comes up and against it the fifteen most beautiful models are revealed, and a few boxes of latex hula-hula girls moving most realistically when you turn the handle underneath. But the flags are the big hope of Badarabad Trading Company. I come from a long line of small capital big hopers, some of whom have not died bankrupt.

When I arrive there Badarabad is just a small place quietly stinking in the sun with a governor and a governor's palace as magnificent as the Blue Dance Hall in the Edgware Road. The governor has got a nice old girl who is his missus, a Lady Duckworth, spends her whole time running round a ruined temple stands just by where the jungle starts, looking at what is carved on the stones. In fact the great tragedy within a couple of days of my arrival is that she has just got a few boys to pull out a stone and what is carved on it gives her such a fright she falls over in a dead faint, and the boys knock off for their rice pudding elevens and when they get back the old girl is completely eaten by a tiger. Sir Duckworth is pretty fed up when he hears this after he comes back from the club where he has been knocking back a few drinks at my expense. And I am pretty worried myself in case, with my luck, he should reckon it against me especially as I am taking up a lot of his time with looking at the fifteen models just once more old chap, and working one of the hula-hula girls till she falls to pieces. Still I gave him a couple more and went back to the tin hut and painted up on the board over the door "By appointment." Which was my second big mistake, the first being ever to come to a fly-ridden, rat-infested, dung heap in a hothouse like Badarabad. Because it was the very next day they got their independence.

Mind you the Badarabadis don't know nothing about this independence business. Posters is being stuck up everywhere in English and Badarabadi but it is all so long and involved the rumor gets round that the British are going to land six regiments of guards and round up all the sacred goats in the place because England is short of meat. The next thing is the streets are full of screaming Badarabadis and Sir Duckworth is taken off in a destroyer with his three ADC's and the two latex hula-hula girls, and a lot of valuable property is burnt down and looted and suddenly I am the only British resident left because I have the sense to dark my face with some brown boot polish and put on a white overall and stand by the shop door shouting and pointing this way and that way while I jump up and down on the flag of the German Republic (what do the Badarabadis know).

And this is where I have my first piece of luck. A whole crowd of Badarabadis comes running past in a hurry since they have just looted the bank. They stop and look at me jumping on the flag and the leader asks me to step aside and has a few jumps himself. Then they all want to, and by the end of the day the fashion has spread like wildfire and my whole stock of flags is sold at a good margin of profit. All of which is to explain how I happen to have twenty thou just handy when his Supreme Highness, the Son of the Morning Star, the Sultan of Badarabad, decided (being as it is the end of the racing season anyway) to visit his home town.

Now this Sultan always has a soothing effect on his people on the
rare occasions he shows up in Badarabad, sometimes after a bad
run of luck on the horses or because there are no good musicals on in
London, or maybe because Paris doesn't happen to be in the spring
just now and who wants Paris in the winter? His Supreme Highness
is only a small-time son of the Morning Star, but as such his perks
are very nice indeed. Every year they make him a present of twenty-
eight fresh girls and the entire crop of dates. That's how much they
love the dear old Sult. But all the wherewithal for spieling in the
casinos of Monte Carlo, Las Vegas and Blackpool comes not from the
two bob's-worth of dates, or even from selling the girls, but from
being not only a sultan but a high priest. This is how the business
works, and you must admit it is rather a sweet racket, and makes
you think that the businessmen of the West can learn a thing or two
from the mysterious East.

The true reason why the Sultan has come back is because as High
Priest of Badarabad he had a duty to perform. This duty consists of
selling through his heavenly land office parcels of land in different
parts of Paradise to all his trusting serfs. They are coming once a
year from far and near to put down a deposit on a nice bit of acreage,
or maybe if they are flush, buying outright a beautiful allotment
where the crops blossom daily in complete contrast to this stony old
Badarabad dump where a handful of rice is a day's pay. And his
agents are selling from a large map parcels at all prices, high for a
good position ranging to however much a coolie happens to have for
not such a good place down low on the map. But they are perfectly
fair about this. If the bloke comes back in a couple of years, or wants
to make a hire-purchase arrangement, they will consider the sum
down a deposit, and who knows, maybe by the time the fellow actually dies he will have the best position in all Paradise. And all the
proceeds (less moderate running costs) are the personal and private
income of the Sultan himself. See?

Now the Sultan had returned a little early because of an un-
precedented run of bad luck at twenty-one, poker, snakes and ladders
and other gambling games, and he needs a few thousand on account,

otherwise how will it look at Monte Carlo when he isn't the heaviest loser? The name of Badarabad will not be respected and they are a proud people. But the fact remains, they tell the Sultan, Badarabad has just had the worst crop in even its history, and the citizens are restive for this very reason, although by the time the Sultan docks and is carried on the bare backs of the multitude to his palace which is as magnificent as the Paramount Dance Hall, Tottenham Court Road, most serfs are quiet again and looking forward to market-gardening in Paradise. Still, the Sultan's agent explains, they haven't been buying too well lately, and there is only a few miserable hundred in the exchequer. Also the bank they robbed was the Sultan's personal bank, and his reserve fund is entirely blued. This is where I come in.

I call on the Sultan and offer him my whole twenty thou (what is the Badarabadi pound worth anyway?) in exchange for Hell, the complete concession, lock, stock and barrel, with a deed of ownership, sealed, signed and delivered, complete with map and all.

"You want to buy Hell?" he says. "Can he buy Hell?" he asks his agents.

"With pleasure," they say. "Who in their right mind would buy Hell?"

So I leave the Sultan's land office the sole owner of Hell, and in the opinion of all and sundry the biggest bloody fool between Arabia Deserta and Seven Dials.

Then with the assistance of my clerk, Jimmy, a Badarabadi who wants to become a company director one day, I draw out a handbill and we get ten thousand distributed all over the state. SPEND ETERNITY IN BADARABAD says the heading on the bill.

> All those who can't afford a pitch in Paradise needn't think they have a hope of going to Hell once dead.

> HELL IS COMPLETELY SOLD OUT Paradise is getting crammed to capacity. Speak to His Supreme Highness

now about it, or look forward to
spending
ETERNITY IN BADARABAD.

The idea is horrifying to all Badarabadis. The first result is a run
on the Sultan's land office so that all plots shown on the map are
taken up at luxury prices. The Sultan and his agents are delighted,
but there is no time to set up new maps, so in a few days the land office and palace are besieged by Badarabadi hordes all demanding
the Sultan should free them from the threat of spending eternity in
Badarabad—than which even the prospect of Hell is more cheerful.

Need I say more? The Sultan comes, crown in hand to me, and I
am kind enough to sell him Hell back, lock, stock and barrel, for a
nominal thirty per cent profit (he always strikes a tough bargain,
the old boy) plus a five per cent royalty in perpetuity on Paradise
(because when it comes to making a bargain I also know a thing or
two, believe me).

So you are now talking to a man who owns five per cent of Paradise and has had the great honor to have been appointed ADC to His
Supreme Highness the Sultan of Badarabad, my partner and a gentleman if ever I met one.

GOOD BUSINESS WITH SENTIMENT

Naturally Mrs. Adamson was excited about the forthcoming marriage of her daughter Elizabeth. She was excited as only an artist can
be—one who has planned and worked and sighed and now sees
the promised end. Or a constructional engineer who has just seen
the last rivet in a fine bridge plugged home. Or a house-agent
who has completed a sale. And yet how can any of these compare with
the supreme satisfaction of a mother who has piloted her only
daughter into a good match?

A good match it was. Elizabeth, only daughter, to Vincent, only
son—and though titles are nice, capital has its importance. The

whole world knew how well capitalized Vincent's father was. And how well they looked together. Mrs. Adamson's eyes filled with joyful tears as she watched her little girl crook her finger delicately.

Ah, that finger. That—to Vincent's astonished sense—that digit scented beyond the musk of exotic dreams, that little, little finger, that dream, that jewel. Elizabeth is altogether a gem not to be priced by a keen eye trained in valuation. She is rare and costly and beautifully polished—like the diamond which glistens brilliantly against her fresh pink skin.

As the day approaches, Mr. Adamson takes an occasional afternoon off from the office. He sits at home by his desk carefully working over the figures for the cost of the wedding. Because he has carefully built up his family's security these twenty years past it is a reflex for him to check and double check. On the wedding, of course, he cannot possibly show a profit. But with luck he will come through without impairing his standard of living. And Mrs. Adamson will be satisfied. Above all she will be content. He sighs as he checks the figures yet again.

Fortunately he has been able to help Vincent in the matter of the ring through a very dear friend in the trade. Not a bad ring, he thinks, for the money. He smiles. As he draws the smoke into his lungs he makes a lightning calculation of the money he has spent in the past twenty years on tobacco.

On such an afternoon Mrs. Adamson's excited girlish face gives in for a moment. Her expression fades, her neck wrinkles, there is an uneven dab of powder on her nose. She sighs and leaves the room to loosen her corset and snatch half an hour's rest before the children arrive for dinner and a discussion of the arrangement of cars. When you get to the outer fringes of large families it becomes difficult to know who is entitled to a car.

Oh, dear, whispers Mrs. Adamson to herself, how complicated life is. She sighs again as she snuggles into the eider-down. She floats far beyond the exhausting details of daughters and weddings, and her features break into wreathing lines of delight. She wriggles her plump little body, and thinks how like her Elizabeth is; so feminine yet such a determined organizer. She has much to learn, but together they, mother and daughter, will triumph, while Mr. Adamson initiates Vincent into the mysteries of being a good husband. Dear Proops, he had never stopped being apologetic. If only Vincent makes half so good a husband, Mrs. Adamson thinks as she turns the ring on her finger. The diamond flashes at her intimately, Elizabeth's ring is much larger of course, but it hasn't the same quality.

At this moment Vincent is being examined by the doctor of an insurance company, and though very healthy decides that the more he pays in premium, the less likely is anything to go wrong. Mr. Adamson is very impressed by the sum for which Vincent insures himself. He shakes him very warmly by the hand. A nice chap, thinks Vincent.

"It was very good of you to take the trouble over the ring," he says.

"It was a pleasure, my dear boy," answers Mr. Adamson, "a real pleasure."

That afternoon Elizabeth drinks tea in a little green tearoom a few minutes from the center of Bond Street. She holds her teacup between two fingers and describes the final alterations in her wedding dress. Elaine listens, cheeks glowing. To think of old Dumpy married! Just fancy her leaving in a car on her husband's arm. Her husband. Elizabeth blushes and looks away.

"Which hotel will you stay at?" Elaine asks. "I mean, you won't leave at once for your . . . holiday?"

"Not likely," says Elizabeth. "I've made Vincent get theater tickets for the evening." She pours more tea for both of them, holding the teapot confidently, her ring finger displayed to the entire room. She is gratified by the whispering of waitresses standing by the trays of tiny pastries just behind her.

"It really is a lovely stone," says Elaine. "Vincent must be terribly in love with you."

"Isn't it?" answers Elizabeth happily.

It was not until after dinner that evening, after the Adamsons and Vincent had arranged and rearranged the seating in the cars some seven times, that any of them noticed what had happened. They had all eaten the excellent dinner with jokes and laughter and little reminiscences of Elizabeth's baby days.

Then Mrs. Adamson had turned the talk to serious matters, and once again the sheets of note paper with the groupings of aunts and great-aunts, uncles and cousins, were produced and shuffled. It was a discussion which always caused a certain amount of heat, but after an hour it was decided that Mrs. Adamson's original arrangement was the best.

"A pity about Uncle Alfred though," murmured Mr. Adamson. "He was very good to me over the Dickinson-Murdock business."

"Now don't start arguing all over again dear," answered Mrs. Adamson in a voice forbidding argument. And then she noticed.

She was silent for several moments, staring, her always too prominent eyes popping like a high-bred Pekinese. Then in a voice high-pitched and cracked with shock she cried, "Elizabeth!"

Elizabeth, dreaming girlishly, looked up blankly. Mr. Adamson and Vincent stopped drawing on their Panatellas.

"Elizabeth," cried Mrs. Adamson, "what have you been up to?" The young couple blushed in harmony. "Look at your ring-finger, you silly girl," shrieked Mrs. Adamson.

As Elizabeth raised her pale face, tears welled from her eyes.

"Where is it gone?" cried Mrs. Adamson again.

"What is the matter, my love?" asked Mr. Adamson.

"What's up, Mum?" asked Vincent anxiously.

"Her beautiful diamond—it's gone!" shouted Mrs. Adamson.

When they had soothed Elizabeth, they retraced all her movements that afternoon.

"You might have eaten it," suggested Vincent, "in a jam tart . . ."

"They were éclairs," said Elizabeth miserably.

"To think a daughter of mine could be so careless," reiterated Mrs. Adamson. But Mr. Adamson just said that he had arranged the insurance at the time it was bought. He seemed quite pleased. He with his skill could recoup such losses. Often with a profit. Jolly good show. Not to worry. There was something to be said, after all, for being a man.

THE BLOTTIK MONOPOLY

It was sure to happen in the end. Ever since the final antique boom in the 1960's dealers had been telling one another it would happen. Regularly every five years someone wrote to the newspapers and complained that "the Nation's heritage is being shipped for a mess of potage." The National Trust might save an old house or two but what could it do as mansion after castle, country house after quaint old cottage, all slipped their roots and went, piece by piece, to foreign parts with harder currencies, there to languish thoroughly out of place among fruit trees and swimming pools and endless sunshine.

But quite apart from the major antique losses—all the minor items were exhausted. Georgian silver, of course, had long since ceased to exist. Sheffield plate was hoarded by a few misers in remote parts of the country. Chelsea and Bow porcelain, Worcester, Swansea and Rockingham—the only pieces ever seen were items imported from the Meissen factories in Alaska (to where they had long ago been removed). Victorian lusters—why, a pair catalogued in very bold type brought 1,700 guineas at Christies and then there was nearly a thousand pounds in the knockout. Wedgwood (it goes without saying) had been exhausted years ago. What was left? What was there for a dealer to live on?

They, those once sleek and prosperous dealers, used to hang about in disorderly groups outside the empty auction rooms, waiting for the auctioneer to call out to whoever was next on the strict rota of subscribing buyers, the item (a broken bit of Woolworth glass or an old doorstop) it was his privilege to buy. As soon as the fortunate bidder received it, the starving dealers would mob him. That miserable item then changed hands perhaps fifty times, eventually rest-ing in the shooting brake of the inevitable American dealer always patiently waiting at hand.

The Antique Dealers' Aid Society had, in the early days of the great antique drought, started a fund for fallen dealers, but very quickly it was found that the dealers' enemy was not starvation but inertia. In one year alone (the year when the last bowl of wax fruit caused that riot at Sotheby's) two hundred and sixty-three members of the Association were certified insane. The cause was always the same—loss of vocation. Nothing to buy, nothing to sell. They couldn't stand it, so that the old ones died off like flies while the younger ones took to arson or robbery with violence. The Delinquent Dealer became a major problem of the day.

It was just after mounted police had been forced to break up a mass meeting of dealers in Hyde Park (they were attempting to tear down the wrought-iron gates to make up an export order) that Morris Blottik (whose vast showrooms in Piccadilly had long ago been converted into an army surplus store) discovered the pan business.

Blottik was a fastidious connoisseur who had, throughout the bad times, kept away from the less reputable groups of dealers. He had scraped a living dealing in respectable goods such as old clothes, bottles, and scrap iron, though only the choicest examples. His thoughts were never far from the historic problem of the antique trade.

"Must those who understand ivory, rot among old bones?" he would suddenly ask the ragged dealers in the Association's soup kitchen. No one answered as he savagely tore a dry baigel to pieces. Everyone was tired of dealer's rant. What was Blottik complaining about? At least he was a respectable rag-and-bone man. What about those poor hunted devils in St. James's? How could they know that this very Blottik was to be the saviour of the antique trade?

It happened quite casually, as most important things do. From the days of his glory when he was exporting his ten thousand pounds worth of goods a week, Blottik retained his habit of retiring to the bathroom for an hour each day. Undisturbed, he would ponder life's problems; when he left for the barrow his careful mind would be soothed. It so happened that one day Blottik had trundled his barrow about the London streets with an unusual feeling of malaise. True, he was intensely preoccupied with the antique problem—but then, he always was. He hastened home and repaired to the bathroom.

Blottik had an early Victorian house in Gunnersbury. The empty rooms echoed to his footsteps as he sped up the stairs. As he opened the bathroom door he had a sense that the moment was one of historic importance. He stood for several seconds as if changed to stone. Then he turned and ran to fetch his tool-box. It took him two hours to prize the lavatory pan free. He phoned an associate and two minutes later was in possession of orders for five hundred decorated basins at £22 apiece. Blottik was a proud man. He was back in the antique business.

Now it was that Blottik's experience told. He did not run about shouting to the wind that he was back in business. No. He had some cards printed, reading:

BOURNE HOLLINGSWORTH
Councillor
Sanitary Cttee.

And he made an arrangement with a little plumber around the corner. Then, one dark night, after having carefully checked to see that no vagrant members of the trade were following him, Blottik and the plumber set out on what was to be the most important buying trip of modern times.

Blottik's method was simple. He would call at a promising house and present his card.

"I'd like to inspect your w.c.," he would say. "I'm from the Council, you know—Sanitary—you don't mind?"

And by this time he would already be glancing into the bathroom. If the toilet was suitably decorated, "George, bring your tools," he called out to the plumber. "We're giving you a brand new toilet,"

Blottik explained to the householder, "the old one's finished—it's an antique."

By the time George had taken out the old pan and put in a new one Blottik's stock had cost him six pounds apiece, and, as in all good business deals, everyone was satisfied.

What pandemonium there was when the news of Blottik's shipments leaped out! The trade fell over itself to buy from him. At once toilets began to be graded—transfer decorated, polychrome —solid body—lead-glazed—and, of course, all the famous old masters of basin molding were listed. Pilkington's Soundless—Beal's Ferrara—Master's Milady, Henry's Invictus. The names are famous today among collectors.

America went mad for the line. Toilet pans were seen all over New York, adapted as hot or cool air vents, set in gilded frames (maker's name foremost), garnished with flowers and trailing ferns. *Vogue* devoted six pages to the more *chic* of what was now called "the basin-maker's art." It was wonderful while it lasted.

Of course it was only a flash in the pan. Within three years there wasn't a fine old toilet to be found in the British Isles. But Blottik was firmly established as an expert and his book, *Famous Basins*, was a collector's *vade mecum*. In those mad months a number of dealers had become solvent and a few of the more conservative ones had died of chagrin, but now once again the wild dangerous groups were beginning to gather outside the empty auction rooms. The recurrent crisis was again imminent.

Blottik himself, the dwindling traders felt, should have at least been knighted, because, although the end of business was again at hand, wasn't Britain the only welfare state in the world where every house had a fine new w.c.?

EIGHT YEARS IN THE MAKING

Mrs. Toshak was forty-two when she first saw the archangel Michael at an auction room off Bond Street. She knew his name was Michael for the auctioneer called it as he made a note of the fact that a small collection of cracked Greek pots had changed hands. And she could see at once that he must be an archangel for he was nearly six and a half feet tall, and his classical features were set in a pale skin and topped with a growth of closely curled golden hair. He for his part —being older than he looked and admiring Mrs. Toshak's experienced figure as much as the encrustations of diamonds about her person—remarked to himself that there was much of the untamed gypsy in this still elegant lady who watched him in so predatory a manner.

Now to tell the truth, Mrs. Toshak was an Armenian carpet dealer's wife who had come to London by way of Smyrna, Budapest and Paris, where Toshak himself had had the decency to die after taking out a very sizable insurance policy with a gullible English company. Thence London, in the area of Sloane Street—with a small elegant shop in gilt and black and stripes, hung with dubious landscapes of blotched satyrs and forced nymphs. Mrs. Toshak was an interior decorator. She could at a glance tell just how well Michael would fit in to her decor and business. As an experienced dealer, she could sense almost to the pound his precise market price.

The archangel Michael, for his part, was a recent importation from Vienna. His sponsor, a collector of Spanish baroque furniture, had picked him up in a café in the Ringstrasse and had recognized immediately how well he would tone with the baroque. As a valet Michael had left nothing to be desired, but his employer, who had at first been quite enchanted by his man's innate sense of the aesthetic, began to worry at the gaps in his collection of Hispano-Mauresque plates. A dealer from whom he was about to buy one of his own pieces was stupid enough to mention an Austrian count who had sold it to him. "Was he six foot six tall and blond?" asked the collector. Michael and his employer parted company that same afternoon. The employer sighed for a week or so and then found a new valet through a fellow collector. And Michael found himself, without surprise, in the fine art business.

Thus it was then that Mrs. Toshak and Michael met in the pur-

suit of business at the very heart of the heartless world of their refined trade. Michael turned to leave the rooms after his last purchase, a slight sneer wrinkling his lips. He always bore in mind the
fact that in the not far distant future he would be buying for much
more than shillings, and he was cultivating a bidding manner suited
to the higher levels of dealing. Mrs. Toshak cut across his exit swift
as a dark cobra, and the two drew level at the swing-doors.

"The last lot—you bought?" inquired Mrs. Toshak with a hard
glitter in her eyes showing to advantage against the velvet of her
voice.

"That is so, madam," replied Michael, making his words drip
slowly with tenderness. "But surely—it must be—but no, how could
it—it is the Princess von Dorfensleben. My dear Princess, enchanted," and he stooped low to kiss Mrs. Toshak's hand.

Although Mrs. Toshak could not resist a smile of amusement at
Michael's methods, she was forced to admire the ease with which he
fell into so patent a lie. In this way he was like her own dead Florio
—a man capable of selling a silk Bokhara every day of the week.
But so tall, so blond, so aristocratic.

She introduced herself and enjoyed Michael's apologies for a
minute or two. Then she returned to the matter in hand.

"Come to my shop at six with this rubbish you have bought," Mrs.
Toshak ordered, and with a scintillating wave of her fingers
she leapt into a taxi, leaving Michael to smile indiscriminately at
the street.

In spite of his willingness to wait upon events with the same de-
votedness he had shown as a valet, Michael was a little perplexed by
his new friend. With mixed feelings but with a delicious sense of an-
ticipation he drew up at Mrs. Toshak's shop front, a discreet affair
of gold and black cupidons surmounted by white brocade drapes
with tassels everywhere. He entered, walking reverently upon the
black carpet, his eyes turned down modestly as Mrs. Toshak came
towards him from the shadowed depth of the room. They had
hardly time to exchange the courtesies appropriate to such a meeting when the door opened again and in came Mrs. Toshak's ex-

pected clients—a portly gentleman with white moustaches, and a lady elegantly dressed as only a woman past her second youth need be.

Mrs. Toshak glided forward to greet them like a *grande dame* afflicted with the intimate huskiness of a brothel madam. She introduced them to Michael by his full title, and then as they looked together at a superb chandelier, she whispered to Michael, "Sell her the Greeks—he is mine." With the formal politeness of an old dance the four then paired off, Michael telling the lady of the glory that is still to be found in Greece. "O Athens," said the lady, "O Sparta— I've never been to Greece. How lovely." For Michael had led from the general discussion to the particular pots he had to offer.

When it was all over, Mrs. Toshak and Michael looked at each other. Their faces were flushed and their eyes swam. Mrs. Toshak put out her hand and Michael's slipped a check into it. Then together they breathed, "Three hundred and seventy pounds." A moment later Mrs. Toshak had clasped Michael to her breast. He settled with her for a hundred and fifty. Only at one point in the discussion it seemed that a promising relationship was in danger. But he looked at her with a sudden, poignant expression of regret in his eyes. Her heart melted like the polar cap of the earth enjoying the first heat in its history. He got his hundred and fifty in cash.

Mrs. Toshak is now fifty. Michael is a little stouter, and he wears glasses. Many are the killings they have enjoyed together, Mrs. Toshak confidently directing, Michael leaping into the battle like a Prussian Guards officer and winning golden commissions every week. Soon he will be earning enough to keep himself in the style to which his employer has accustomed him—and a little later on, perhaps, he will be able to steal enough from Mrs. Toshak to buy a full half-share in her prosperous business.

SHORT STORIES

EXPRESSO BONGO

THE PICTURE IN THE FAN-MAG SHOWED THIS GANGLY KID IN JEANS and a sweat shirt, his face contorted, mouth wide open, beating with both hands on a bongo set round his shoulder, over it the headline BONGO SCORES AT TOM-TOM. The same terrible stuff, but this time it was good, because it was me who dropped the dead-beat drunk columnist a fiver to run it. Because this new boy Bongo Herbert, playing nightly for the past week at the Tom-Tom expresso back of Frith Street, is under contract to nobody but me. Half of the ten pounds he picks up this Friday comes to me. Half of everything he beats out of those little bongos for the next three years comes to me.

I checked my capital of twenty-three pounds and some shillings useful for unavoidable tips, the balance of a fifty-pound fee for publicizing the Wally Burn Flames tour. Free as a pimp or an artiste's manager I walked over to the Tom-Tom to collect my first week's unearned income.

Not so unearned. For three weeks after I found my property beating and shouting himself into a frenzy on the corny Jazz Boat Stomp which the Flames signed off with, I had wet-nursed that kid along, bought him cigarettes and coffee and sandwiches, a couple of sweat shirts with bongos painted on them, a pair of tailored black jeans, and a fancy haircut, turned him from Bert Rudge, snotty-nosed nobody, to Bongo Herbert, Britain's latest answer to America's latest solution of how to keep discs selling by the million. Not that Bongo was answering back yet. I wouldn't be in profit for another couple of weeks, and then only if Leon at the Tom-Tom kept him on that long.

"The boy's great, isn't he Leon?" I said.

"I'm getting my Italian peasant-style cups and saucers broke," Leon complained, "from where these mad kids keep time bashing on the tables. Two tables also is already broke in the legs."

"You're doing great business Leon," I told him, and showed him the fan-mag.

"It's a good publicity," he said. "How much costs a whole page in this paper?"

"More than the ten you're paying my boy," I pointed out.

"I keep him another week maybe," Leon said grudgingly as he handed over ten dirty but attractive notes.

"You take him for six weeks Leon," I replied, "or we beat our tiny brains out in some other expresso."

"Six weeks at ten," he said.

"At fifteen," I corrected.

So I sold Bongo to Leon for twelve a week for six weeks. At this rate Bongo would be a very old teen-ager before I could retire to the South of France. Kids with imitation American gimmicks were rocking their managers into comfort while I wasted my life on café expresso and doughnuts. It was humiliating.

Still, Bongo was a good boy—a good simple unspoiled boy. When I gave him his five, his first week's money, there were great oily tears in his eyes.

"That only leaves you five for yourself guv," he muttered. "You should take more. I wouldn't get nothing without you."

Such trust and honesty deserved my support.

"Take it Bongo," I told him with a he-man pulled-punch to his jaw. "Half of everything you make is going to go to you kid."

I knew Bongo could be the answer. After all, Tommy Steele had been standing in for Elvis Presley (who was too busy counting his dollars to bother coming after softer currencies in person) for a year now. A year is a long time in the life of a teen-age idol. The seventeen-year-olds make the most capricious public in the world. They want someone new to get excited about every few months. It has to be someone who is (or can act) not much older than themselves, and since the mob is mostly female, the talent has to be male and sexy (or able to act it). It has to be someone with a nobody background—rags to riches in five yelping stages—from dirty sweat shirt to gold lamé sweat shirt. It had to be Bongo.

That night at the Tom-Tom it was.

The place was stacked with sweating teen-agers (and a few who would like to be) wearing Vince Man's Shop jeans with heavy roll-necks, close-fitting Charing Cross Road teddy trousers and velvet-collared coats bought on the hire-purchase, string ties hanging in the cold coffee, suede Jeff Chandler lumber jackets, and bright strained cotton sweaters dashed with cigarette ash and crumbs from Leon's special pizza. There was smoke in the Tony Curtis hair styles, and smoke around the pony tails. Thick badly applied mascara ran down the face of a girl in a black jersey and ski pants crying in a corner, while a spade with big white teeth chipped one of Leon's valuable cups beating it out with Bongo.

Backed by a frantic skiffle group called the Beasts (hungry for pizza and applause), Bongo found rhythms which were crude enough for these simple-minded low-budget good-timers to believe in. He bashed the baby drums, twisted like an electric eel, and shouted a meaningless string of words we had thrown together.

The boy had something—a something which wasn't commodity in the days when talent with polish was expected. He was contemporary-style: elementary violent energy coupled to an inane but genuine gaiety (at this price what did he have to be gay about?) which hooked these yokels from Elephant and Castle and points south by the grubby scruffs of their immature emotions and flung them far away from the kitchen sink, the stale oilcloth, the nagging mothers, and the bellowing bewildered fathers, and dropped them writhing into a synthetic tropic confusion. Or, as Bongo, yelping and chi-yiking in his hoarse Hoxton voice, put it:

> Ex-presso—bongo
> Fla-menko—bongo
> Tooo-baygo—bongo

Caa-lypso—bongo
Bongo—bongo—calypso—bongo
Ole.

While Bongo broke off for a while to pour coffee down his gravel throat and let his bongos cool off, I turned to the thin, oily-eyed dyspeptic whose poker face had grown longer with every *bongo!*

"Another *cappuccino* Mr. Mayer?" For it was no other than the hard-to-get talent spotter from Garrick Records himself whom I had caressed through an expensive dinner and dragged into this hellhole to hear my talented client. His eyes showed the glaze of six brandies and a genuine dislike for this kind of music.

"Have another, Mr. Mayer?"

"Keeps me awake," he complained.

I might as well get it over with, I thought. "What's your feeling about the boy?" I asked him.

"Nausea," he replied.

Well thank you and good night, Mr. Mayer, I thought.

"The kid's got a great gimmick, Mr. Mayer," I said, my eyes bursting with enthusiasm, my teeth bared in the full smile of the confident loser.

Mayer wiped coffee stains from the corners of his dry mouth on a grubby handkerchief monogrammed "O"—must be for ostrich. He refused to see something great when it happened.

"You know," he said, "I am really by nature an opera man. I think *Aïda* is a work of beauty and excitement. All this"—he waved a thin, contracted claw in the direction of Bongo and the Beasts—"all this kind of thing is deeply sickening to my temperament. It so happens, due to the irony of fate, in opera I lost my shirt . . ."

"You put on some great shows, Mr. Mayer, show business doesn't forget," I said, sycophantic as ever. I waved the fan-mag with the Bongo headline under his nose like potpourri. "This boy's not doing bad."

Mayer sighed. "I lost my shirt," he repeated. "Yet from this disc lunacy I make money."

It was getting too late to sit listening to the reminiscences of an old O-for-ostrich has-been impresario.

"Well thank you Mr. Mayer for being so frank," I said (he should be this frank once more and drop stone dead).

"Like I say," he continued sadly, "for me personally this kind of thing is torture. I'll give thirty-five pounds for your client and the group, two sides, no royalty, one-way option to the company. Record next week. All right?"

"Mr. Mayer," I said, blinking, "so you really think the boy has something?"

Mayer got up to go.

"I don't know—I don't care," he said. "These young idiots seem to want this kind of thing so let's sell them what they want. Maybe next week, with this Bongo boy, we lose a few pounds. So what? The week after we find a Tommy Steele and make a profit."

The mob had gulped down the pizzas and expressos and was shouting for more Bongo.

"Listen to them Mr. Mayer," I said with missionary fervor, "they want him—they want him, Mr. Mayer."

"Don't get so excited," he said, as he rose, a thin lost waif of an impresario. "Here they don't have to pay for him. A record costs six shillings."

As the kid, fresh again, began to beat on his little skin money boxes, I worked out how many discs at six shillings Mayer had to sell before Bongo earned me my first thousand.

Assuming we got onto a royalty basis of 1½d a disc with our second recording, it came to almost half a million.

Meanwhile, take off a fiver for the skiffle Beasts, and the evening's work showed me and my boy fifteen apiece cash. Not exactly the late Mike Todd's kind of money—but I was in profit.

In profit.

I love those words.

When I came out after the recording session Regent Street looked mellow in the late afternoon sunshine. The traffic was soothing after the six hours of bongo and skiffle, bad jokes and adolescent exhibitionism which we had condensed into two sides of a wax disc.

I crossed by Liberty's and cut through Poland Street to take a late lunch at the Roll-Mop.

It took two salt-beef sandwiches to revive me. Then I started to sketch a review of our great contribution to teen-age dream life.

BONGO HERBERT
Expresso Bongo/Bongo Calypso
(Garrick Pop. 786)

The up-and-coming bongo boy starts to beat his way into tomorrow's hit parade with his own number, *Expresso Bongo*, a foaming, furious farrago of tropicality powerfully supported by the Beasts bongo group. Hate or hug him, Bongo has something that's new, a swaying calypso beat woven around a rock foundation. Here it is kids. Bongo you beasts.

Good, I told myself, that earns you the giant slice of cheesecake.

I forked the cheesecake up, but I can't say I enjoyed it. Because supposing Bongo's disc did get the notices—so what? The only way you ever sell a record is by getting it heard—which means plugs by TV or radio, preferably both. I'm not saying such plugs can be bought—but supposing they could, was I in a position to outbid the established managers? Even this cheesecake was, strictly speaking, a luxury I couldn't yet afford.

Now we were started on this success kick and I saw the whole terrible long drag stretching before me, Bongo didn't seem such a wonderful property any more.

I looked him over as he sulked in the kitchen of the three-up and two-down Hoxton hovel he lived in with Mum, a baggy old harridan, Dad, a brick-faced bricklayer, and younger sister Edna with adenoids stunting the growth of nothing except her brain.

Bongo, the hope of Hoxton, his cockscomb of platinum-tinted hair drooping under Mum's accusing predatory hen's eye, our breadwinner—with both of us doubtful for the moment.

"You say, mister whatsit," she gobbled. "How much is he making at that West End place where he's been night after night?"

"Just a fiver a week Mrs. Rudge," I said, "but it'll get—"

"A fiver," she whispered hoarsely. "A fiver!" she screamed as if it were a swearword. "The little bleeder's still giving me two pound a week when he's knocking up a fiver?"

"Haven't I got expenses?" Bongo muttered. "I got a lot of expenses."

"Have kids," she told me, "go on, have kids. I don't know what we have them for."

"He's a good boy Mrs. Rudge," I told her. "He'll look after you fine."

"Have kids," she went on. "I got that drunken loafer can't have two h'pennies in his pocket without being a good-time Charlie with drinks all round for every Tom, Dick and Harry. And that Edna always after the boys—where's she going to end up? And *him,*" she pointed accusingly at poor beaten-up Bongo, high-living his way out of her heart on three pounds a week. "I don't know what we have kids for," she repeated querulously.

Then it was Bongo's solo. "I know what for," he said quietly. Then all that energy came roaring up like a hot geyser. "So you can bleed the poor bastards white," he screamed. "Call yourself a mother," he hissed. "I never had a mother. Just you, that's all—you."

When Bongo finished telling her, she looked like a pricked bladder of off-white lard—a tired, gray old char who had scrubbed millions of square miles of floor to find at the end that the earth was flat and the edge of it a precipice complete with only son to push her off.

So Bongo walked out, leaving the home fire doused and faintly smoking behind him.

By the time we'd got back into Town with Bongo simmering his injustices fitfully all the way I had enough case history. I wasn't strong enough to sustain another bongo that night. So I dropped him at the Tom-Tom and wandered over to a small-time nude revue off Brewer Street which included an occasional friend of mine called Maisie whom in her way was very fond of me—or you—or whoever paid for her singing lessons, a subject on which she was hipped as a result of having the ambition to be a Judy Garland but not the voice yet.

Maisie was representing Coventry that night, by wrapping her legs round the neck of a stuffed horse behind the chorus. Neither she nor the horse was permitted by law to move. After the tableaux (laughingly called "Vivant") were finished, we had some dinner in a Chinese restaurant and she complained for a while about how everybody neglected her voice. Then we followed the indigestion and neglect up with a bottle of Irish whisky at a club where a Negro sang a calypso about how much worse than a man-scorpion a woman-scorpion can be. Then we two scorpions went back to her nest. In the morning I had two pounds left but there was still the indiges-tion. I also seemed to have won the calypso singer, because I couldn't get the song out of my head. If I ever write a book I'll call it *What Maisie Did* and sell it in purple cellophane covers.

You can tell the temper I was in when I walked into my flat at midday and found the kid sleeping slob-like in his sweat shirt on my bed.

I dragged the blankets from under him and he shouted, "No Mum," and woke up.

"You missed a great night at the Tom-Tom," he grunted.

"I'll live anyway," I replied. "Thank you for keeping my bed warm and get out of it."

"The telly boys were there last night," he said as he pulled on his jeans.

"The who?" I kicked Bongo's shoes over to him and opened a win-dow.

"The television film boys. They was there all night shooting."

What was he saying? Could I have, after so many years, this kind of luck?

The short answer to that was—I couldn't. I checked up with the television boys and, yes, it was true they'd been filming Bongo at the Tom-Tom all evening—for a big documentary program called

Teen-age Rebellion. The bill co-starred Bongo and other delinquent types with a magistrate, a psychiatrist, and the governor of a Boys' Remand Home. This was exactly, I told them, the kind of plug Bongo needed.

"The material is magnificent," the eager young director told me. "That boy is demonic."

He agreed to do his best to get the demonic boy a variety spot if we didn't object to the documentary.

"The way things are," I told him, "just get us a few quid in cash and you can insult my client as much as you like."

Every cloud has its silver lining, as Mrs. Rudge herself must have observed more than once during her long, dreary, silverless, and clouded life.

We didn't know that the cloud had turned and was shining for us until a fortnight later when *Teen-age Rebellion* turned out to be a big hit. And it wasn't for the magistrate, the psychiatrist, and the Remand Home governor either. It was Bongo who got the notices.

They had used his sound track all the way through the program. The shots of him beating the life out of Mother and Hoxton in the shape of a pair of midget drums had real power. When the camera moved right close in on Bongo's face those tired TV critics woke up and reached for their adjectives. Myself I just felt frightened of what was going on there behind the bright eyes and that twisted dry mouth.

Mayer moved fast and got Bongo's disc out ten days early, and now we didn't need any help to get bookings. In quick succession Bongo skinned the black cat on Jack Jackson's program, was introduced by Jack Payne as "that terrifying teen-ager," and was discovered by four radio disc jockeys in the same week. Whereupon Cyril Stapleton gave *Expresso Bongo* the lead in his *Daily Express* column, and the fan-mag that had been the first to feature Bongo ran him as a cover story, giving Mum big play for her golden heart and undying faith.

Bongo, you beasts.

People who don't know (and this includes quite a few who should) see a lot of pictures, headlines, blurbs, and puffs, they hear a name being talked around, and straightaway they start counting how much money it means in the bank account of the overpublicized one.

But if publicity was dough, every little starlet in Town wouldn't be plotting how to marry a millionaire—she would be one. Similarly with me and Bongo. We were making a big impact but there was still a lot of merchandising to be done before you could say that my property was a solid investment.

Certainly *Expresso Bongo* was running away but, if you remember, I had sold Garrick Records the whole show outright for thirty-five pounds. Stupid of me—but poverty and Mayer had taken advantage of both my good nature and my judgment. All the good that particular best seller was doing us was in those newspaper clippings.

Of course, Bongo was picking up television fees here and there, but booking agents just laughed and laughed when I asked a hundred a week for him on tour. According to them, in the provinces the public didn't watch television or read the newspapers. But the fact of no bookings apart, maybe to let Bongo get lost up North for a few months would be bad businesswise. The reputations were made here, in the Smoke. So what the hell, so long as a few pennies were tinkling in nicely—why be greedy? In fact, how be greedy, when no one is offering you enough to get greedy about?

Still we didn't need the Tom-Tom any more. It cost him blood, but Leon went as high as thirty a week for Bongo to stay on. "It's not the money Leon," I told him, "it's just that we need a little more class than you can offer."

As to class, at the top there's the Café de Paris booked solid with Dietrich, Coward, Bankhead, and Steele. After that there's the Diplomatique—not in the same team but trying hard and spending plenty. In fact the Dip had spent so much, their publicity boy Mavers told me (over a drink in the Café de Paris), that the cabaret budget was going to be axed for a while.

"What?" I asked, luxuriating in the champagne cocktail he stood me on his as yet unaxed expense account. "No more of those great, completely unknown American artistes hot-foot from their phenomenal success at a barn dance not far from Las Vegas?"

"No more," he replied. "We had Danny Reno, fell flat on his face; Beulah Heat, fell flat on her back; Gig Rand—the Tommy Steele of America—would've been a better show if his guitar had electrocuted him."

"Not to mention," I mentioned, "that animated corpse delectable of the silent screen—"

"Don't mention her name," Mavers sighed. "She fell flat in her coffin. So anyway," he continued, "you can see why the Dip is dipping. Don't I hear that you are now operating as an honest manager, if you'll pardon the contradiction in terms?"

Suddenly I could see it all clearly, and so, within another champagne cocktail (which I sportingly paid for) could Mavers. For patriotism, youth, vitality, and the business graph of the Dip, why not try Britain's own new star—the only boy with a gimmick the Americans hadn't thought of first—Bongo Herbert.

"What have you been paying these transatlantic hams?" I inquired discreetly. "Your press stories, possibly exaggerated, said thousands."

"You might get a hundred a week on a single week booking," he replied. "Provided you agree to announce that we're paying him five."

"For you," I said to him, putting my arm round his shoulders, "I'm prepared to make that sacrifice."

You've got to hand it to Mavers. True, he was in danger of being axed himself if the Dip's business didn't improve. But Mavers deserves all the credit in the world for stage-managing Bongo's first night.

The Dip was crammed with those indispensable free-eaters who carry knives under their Moss Bros. dinner jackets, accompanied by the pretty publicity-hungry pouter pigeons who settle wherever there's a flashlight. My pigeon these days was usually Maisie. She was after all perfectly equipped to be a temporary fixture, except she wouldn't give up learning to be Judy Garland—but I am a man who, when in funds, does not object to wasting the price of a few singing lessons. All of us there that night agreed that whether Bongo was good or not, Mavers' production had star quality.

Because suddenly, out of nowhere, there was a Fan Club complete with bongos beating its way past the *commissionnaire* to mob Bongo as he came down the stairs at the end of his act.

Who bothered to ask wasn't this the Danny Reno fan mob divorced from Danny; who cared that six weeks ago they were screaming for Gig Rand, or that next month they would foam and swoon for some as yet unbooked talent? Fans all look alike and are expected to materialize magically from nowhere like maggots. Normally they're kept outside on the pavement. Mavers' innovation was to tip off the *commissionnaire* to let them break through. The resultant pictures were much appreciated by all.

There was a good selection. Golden boy acclaimed, hysterical bobby-soxers swoon, a fine set of grainy action shots. But the best of all was the dressing-room picture of Dixie Collins, the well-known myth, giving Bongo the look that had sold sixty-eight films and withered about the same number of leading men. Dixie was always good for a quote, and this time the quote was really quotable. "This slim, vibrant boy doesn't need talent," she said throatily. "He has more life in him than a dozen talents. Vitality is the greatest talent of all."

Call it vitality, talent, or genius if you like, but personally I am not inclined to kid myself. I am rather one who prefers to kid others. And this is something you can only do so long as you have a strict regard for the truth. If you really believed you were selling gold bricks how could you offer them so cheap? The gold on Bongo was no more real than the white beard on the Father Christmas at Selfridge's, yet look how that show runs year after year.

So far as I could ever see, Bongo was a normal healthy crazy and mixed-up kid, plus a crude sense of rhythm and an amateur-night talent, which altogether looked like a big gay escapist time to a younger generation which didn't know where to go. The older generation, with a belly full of wars and post-wars, was too tired from jumping over rising costs and crises to see the worry behind its children's gaiety. So the kids were on their own—except for their discs and their fancy dress, and scrappy bits of excitement like Bongo.

But whatever Bongo had, that first night at the Dip it rattled like a pair of loaded atomic dice, and even if you thought it was mad or had nothing to do with art or talent, it made a fascinating show.

I happened to know why Bongo was more hopped-up than usual that night. In the afternoon he had been tracked down by his mum who, like the rest of us, needed money. You know all the dancing around that these Spanish performers do to get a bull excited? With Bongo all you had to do was produce his mother, or if she had a sick headache and was lying down, just mention her. However, the public is always right, and if Bongo was great for the public, then with me too he was great, just great. If anyone had any doubts about it, that picture and quote from Dixie clinched it.

There is no doubt in anybody's mind that Dixie Collins is great because she has the name, the credits, and the important and celebrated friends to prove it. Furthermore, everybody feels a little proud that Dixie, the daughter of a Brixton bailiff's man, has been a fabulous American success without taking out citizenship papers. When Dixie resettled in England she was accepted as a pillar and oracle of café society. For a woman admitting to fifty she didn't look too bad either.

So there he was, my little gutter lily, glistening up at the fabulous Dixie Collins in the fabulous star dressing room of the fabulous Diplomatique. The headline over the picture quite rightly recited "Hoxton Boy Hits High Society."

If it all hadn't been so fabulous I would have been warned.

In Bongo's third week the Diplomatique was doing capacity business. I'd had six numbers written for him, and Mayer rushed out another record which was climbing the hit parade very steadily. I was now working from a furnished apartment-office off Bond Street with

Maisie as not the only secretary in London who couldn't write short-
hand or use a typewriter.

But she could do other things, like try to sing *Over the Rainbow*
between answering the telephone. It wasn't too hard to bear because the telephone hardly stopped ringing. The Dip was paying
two hundred and fifty a week, we had a regular spot on a weekly
television program for teen-agers, and Mayer was so embarrassed
by the success of *Expresso Bongo* he had changed the habit of a lifetime and was now, after the first half million, paying us a small—a
very small—percentage on it. True, Bongo was signed to Garrick
Records for life, but then as Mayer himself put it, "Nothing is for
nothing."

I saw plenty of Bongo, rehearsing and polishing him till, with his
natural audience sense and all the experience he was getting, he was
beginning to look like a star, even to me.

So that Bongo's life was now not only his problem, it was mine
too. Not that there was any danger in that motley band of badly
dressed and grubby girls who hang around every backstage. It was
high society I didn't trust, which though it includes some equally
badly dressed and grubby fans, also comprises more dangerous animals. In this jungle, like in every other, the enemy is the dog with
the bone. After years of fighting for other dogs' bones, I now had my
own. Experience told me that I would need to protect it.

I watched Bongo being salivated over bone-like by hordes of hy-
brid managerial canines. They didn't frighten me because I have
the same kind of teeth.

No—it was these classy kittenish debs, the doggy younger sons of
dukes, and the tired old fashion-wise operators of neither sex I
had to watch. And listening one night with my friend Maisie and
her friend (whom he ignored) to Bongo talk, I realized that the
favorite in the race for the bone was Dixie Collins.

It was all Dixie says this and Dixie says that, and what it amounted
to was that now we were a success whatever the management said
was corn for the birds, while Miss Collins was all of a sudden the female Gandhi of show business.

And Dixie had plenty to say. First she completely re-dressed us. That sweat-stained reality which had caught the reporters' eyes was slicked up and deodorized out. We were a very chic Bongo when Dixie had finished having us dressed by the most chi-chi *couturier* her influence could get wholesale. Our hair was shaped into the Bongo bob featured by four women columnists on the same Sunday. Even our bongos were studded with rhinestones. We were now a pretty slick Bongo. We were also a Bongo that didn't want to know whatever I had to say.

"Look kid," I told my fast-growing love child, "you are great with the teen-age public just so long as you're one of them. Start going fancy on them, just think of creeping out of your bracket, make as if you were, for one brief moment, superior to those immature big-hearted cats who think you are themself only successful and rich— and you, my chick, have had it."

"What do I care?" replied the sophisticated star. "What do I care about those grimy yobs? What do they know?"

"They know when you're going high-hat on them," I told him. "And furthermore, what do I care what you care? I am the one who cares. You think I am working to provide for your middle age, or maybe endow a bed in a children's hospital? Your job, my sweet unspoilt Hoxton beauty, is to beat me out more and better hangovers in plushier settings. Don't get ideas above your station, Bongo boy. There's plenty more where you came from."

Maybe I overstated my case, because that sensitive kid didn't say another word. He just treated me as if I was his mother, and walked out. After the show that night I went round to his dressing room and saw that he had walked in on no one less than Dixie herself.

From now on it was Dixie and Bongo together in every column. She made him smart—so smart he even got into the habit of having his fingernails manicured, learned which fork to pick up when the forks were real silver and there were several of them, and knew that with meat you took red wine. He was now so fashion-wise and pound-foolish he actually performed at a couple of important deb dances without being paid. It was at this point I felt compelled to object.

"Do what you like in your own time—I don't worry," I lied. "But when you take a booking, you fix it through me. We are not in this business to give your society friends inexpensive laughs. I still own 50 per cent of you no matter which part you're giving to Dixie Collins."

Afterwards I phoned Mavers at the Dip to tell him that one more week was all we could give him. Tomorrow I was signing in Bongo's name a contract for a twelve-week tour at four hundred a week, and nothing the Dip had to say could be more interesting.

That tour was a perfectly planned operation. Mayer was to issue another disc, the fans and the publicity were ready and waiting, and even if Bongo looked too clean and had ideas above his station, nothing could stop us from making real money.

Nothing, that is, except that slumming bitch Dixie Collins. Although there are so many ways to break a contract, and she knew them all, the one she put Bongo on to was the dirtiest ever.

Like any innocent manager might, I had signed the deal for the tour on behalf of my client. But where, when the tour opened at Birmingham, was my client?

I'll tell you where. He was staying at the villa near Nice of a lady in her own right. Among the distinguished guests was none other than that fabulous fifty-year-old female grifter, Dixie Collins. And among the undistinguished gate-crashers was me.

He was frying himself to a deep brown expresso tan when I arrived, sweating under the palms in the two-acre garden of the Villa Esperanza. His friend was out shopping with her ladyship, so we were able to be cosily boys together.

"Why are you crucifying me, Bongo baby?" I asked him gently.

"You've been a good start for me," he generously conceded. "But can't you see I've outgrown your kind of show?"

"Outgrown? I invented you, you big-headed moron."

"That tour isn't a good thing for me. A tour with a lot of kids screaming their heads off. Is that the best you can do for me? Is that all you want for me?"

"Four hundred a week is bad?" I asked.

"With you anything that's money is good," he shouted. "You're just like that old woman of mine. You don't care about me—it's only the money. Dixie and me are talking about a film together."

I see. He was an actor all of a sudden.

"I see," I said. "I suppose it's about this great star who is underneath it all just a lonely woman, and this great boy who is underneath it all just a cheap rotten little scut."

Then Dixie and Lady Rosemary arrived back, wearing bright-colored sailcloth sun suits and loaded with expensive shopping. They had that elegant sinewy leathery smart look which is the sterling mark of the middle-aged woman-about-town. Dixie had never spoken to me direct before. This time she did.

"This is one artiste you won't be cheating any longer, you Soho Square shark," she said concisely.

"Don't think I'm pushing myself forward Miss Collins," I replied, "but this artiste has a three-year contract with me."

"In a pig's eye you have a contract," she spat back, so unladylike that Lady Rosemary left the patio. "That contract is about as legitimate as you are. It gives you 50 per cent and doesn't even guarantee him cigarette money."

"What's more," she continued, her eyes glinting with the same kind of vitality she found so admirable in Bongo, "he was underage when he signed."

"I can get his parents to sign that contract any time," I countered confidently, but my heart was shrinking with fright.

"No you can't," she said, and it sounded like a rattrap snapping. "Because I've seen them and explained how you took them for a ride. The contract's null and void so far as they're concerned—and so are you. Bongo's underage."

I gave her that slow, dirty look that doesn't change anything but is guaranteed to hurt a woman's feelings.

"To me," I said, before I turned and left her my property, "to me he looks all of a sudden very, very grown-up."

When I got back to Town the sky was hot and tired and heavy, the air dusty, each breath another stale coating on the lungs. I should smoke tipped cigarettes and have my cancer later in life I thought, standing in the apartment frowsty with Maisie's clothes and phone messages from the Tovey Agency scattered all over. I read a letter from Tovey's solicitor and lit an uptipped cigarette. I might as well get my cancer as quickly as possible because the agency was suing me for failure to produce Bongo for the tour I had contracted.

For those who don't get the strategy let me draw a sketch map.

I had been maneuvered by Dixie into a situation where, in order to protect myself, I had to disown my client. I had no alternative now but to go down on my knees to Tovey and try to crawl right out of the Bongo business. Of course I could go to Court, but that is something which, if you are a manager, you try not to do because everyone knows how artistes are so terribly exploited by us managers.

So with one sweet old-fashioned Dixie-style number here I was— off the gravy train.

Can you understand now why I smacked Maisie hard enough across the left eye to turn it black when she came in gaily chattering that she had found herself a new singing teacher who specialized in Judy Garland style?

Things were even worse by the end of the week, because although the Tovey Agency, having made me crawl and sweat, had finally let me off with a warning, they at once announced that henceforth they were solely and completely acting for that great new British star, Bongo Herbert—unfortunately forced to cancel his announced tour because of a slight operation. They didn't say the operation involved was cutting me off Bongo.

I walked down Shaftesbury Avenue and it had never looked so grimy. A sandwich-board man, his gray jowls hanging hound-like below wet bloodshot eyes, puffed and blowed along the gutter. "The End of the World Is at Hand" was the message on his board and so far as I was concerned this rancid summer, he was right.

I walked slowly through the jammed, irritable traffic into Frith Street. As I turned the corner I noticed a fat man trimming delicately between two buses, holding onto his stomach with both hands, placing his feet carefully as if they hurt badly. By the time he caught up with me his face looked like a freshly boiled hunk of silverside. Naturally, on such a day, who else should buttonhole me but old gray squirrel-eyed Kakky Katz, formerly K. Arnold Katz, an extinct Hollywood producer. "I didn't see you in a month of Sundays," he said.

"You certainly didn't," I agreed. "It's a small world but not really small enough."

"At last I got a proposition which is hunderd and ten per cent," he wheezed. "Such a heat today. Come in for a ice coffee, with whip cream, delicious."

He put his arm round me and steered me into my least favorite expresso—the Tom-Tom. I looked round for Leon. He wasn't there. Instead, there was an "Under New Management" sign and a pretty young man playing the Gaggia coffee machine with the dash of a theater organist. How quickly things change in this town.

Kakky squeezed his backside into a stall. It was an encouraging thought that someone as passé as Kakky could still keep fat. He was so dead that the long-haired cineastes (who hate live film makers) put three of his pre-accountancy-era movies into a National Film Theater series. There was a hundred-word tribute on the back cover of the program. "Pioneer of Spectacle" they called him.

The pioneer of spectacle bubbled contentedly until his iced coffee was finished. Then, as he sucked up the blob of whipped cream from the bottom of the glass, he told me his news.

"To cut off a long story short, Feigele-Lox want the remake rights of my great picture *Rubáiyát*. You remember my *Rubáiyát?*"

I remembered—a rambling, magnificent, phony-poetic, sex-saturated epic which, a quarter of a century before Todd, had taught housemaids the world over the secret life of Omar Khayyam.

"They want to make from it in the first place a stage musical in the West End. In the second place a musical on Broadway, and then, if everything goes, in the third place they will make a panoramic movie."

"How can all this," I asked with tired patience, "concern either you or me?" To twist the knife, the jukebox had started to play *Expresso Bongo*.

He belched delicately, settled back, and smiled. "By a slight oversight on the part of those hyenas that threw me out of Hollywood at the peak of my career, I happen to own the stage rights. Who thought the stage rights will ever be worth something?"

"So you'll sell out," I said, "and retire for the second time. Congratulations. It couldn't happen to a nicer pioneer of spectacle."

"Sell out nothing," he replied. "I told Feigele it can be a musical only if I produce it."

I chewed my straw slowly. "You know something K.A., I have on contract to me exclusively someone who could be great for Rubáiyát." I spat the straw out.

"You made that Bongo Herbert wasn't it?" he said shrewdly, doing a quick recheck on my credits as a talent judge.

"I certainly did," I replied. "I don't want to sell you anything K.A. Another iced coffee?"

"*Rubáiyát*, the way I see it"—he spread his hands wide to show the scope of his vision—"*Rubáiyát*, is like for a new Judy Garland."

"Kakky," I said, "K.A.—you are so right. That's what this kid of mine is—an absolutely brand-new, all-British, entirely gorgeous, real sexsational Judy Garland."

THE BATTERSEA MIRACLE

All Christmas I hadn't been feeling quite up to the mark. It's a hard time anyway for us in Bancroft's Grand Circus getting everything set up for the Boxing Day matinee, so what with feeling a bit dicky plus the normal fatigue I thought I'd treat myself to a couple in the pub opposite the bombed lot in Battersea where we've been pitching our little show ever since the end of the war.

I hadn't downed the first pint before, tired as I was, I knew I'd I'd made a pickup. Squinting along the side of the glass, I saw him on my wrist. I knew at once he was different, because you don't spend thirty years of your life training fleas without becoming a fair judge of character. And though I've never been more than a cage cleaner and interval clown around what was never a great circus, I run as a paying hobby a fairly distinguished little show of my own which gets a lot of respect among flea lovers. I bow to no one in the flea world. So as soon as that tired, bedraggled flea hopped feebly onto my wrist I knew he was exceptional. Mind, he didn't have what I call the "hop" of a healthy flea. He was quiet and sad, and I could see why when, back in the boxcar I sleep in, I introduced him to my troupe. I never saw it happen before with fleas, because they're matey creatures unprone to the pettiness you find elsewhere in life. Yet when I flipped him into the box, like one flea the troupe turned its back on him. I called him Pete.

That night I was just dropping off after a hard session trying to get the troupe to work with Pete in the royal-carriage-drawing act, but no use, they kept shying away from him, so I was just going to sleep when I heard this voice in my ear.

"Don't panic, Joe," it said in a soothing chirruping kind of way, "this is Pete speaking."

I've been working too hard, I thought, I've been a bit off-color all day.

"I'm Pete the Talking Flea," the voice said. "And I've got to talk to you, Joe."

"I've been flea training for thirty years," I said, "and I'd be the first to give credit to them for intelligence, willingness, and humanity, but I never heard of a talking flea."

"We are living in an atomic age, Joe," he replied. "And I am an atomic flea hatched in the pocket of one of our greatest scientists in our biggest nuclear energy center. In the same historic moment both I and the H-bomb were born."

Now personally I don't understand these things any more than you can explain why it takes nine months for someone to get born and only nine seconds for a few million someones to die. But when a flea speaks you listen.

"In every force there are both death and life. I am life's answer to the Bomb," Pete continued.

"You're a bit small in comparison," I suggested.

"I am," he agreed, "and though I have superhuman intelligence and the accumulated wisdom of mankind, it is my size that is worrying me."

I've known the nicest, cleverest midgets to suffer with the same problem. "Some very good things come in small parcels," I said comfortingly.

"Never mind all that," he replied irritably. "I have to tell men what no man—and I include Moses, Jesus, and the Buddha—has ever been able to get them to listen to for long." He quickly whistled, piped like an oboe, squealed bat-style, sang a few bass notes, turned treble, and wound up with a sound no human had ever heard before. "Fortunately," he said, "I have a gimmick."

All through that night Pete told me about his ideas. "One man is equal to the whole of Creation" was his attitude. "Whoever destroys one life it is as if he had destroyed a whole world. Whoever saves a life has saved a whole world. There are millions of worlds to be saved, Joe," he explained. "What is hateful to yourself, do not do to another. That's all I have to say," he concluded. "The rest is gimmick and gloss."

"Forget it, Pete," I told him. "The world doesn't want to know. You can't go hopping around telling men to love one another and not expect them to kill you for it. It's human nature."

"Who is mighty?" Pete replied. "He who turns an enemy into a friend."

"But, Pete," I begged him, "you're only seven months old and you don't know what you're up against. You're all mind and soul, but I've been a man for more than fifty years. I know some shocking things about the beast that mind and soul will never understand."

"I know more than I want," he answered sadly. "Ever since I was born in that radiant blast of life and death I've been running away from what I know. But it runs after me, Joe. The hope of man is but a flea." A soft tremulous piccolo note came from him.

"You'd better spend the night in my ear," I said. "You're all tired out."

Bancroft's Grand Christmas Circus at Battersea is an old-style show which normally opens with the March of the Gladiators and the Torino Tumblers as a warmer. But this Boxing Day it was different.

The old ones sat back sucking their humbugs, and the young ones leaned forward chattering over their monkey nuts. It was nearly a full house, and chasing round the ring in my red balloon nose and checkered jacket and trousers with Fred, our chimp, after me, I saw old Bancroft signal the electrician to switch on the Tannoy and give them that opening blast of Sousa which means the show is on. The sparks flicked the switch, but it wasn't Sousa that came out of the Tannoy. It was Pete's unearthly twelve-octave voice singing, playing, and chirruping like a huge soul filling the tent.

Pete had ordered me to slip him into the Tannoy and keep quiet about it. And that was really all I had personally to do with what is now being called the Battersea Miracle.

I didn't quite cotton on to what Pete had in mind until that weird singing of his started. By that time, like everyone else in Bancroft's Circus that Boxing Day, I just went into a sort of trance without time, listening to Pete's words.

For after he had knobbled us with his gimmick he started to talk seriously, like a lot of wonderful quotations you had always known, explained by a master teacher with the great art of making you feel and understand. By the time Pete finished we really felt that each one of us was like the whole of Creation. We were convinced that it was worth keeping one another alive. I realized afterwards I had never been too sure about that before—neither for myself nor for anyone else.

"You see, Joe," Pete explained after his first show was over and the public had left more joyful and hopeful than after any other circus in history, "the reason why the Aztecs with all their civilization died so easily was not because the Spanish pirates under Cortes were so wonderful. It was because those Aztecs believed their time was up. They let themselves die inside and annihilation inevitably followed. Man is not destroyed by life. He commits suicide by ceasing to love it."

With Pete snugly back in my ear, the whole circus was ransacked for concealed tape recordings or such-like by two reporters. All they found were our old scratched Sousa records, so, writing about Pete's performance (HYPNOTIC VOICE FROM NOWHERE), they raked up what they could and quoted a cranky old lady who said it was the voice of God. "I recognized it at once," she said, "because I heard it often as a child."

They were queuing six deep for Pete's second night. "I know one thing," said old Bancroft, as business built higher and higher (matinees included). "Nothing less than a bloody miracle could ever have filled this house."

With thousands of people converging on Battersea day after day to listen to him (because, as we always say in the business, nothing sells a show like good word of mouth,) Pete was very happy, and I know it wasn't just vanity either. Although it is a great satisfaction for an artiste to play to enthusiastic houses night after night, Pete wasn't getting any good notices for being Pete the Superhuman Talking Flea. He was the Battersea Miracle, the Space Voice, the Voice of God and the dozen other fancy stage names they pinned on him.

"It says in tonight's paper," I told him, "that a well-known ecclesiastic is convinced you're an archangel. The quality of your voice he says is distinctly described somewhere in the Armenian Apocrypha."

It also said in the same paper that the Tannoy was going to be taken away from Battersea by Cabinet instructions.

"The laugh will be on them," I sniggered, "when they find it's just a rough old Tannoy blaster with not even a flea in it."

"It won't be empty," Pete replied.

"What do you mean, Pete?" I asked.

"I'm going with it," he said.

"But, Pete," I spluttered, "be sensible. How will you live without me?"

"The laborer is worthy of his hire," he replied. "I'll just have to take a quick nip whenever I can from whoever comes to listen to me."

"But it says here they're going to use you exclusively for top-level discussions and Summit conferences. You can't take a quick nip off gentlemen like the Prime Minister."

I rubbed my forearm ruefully because, to tell the truth, intelligence was not Pete's only super quality. I suppose his work took a great deal out of him, but the fact was he had an appetite so super that, even with thirty years of flea training behind me, I felt it.

"Do you mean to tell me," Pete replied with irritability, "that a full course of instruction in solving the world's greatest problems is not worth the piddling inconvenience of a few fleabites?"

"My human experience tells me, Pete," I warned him solemnly, "that leaders who can stand for any number of the people they lead to suffer any amount of agony don't take kindly to personal inconvenience. I wouldn't chance it if I were you. Come clean and tell them you are only a little atomic superhuman flea."

"They wouldn't listen if they knew," he replied. "There isn't a man living, no matter how bestial, craven, and ignorant, who doesn't believe himself superior in thought and feeling to a flea."

"But you're different from other fleas, Pete," I argued.

"Not so different," he answered. "Even the dumbest fleas love life more than most men do."

They carried Pete off in the Tannoy the next morning. For a couple of days now I've been hanging around that big bunker in St. James's Park where they put him, watching the generals and diplomats coming out to their cars discreetly scratching themselves.

Tonight's paper says that Mr. Eisenhower and Mr. Khrushchev are flying in next week to consult the Miracle.

This afternoon it started to snow, and two soldiers with holly in their caps unloaded six cans of special insecticide, no doubt trying to save the visiting dignitaries any personal discomfort.

I hope Pete is strong enough to stand up to it all, because while there's Pete there's hope.

MY FATHER AS A DEALER

On Thursdays, my father always went to an auction in Lillie Road, Fulham. The auction room led into a yard stacked with furniture no one ever bought. It stood there in the rain and the sleet, and now in the cold spring sunshine, quietly rotting. At the other end of the yard, steep wooden steps led down to a basement. Down there, round a stove, the auction porters ate their dinners off thick white plates brought over by a cross-eyed teaboy from a café down the road.

One Thursday, there was nothing in the auction cheap enough for my father to buy. He crossed the yard to the basement and sent the cross-eyed boy out for a cheese roll and a mug of tea. Then, as he slowly chewed the hard crust of the roll and listened to an old porter named Bert tell how they protected theirselves against mustard gas poisoning at Ypres, he suddenly stopped worrying; which was anyway something he could usually do at the drop of an auctioneer's hammer.

With a cavalier gesture, he threw the remains of the cheese roll into the furnace, congratulated Bert on his anti-gas precautions, and went over to a pyramid of tea chests which all this time had tortured his curiosity. They contained a large quantity of lace edging —"cabbage," Bert told him, which the porters had "found."

When the foreman porter came back, he said, "I have seen in my time (and who hasn't) some dead lousy sales, but this sale is so dead lousy even the lice dropped dead waiting for something to happen." Then, on behalf of himself and his colleagues, he sold my father the lace for ten shillings a case, plus five bob for a pint all round. He even unpadlocked his tool chest and threw in a quantity of valuable brown paper and string. My father was expert in making parcels. The two enormous ones he made out of the lace were so heavy that getting them onto the Underground train would have ruptured a horse. But man, said my father, has his unconquerable soul, and so he doesn't rupture so easily.

At that time, my father worked a lockup stall in East Ham Shopping Hall, a kind of semi-enclosed market, where the green shutters of the shops come down onto trestles to make stalls. Thursday was early-closing day, and when he rattled the gates of the market to call the boilerman to open up, there was no one around except a mangy dog, which, like the other stall-holders, somehow made a living.

"What you got there, Guv?" the boilerman asked.

My father, rubbing the weals the string had cut in his hands, said, "With luck, meat and potatoes for five for one month. Give us a hand, Charlie."

That Friday he passed happily sorting the lace. My mother held lengths of it round her sleeves, her neck, and the hem of her dress, because at one time she had worked as a trimmer in a clothing factory. In lace trimming she was, she kept pointing out (though she shouldn't say it herself,) something of a connoisseur.

"Look at this, Solly," she said, putting a length of fine black lace round her hair. "Lace like this when I was a girl you couldn't buy for a pound a yard."

"And in those days," my father remembered, "a pound was real money. Not that it mattered, because who had it?"

Saturday was a big day in the market. This Saturday, my father's stall was eight inches deep in lace trimming, all at fourpence a yard.

The next few weeks, there wasn't a petticoat within five miles my father hadn't put lace trimming on. He reckoned he had saved a lot of marriages and helped more than a few engagements.

"Come on, girls!" he shouted. "Three yards of black lace for a bob makes you a new woman!" .

For a few weeks the tin biscuit box we threw the money into was half-full of sixpences and shillings and pennies. About half past ten in the evening, when business slacked off, I went to the Ocean Fish Bar with everybody's orders for chips with plenty of salt and vinegar. I ran back, my hands warm and damp from the vinegar soaking through the newspaper, the acrid smell of oiled newsprint making my mouth water. While we ate the chips we counted the money in the biscuit box, and I knew my father was at last rich because there were so many small piles of coins along the back edge of the stall.

As he tipped the coins into two bags—a gray one for silver and a blue one for copper—I said to him, "When I have my own stall I'll sell things like you do for pennies and sixpences, because that way you can see how rich you are." Then my father told me of the meaning of objects like lace and money and chips with plenty of vinegar.

Supposing you are starving, my father asked, what is the value of two pennyworth of chips? It saves your life. But is your life worth no more than tuppence?

"Take three yards of this lace," he said, holding it out at arm's length. "A woman is miserable because there are too many children, the house has to be cleaned every day only to get dirty, the fire has to be made only to burn out. She feels old, older and older, every day the beat of a hammer nailing up the coffin of her life, daily. What's a piece of lace to such a woman? I'll tell you. On such a thing she can build a new life. It is frivolous as she has not been frivolous for years—extravagant as she thought she had forgotten how to be. From these things (and to be honest, there is no new life to be built) at least some sort of hope—for a short time, some touch of something. If you ask what difference will it make in the end, the answer is simple. No difference at all. But for the time being, it helps. How much is that help worth?"

Quick as a needle, I pointed out that three yards of lace at the present market price was one shilling. My father agreed, "The lace is worth a shilling, or more, or less. But what is the unthought-of moment in the time of such a woman's life worth?"

Then he concluded the lesson. "In all accounts, you must keep a margin for error. In life, there is a margin, a narrow margin, for vain errors like lace, and they have no value. They are consequently beyond value, valueless, priceless. As for these—" (and with quick movements he scooped the piles of coins into their proper bags) "as for these—these three are for the man who lent me the money to buy the lace; and these two pay the rent so that the lace may be sold. And this one is for your mother to buy food; and these two are for me, so that I may buy some other error next week to sell again so that it will all go on and on."

For my father, no story ever had an end. When the lace was finished, he discovered wallpaper; and when the wallpaper had been pasted to a thousand walls, he bought fancy buttons, six on a card for three ha'pence. And when East Ham had enough fancy buttons on its coat, it was something else, and so (as he said) on, and on.

Because of this feeling he had for objects, that they were valuable for what they meant to people and for no other reason, my father found himself buying at the Lillie Road auction one Thursday morning several mixed lots of china and glass, and a basket containing a quantity of Egyptian antiquities. So easily can a dealer become an antique dealer, if he has this sense of value, not objective value.

RULE ONE: *To be an antique dealer, you must know about subjective values—that is to say, what objects mean to people at the level of feeling. To be able to appraise an object at its current market value is not enough. You must be able to communicate to your clients the meaning of the object to you. If the operation is successful, your meaning communicates with his meaning; he suddenly wants to possess the object and a deal can be negotiated. Of course, at this point you must remember current market values.*

My father's method of appraisal for a mixed lot was to look through it, decide how much someone might pay for the most exciting thing in it, and try to buy the lot for about that price. Sometimes no one came along who agreed with him about that particular object and he, as he put it, "fell in." The stall was always cluttered with strange junk which excited my father but no one else. But this, he said, is the way in which an antique dealer builds his stock. It took about a year, but in the end we had enough stock to reckon ourselves qualified junk dealers.

The junk is raw material, but you can buy fresh merchandise every week, it will freshen up the junk, and perhaps sell it. More often the junk is a dead-weight background; it remains after the interesting things are sold. But when business or credit is not good enough, and he can't freshen up his stock, it is purely raw material for the dealer's free and enterprising imagination.

In East Ham Shopping Hall marble-topped washstands were always good basic merchandise, because although no one wanted them for washstands, they could be sold as washable kitchen tables, the marble might be taken off and sold for crazy-paving, and the frames converted into usable dressing tables. But, for my father, marble-topped washstands were not a difficult enough test. They were a tedious concession to necessity, dull against the useless, fascinating lace trimming of life. To sell a lacquered image of the Chinese god of plenty to a customer who combined an exotic taste with an eye for a bargain was more uncertain and artistic. "Otherwise," my father said, "I might as well sell tinned onion soup." One week, as a matter of fact, he did sell three cases of tinned onion soup which had been in a fire. But it was with relief he returned to the Chinese god.

RULE TWO: *An antique dealer is a dealer like any other, except that he is not merely interested in exchanging goods against money. If he were, he would handle all merchandise with the same disinterest. It is because he has a characteristic prejudice in favor of Chinese gods that a dealer becomes an antique dealer rather than a chronic purveyor of canned onion soup.*

My father, like all natural-born dealers, suffered from buying compulsion associated with deflated credit—an occupational disease of the dealing classes. When I was not at school I went to the auctions with him. He always stood near the auctioneer's rostrum, his mouth turned down, his face expressionless, bidding with short jabs of his catalogue. When he stopped bidding and the auctioneer looked at him inquiringly, he shook his head and said quietly, "No more, thank you, sir." Sometimes he impulsively decided to continue bidding. Then he would say in a gentle voice, "Make it guineas, sir," and the price would go up to two pounds, two shillings.

Occasionally, carried away by the credit which regular buying at a particular auction room creates for a dealer, my father would discover that he had spent more than he had. Then, whistling the aria "Softly Awakes My Heart" from *Samson and Delilah* tunelessly through his teeth, he went back to the market to speak to one of three friends he had there who operated more regular businesses than he did.

One of these was a grocer, a short, round-faced man in a white coat who, on a Saturday night, auctioned off cut-price groceries with an explosive stutter. Another was a butcher, greatly respected as the most solvent man in the market. He wore a straw hat all the year round, changing the colored band on it to indicate which season was which. The third was an uncle of mine who had a fruit and vegetable stall where he did a fair business. Being a gambler on dog races, he was easy enough to borrow from if he happened to have won recently.

My father borrowed a check for the amount he needed, giving in return his own postdated check for the end of the next week. The system had its complex variations; but then, as my father pointed out to my mother (who worried about money): "Finance is always the problem of an expanding economy; credit was invented by men who believe they will still be alive and working next week. Both of which I fully intend. Furthermore, how can I sell goods if I don't buy them first?"

RULE THREE: *You can sell goods best if you buy them first. If you have capital, things are much more straightforward; but a real dealer will deal even without capital. To be an antique dealer you must have an absolute conviction that what you buy today you will be here next week to sell at a profit. What my father did not at this time realize was that in dealing at the highest levels goods are frequently sold first and paid for afterwards. But this is just a more sophisticated version of the same basic credit system.*

My father had his own system. If he bought something at one pound and sold it at ten, he considered that he was working on a mere 10 per cent, meaning that 10 per cent of the total sum realized was the money that he worked with. On the other hand, if he bought something for five pounds and it kicked around for months until he finally sold it for two, he considered he had done very well. He would point out that keeping the item any longer could send him bankrupt paying rent to house it.

Another aspect of my father's system was his refusal to sell in bulk to other dealers, because he resented their assumption that they could sell his goods. He liked to believe that his goods were so eccentric that only he could ever sell them. If even he failed, he put them on one side. The market, he said, was not yet fit to accommodate these goods. Soon they would come into their own. Meanwhile the shelves at the back of the shop were choked with goods packed tight into boxes which my father labeled in chalk. The chalk rubbed off, and he forgot what was in the boxes. But by now he was too busy negotiating the future to be bothered with the debris of the past.

His system caused my father's business to expand until he had four shops in the same market, all choked with goods. One Sunday he and I were in the market unpacking a quantity of Bohemian colored glass vases we had unearthed recently in one of the remoter shops. I noticed that his expression was distracted; he was whistling "Softly Awakes My Heart," a certain sign of pending developments. Then he suddenly announced his intention of becoming a wholesaler. "All the time," he said, "I have been a wholesaler, and I only just realized it; but so impossible is it to go against one's own nature that here" (and he indicated the stuffed shelves in the background) "I have accumulated a wholesaler's stock without knowing it."

It was a magnificent theory, delivered with superb confidence in the hidden forces of a dealer's life. There was only one thing wrong with it. No one wanted to buy the rubber soles and heels, the pepperpot lids, the tea cosies, and the leather bootlaces which the forgotten boxes contained.

RULE FOUR: *There is a difference in genus between retailing dealers and wholesalers. The general dealer (like my father) who pits his imagination against the intractability of unlikely merchandise is essentially a retailer. He operates best with a variety of different objects, about each of which he can build a different story. Your wholesaler is a man capable of calculating in a moment the difference between 12½ per cent less carriage, and 10 per cent plus carriage.*

Alas, you can't wholesale against your nature. Useful goods in quantity are sold in a highly competitive market; once you have supplied your retail public with useful goods at cut prices, you may as well throw the balance of your stock away. "Or," my father said, unbowed, "why not take it to another market?"

He at once bought a small lorry for twelve pounds. Loaded with the excess, it visited the markets in such provincial places as Romford, Catford, and Lewisham. At one time or another I went to all of them, but I remember Romford best because when we had eggs on chips there, they were goose eggs. Maybe geese did well in Romford. My father didn't. The van drank oil with an alcoholic's unconcern for wear and tear on the financial system. On a good stretch of road it made about fifteen miles to the gallon, complaining constantly. The radiator leaked, steaming like a boiled pudding; something called the big end knocked; the gear change ground. It was a secondhand van special for secondhand dealers. It broke down, always in the middle of traffic. When we arrived at the market, the best pitches were gone.

Travel didn't broaden my father's turnover, but it brought him into touch with people who had junk to sell. He kept himself busy during the trade recessions calling at private houses in the locality —on "the knocker," as we called it. Traveling markets and buying junk led inevitably to a pitch on the stones in the Caledonian Market, a vast bazaar of bric-a-brac which bombs and the shortage of goods destroyed soon after my father started to use it. If he had started five years earlier, he might have become a successful antique dealer. As it was, he remained an unsuccessful antique dealer. In the first few months of the war, the four pounds a week a professional air raid warden was paid began to look like a good living to him. The market was empty—trade was a post-war credit, and the war had barely started. But it had already been there long enough to show that prices for things which you couldn't eat, or drink, or hide in were fictitious. Consequently antique dealers of all sizes found themselves in difficulties. The great trade secret was out.

RULE FIVE: *The great secret of the antique trade is simply that all values other than aesthetic are approximate. That is to say, they are approximated as nearly as a dealer can guess to what the buyer with an aesthetic inclination towards a particular nonuseful object can pay for it.*

My father had always poetically comprehended the facts of dealing life, and I started as an antique dealer aware of them in the same vague way—as in a relay race, the baton is snatched by a fresh man from one who has already covered the toughest section of the course; but it's the same baton. The war, however, stopped play for the time being. When we got back to the game a few years later, it was faster, but the rules hadn't changed.

PLAYS

THE BESPOKE OVERCOAT

Author's Note

Love is a luxury which very poor people can afford, and *The Bespoke Overcoat* is a story of this love. It is not a love which conquers all. FENDER does not get enough food or a tailor-made overcoat, in this life. In life he does not find satisfaction, except in so far as he is able to accept with humor and humility the deprivations forced upon him. It is because this humor and humility is shared with his friend that FENDER, is spite of everything, would prefer to go on living. To prefer to go on living is to love in the context of this story, and because this is loving at its most deprived the story is a sad one.

In producing *The Bespoke Overcoat* that remarkable artist Alec Clunes concentrated entirely upon this feeling which, by its intensity, animates a piece which is not well-constructed. The story was written without any directions for staging or the production of effects. The only stage, the only effects, the only theatre I had in mind were in the heart of a drunken tailor. There was no indication of time past or present, because a twinge of conscience lasts a moment or a life-time, and *The Bespoke Overcoat* is about the unreasonable conscience felt by the poor who love the poorer with a love which conquers nothing.

So Alec Clunes' production, which was, in effect, the writing of the play for the practical stage, dispensed with sets, used the barest properties, used darkness broken by three constantly moving areas of light, to tell a simple story with great simplicity. He realized that Fender was not a ghost and that this story was not a ghost-story; he understood that *The Bespoke Overcoat* was a sustained, typically over-long Jewish joke—than which there is no sadder and no funnier story. And I am deeply grateful to him for having understood so much, for having made it available to other people, and for having taught me in the process, as he has taught so many other artists, something of the meaning of theatre.

CHARACTERS

MORRY, a tailor
FENDER, a warehouse clerk
RANTING, his employer
A CLERK

SCENE 1

The action of the play is distributed among three separate areas permanently set and used in turn.

Area "A," midstage R., is RANTING'S *warehouse, which consists of a sizable table, placed obliquely, with a chair or stool L. and to the* U.S. *end of it.* U.S. *of the table, and rather behind it, a large rack supports a selection of overcoats on hangers.*

Area "B" is D.S.C. *and has no furnishing.*

Area "C," midstage L., is MORRY'S *room, which consists of a mattress lying obliquely on the floor, and beside it R., at the* U.S. *end, a chair.*

These three areas are encompassed by a black surround with entrances D.R., D.L. *and* U.C. *During the entire play, these are in total darkness, as are any two of the acting areas not being used. Throughout, the stage directions will be related to the three areas described.*

When the curtain rises MORRY *is standing in the area "B," with a navy blue overcoat over his arm. A barrel organ is playing, off, and fades out as the light at "B" fades in.*

MORRY. Fender dead. That old man Fender dead. Funny thing. You're a good tailor, he used to say. You're a good tailor. Nu, you're a good tailor. Look around. I don't care where you look, he says, you are a number one tailor. Look at this coat, he says. What, that old coat? A coat must be twenty years old. Mind you, I can tell straightaway by the cross-stitch it's my coat. It's your coat, he shouts. You made it. Twenty-two years ago I come to you for a coat. This is him. I still got him. You got a good point. I tell him, I'm a good tailor. It's only the truth. I'm a good tailor. Straightaway, I see I made a mistake. I fell in. How much, Fender says, will you take to mend a coat like this? I ask you. It's falling to pieces on his back. I told him straight, no nonsense. Look, Fender, I told him, I can run you up a pair of trousers from lining canvas you can walk up Saville Road nobody can tell you from the Prince of Wales. But, Fender, do me a favor. Take the coat somewhere else. A new coat I can make, but the Union says no miracles. A rag, that's all. I got my clients to think about. Good afternoon. A lovely piece of worsted. Mind you, I got a suit length here: in a hundred year you wouldn't see nothing better. Clients. Fender dead. An old man. (*Turns* U.S., *still speaking.*) He sits in that stone cold warehouse all day long. (*Turns head round to audience.*) Who could mend such a coat? (*Moves slowly* U.S. *to* C. *exit.*) That's enough. (*Light starts to fade.*) Leave me alone. All this nagging, nagging. (*He has gone, and so has the light.*)

SCENE 2

*As the light fades in on "*C*," sitting cross-legged and hunched on* MORRY'S *mattress is* FENDER. *He rubs his hands.*

FENDER. Oi. How that Morry can thread a needle in this cold, I don't know. Such a cold.

MORRY (*entering* U.S.C.). I got trouble of my own. After all, I'm in Bond Street? I'm a merchant prince? I'm not even a limited company.

FENDER. I thought you was a limited company.

MORRY (*turning*). Me? Never. What do I want with shares and directors? So—what can I do for you? It's late, but . . .

FENDER. To be managing director is not a nice thing? You got no ambition? Terrible cold in here. My old guvernor—managing director three companies. Chairman—six companies. But what a man! (*Rises.*) Look, Morry. I still got no overcoat. Put on the gas ring.

MORRY. Fender! You ain't dead?

FENDER. Sure I'm dead. Would I sit up half the night in the freezing cold if I wasn't dead? I can tell you, I won't be sorry to get back. They got central heating, constant hot water, room service. And the food—as much as you like. Kosher, of course.

MORRY (*holding his head*). I won't touch the rotten brandy.

FENDER. Drinks? You can have what you like, any time, day or night, on the house.

MORRY. Go on. So tell me, Fender. Is it really you?

FENDER (*holding out his hand*). Feel my hand. Feel.

MORRY (*taking his hand*). Believe me, you are cold. That lousy brandy. It kills you. (*Sneezes.*)

FENDER (*sitting on chair*). Gesundheit.

MORRY. Thank you.

FENDER. All I want is to get back. Listen, Morry. You know the first person I met down there?

MORRY. Down there?

FENDER. I tell you, Morry, a secret: everybody goes down there. You know who I met? Lennie.

MORRY. Lennie from Fournier Street?

FENDER. Who else? He's doing the same job. And *what* herrings! I tell you, Morry, I won't be sorry to get back.

MORRY (*kneeling on mattress*). Fender! You don't hold that overcoat against me, do you Fender? Believe me, if I had known you would catched a cold and died I would give you my own coat.

FENDER. That blankety coat. For that coat I'm here and not at the hotel. Look, Morry. I got nothing against you.

MORRY (*rising to one knee*). You ain't going to haunt me, Fender? You wouldn't haunt an old friend?

FENDER. Don't talk silly, Morry. That haunting is a special job. They don't give it to new residents. For haunting you get a commission.

MORRY (*rising and moving behind* FENDER. *Crossing arms*). So listen, Fender. It goes without saying I am pleased to see you. I'm glad you enjoy being dead. But you won't think I am rude, if I ask what you want of my life?

FENDER. I'll tell you. But first light that gas-ring so at least I won't freeze—listen to me—to death, I nearly said. You don't know, Morry, (*The light begins to fade.*) what sort of life it was at that Ranting clothing company. No wonder I didn't lose any sleep about dying . . . (*The light has gone.*)

SCENE 3

*The light fades in on "*A.*"* FENDER *is sitting on the stool with his notebook and pencil on the table in front of him. The conversation continues from the previous* SCENE.

FENDER. After that warehouse for forty-three years, any change would be a pleasure. Forty-three years a shipping clerk.

MORRY (*off*). So long?

FENDER. Forty-three years next Purim, if I didn't die before. (RANTING *enters* D.R. *carrying a board with lists.*)

RANTING (*to behind desk*). And sixty gross denim trousers.

FENDER (*writing*). Sixty gross denim trousers.

RANTING. And forty gross cellaloid collars.

FENDER. Cellaloid collars. Forty gross cellaloid.

RANTING (*tapping with pencil, impatiently*). Cellaloid makes with a C, no S.

FENDER. And what more?

RANTING. Eleven dozen raincoats, Prussian collar.

FENDER. Eleven dozen raincoats.

RANTING. Prussian collar.

FENDER. You know something, Mr. Ranting? It's cold in this warehouse. I said it's cold, Mr. Ranting. I feel the cold something terrible.

RANTING. Fender, I don't think you enjoy your work like in the olden days. (*Sits on table, head turned half* D.S. *towards* FENDER.)

FENDER. What an idea! I enjoy my work? Certainly I enjoy. I feel the cold, that's all.

RANTING. Naturally, you are getting on. The work is hard. Nobody is as young as he used to be.

FENDER. What are you talking, Mr. Ranting? Nobody is as young as he used to be? And how could he?

RANTING. I am saying, Fender, an old man is an old man.

FENDER (*rises*). Certainly. Of course. An old man is an old man. Mr. Ranting, I tell you something: my father, when he was seventy —no, over seventy—he can bend a horseshoe straight with his bare hands. And even he felt the cold.

RANTING (*getting off table*). All I am saying, Fender, is stop driving me mad with your crying "it's so cold, it's so cold." Get a new overcoat; you won't feel it.

FENDER. I make an arrangement with you, Mr. Ranting. I'll take one of the overcoats, the big ones with the sheepskin lining, and every week from my wages take off a certain sum. (*Holds out his hands.*) A proposition, Mr. Ranting?

RANTING. One of them coats, Fender? Leave me alone. (FENDER *moves as if to speak.*) Hup! A coat like this is worth twenty pound anybody's money. What do you make? With all due respect, Fender, what do you make? You won't live so long to pay off such a coat.

FENDER (*sitting on stool, again*). That's true. So what can you do?

RANTING (*reading from list*). Seventeen dozen pair shooting breeches.

FENDER (*writing*). Seventeen dozen pair breeches.

RANTING. Shooting.

FENDER. Shooting, shooting. (*Indicates the entry in his book.*)

RANTING (*in disgust*). Ah! (*Exit* D.R.)

FENDER (*rising and taking off his coat*). Maybe Morry can mend the old coat again. (*Cross fade lights from* "A" *to* "C.") After all he's a good tailor. (*Turns* U.S. *as the light goes.*)

SCENE 4

*As the light fades in on "*C*"* FENDER *is standing* U.S. *of mattress.* MORRY. *enters* D.L.

MORRY. Look, Fender, look. The seams is all rotten. Look, the lining is like ribbons. Look, the material is threadbare.

FENDER. A tailor like you, Morry, to make such a fuss. You should be ashamed.

MORRY (*sitting on chair*). The padding is like an old horse blanket.

FENDER. Who asks for new padding? Only make the coat good. Who cares about the padding, so long as the coat is warm?

MORRY. It can't be done.

FENDER. Don't make jokes, Morry.

MORRY. If I say it can't be done, it can't be done.

FENDER. So, all right, charge a little more.

MORRY. Charge! What does charge matter? It can't be done.

FENDER. Why are you so hard for, Morry? After all, you can patch with off cuts. (MORRY *holds head in hands.*) I am not asking, after all, for West End style; I should look so smart. I don't care how smart. Only mend the coat, Morry.

MORRY. Fender, listen to me, Fender. A good coat like I make has got twenty years wear. I double stitch the seams with best thread, no rubbish. Every stitch I test, (*Bites imaginary thread.*) so it's good and strong. I use good material: crombie, tweed, what you like. The best. I use a lovely lining; someone else would make a wedding dress from it, such a lining I use.

FENDER. You use marvelous lining, Morry.

MORRY. I make the whole coat, the buttons holes, the pockets, everything.

FENDER. Don't I tell everybody? Morry—a needle like Paganini. I tell everybody.

MORRY. I would make you such a coat for cost, Fender.

FENDER. How much costs such a coat?

MORRY. Three yards, say.

FENDER. Say two and a half.

MORRY. And lining.

FENDER. Don't worry yourself with lining.

MORRY. I can make you a good coat for twelve pound.

FENDER. You can't mend the old coat?

MORRY. Please, Fender, do me a favor.

FENDER. I can ask? Twelve pound is money.

MORRY (*rises*). Listen, Fender. I break my neck: ten pound for the coat. You got ten pound?

FENDER. I look like a banker? I can save ten pound.

MORRY. So.

FENDER (*as he starts to put on his old coat*). So. So I'm going to have made a bespoke overcoat.

MORRY. Bespoke is good.

FENDER. Certainly bespoke. You think I would wear Ranting's rubbish? (*Sits on chair.*)

MORRY (*moving* D.S.L. *and reaching off-stage for patterns*). What material you like?

FENDER. I can choose material?

MORRY (*to* FENDER *with patterns*). Here, patterns.

FENDER. The gray is not nice for me. The blue is better?

MORRY (*fingering the blue material*). Blue is nice. You can wear blue for any occasion.

FENDER. Nigger brown is smart.

MORRY. For a young man.

FENDER. Black is always good.

MORRY. Black is good, but a nice, dark blue is nicer.

FENDER (*rising, and moving* D.S. *of mattress*). Believe me, Morry, I think you are right. The blue is good—and thick. What a material!

MORRY (*down to* FENDER). I should say. So you can save ten pounds?

FENDER. Save? Sure I can save. An old man like me, if I got an overcoat, what do I need? (*Moving* D.S.C. *to* "B."). If I got a bespoke overcoat, what more can I need? (*Exit into darkness* D.R.)

SCENE 5

MORRY *takes out black bread etc. from his pocket and moves to his chair.*

MORRY. With a piece of black bread and a herring you can't go wrong. You got in black bread vitamins, nutriment *and* a good flavor from herrings. In the old days, (*Sits.*) sometimes six clients a week, all wanting coats, suits, a spare pair of trousers, something. The trade is not good any more. Believe me, if I had a boy I wouldn't let him see a needle and thread. It's a thing of the past. Things are so bad now, you know what I'm doing? I'm making a ten pound coat for Fender. For ten pounds, it's a wonderful coat. The material, the seams. No wind can blow through a coat like this. (*Rises and moves* D.S. *a few paces.*) Let it blow as much as it likes. I read an interesting thing somewhere. When it's cold, it's not really cold. You are hot; that's why you feel the cold. Also you pull in your muscles. That's bad. Fender: his trouble is he's pulled his muscles so far in they won't pull any more. (*Moving* D.L. *to exit, as light fades.*) I was always interested in science things like this. (*Cross fade to* "B.")

SCENE 6

RANTING *enters* D.R. *with a plate of chopped liver and a fork.*

RANTING. The chopped liver is tukke good, Alf. You want some? Good boy. (*Stops* D.C. "B.") Bring some more chopped liver, Maisie. So I was telling you, Alf: this exhibition they got such machines you wouldn't believe. They got a machine there, (I'm not telling you a word of a lie, Alf) they got a machine can add up how much you made last year, take away your overheads, knock off your income tax, and show you if you got anything left. By my life. It has a dictation machine, a suspended filing system, a place special for telephone directories, and a permutator for working out football pools so they should win. And I worry myself to nothing, worrying, worrying the whole time over an old clerk's mistakes. What you say? Can a machine laugh like a man? Can it cry like a man? What difference? So long as a clerk clerks good, what difference he's laughing or crying? (*Exit* D.R. *in blackout as we hear* FENDER *laugh, off.*)

SCENE 7

The light fades in on FENDER, *laughing quietly, as he enters* D.R. *and moves to* "A" *below table, with the baigel half eaten and wrapped in paper.*

FENDER. A marvelous story, I must tell it to Morry. I enjoy a good laugh. (*He sighs and looks at the baigel.*) A baigel is enough. After all, bread and salt is food. It's the same dinner, only I leave out the soup. That woman, terrible, but what soup. I'm not saying it's not worth a sixpence. A bowl like that, where could you get it for sixpence? In a big restaurant they bring you half as much, and charge terrible prices. A woman cooks soup like that must make somebody a marvelous wife. Mind you, boss-eyed and what temper, a terrible woman. Still a baigel is plenty. Eat it slow, careful, every crumb does you good. Soup! who wants soup? (*Moves* U.S.) When I get the coat, I put it on. I walk up to a table, (*Sits.*) I sit down in the overcoat, blue, nice: a bowl of soup, missus, and a baigel. (*Rises and moves a few paces* D.S.) Be careful! You want the soup should drop on this new overcoat—a bespoke overcoat—ruined. (*He laughs as, lifting the flap of his torn coat, his hand slips through a hole.*) I don't think I got room for these bits. No, I'm full up. I couldn't eat another thing, not even a fresh lutka or a piece of cheesecake. (*Turns to his accounts.*) Sixteen dozen flying jackets. (U.S. *to sit.*) With such jackets you can fly?

RANTING (*enters* D.R., *moves behind table from which he brushes crumbs*). How many times, Fender? Don't eat in the warehouse. It brings the mice. The mice eat the clothing.

FENDER. How many clothing can a little mouse eat?

RANTING (*reading*). Twenty-eight gross denim trousers. (*Fade out.*)

SCENE 8

Area "C." Fade in on FENDER *entering breathlessly* U.C.

FENDER (*calls*). Morry, I come to see how the coat is coming, Morry.

MORRY (*footsteps, off*). The coat is all right.

FENDER. Which is the coat, Morry?

MORRY (*entering* D.L., *with half-made coat*). Here! Here!

FENDER. Should I try it on?

MORRY (*holding out coat*). Try it on. Don't be shy. What's a matter with you? You're a film starlet, you got to have a changing room else you can't take off the old coat. (FENDER *removes coat.*) So. That's right. Take it off.

(FENDER *gives his coat to* MORRY, *who puts it on chair, and puts on the new coat.*)

FENDER. If I knew, I would put my other shirt on. You see it, Morry? The drill shirt, with tabs on the shoulders, very smart.

MORRY. And why should you? Today is a bank holiday? Look. My own shirt. Everybody wears his old shirt for a working day. Nu. Try it.

FENDER (*as* MORRY *fits the coat*). In Clacton the sun is hot. This makes him the sun, you understand. What a hot! You got a nice deck chair, Mrs. Felderman. I can see. A comfortable deck chair. Certainly a new overcoat—a bespoke overcoat. (*Lifts the left arm with sleeve in it.*) Suits me? Under the arms is a bit tight.

MORRY (*feeling armhole*). It's fine. You got plenty room, look, look.

FENDER. A coat like this makes a difference.

MORRY (*kneeling in front to fit coat*). Fender, you like the coat? What about a couple of pound on account? I got expenses. (*Rising.*) Can you manage a couple?

> (FENDER *takes out purse, sorts out notes and silver, and hands them over with great dignity.*)

FENDER. Certainly. You know, Morry, twenty shillings, if you saved money like I do, thirty shillings, and didn't throw it away on that rotten brandy, thirty-five shillings, you would be a rich man. Forty shillings.

MORRY. And what would I do with my money?

FENDER. A question. What can you do with it?

MORRY. I can take an off-license.

FENDER. An off-license is a good idea. (*Taking off new coat.*)

MORRY. I use my knowledge. A special line in brandy. Old stuff— Napoleon—something good. (*Takes overcoat from* FENDER *and hands him his old one.*)

FENDER. How can you know it's good?

MORRY. I try every bottle, personal. I put up a smart notice, Morry's Napoleon Brandy; every bottle personal tasted. Thanks for the two pound. You can spare?

FENDER. Sure I can spare. The coat won't be long now, Morry?

MORRY. This week I make an exception. I have a drink tonight; that way tomorrow I take less.

FENDER. Tukke?

MORRY. Listen, Fender, drinking is by me not by you; its my hobby so I shouldn't know? (*Exeunt. Cross fade to* "B.")

Scene 9

When the lights go up on "B," Ranting *is straphanging* D.S.C.

Ranting (*in a new coat*). On the Central Line is always hot. You like the coat? Yesterday I picked it up. America style. (*Lurches.*) Sorry, miss. Dear? I should say it's dear! You want me to wear one of me own coats? Twenty-five nicker—a pony, this coat—I beg your pardon. Knock off the booze and you'll be able to afford. My advice to you friend, is—knock off the demon drink.

He goes out D.R. *Cross fade to* "C."

Scene 10

Fender *is asleep on* Morry's *mattress, covered by the half-finished overcoat.* Morry *enters drunkenly,* U.S.C., *singing and carrying a bottle.*

Morry. It says on the label extra special reserve, cognac Napoleon brandy, old special reserve. A brandy like this is a brandy like this. This. (*Drinks.*) A brandy. (*Turns to mattress.*) I got company? So late? (U.S. *to put bottle on chair.*) Hey, wake up. I got company. You sit here a minute. Don't go way. I'll come back. (*Kneeling* U.S. *of mattress.*) Wake up, Fender, it's you? What an unexpected pleasure.

Fender (*sitting up*). I was having a dream. A flying overcoat and inside the pockets bowls of soup. And do you know, the soup never upset in the coat.

Morry. I got here a brandy; you never drunk such a brandy in your life.

Fender (*peering at the label*). Special reserve. Must be good.

Morry. Take a little drop. Go on. Take.

Fender (*trying it*). Ahh, like fire. (*Hands bottle back.*) A good one all right. Morry—Moishele.

MORRY (*holding out bottle in front of him*). It's good brandy.

FENDER. I got bad news, Morry.

MORRY. Where can you find a brandy like this?

FENDER. That Ranting. He give me the sack.

MORRY (*as he sits back on his heels and puts bottle on floor with a thud*). He give you the sack?

FENDER. He give me the sack.

MORRY. After so long he give you the sack?

FENDER. He give me.

MORRY. He give it to *you?*

FENDER. The sack.

MORRY. Oi.

FENDER. I have with great regrets, Morry I must tell you, to cancel the coat. I came to tell you. Cancel the coat.

MORRY (*trying to give him the bottle*). Take another drop brandy. Good for your cough.

FENDER. I don't fancy.

MORRY. Take. Don't be shy. Take. (FENDER *drinks from bottle, and as he lifts his arm we see that the old coat is torn under the arm.*) If I could mend that coat, Fender, I would mend it, I want you to know. I defy any master tailor to make that coat good.

FENDER. What can you do? It's just an old coat, that's all.

MORRY (*rises*). You can't find the rest of the ten pounds? I'll finish the coat.

FENDER. How?

MORRY (*puts arm round* FENDER *and pats him on shoulder*). With a needle. How else?

The lights slowly fade.

SCENE 11

FENDER (*at* "B," D.S.C.). I told him, polite, but strong. Mr. Ranting, I been with this firm with your father and your uncle so many years. All this time I done the same job; nobody complains. Suddenly business is so bad you have to turn me off? Let him answer me that. No good. Excuses, anybody can find excuses. What I ask you, Mr. Ranting, is, is it right? Let him answer me that. That's what I should have said. I should have told him off, big as he is. The governor, (*Turns* u.s. *and spits.*) I used to give him a handkerchief he should wipe his nose. A little boy crying round the warehouse with his stockings down gives me the sack. Why didn't I tell him? Fender, he says, you got something put by, an insurance policy, something? I got something put by, don't worry. You got no family? Don't worry, I got plenty of family, I got friends. He worries about me. I even got a niece with a boardinghouse in Clacton, and can she cook? Lovely weather the whole time. (*Turns* u.s.c. *and then back to audience.*) Mind you, Morry is a good friend. In the morning I put on my new coat. I go to Ranting. I tell him. Give me that coat with the sheepskin. (*Coughs.*) Funny thing, a cough like this, comes right through you. Like a bowl of soup. It flies up through you like a flying jacket. There he goes. (*He traces the path of the imaginary jacket round the theater. It returns as the threatening celluloid collars.* FENDER *is dying.*) Seventeen dozen cellaloid collars, cellaloid makes with a C, no S—or S, no C. (*Weekly.*) Funny thing, I don't seem to know nothing any more. (*Sinks down as the lights slowly fade.*)

SCENE 12

*The lights fade in on area "*A*" as a* CLERK, *followed by* RANTING, *enters* D.R. RANTING *goes* U.S. *to behind table.* CLERK *sits at table with notebook and pencil.*

RANTING. Thirty dozen pair shooting breeches.
CLERK. Thirty dozen pair shooting breeches.
RANTING. And a hundred dozen Balaclava helmets.

(MORRY *enters* U.S.C. *with finished overcoat over his arm.*)

MORRY (*coming to* U.S. *of table*). Mr. Ranting. Excuse me, Mr. Ranting.

RANTING. And sixty various drill jackets. Can I help you, sir?

MORRY. I come for Fender. I finished him a coat.

RANTING. And two gross khaki drill shorts. He don't work here no more. I say work, but you should understand he was past it.

CLERK. Two gross shorts.

RANTING. Khaki drill.

CLERK. What?

MORRY. Khaki drill.

RANTING. Thank you. Fender lives by the arches in Flower and Dean Street. Or maybe with his niece at Clacton or somewhere. Pardon me. And twenty-eight pith helmets. (*Exit* D.S.R.) Ah!

CLERK. Twenty-eight pith helmets. (*Rests his arms and head on table.*)

*Cross fade "*A*" to "*C*."*

SCENE 13

*Area "*C*," continuing as from* SCENE 2; MORRY *is* U.S. *of mattress, level with* FENDER, *who sits in chair.*

MORRY. So I go to your lodging. I knock on the door. No answer. I knock again. An old woman comes. She's a bit deaf.

FENDER. She's stone deaf. A bit, he says.

MORRY. I shout in her ear, where is Fender? Fender—Fender! where should he be? He's dead. He didn't have my age, but he's dead. You can knock me over with a feather bed.

FENDER. She got her head screwed on, the old girl. I was dead all right. Mind you, she makes out she's older than she is. I don't like that sort of thing.

MORRY. But so sudden.

FENDER (*rising and crossing in front of* MORRY). Listen, Morry. You die when you are ready? You die when you have to, that's all. Still, I haven't done so bad. I can't complain. If only I kept my mouth shut I would be all right.

MORRY. I made the coat as quick as I can, Fender. (*Sits in chair.*)

FENDER. Look, Morry, I got nothing against you. You behave like a perfect gentleman. I told everybody at the hotel. Morry's a wonderful tailor. You think you look smart? Wait until Morry gets here. No. It was that Ranting. You see, Morry, I didn't take too long dying, but the whilst I am screaming and cursing, using terrible language, all against that Ranting. And when I get down there, it must have been on my mind. So the first couple of weeks, I am stopping the porter, the commissionaire, the chambermaids, even the guests, telling them about the overcoat. At last, they can't stand it any more. The manager sends for me. Fender, he says, you like the hotel? It's a wonderful hotel, I tell him. Everything of the best. I am very satisfied. Look, Fender, he says, I am very glad if you are comfortable, but I have to tell you everyone has a headache with your overcoat. Do me a favor: go down to the cloakroom, pick yourself any coat. Thank you, I tell him. It's not the same. I can see he is upset. I can't have the place turned upside down, he says. (*Pointing upwards.*) You'll have to go back for a while. When you get it, (*Points downwards.*) come back. It's on my mind, I told him. Next thing I know, I'm here. And here I am.

MORRY (*half rises*). And I got your overcoat all wrapped up ready, Fender. Take it and good luck to you.

FENDER (*moving* D.S. *level with bottom of mattress*). It's no good, Morry. It wouldn't make me happy. Somehow, I got to have that sheepskin coat from Ranting. I am not saying your coat isn't wonderful. It is. But I must have from Ranting a coat. I give him forty-three years nearly. He must give me a coat.

MORRY (*moving down to* FENDER *with bottle*). You know what?

FENDER. What?

MORRY. We go to Rantings and take the coat. That's what. (*Drinks.*)

FENDER (*as* MORRY *offers him the bottle*). Not a bad idea. (*Drinks and returns bottle. Exeunt* D.S.L. *with* MORRY'S *arm round* FENDER. *Cross fade to* "A.")

SCENE 14

As the light fades in on "A," RANTING enters from u.s.c., singing. The CLERK is seated at the table, writing in his notebook.

RANTING. That book you been making up for the past hour, what's the matter, you can't read?

CLERK. The old clerk had his own way of doing things. It takes a little while to work out. But I mastered it.

RANTING (*taking hat off*). You got your head screwed on right. You go to the dog tracks in the evening?

CLERK. Not for me, Mr. Ranting.

RANTING. Horses?

CLERK. No horses, neither.

RANTING. You must spiel something. Poker, shemmy?

CLERK (*rising and moving behind his stool*). I'm developing myself, Mr. Ranting.

RANTING. Something new?

CLERK. The human frame has nine hundred seventy-six individual muscles, each of whom can be developed up to peak power, give proper exercises and consideration.

RANTING. Nearly a thousand? So many?

CLERK. It has been proved by the best efficiency authorities that each of these muscular resources is vital to one. And what do we do? You sit cramped—like this. The muscles get slack and useless. You stand like this. The muscles suffer.

RANTING. Sit and stand you can't avoid.

CLERK (*taking off his overalls*). Look at this, Mr. Ranting. (*Rolls up sleeve and demonstrates muscle.*)

RANTING. Marvelous. Like Kid Berg. You should be a boxer.

CLERK. Worse thing you can do for the muscles, boxing. Fatal to the muscle tone.

RANTING. So what can you do with all them muscles?

CLERK. So far, I still have four hundred and eighty-nine muscles undeveloped.

RANTING. And then?

CLERK. I hope to stand as Mr. Universe.

RANTING. A meshuggus. Put back the coat.

CLERK (*restoring coat and moving* D.S.R.). When I get these pecs up I'll take my first competition.

RANTING. Local? (*Picks up clerk's notebook.*)

CLERK. Down at the Roxy.

RANTING. Maybe I'll come.

CLERK. You'll enjoy it, Mr. Ranting. The body beautiful.

RANTING. So I'll enjoy it. The whilst Mr. Universe, go shut the door. (*Pushes* CLERK *out* D.R. *and follows him.*)

SCENE 15

MORRY *and* FENDER *enter* D.L. *and move towards area* "B" *where the light now is. They come in arm in arm, singing and stumbling.* MORRY *carries an empty beer crate.*

MORRY. In your position, Fender, it's not professional to drink so much at once.

FENDER. You know I met Lennie?

MORRY. You were saying before. How is he doing?

FENDER. Very nice. They let him open a little stall outside the hotel, on the promenade. You can get any kind of herring from him.

MORRY (*puts crate down and stands on it*). I get in the window and give you a lift up. Just a minute. (*Gets down.*) See if you can walk through the wall.

FENDER (*crossing to* R. *of* MORRY, *pauses*). Don't talk silly, Morry.

MORRY. If you're a ghost you can walk through walls. And if you're not a ghost at least it's scientific experiment.

FENDER. It's true. I'll try. (*He tries.*) I feel silly. Get through the window, Morry. Just a minute. (*Takes key from pocket.*) A solution. I'll go round and open the door. (*Exit* D.R.)

MORRY (*gets on crate and tries to open window*). I can give myself a stricture with this. Shift, you—it don't budge. Get up.

FENDER (*off*). I done it. Come round. It's cold in here.

MORRY (*getting off crate and picking it up*). It would be nice if he walked through the wall, like I told him. (*Moving* R.) I even got to tell him how to be a ghost proper. (*Exit* D.R. *Blackout.*)

SCENE 16

Area "A." FENDER *enters* U.S.C. *with a torch and crosses* R. *to switch on imaginary light.*

FENDER. It's easy. You should try. I'll just switch on the light.

MORRY (*follows him in as the lights come on*). Right. Now, let's see. You remember where the coat is?

FENDER (*moving* U.S. *of stool*). Wait a minute. Trousers over there. Jackets here. (*Turns to audience.*) Would you believe it? I haven't been away five minutes and they shift the jackets.

MORRY (*moving to* U.S. *of coat rack*). Here are the coats. What about this? What a terrible cut. This one?

FENDER (*taking his old coat off and examining coat rack*). Not for me.

MORRY. The blue is nice.

FENDER. No.

MORRY. It's a silk lining. A good lining.

FENDER. For what?

MORRY. This?

FENDER. Too short. (*Takes out coat with sheepskin lining.*) Ah! Ah! This is different. This I'll take.

MORRY. It's a nice weight, Fender, (*Helping him on with it.*) but the workmanship. Not nice.

FENDER (*moving* D.S.C.). How many times do I have to tell you, Morry? It's not personal. Only I must have one of Ranting's coats.

That's all. He owes me. (*On these lines* FENDER *becomes, it seems to us and to* MORRY, *less mobile, more like a dead man.*)

MORRY (*moving* D.S. *to* R. *of* FENDER). Terrible cold in here. So. Can you go?

FENDER. I can go.

MORRY. My work is better.

FENDER. Certainly your work is better.

MORRY. So now you're all right, heh?

FENDER. I feel all right.

MORRY. Fender, you know something. (*Hesitates.*) This brandy is good.

FENDER. So—thank you, Morry.

MORRY. So, Fender, you're going now? You'll go back to the hotel?

FENDER (*turning* U.S.). Where else have I got to go to?

MORRY. Fenderler—you should give to Lennie my best regards.

FENDER (*turning back to* MORRY). He's selling herrings like hot cakes, all day long. (*Moves* U.S.) He'll be pleased. A long life to you, Morry. Pray for me. (*His voice fades on this line and he has gone.*)

MORRY (*calls after him*). May you come to your place in peace, Fender. (*Putting his hat on to pray.*) Yiskadal, Veyiskaddish, . . .

The Hebrew Prayer for the dead is broken by barrel-organ music, off, as MORRY's *head sinks upon his chest.*

Slow CURTAIN *as light fades.*

IT SHOULD HAPPEN TO A DOG

Author's Note

It Should Happen to a Dog is a serio-comic strip, which, those who know the story of Jonah will see, is faithful to the original. If the characters speak as people we know personally, it is because there is no other way for us to know characters. If Jonah is somewhat familiar in his manner of address to the Almighty—it is because one may assume that a greater intimacy exists between Prophets and their source of instruction than does for the rest of us.

In the staging of *It Should Happen to a Dog,* a coatstand is required from which the rope of the ship is hung, and upon which any practical props may also hang. The coatstand becomes the tree in the last scene, and should be placed behind Jonah's back in full view of the audience by the Angel or by a property man who may be written in at the director's discretion. A thunder-sheet will be found useful. The characters should be dressed in an anachronistic selection of garments suggestive of our own time and of biblical times, and the piece should be played at a fast tempo.

As to the message of the story—"Why should I not spare Nineveh?" This is, one hopes, how God feels about Man—unlike Man, who is less tolerant of himself.

CHARACTERS

JONAH
A MAN

SCENE I

JONAH. Please, please, what do you want from my life? He won't leave me alone. All these years I've been running—a traveler— Jonah, the traveler, representing Top Hat; Braces For The Trousers; Fair Lady Fancy Buttons; Hold Tight Hair Grips—only good brands in the suitcase. Ask them in Tarshish, ask them in Aleppo, in Carthage even; they all know Jonah ben Amittai, regular call once a month for more than thirty years. I don't complain, only I'm tired of running, that's all. Now at last I'm tired. I get this good pitch here—at last—so I shouldn't have to run with a suitcase any more. And still he nags me. All right. I heard. I'm going. What happens to me shouldn't happen to a dog.

(*A man stands in his way.*)

MAN. It's a nice pitch you got here.

JONAH. It's nice.

MAN. So what are you looking so down in the mouth for?

JONAH. What's the use of talking? It has to happen to me.

MAN. What happens?

JONAH. This dream.

MAN. Dream?

JONAH. I tell you, this is a most terrible dream. The voice comes like the voice of a bird. In the middle hours of the night it comes chirping, chirping, "The end of the world is at hand. The end of the world is at hand."

MAN. Could be right. It wouldn't be the first time.

JONAH. So all right then, let it be the end of the world. Is it my business? Am I to blame?

MAN. And this is *all* the voice says?

JONAH (*lying*). Certainly that's all. Isn't it enough? What else should it say?

MAN. Nothing. Only if that is all the voice says you got nothing to worry about. Look—if it *is* the end of the world, what can you do? On the other hand—if it isn't—you got nothing to worry about. I'll take a quarter ounce Archangel Gabriel tobacco.

JONAH (*handing him a small packet of tobacco*). That's a good brand. I opened up the Tarshish territory for Archangel Gabriel.

MAN. I never smoke nothing else. (*Starts to go out.*)

JONAH. Ay, ay.

MAN. Oh. (*Giving coin.*) Chirp, chirp? Chirp, chirp, heh, heh. (*As he goes.*)

JONAH. I hate birds. You know what it says? "Arise, Jonah, arise. Go to Nineveh, that great city, and cry against it." I ask you. Why pick on me? Why sort me out? Chirp, chirp. It's in my head the whole time. Once I could sleep fifteen hours—like a short course of death. No more. I don't sleep that good no more. I hate birds. (*To God.*) All right, I'm going—to the docks—for a ship—I'm going. (*He walks into the next area and set-up.*)

SCENE II

The same man as before, as a sailor, is untying a rope from a capstan as JONAH *enters.*

JONAH (*to God*). Certainly I'm on my way. By ship. You expect me to fly? If you are so clever and in such a hurry, make me sprout a couple of wings so I'll take off. It's quicker by air. But so far is only invented the ship. (*To the* SAILOR.) Which way you going, shipmate?

SAILOR. Tarshish.

JONAH. You don't say. I got a lot of friends there. It's a beautiful place. In Tarshish they got more people over a hundred years old than anywhere else.

SAILOR. Who wants to live so long?

JONAH. In some circumstances, chirp, chirp, who gets a chance to live so long? Tarshish, eh? (*Aside.*) It seems silly, if I'm going all this way to Nineveh (where I am certainly eventually going) why don't I break my journey and look up a few old friends in Tarshish. Why not? (*To the* SAILOR.) It's a crime? You can take passengers?

SAILOR. First class or tourist?

JONAH. In the old days when I was traveling for myself, nothing but first class for J. B. Amittai. But in these circumstances, one tourist.

SAILOR. Single or return?

JONAH. What's the matter with you? Return, of course. I got a wonderful little business waiting for me when I come back.

SAILOR (*shouts*). One more tourist coming up. Tarshish return.

JONAH (*aside, as he begins to board ship*). I'll spend a couple of days there to build my strength up and then I'll give such a shout against Nineveh. After all, it's a tough territory, and what difference can a couple of days make? Thank you. (*Sits.*) Oh, it's a beautiful day for sailing. Any more for the Skylark?

BLACK OUT

SCENE III

JONAH *asleep on some bales of goods. The* SAILOR *wakes him.*

JONAH. Chirp, chirp. The end of the world is at hand. (*He wakes up.*)

SAILOR. If it isn't troubling you.

JONAH. The weather's come over black all of a sudden.

SAILOR. In all my years I never knew a storm this time of the year.

JONAH. Are we far from Tarshish?

SAILOR. Are you barmy? We been stuck out here the past five hours, and all the wind does is try to blow us back. In all my years I never see anything like it.

JONAH. Very interesting phenomena. Like St. Ermin's fire; caused by electricity in the atmosphere, you understand? And take the sea serpent, for example.

SAILOR. I will.

JONAH. The sea serpent is really a very big eel. Science proves it.

SAILOR. I don't take any chances. After I tried every trick I know, I pray. (*He prays for a few moments. Then he looks at* JONAH.) You too, guv'ner.

JONAH. I already said my prayers today. To duplicate is just silly. When it comes to the evening I'll say my evening prayers.

SAILOR. Don't take no chances. Pray now.

JONAH. It should happen to a dog what happens to me. Listen, God. Stop messing me about. Didn't I give you my word of honor I will go to Nineveh? Ask anybody anywhere in these territories. Jonah's word is his bond. (*A gale begins to blow.*) Do me a favor just this once. I will catch the first boat from Tarshish to Nineveh. The very first boat. (*The gale blows stronger.*)

SAILOR. Did you make a sacrifice yet? We got all the passengers making sacrifices to all the different gods. That way we must hit the right god sooner or later and he'll stop the storm. Guv'ner, did you make a sacrifice yet?

JONAH. Here. I sacrifice this beautiful meat pie. I only ate a small portion of it.

SAILOR. Right. Throw it overboard with an appropriate prayer.

JONAH. Here, God. And remember I'm catching the first boat from Tarshish. All right? (*He throws the pie overboard. The pie is thrown straight back, and* JONAH *catches it. The* SAILOR *looks at him significantly, then calls out.*)

SAILOR. Aye, aye. This is it folks.

JONAH. It's a perfectly natural phenomena.

SAILOR. This man is the troublemaker.

JONAH. It's got a perfectly natural explanation.

SAILOR. His sacrifice was definitely refused. He's the one. Overboard with him—overboard. (*He advances on* JONAH.)

JONAH. You can't do this to me. I am on very important business. I can drown in there. What happens to me should happen to a dog. (*He backs away from the influence of the* SAILOR *till he falls overboard and the gale stops and the sun comes out.*)

SAILOR. I never did like the look of that fella. To me, he always looked a troublemaker. Uh? What? (*He follows the progress of* JONAH *in the water.*) You could live a thousand years, you wouldn't see a man swallowed by a whale. But who would believe such a story.

BLACK OUT

SCENE IV

JONAH *gropes in the dark, then strikes a match.*

JONAH. Faugh—it smells like Billingsgate in here. All right. Now what am I supposed to do. Now I can't go to Nineveh. All I wanted to do was to go to Nineveh and cry against it, and look at me. Maybe I'm dead. I must be dead. Who would have thought that being dead was a blackout in a fish shop? Maybe *this is* the end of the world. But if it isn't, if, for example, don't laugh, I happen to have been swallowed by a whale, tee-hee, I categorically put it on record that if I could go to Nineveh at this moment I would definitely and unconditionally go to Nineveh at this moment (*A crash of thunder; lightning.* JONAH *executes a double somersault into the light. Looks round, amazed.*) Honestly, God, sometimes I can't make you out. You've got such a mysterious way of carrying on. (*He stretches himself.*) So where's Tarshish? Tarshish. (*Disgusted.*) If I'm not dead and if I'm not mistaken and if my memory serves me right that great city in the distance is— Nineveh. It should happen to a dog. (*Exit, towards Nineveh.*)

SCENE V

KING (*enters, sits, sorts papers, looks up*). Jonah B. Amittai.

JONAH. Yes, Your Majesty.

KING. You are up on a charge of vagrancy.

JONAH. Uh?

KING. Vagrancy.

JONAH. Oh.

KING. Also it seems you have been talking a lot of seditious nonsense about the end of the world is at hand. Also—what's this? Also you keep saying "chirp, chirp." This official work is beginning to get me down. All night long I get the most terrible dreams. Mmm— what have you got to say for yourself?

JONAH. Just a minute. (*He mounts the throne and sings*). The Lord saith: Cry out against Nineveh, that great city, for their wickedness is come up before me. Stop. Yet forty days and Nineveh shall be overthrown. Stop. The end of the world is at hand. Stop. Repent lest ye perish. End of message. And that, Your Majesty, in short, is what I am instructed to tell you. (*Sits.*) Personally it make no differ- ence to me. I should be just as pleased for Nineveh not to be de- stroyed. For my part it can go on being as wicked as you like, though, if you was to ask my opinion, as a business man of some experience, I'll tell you straight out that honesty is always the best policy. A satisfied client is better than Government consuls. Especially as, I am instructed to tell you, the Government is not going to last too long, anyway.

KING. What's the source of your information?

JONAH. A little bird tells me every night.

KING (*alarmed*). A bird?

JONAH. A little bird. Chirp, chirp. It makes just like that.

KING. What color the feathers?

JONAH. The feathers! One wing is blue, the other wing white, the breast red, the tail purple, but the funny thing is, this bird has one brown eye and . . .

KING. . . . and the other a blue!

JONAH. You are familiar with it?

KING. I have been getting the same dream.

JONAH. Oh. So *your* little bird tells *me* one hundred times nightly to come to Nineveh and inform *you* that in forty days from now *you* are completely in liquidation. And that's what *I'm* telling *you?* It's a madhouse here!

KING (*stands up and tears his robe*). Let neither man nor beast, herd nor flock, taste anything. Let them not eat food nor drink water; but let man and beast be covered with sackcloth and cry mightily unto God. Yea, let them turn every one from his evil way, and from the violence that is in their hands. Let them turn from the violence that is in their hands for the sake of the smallest bird, for the bird also is God. (*To* JONAH.) Who can tell if God will turn and repent, and turn away from his fierce anger, that we perish not?

JONAH. Who can tell? But if you ask my opinion, I don't think so. Otherwise he doesn't go to all this trouble. No, king, this is the end. Still, you can always try. There's no charge for trying.

(*Exeunt.*)

SCENE VI

Jonah is sitting on a rock in the scorching sun. In the background a celebratory fairground noise, like a Bank Holiday Monday.

JONAH. It should happen to a dog, what happens to me. Here after all this the King himself takes my personal word that in forty days it is the end of the world; and what happens? The forty-first day is proclaimed a national holiday. Government stock rises, and I am the biggest bloody fool in the Middle East. I am a laughing stock, that's all, a laughing stock. I don't move. I'm going to sit here until I get a sun stroke. You can do what you like with Nineveh, Miniver, Shminever. I'm finished. "Yet forty days and Nineveh shall be overthrown." (*Laughter off and voices singing: "Jonah, Jonah— He pulled a boner."*) Listen to 'em. Laugh your heads off! Three-four hours I won't hear you any more. And I won't hear that damned bird either no more. I hate birds. (*A shadow is thrown over* JONAH.) What's this? By my life. A tree! (*A palm tree has sprung up from nowhere. He reaches down a coconut.*) What do you know? Coconuts as well with a patent zipper. You just pull it open and drink the milk. Ice cold. Delicious. And what's this. The *Tarshish Gazette*. Well, this is certainly a novelty. (*Reads.*) Aha. I see that Mrs. Zinkin has been presented with her third daughter. That's bad. Young Fyvel is opening a café espresso bar on the High Street. That's a good position. He should do well. It's just like a summer holiday here now, and believe me, I earned a vacation. This is certainly a wonderful place you made here, Lord. I got to hand it to you. For land development you're the tops.

(*Standing beside him is the* MAN *dressed as an angel.* JONAH *sees him and looks away, back to his paper.*)

ANGEL. A beautiful day.
JONAH. Yes, it's certainly marvelous weather we're having.

ANGEL. That's a remarkable palm tree. (*He reaches out for a coconut.*) This I never saw before.

JONAH. It's got a zipper.

ANGEL. What will he think of next, eh?

(*He offers the coconut to the irritable* JONAH.)

JONAH (*throwing down the newspaper*). All right. Cut out the performance. You are an angel, right?

ANGEL. I must give you credit, Jonah. You're certainly quick off
the mark.

JONAH. But an angel?

ANGEL. Archangel.

JONAH. Oh—so now what do I have to do? Go back to Nineveh? Tell
the King the Lord has changed his mind again? He is going to give
him ten more days and then bring the world to an end? He made a
laughingstock of me.

ANGEL. What can you do?

JONAH. Admitted. But at the same time this is a terrible way to
treat someone who goes through all the trouble I go through. For
what—only He knows. And He won't tell. (*Turns, bangs into
tree.*) Feh! Fancy trees yet!

ANGEL (*wheedling*). That's certainly a *wonderful* tree. Help yourself.

JONAH. Perhaps just another coconut. These coconuts are delicious.
(*As he turns the tree withers, collapsing into dust; that is, the
coatstand is removed.*) What a terrible thing to happen. Such a
wonderful tree. With such trees mankind could live in plenty for
ever. A quick death from some palm tree disease, I suppose?

ANGEL. It's a small worm crawls through the arterial system of the
tree, cuts off the life from the heart. And boom.

JONAH. A quick death to that worm.

ANGEL. Ah. You notice something. How annoyed you are with this
worm which after all only killed a tree, which after all didn't cause
you an hour's work. After all, you don't hear God complain; He
made the tree to come up in a night. He can make it go down the
night after.

JONAH. It cranks me such a beautiful tree should die like that, apart from now I am in the sun again and can catch a sun stroke any minute. Pity about the tree. Hey-hey. This is some kind of parable, ain't it? You are trying to teach me something, isn't it?

ANGEL. That's my boy. By this little experiment He is saying, if you feel sorry for the tree, which after all didn't cost you anything, why shouldn't He feel sorry for Nineveh, that great city, in which there are one hundred and twenty thousand human beings on whom after all He has taken a great deal of trouble even if they still don't know what time it is, or their left hand from the right hand. Also much cattle.

JONAH. You got a point there, there was never any harm in those cattle. But if you don't mind a question . . .

ANGEL. Any help I can give you.

JONAH. If God knew right from the start exactly what He is going to do about everything—right?

ANGEL. That's right.

JONAH. Then He knows He isn't going to destroy Nineveh. Right?

ANGEL. Right!

JONAH. Then what does He want of my life? What's the point of all this expensive business with whales and palm trees and so on?

ANGEL. You mankind, you can't see no further than your nose.

JONAH. So what's the answer?

ANGEL. You see— (*Long pause.*) frankly, I don't know.

JONAH. It should happen to a dog.

ANGEL. Me too. After all, it's no joke following you or any other prophet I happen to get assigned to around the whole time. You think it's such a wonderful thing to be an angel and do a few conjuring tricks? It *should* happen to a dog.

JONAH. On the other hand, come to think of it, whose dogs are we?

ANGEL. We are the dogs of God.

JONAH. So . . .

ANGEL. Nu?

JONAH. Whatever happens to a dog . . .

ANGEL. . . . must happen to us, eh? (*He chuckles with admiration.*)

70
71
72
74
75
76
77
78
82
85